The
Murder
Quadrille

The Murder Quadrille
By Fidelis Morgan

PRAISE FOR FIDELIS MORGAN

THE COUNTESS BOOKS

If you haven't yet made the acquaintance of the Countess and Alpiew, I urge you to do so at once. You will be rewarded with thrills and laughter aplenty.

—*Steven Saylor*

Fidelis Morgan's books are meticulous in their historical accuracy, zestful in their crime plotting, and very funny.

—*Simon Brett*

A delicious, rollicking romp of a mystery that kept me enthralled. Fidelis Morgan writes just the sort of story I love, full of sensuous details that make history come alive... I can't wait to read her next one.

—*Tess Gerritsen*

I challenge you to open a Fidelis Morgan at any page and not to be grabbed and plunged into a story where the action is non-stop and outrageous. The Countess Ashby de la Zouche books are a joy, written with tremendous energy and flair. It goes without saying that Fidelis has done her history homework, but no one ever made history more fun.

—*Peter Lovesey*

UNNATURAL FIRE

Hilarious 17th century romp, which combines an authentic slice of history with a tantalising storyline. An authority on the era, Morgan has created an inventive book which wears its learning lightly. Colourful turns of phrase and witty descriptions –like a bawdy P.G. Wodehouse leave you with a keen sense of the period. This is a frolicking good read.

—*Daily Mail*

THE RIVAL QUEENS

A 1699 version of bawdy London is splendidly brought to life in Fidelis Morgan's *The Rival Queens*, the second rollicking novel to feature the wiles and conniving intrigues of Countess Ashby de la Zouche and her maidservant Alpiew... Restoration comedy and action, artifice, gunpowder and Samuel Pepys a perfect historical menu of crime and mystery, with the bonus of laughs aplenty.

—The Guardian

Steeped in period detail and wit, it's a mystery that is as much fun to read as it is to try to solve.

—Minneapolis Star Tribune

THE AMBITIOUS STEPMOTHER

A third irrepressible outing for the ebullient Countess Ashby de la Zouche and her awesomely bosomed maid, Alpiew, a pair of Restoration detectives dubbed Cagney and Lacey in corsets, although I'd add a strong dash of Laurel and Hardy to the mix....Plots within plots, culinary eccentricities, the Bastille's most mysterious prisoner and the discovery of Lord Whippingham's favourite depravity, involving women with strong teeth, pepper the uproarious progress of our two unconventional heroines. Fun never came so lusty.

—The Guardian

FORTUNE'S SLAVE

Morgan's novels are a hoot, and packed to the hilt with parody, drama, luscious costumes and gruesome re-enactments. Hangings, shootings, dismemberings and a glorious lack of morality abound. Morgan is adept in contrasting her characters with their surroundings and with each other... She brings dank, disease-ridden London vividly to life, with great humour... The Countess and Alpiew are comic creations of genius. Morgan's roller-coaster romp of a novel is a hard act to follow.

—The Herald

FIDELIS MORGAN

The Murder Quadrille

1

Foxtrot

*A pace with short steps, as in changing
from trotting to walking*

HALFWAY THROUGH THE dinner party Sarah Beaumont decided that she would definitely leave Martin, her husband of ten years.

As the thought blossomed in her mind she blushed. Bowing her head to hide her flushed cheeks, she toyed with the peas on her plate, chasing one behind a piece of sautéed potato before stabbing it with her fork. To tell the truth, she wished she wasn't there at all, sitting round the table with a bunch of jabbering strangers, one of whom was Martin.

How had this happened?

She should have left him a week ago.

Sarah had never wanted to be a housewife, throwing dinner parties, cooking for her husband's clients. Yet here she was playing the unlikely role of hostess-with-the-most-ess, straight from the Technicolor pages of some 1950s magazine.

Last week Sarah had turned thirty. There had been no wild party, no drunken marking of the years. Rather, Martin had opened a bottle of champagne at home, they'd each drunk a couple of glasses, then he had taken her out for a quiet meal in an elegant restaurant, and just before dessert, (dark chocolate profiteroles for her, sticky toffee pudding for him) he had given her an eternity ring. Sarah put it straight onto her finger, stretched out her arm and admired the sparkling gewgaw.

It was a strange looking thing, a gold band inset with a row of precious and not so precious stones, the initials of which spelled Sarah: a sapphire, followed by an agate, a ruby, an amethyst and a gem she had never before heard of—hauynite, a vivid royal blue in colour, which she suspected was worthless. The assembled colours, a string of dark reds, blues and purples, reminded her of a bruise. She thought it a splendid bauble, marvellous and camp.

As she had twirled the ring with the tip of her thumb, Sarah had asked Martin why he had not given her a ring displaying his own initials, as she thought it would be nice for her to carry his name on her finger, rather than her own. He explained somewhat bashfully that that had actually been his first intention, but that there was no gemstone in stock representing the initial N. Using the available jewels his ring could only have spelled out Marti.

The morning after, when she was thirty years and one day old, Sarah found that, delightful as the present was, there was a price to pay.

'You like the ring, don't you, darling?' asked Martin, wearing a little-boy-lost smile. 'I wonder, could I ask a little favour in return?'

Putting aside the fact that she was miffed that he thought there was some unwritten tit-for-tat, I'll show you mine if you show me yours agreement on birthday gifts, Sarah listened to his proposition. Although he knew it was something she had never done before, Martin wanted her to throw a dinner party. The occasion was business—"a honey trap" he called it. That sounded dodgy enough, but then he declared, 'Actually, I just want to show you off.' He nuzzled up to her neck. 'After all, not many men have such a beautiful wife. I want people to meet my own personal Vivien Leigh.'

'Thanks.' Sarah pulled herself away.

'What?'

'Well, apart from the fact that she's dead...'

'You have those bright but kittenish looks.' Martin kissed her on the tip of her nose. 'Truly. But you're sexier.'

'I think that can hardly be possible,' Sarah replied, dimly recalling some article she had glancingly read which made out that Vivien Leigh had been a bisexual night-prowling nymphomaniac. 'Well, fiddle-dee-dee,' she added, in a weak attempt to lighten the atmosphere.

Against her own instincts, Sarah agreed to the dinner. Martin presented a small business card revealing the guest of honour, for whom the trap was to be set: Martin's new bank manager, a young man who went by the name Kevin Kruszynska.

Sarah peered at the card. 'There's a moniker for you.'

'What do you mean?' Martin gave her a beady look.

'Kevin Kruszynska. A mouthful of a name. A strange blend of the banal and the exotic.'

'What's wrong with that? He's a Czech from Tooting, or was it Streatham?'

'Let's hope he doesn't bounce.'

Martin frowned and pocketed the card. 'What are you talking about?'

'A Czech...from the bank.' Sarah watched Martin's cold panicked eyes, and without warning realised that she no longer knew him. Sometime over the years her husband had vanished and before her stood this gormless stranger.

'A bouncing Czech?'

Sarah laughed.

Martin did not. Instead, he gave her a blank look, then turned and expressed a sound filled with irritation and impatience.

Sarah left the room, heading for the kitchen and the remains of that champagne bottle in the fridge. What on earth had happened to Martin's sense of humour? She had fallen for him all those years ago at university because he was such a comical boy, solemn and flip at the same time. It had always been hard combination to keep up with, a kind of deadpan joviality.

Like an earnest though grumpy puppy, Martin followed her into the kitchen, saying: 'I hope you won't ruin this dinner, Sarah.' He picked up a biscuit from the table and crunched. 'It's important to both of us, you know. At this point in time it is imperative to expand the business...'

At this point in time?

'And for that I need to know that the bank is behind me...as 'twere, singing from the same hymn sheet.'

As 'twere? Singing from the same hymn sheet? Sarah poured the entire contents of the bottle into a tumbler, while watching

the stranger called Martin, as he used his sleeve to wipe away
a sprinkle of crumbs which he had sprayed onto the kitchen top.

'It is imperative that we make an impression.'

'You'll certainly make an impression if you go on behaving
like this.' Sarah handed him a cloth to wipe away the smear
of biscuit, and downed the glass of champagne. 'Just fill in the
forms, Martin. You know, these days, all banking decisions
are made by computer.'

'I've already filled in the bloody forms.' Martin glared at her.
Sarah was transfixed by his enormous, frantic pupils. 'And I
also know all about computers, you know. What do you think
I am, a blithering plonker?'

Sarah searched his face for signs of irony. Plonker? She
couldn't believe he had just used that word. She felt embarrassed for him. She made another feeble attempt to diffuse
the tension.

'Come on Marti, keep your hair on.'

'Martin actually.'

'Joke!' Sarah waved the ring at him, but a dark disquiet
flooded her belly. 'Look, Martin, wouldn't it be better to invite
this nice Czech over for drinks? Just the three of us. Cocktails?'
He gave no response so she pressed on. 'I'm quite good at that
kind of short-form, brisk entertaining.' She smiled, touching
his elbow. 'You know what dinner parties are like, darling. Too
many people jostling for attention. All those loose cannons.
No good will come of it.'

'I want a dinner party, Sarah.' As though to control himself,
Martin ran his fingers through his hair. Sarah noticed that it
seemed greasy.

'Far cooler to invite people round, pop open a good champagne and serve up something from a take-away. For instance,
battered haddock and chips.'

'Sarah! We are having dinner. Okay?'

Sarah watched his sallow skin, pale and gleaming with anxious perspiration. He looked as though he was about to faint. Now she felt sorry for being so stubborn.

'Calm yourself, darling. It's all right. If you really want me to I'll do a lovely meal.' She filled the kettle ready to prepare a pot of tea, to calm the situation.

Martin stood before her, his nostrils flared, his face drained, ash coloured.

'As my wife,' he said through gritted teeth. 'It is the least I would expect.'

This 'as my wife' remark changed Sarah's stance again. She was not in the mood to let it go.

'You can expect what you like of me. If it's a servant you really want I will serve you. However if it's a loan you're after, Martin, I wouldn't expect any great things to come of any dinner party. As I said, computers make the financial calculations and computers don't eat dinner. It will be an expensive, not to say interminable way of buttering the fellow up.'

As the kettle rattled away, Sarah gave up on the idea of a healing pot of tea and made for the stairs.

When had this happened? When had her husband vanished and been replaced by this bizarre trembling hysteric. What was going on? Was he on drugs?

Sarah knew she must escape momentarily from his presence and regain her equilibrium.

But Martin had got to the stairs first and was hanging onto the newel post, blocking her way. 'You never want anything to go right for me, do you, Sarah?' His face was flushed now, his knuckles showing through his skin, white jewels emblazoned on the orb of his fist. 'I thought the whole point of wives was to support their husbands, not to undermine them at every given opportunity.'

'What are you talking about, Martin? No one could accuse me of not supporting you.'

Only two years ago Sarah had given up a well-paid job in publicity to promote his new company—a small advertising firm. Martin himself had worked for years as an underling in a big PR company, writing slogans and spin for celebrity clients—writers, actors, politicians. Then he decided to break free and set up as an independent, be his own boss.

At about the same time the publishing firm for which Sarah worked declared its plan to 'rationalise' the workforce. 'We are restructuring for a bright new future' trumpeted the official press release, whereas in reality they were sacking people by the score. Some golden handshakes were proposed for the chosen few. Despite being safe from the prospective chopper, Sarah offered herself for redundancy. The total of that lump sum, received in exchange for sacrificing her job, Sarah invested in Martin's new business.

She didn't bother to look in the trade papers for similar jobs. She had had enough of the way publishing was going. Her decision to quit had been made easier by the mental image of her female bosses booting their more intellectual colleagues off the upward steps of the ladder with winkle-picker toes, then they used the sharpened spikes of their stilettos to kick off the venerable but genial old men beneath them. Sarah preferred to work for someone she knew and liked rather than for a hard-faced team of cold, tight-skirted women whose lives were driven by statistics, board-room jargon, and a ruthless desire to climb to the top, preferably using their friends' heads as stepping stones.

Sarah knew if she stayed in publishing for the big firms, she wasn't going to find much except more of the same.

From Martin's company she took no pay. As long as the two of them could survive and live in comfort, she sincerely believed that the most important thing was to build up the company's profile. To Sarah financial prosperity came second to getting the firm a good reputation. Once the company was thriving they could pay themselves a great whack, maybe float on the stock market and pocket a million or two.

For a year Sarah and Martin had worked together in a small office above a newsagent's shop in Vauxhall. The company flourished.

It was soon necessary to engage Justin and Mike, a couple of new employees to deal with the burgeoning client list. The Vauxhall office seemed suddenly too small. Rather than splashing out capital on new premises, it seemed more sensible to Sarah that she handed over the second office/reception room to the new boys while she worked from home.

And now Sarah found herself standing at the foot of the stairs, being told by an alien who was her legal spouse that she did not support him.

'If we're to compete with the big fish we need an injection of capital,' said Martin, gripping the banisters as though they were prison bars, and looking down at her from his elevated position on the fourth step, enunciating every syllable as though he was addressing a simpleton. 'We have to expand. More employees. Bigger premises—Maybe in the centre of town— or The West End.'

Silently Sarah stepped back, rolling the eternity ring round her finger with the tip of her thumb. Apart from the fact it sounded like lunacy to expand now, she wondered when she had she been squeezed out of the decision making process? And wasn't the centre of town and the West End the same thing?

Although she had voluntarily removed herself from the cut and thrust of working life by working from home, as far as she knew she was still a director of their company, and had responsibilities, if only to counsel Martin, her co-director. She had already once saved the company from making a wild and extravagant move which they could not afford. Now Martin wanted to make an even bigger one. This was the first time he had ever made a business resolution without first consulting her.

Suddenly Martin let go of the banister and stepped down to her level.

'I'm sorry, Sarah. I've been a twerp. I'm just a bit tense at the moment.' He lowered his face towards her and put on a baby voice. 'You will do the dinner, won't you, sweetheart? Do it for Marti.'

He held his arms open for a hug.

Sarah stepped into his embrace. When his arms were around her she wondered why she had demurred. Poor Martin. He had got himself into a state. Like a child deprived of its teddy.

She'd do the dinner and she'd try her best to make it work for him. Perhaps then the bank would refuse anyhow, and it would all be over with. But at least she would have done her bit and the bank would, as ever, make the final decision.

This morning Sarah had gone shopping, buying the best fresh produce, and during the afternoon she prepared the meal for her husband and four people whom she hardly knew: Martin's lawyer, Max Latham and his live-in girlfriend, Lisa Pope; their next door neighbour, a surly and brash American writer called Tess Brandon (whom Martin invited not only to make up the numbers but to impress the others with a famous-ish name, and perhaps to snare her as a future client) and, lastly, of course, the bouncing Czech.

Only an hour ago the guests had all arrived and stood in the dining room/conservatory, clutching drinks and making small talk.

The Yank author doled out her business cards to everyone present, and started describing in nauseating detail her morning's work—sitting in on a particularly grizzly inquest at the local coroner's court.

Sarah smoothed the edgy moment by calling everyone to sit.

As the guests took their seats round the prettily decorated table Kevin asked Sarah what she did—what was her job.

But before she had a chance to open her mouth Martin replied on her behalf.

'Sarah's a housewife.' He gave a self-deprecating smile. 'I am the hunter-gatherer in this household.'

Sarah suppressed a gasp. She was about to laugh when she caught Martin's forbidding eye. She wondered what on earth he must have put down on those banking forms.

Then she remembered that though she was Martin's business partner, and wrote the lion's share of slogans and strap-lines, she wasn't actually on the payroll. Maybe Martin was thinking about some legal point in the accounts, like National Insurance or pension contributions.

From that moment, once she had been introduced as a house-wife, Sarah was ignored. As the guests chatted and champed their way through the crispy salad starter it was as though she was a mere ghost looking on from her position in an empty chair.

She never usually went to dinner parties. Now it seemed that by trying to have one of her own, she had become not so much the domestic goddess as the domestic slave.

In silence Sarah watched the guests rattle on about weather, traffic, holidays and all the other tiresome subjects which oil the discourse of society while regretting utterly having got herself roped into this make-believe, table-napkin-candles-and-cruet state of affairs.

After she had cleared away the dirty salad plates and served the main course, Sarah stretched out for the wine and topped up her glass.

It was a pleasant smooth red, a sturdy Chateau Neuf du Pape.

Throughout the meal Martin had referred to the wine by name—Clos de l'Oratoire des Papes. 'Some more delicious Clos de l'Oratoire des Papes, Max?' and 'Jaunty little wine, Clos de l'Oratoire des Papes, don't you think, Kevin? Trips across the tongue.'

Sarah sighed inwardly. It was embarrassing. It's not as though the wine was some nineteenth century Chateau Lafitte or even a rare Chateau d'Yquem. Martin had bought it in the supermarket—a pick on the "special" wine shelves. It had cost him less than fifteen pounds. But from the way he handled the bottle you'd think the wine was from the long lost caves of Napoleon or had gone under the hammer at Sotheby's for over a grand.

She took a glug and rolled it round in her mouth.

Although she was quite happy to be excluded from the small talk, all the same she was profoundly irritated by her new-found invisibility. Some years ago Sarah had seen documentaries about out of body experiences: incidents involving people who had technically died and then been brought back to life. They all described the same thing. First came a bright white tunnel. Then they were suddenly floating around on the ceiling watching themselves on the bed below.

This dinner party, Sarah thought, was something akin to this. Somehow she had been wiped out of the actual happening but could still see and hear everything with astonishing clarity.

She looked round the table. It was like scrutinizing bizarre creatures in a brightly lit display case in the zoo—a vivarium of human life. These strangers seemed so relaxed and at home here in her house. Martin caressed the crystal glass containing his precious wine. Max leaned into the conversation, occasionally slipping an almost imperceptible wink at Martin, while his flabby hand rested lightly on Lisa's thigh. Lisa, apparently unaware of Max's paw, chewed earnestly, glancing now and then at Max with dog-like devotion. Kevin the Czech (or was it really Kevin the Cheque?) was smiling blithely at Tess as she reeled off gruesome details of crimes she had researched for her novels.

'There was this case back in the States a few years back where a man killed a woman and used a grease gun to fill every one of her orifices with highly flammable foam. Then he heaved her into a tin drum, poured on petrol and set the whole thing alight.'

'Recipe du jour: femme farcie et flambée,' Sarah said.

No one laughed. They didn't even pause or look in her direction. It was as though she had not uttered.

'But you see, that's exactly what I mean,' said Max, his voice slightly raised in eager animation. 'The very fact that you, Tess, know about this means it was in no way a perfect murder. A murder only becomes perfect when there is no body –'

'No, Max. No. No. I tell you, it's been zillions of years since that was true. Lookit, I've done the research. Way back before World War Two there was your John Haigh—The Acid Bath Murderer. It made legal history worldwide: no corpse, just a couple of kidney stones.' Tess was combative, taking Max on, man to man. 'Since then—well, it happens all the time. Presence of a corpus delicti is not necessary to prove murder. Even without a body or a murder weapon they can catch you, incriminate you and execute you.'

'You should tighten up your studies, Miss. You don't mean Corpus delicti, which means the body of a crime—the presence of money, for instance, being proof of larceny. Corpus Delicti has nothing to do with dead bodies. You mean a corpse. You will find it's the presence of a corpse which is not necessary to prove murder. Peter Falconio for instance.'

'So what are you trying to say?' Tess jutted her head forward and kneaded her napkin with nail-bitten fingers. 'You agreeing with me on this, or what?'

'No, I am not agreeing with you. The Falconio case came to court, therefore the murder was not perfect. But, I mean to say, you could commit a perfect murder. But for that to be necessary there must be no actual body—not even a living person who is known to be missing. I feel sure you could kill a vagrant, for instance, and, if you successfully disposed of his remains, and, if no one was around who knew or cared that he was missing, then there would be no murder investigation, no case, no trial. Therefore...' He gave a magician's flourish, '– a perfect murder.'

'So that girl, the librarian.' Lisa, anxious not to be seen as the bimbo she so clearly was, piped up. 'What do you think, Tess? Run away or dead?'

'Dead as a dodo,' said Max, stuffing his mouth with a chunk of bread roll smothered in butter. 'Lying in a ditch somewhere. Soon to be found by the ubiquitous "man, walking dog".'

Sarah knew the case they were talking about. It was all over the papers. A young woman, Jane Grimshaw, had gone missing. A week had gone by since anyone had heard from her. Her mobile phone had been found down a drain, near to the pub where she had gone for a drink before she vanished.

Police feared the worst.

'I saw that,' said Tess. 'Her folks and co-workers were on TV, begging for her to phone home, to contact them.'

'Utterly unconvincing,' said Max. 'A lot of ghouls. They love the cameras, these people. Think it's an audition for *The X Factor*. Either that or they couldn't stand the girl.'

'Max says the police aren't fools,' said Lisa, reporting the information as though Max was not sitting beside her, his hand resting on her lap. 'They usually put people on the telly only to expose them, cos they know they're as guilty as sin and the victim is already lying in a ditch somewhere.'

'All these ditches,' said Sarah, still hovering on the ceiling. 'Where do these killers find ditches in London?'

'Exactly! Look at Soham.' Tess topped Lisa's remark, and ignored Sarah's.

'Plus,' Sarah shrugged. 'Why do people wrap up dead bodies in carpets? As though a body isn't heavy enough to start with!'

'The killer himself made an appeal for help.' Tess held her knife and fork in the air and laughed. 'Can you believe it?'

Sarah wondered if perhaps she really was undergoing a near-death experience.

'The egotism of the guilty mind! It's unparalleled.' Tess laughed, then furrowed her brow and grew very serious. 'Profilers can see through it, though. Once these people are on film, profilers watch the tapes frame by frame, noting each tic, each tiny gesture—the flickering eyelid, the twitching toe, "the tell" which ultimately betrays them.'

'According to the TV, the profiler on this case reckons it was the same man,' said Martin. 'The same man who killed that girl last year.'

'Marina Sutton.' Max interrupted with a show-off matter of fact delivery, which Sarah perceived was aimed at showing Tess that he also knew everything to do with anything about murder. 'Body found on the Common, partially submerged in the fishing lake.'

'A lake this time, not a ditch,' said Sarah to herself.

Martin talked over her: 'A loner, they said.'

'Yeah! Like the partying, pub-going Yorkshire Ripper was a loner! Didn't he slip out of one of his own shindigs to kill some whore then slipped back to party a bit more? And wasn't Dennis Nielsen the life and soul of the Welfare office where he worked. Loner! I don't think so.' Tess spoke with the sing song of the professional know-all. 'It's just easier for Society to blame loners, or to believe that loners are more capable of depravity, because Society doesn't like loners.'

'You only say that because you yourself are a loner.' Sarah spoke a moment before she realised that, though what Tess said might be true, it was rude to point it out. But Tess hadn't heard her, and ploughed on without caring about her opinion. 'Society wants everyone to be one of a couple, like y'all. Society detests individuals.'

'Don't be silly, Tess.' Lisa cuddled up to Max. 'I think it's nice when people are couples.'

'Like Bonnie and Clyde, you mean.' Sarah found Lisa's loyalty even more irritating than Tess's confidence. 'Or Myra Hindley and Ian Brady?'

'Exactly,' said Lisa, who clearly did not appreciate the references. 'It's natural to live in pairs. Look at Noah's Ark!'

Sarah laughed aloud as Lisa leaned forward and bestowed one of her irritating winsome smiles upon Kevin the Czech and said: 'I'll bet you have a lovely wife, Kevin.'

Was Lisa finally making an unforgivable social gaff? Kevin had a distinct air of gayness about him. The wedding finger, Sarah saw, sported a gold band—but then, maybe he had gone through a civil partnership.

'My wife has only just moved over from the Czech Republic. She doesn't speak good English, I'm afraid.'

Sarah wanted to take hold of Martin and shake him. They had done the unforgivable thing: not inviting the man to bring his wife to dinner. Why hadn't Martin bothered to find out? How much easier the evening could have been with a nice Czech wife instead of the insufferable Miss Know-it-all from next door?

Kevin lifted his hands, as though guarding himself from criticism. 'My wife prefers to stay at home in the evening, as we have two young children.'

'Two!' Lisa radiated joy on his behalf. 'How lovely. How old are they?'

'The little girl is three, and the boy is still a baby—ten months.'

Sarah could not believe that despite this eruption of cosy domesticity at the table, Max and Tess were still on the trail of serial killers.

'There you have it.' Max took his hand off Lisa's thigh and slammed his palm down on the tablecloth. 'People are stupid. Their arrogance betrays them.'

Sarah had to stop herself laughing aloud. *Boston Legal*'s Denny Crane in three dimensions. Even more pathetic actually—embarrassingly stagy, like that ancient old ham, *Perry Mason*. Similar bulky figure too.

'I say that there is a recipe for the perfect murder, but it can only happen if the perpetrator is able to override their inevitable arrogance. Let's face it, such a person feels superior because they have taken that one thing which can never ever be replaced—Life. And if they want to get away with their achievement and all its glory they must suppress their pride in their super-human act, or at least keep it to themselves, while shrouding it in quiet reason and empathy.'

Sarah watched Kevin. Was he bored by all this gory talk? He looked perfectly at ease. His elbows rested on the table, his chin balancing on the tip of his steepled fingers, his dark rat eyes darting from one pair of moving lips to the next. Perhaps when you usually spent your days adding and subtracting numbers, it was fun to be included on gruesome little junket like this.

'So where are you from Kevin? Prague?' she asked.

'No. Javornik. It's a small town in Silesia.' He glanced in Sarah's direction, his concentration momentarily distracted. 'The Mountains. The Sudetes.'

'Psychopaths don't feel empathy.' Tess spoke with her mouth full. Sarah caught a flash of green and white—chewed potato and pea. The Nigerian flag. 'But they are also particularly good at acting, therefore could easily assume the mantle of empathy to protect themselves. Most psychopaths are extremely intelligent narcissists.'

'I'm sorry, Kevin.' Sarah thought she might try to steer the conversation away from murder and back to geography. 'The Sudetes? Is that what we learned in school history as The Sudetanland?'

Kevin smiled and nodded. 'That's right.'

'I'm not talking about psychopaths.' Max sighed, implying Tess's information was irrelevant. 'Any Joe Bloggs can murder. You should meet some of my clients. I can assure you they're hardly in the MENSA league.'

'I thought you were a company lawyer, Max,' said Kevin, turning briskly away from Sarah to join the clan. He shot

Martin a quizzical look. Sarah wondered whether this had been some vital information previously supplied on the bank forms. Lawyer: Max Latham, specialities include company law and murder.

'I am a Tom of all Trades, Kevin.' Max spoke with a flourish that would put a Victorian actor-manager to shame. 'Master of all.'

'Jack, don't you mean?' said Lisa quietly. It was obvious she was not in the habit of contradicting the great man.

'Either appellation will serve the purpose.'

'He's very modest,' said Lisa, the vanguard, bearing Max's blazon. 'Max is a genius. He can do everything. He's one of those—oh what are they called—I think it starts with R...'

'Rottweilers?' said Sarah, slumped back in her undetectable bubble.

'Ranph...something...Rrr...Rrr...Rrr...' Lisa sounded like a child impersonating a motor car. 'Oh, I remember.' She squealed and clapped her hands. 'Max is a Pre-Raphaelite.'

Sarah snorted, imagining Max with long red crinkled hair, wearing a mauve velvet dress, floating lifelessly along in one of those water-filled ditches of his.

For the first time since they had all sat down Martin made eye contact with her, giving a breathy tut.

The ignominy of her husband's rebuke was the final straw.

Sarah decided to interpret his exclamation as a signal for her to take away the plates and bring in pudding.

It was going to happen. Tomorrow morning she would leave him.

'If one of us, for instance, wanted to commit a murder and get away with it, the first thing we would need to understand is the difference between the egotism of the guilty mind and the anxiety of the innocent.'

Max continued sounding off, his back slightly turned away from her as Sarah gathered his plate.

She felt as though she was playing the role of a parlour maid in some seedy Patrick Hamilton boarding house. She was almost tempted to say something like 'Cor blimey, sir, these crocks ain't 'arf slippy,' before pulling an imaginary dangling cigarette butt from her clamped scarlet lips and grinding it out with a peep-hole-toed sandal.

'Can't we talk about something nice now?' Lisa gave Sarah a lingering patronising look. 'After all, poor Sarah's gone to such trouble.'

Poor Sarah! Grateful as she was to know that someone had noticed her, it was all Sarah could do not to smash the pile of plates down on the simpering woman's head.

Yes, she had indeed spent the best part of the day peeling and chopping and shoving things in and out of the oven. Yes, she knew that these days dinner party hostesses got caterers in, or bought pre-prepared stuff and passed it off as their own, but if Sarah was going to do anything, she wanted to do it properly. The reaction she wanted was admiration, commendation, applause, not sympathy, not 'poor Sarah'.

'So, Max, what are you trying to say?' Martin bent forward, as Sarah stooped to retrieve his fork which had fallen onto the white cloth, leaving a brown spreading stain. 'That the secret of the perfect murder is to understand the essence of guilt? For surely that is what it must be.'

'Like Martin,' said Kevin, 'I am lost.' Wearing an ingenuous smile, he smoothed his napkin across his lap. 'A while back, Max, you said the secret was to leave no corpse. Which is it?'

'No—that's not what he said.' Tess, ever the earnest professional, shuffled her chair nearer the table. 'Max thinks that the important thing, and I have to agree with him, is that no person appears to be missing—thus there is no murder hunt. Ergo, as long as the body remains undiscovered, and no person is actually missed, apparently there has been no suspicious death. And that is the only secret of the perfect murder. Right, Max?'

Sarah piled Kevin's plate on top of the others, and he turned to her, gave her a curt smile and briskly bobbed his head. She wondered whether it was a tic.

'That's not the only rule.' Max leaned back in his chair while smoothing his chubby hand down his tie. 'The other secret for the perfect murderer is to hire the perfect lawyer.'

Sarah strolled out to the kitchen, suppressing the urge to yawn.

She put the dishes on the draining board, relieved to be out of the dining room and away from this gathering from hell.

Even with the tap running she could still hear Max pontificating. God, he was an arrogant arsehole. Didn't Dante Alighieri send lawyers and their cohorts to the seventh circle of hell, the Malebolge. Marvellous name for him: Max Malebolge. Come to think of it, wasn't the Malebolge made up of ditches? How at home Max would feel there, when the time came, floating along the ninth ditch of the seventh circle of hell in his fetching purple velvet Pre-Raphaelite dress.

Laughing silently till tears spilled down into the swing bin, Sarah scraped scraps off the dirty plates.

She could hear Tess rabbiting on about how her agent never called and her friends "back in the States" had strict instructions not to contact her while she was over here working, so, if it came to it, she herself would be an ideal candidate for Max's scenario of not being missed.

Tess Brandon an invisible person who would not be missed? That was a joke. Tonight alone how many times had she managed to drag the conversation back to herself? Invisible? It was laughable.

Sarah took her time in the cool kitchen, methodically packing the dishwasher and setting it off.

She wondered whether she would ever set off this machine again. If she had been dithering before, now she was certain. She really was going to leave Martin.

She pondered the method of her departure: should she have a row with Martin first, or just quietly pack a bag and slip away, leaving a polite note on the hall table for him to find when he came home from the office? Should she leave the rings: wedding, engagement and eternity, or would that be petty?

There were other questions too. Where would she go? And what would she live on?

But none of that mattered really as long as she got out of this awful, oppressive domestic world. Once, like Ibsen's Nora Helmer, she had slammed the door behind her, she could work out what came next. Earlier in the week Martin had called her his very own personal Vivien Leigh. Now Sarah would do what Miss Leigh had been so famous for, and be *Gone With the Wind*.

Sarah smirked to herself as she stirred whipped egg yolk into the custard mixture. The others were still banging on about murder. She was tempted to put on the radio, some dance music or jazz to drown them out with soft tones and mellow voices.

She felt sorry for the poor Czech. Fancy thinking you are coming to a semi-business meal with a client and finding yourself in the middle of this morbid catalogue of slaughter.

'My father always used to say—"Follow the eleventh commandment, my son."' At first Sarah thought it was Max, but it was in fact Martin who was speaking. '"Thou shall not be found out."'

Oh Martin!

Why was he bringing this up? His father was a pompous little popinjay.

Sarah checked the oven to see the blackcurrant pie. Some of the filling had bubbled over and was forming a caramelised lump on the baking tray. Sarah scraped it off before it sent the acrid smell of burning back into the dining room.

Brimstone and treacle.

How appropriate.

By the time she turned back to the custard it had curdled.

Damnation!

Sarah always kept tins of custard for eating on ordinary occasions. She adored curling on the sofa on a cold windy night, dropping hunks of dark chocolate into the hot bowl and eating it just as the chocolate melted.

Hastily she snatched the can opener and poured some ready-made custard into a milk-pan

'Your father is quite right, Martin. Everything must stay normal.' Max was back on his soapbox. 'Too many coincidences give a murderer away: his boat caught fire, the life-raft sprung a leak, they were just that little bit too far from the shore to swim, and, anyhow, although he had medals for butterfly and the crawl, his wife had never learned to swim, not even doggy-paddle. And at the moment he went to rescue her he was inexplicably seized by an uncontrollable fit of cramp. Next thing she was swallowed up by the broiling briny. I don't think so.'

While Sarah waited for the custard to heat, she hovered in the gloom of the doorway, watching from the shadows.

'I saw a case where the detectives found blood on the hall floorboards.' Tess licked her lips as she told the tale, as though she was a cook describing a scrumptious dish she was about to present. 'The husband explained how he had just thrown out the hall carpet, his dog had been in a fight and run along the hall, bleeding, he'd apparently mislaid the big kitchen knife from the wooden block, maybe at a friend's barbecue a few weeks before, and it just happened his wife had...' She put up her forefingers and mimed quotation marks '...suddenly gone missing.'

The custard slurped and bubbled. Sarah pulled out the pie, and put it next to the bowls laid out on a large melamine tray. She picked up the empty custard tin by its lid and tossed it into the pedal bin.

'Exactly,' snapped Max. 'Too many coincidences. Take packing. A person is reported missing, they've apparently left home—but they've gone without their clothes, their passport, their jewellery, their credit cards, their favourite photo of their kids...No way.'

Sarah poured the heated custard into a gravy boat. When would this purgatory ever end? As she picked up the tray she noticed a bead of blood grow from her finger tip. Damned tin. She walked through into the hall looking for a tissue.

The phone rang.

Bloody fingers splayed, she picked up.

A shrill voice. 'Maureen, is that you?'

'Wrong number. Sorry.'

A large drip of blood fell from her finger onto the rug.

Sarah replaced the receiver and grabbed a tissue, packing it round her finger tip as she looked down at the beige mat with a typical middle eastern pattern, Indian paisley swirls in green. Wherever had they found a horrible thing like that? It looked so nasty Sarah was pleased that she had interrupted its symmetry with a splosh of scarlet. She hoped the stain would spread but it didn't. Dire thing must be acrylic too, the type of carpet which would make you itch if you were mad enough to walk on it in bare feet.

She returned to the kitchen.

Martin was talking very loudly, and sounded almost manic. What had come into him? As she ran her finger under the cold tap Sarah remembered an episode a few weeks ago when, quite irrationally, Martin had shouted at two women who were standing chatting in a parking bay at the supermarket next to the library. He had thrust his head out of the window and literally screamed at them to get out of the way, calling them 'lazy, lolloping lesbians'. Afterwards in the shop when Sarah had challenged him he had laughed away the episode as a piece of 'parking rage'.

Once her hand was cleaned up and the cut covered with a large elastoplast, Sarah rooted in the drawers for a knife, tossed it onto the tray and carried the thing halfway across the kitchen before she saw she'd picked up the frosting knife, which might look scary but which would be no good at penetrating a baked pie. She threw it back into the drawer, and grabbed the big Sabatier, which could probably carve through granite let alone pastry, and returned to the fray.

'So, what about that librarian who's gone missing?' Lisa, dim-witted enthusiast, idiotically stirring a dying conversation back to life. 'What do you actually think happened?'

Sarah laid down the tray and went to work serving the dessert. Whereas she expected at least the Bisto-family 'Aaaaah!' of appreciation when she sunk the knife into the pie, releasing its spicy fruit scent, the conversation rolled on with no acknowledgement.

'I disagree with Max. I think she's probably got bored with her life, her job, her husband,' said Martin, little realising how closely his remark mirrored Sarah's own thoughts. 'Got a new lover now, and is living in sexual splendour on the Riviera, or somewhere.'

The Riviera with a lover! If only!

Sarah peered down at the balding patch on the back of Martin's head. She could see tiny flecks of dandruff on his shoulder and a small boil coming up beneath his collar. She could also smell his sickly, bitter aftershave. Revulsion swept through her. How had she ever liked him, this tight little cur of a man, creeping and grovelling at Max Malebolge's pompous heels?

She took her seat, getting a view of her husband's face. He was grinning inanely, the exact image of the gift in Portia's silver casket—the portrait of a blinking idiot.

'Rubbish,' barked Max. 'As I said before—She's dead. Under the patio. Or lying in a ditch.'

Sarah thought back to her mother's famous dinners and wondered what she would have made of all this. Then it was usually artists and musicians round the table. But there was at least one bank manager episode. And those were the days when buttering up the bank manager really did make a difference.

At eight years old, Sarah and her five year old sister, both shiny from the bath, had been led in to just such a dinner to say goodnight. It was artfully staged. Two angelic girls in lacy floor length nightgowns, animated Victorian dolls, a delightful feature displaying a sentimental picture of the perfect family.

The bank manager, a rotund avuncular bald man, had beamed delight. But in the slight pause between the kisses goodnight and the pretty young baby-sitter gathering the children to take them up to bed, her sister had pulled the bank manager's sleeve and said: 'I saw Daddy's plums.'

Earlier in the day Sarah's sister had walked into the unlocked bathroom and accidentally caught her father rising naked from the bath.

'Victoria plums!' her mother yelped, nodding frantically at the babysitter to take the children away, pronto. 'My husband grows them. Prize plums. In the garden.'

Sarah sniggered at the memory.

For a fraction of a second everyone glanced in her direction, then carried on with their homicidal conversation.

'Let's say, Max, you have murdered Lisa.' Tess shovelled custard-drowned pie into her mouth and waved the spoon around, pointing towards Max and Lisa as though they were soloists in an orchestra, and she the conductor.

'Eeeuu!' Lisa emitted an unearthly sound which the world judged feminine. 'Why me? Why not the other way round?'

'Statistics say when spouses fall out (and most murders, I should point, out are carried out by partners, lovers, husbands) the male is far more likely to kill the female than the other way round, but hey, Lisa, this is only a game—so, come on y'all, let's do it.'

Fat Max assumed the sly vulpine look of a stage villain, twisting an invisible moustache.

Hi diddle dee dee. Max, the fat fox, thought Sarah, then realised that that was something you'd never see—a fat fox. She glanced round the table again. They were foxes all, yapping and squealing, playing furtive games in the moonlight.

Sarah knew all about foxes.

Her mother made pets of them. Early in the winter mornings tender cubs were frequently discovered curled up on the edge of the warm grey embers in the open fireplace. Every night, rain, snow or shimmering heat, Sarah's mother would disappear into the black of the garden to put out food for the more tentative animals who were fearful of coming inside.

As a token of gratitude the foxes left shit where the food had been.

'It's their way of saying thank you,' said her mother.

'Some gratitude,' said anyone who saw the crap-strewn table.

'What would you have them do?' her mother would reply. 'Write me a note?'

Sarah sniggered, imagining the same thing happening here—the crisp white of the Irish linen cloth scattered with long brown glistening turds of appreciation.

She reached out to top up her wine.

With a winsome fraternal shake of the head, Martin placed his hand across the mouth of her glass.

Still holding the bottle Sarah tried to swipe Martin's hand away.

He was wearing that little-boy-lost, furrowed-forehead look again.

She wanted to smash the bottle into his idiotic, patronising face.

'Enough wine, I think, Sarah, for tonight.'

'I cooked all this food, darling.' Sarah yanked the glass onto her lap and filled it to the brim, the false dinner-party smile frozen on her lips. 'The least you can do in return is permit me a second glass of your precious Clos de l'Oratoire des Papes.' She exploded in laughter and gulped from the brimming glass. 'Bottoms up!'

Martin stood and snatched the bottle away, spraying her white blouse with red.

'As you said earlier, Martin, this "jaunty wine trips across the tongue".' Sarah rose too, white-lipped, any pretence of bourgeois decorum gone. 'And speaking entirely personally

I won't be happy till it has done the fucking can-can all the way down to my stomach.' Grasping the glass by its bowl, she marched to the kitchen door. 'I'll leave you all now to your little murders.' As she left she turned and pulled down her lower eyelid. 'And, as they used to say on *Crime Watch,* "Keep 'em peeled. Don't have any bad dreams, now."'

Up in the bedroom a few minutes later, Sarah lay in the dark, hearing the hushed apologetic sounds of the embarrassed guests trying politely to leave.

Fuck it. What did it matter? She'd be gone tomorrow. With any luck she'd never see any of them again.

She got up, pulled a small case from the top of the wardrobe and started flinging in pieces of clothing and make-up.

If only she could run to her mother. But that could not be.

Her mother was gone.

Sarah heard the front door slam. She glided silently to the window and peered down through the net curtains: Mrs Danvers, lit only by the shadowy street light.

Max and Lisa pulled faces at each other and giggled as they climbed into a huge sporty Jaguar. The car roared away into the night.

Another minute and the door banged a second time. Tess, this time, strutting along with that odd, bouncing gait of hers, fidgeting in her trouser pocket. She pulled out keys and tossed them a couple of times in her palm as she climbed the front steps to the house next door. Tess turned the key, and disappeared inside. A few moments later Sarah could hear her muffled footsteps padding up stairs to her lonely flat.

She moved out to the landing and listened over the banister. She could hear the muted hum of male voices coming from the dining room, low and respectful, like distant relatives round a death bed.

Martin must be trying to make things good with Mr Kruszynska, perhaps setting up another meeting in more convivial surroundings, like the bank, where it should have been in the first place.

She felt sorry now for her behaviour, but realised it would have been both simpler and better if Martin hadn't pestered her, and that she had simply refused to host the dinner.

Sarah returned to packing, taking a small bag of costume jewellery, a pile of paperwork, chequebooks, and the photograph of her mother from her dressing table.

The face in the black and white print was dark, handsome, smiling. A proud Irishwoman.

Poor Mama now, shrivelled, grey and gummy, all alone in a dim solitary world of her own.

Although Sarah went to see her most weeks, it was three years since her mother had recognised her. If anything, she was irritated by Sarah's visits, which broke up the calm docile hours spent in front of the television. Clever old Ma, who once delighted in the barbarities of Seneca, Laclos, and the Jacobean playwrights, now clapped with glee in front of a noisy screen showing *Bananas in Pyjamas*, sat tranquil and transfixed by The Hoobs and Spongebob Squarepants.

Sarah briefly squeezed the photograph to her breast before kissing it, placing it on top of her clothes and shutting the case.

Martin and Kevin moved along the hall towards the front door. Kevin must be putting on his coat.

Sarah swung her case off the bed and tiptoed downstairs. Now to face the music.

She winced at the brightness of the halogen-lit kitchen after being in the darkness of the unlit bedroom. Holding her hand up against her brow, she tucked the case under the breakfast bar, and took a casual position, leaning against the worktop near the sink, waiting for Martin to come back from his door-step farewell with the bank manager.

The front door clicked shut.

Sarah stepped away from the counter and folded her arms, ready for the barrage.

Martin slouched in. He looked at Sarah then shook his head, like a patronising driver overtaking on a country lane. He moved to the sink, hissing under his breath and ran the tap, testing its temperature with his fingers.

Sarah didn't mind the silence.

She made up her mind she would wait for Martin to speak first.

He poured a glass of water, and drank it in long, loud glugs.

With a fascinated revulsion, Sarah watched his Adam's apple bouncing up and down beneath the turkey skin of his neck.

When he had emptied the glass, Martin slammed it on the draining board making the dirty pudding bowls rattle.

'I suppose you think it's hilarious to humiliate me.' He picked up a cloth and started frenetically wiping down the worktops. As he passed her he swept his eyes up and down her body like a reptile eyeing up an unappetising lunch.

Sarah looked down at her feet. How silly and huge they looked in these high heels. She had a ladder in her tights. It ran up as far as her knee.

'I'm leaving you tomorrow, Martin.' She raised her eyes and watched for his reaction.

He stood still, his breathing shallow.

'Don't worry.' She smoothed down the front of her absurdly short skirt, worn only for the dinner party. 'You won't have to suffer any more embarrassment from me.' She straightened up and faced him, this stranger-husband of hers. 'I'll be off now, if you like. Though it would be more convenient, obviously, if I could wait till morning.'

Emitting a strangled growl, Martin flung the dishcloth into the sink. His lips were tight as string round a brown paper parcel. 'Fuck you, cunt!'

'Is that a yes or a no?' asked Sarah. 'Staying the night I mean, not fucking.'

'You're a bitch and a slag.' Martin paced the kitchen, waving his arms, barring her exit. 'Why did you have to show me up all night, making me look like a sodding twat in my own fucking home?'

'You think that I made you look a twat? While you were trying to pass me off as a suburban Stepford Wife?'

'Pity you're not one, at least the food might have had some taste. And you wouldn't be standing there now abusing me. You'd know your place.'

'My place?'

'After all, I've kept you for the last two years, while you just lounged around here at home, watching TV and playing on the computer.'

Sarah knew the rules of engagement. She knew she must take a deep breath, count to ten before she spoke, but it was impossible. She wanted to slap his smug, patronising face.

'This last year, while playing on my computer you might remember I have written all the company's best slogans. Much better slogans than your pathetic in-house team ever dredged up. And I might remind you Martin, that it was my redundancy money which set the business up. I could still have had a perfectly good job.'

'Oh, so that's the game is it? You want your money back.' He oiled across the room, nodding his head before abruptly spinning round like a bad actress in a cheap TV soap. 'Well, tough! It was all used up months ago.' He gave a manic laugh before licking the front of his teeth with the tip of his tongue and assuming a condescending smile. 'You can go now if you want. Otherwise...' He gestured towards the living room door. '...the sofa is through there. And when I come down to leave for work in the morning you'll be gone. I'm off to bed now. Some people have serious responsibilities, you know, things to do, offices to run.'

Martin gave her another withering look and turned for the stairs. He was walking away as he said:

'My father always said one day you'd turn into your mother. All women do. That is their misfortune.'

Sarah groaned. 'Your father didn't say that, actually, Martin. It was Oscar Wilde.'

He turned round, and moved slowly towards her. 'He also said that whenever a woman uses the word "actually", it means they're going for your balls.'

'If you had any intelligence, you know, you wouldn't go around quoting your father. He's a pompous fart.'

'Is that what you think?' Martin was right in front of her now, his eyes cold. 'Well, at least he isn't barking mad.'

'Are you trying to imply something about my mother?'

He shrugged and started pacing the kitchen again. 'If the cap fits.'

'She's got Alzheimer's, Martin. Alzheimer's.'

Martin started to chuckle. 'I'm not talking about now. I'm talking about way back, when I first met you. Your mother's a batty old bitch, with her foxes and rats and all the other vermin she surrounded herself with.'

Sarah thought back to the last few years her mother spent in her own home. She had been confused, had started leaving food out for the rats as well as the foxes. But that surely had been the onset of the disease which had now reduced her brain to mush.

Sarah's guts clenched with the memory. Her mother's cooker had broken. Sarah went round to sort it out. The electrician pulled the ancient white American range away from the wall, and said 'I think we may have found the culprit.'

He had stepped out of the way to let Sarah take a look.

The charred mummified remains of a rat were stuck to the blackened kitchen wall, its long curved teeth sunk deep into the mains cable.

Sarah had got the council in. The vermin exterminator found the little bowls of food in the garden, and also under the stairs. He sent in the social workers.

And so, bingo, proud, Irish-to-the-core, Ma was put into the home, where she remained to this day, spending her days sitting alone in that grim, bleak room staring out of the dusty window at leafless winter trees, perpetual tears running down her crinkled paper cheeks.

Sarah gave a dry sob.

'There you go,' sneered Martin in a sing-song voice. 'On with the waterworks. Exactly like her.' Throwing back his head, he guffawed. 'Preposterous old cow.'

After that everything happened very quickly.

Sarah picked up the fruit-smeared carving knife from the draining board and ran at Martin, holding it up above her head.

Hearing the rush, Martin turned in time to see the flash of the blade swing down towards his left shoulder.

He flung up a fist and knocked Sarah's arm away, grabbing at her forearms, trying to shake the knife out of her grip.

They grappled for a couple of seconds before Martin managed to seize hold of the knife's handle.

Sarah moved in to smack his face and stumbled.

Martin swung round, ducking to avoid her. With the flat of her palms she slapped out at him. Martin pushed her shoulder with his empty hand and they struggled, bodies close, almost wrestling.

Sarah managed momentarily to snatch the knife from Martin's grasp. Once she had hold of it, Sarah felt suddenly calm.

Then she saw the look on Martin's face. His expression seemed to crumple, his sinking eyes wide in horror. He stumbled backwards a step. His complexion suddenly took on a grey, putty-like sheen.

He lurched backwards until his spine hit the counter.

During a slow-motion second he remained there, pointing towards her with an accusing finger.

Sarah could hear nothing but her own heartbeat, the whooshing of blood in her ears. Now that she looked she could see spots of blood spreading across Martin's shirt front.

'Oh, my god,' cried Martin, in a high pitched whine. 'What have you done?'

His voice seemed strangely distant, as though he was underwater.

Sarah felt suddenly frightened.

Her slippery fingers, she realised, were still clenched around the sticky knife handle.

Someone must be playing with the dimmer switch, she thought, for the kitchen lights faded then suddenly grew brighter.

She tried to drop the knife, but it would not budge.

She looked down, pushing at the handle, trying to get rid of it.

It was only then that she realised the long steel blade was lodged in her own abdomen.

A white rushing sound filled her ears as Sarah slid slowly, irrevocably to the ground.

2

Jitterbug

A fast dance performed to swing or boogie-woogie music, consisting of a few standard steps and much improvisation

*O*H *FUCK!*

In a kind of stupefied paralysis Martin watched Sarah slump, blood streaming from a scarlet slash in her white blouse.

Fuck, fuck, fuck, fuck, fuck!

His heart thumped so hard he could almost hear it.

As he stumbled forward, his legs seemed to give way under him.

He fell to his knees and fumbled about, pressing his trembling hand to Sarah's neck, her chest.

Nothing.

She was dead.

God.

Dead!

What to do?

He pulled himself back to his feet and ran into the living room.

He picked up the phone, one finger poised on the 9 button.

Which service—Ambulance?

What for? Sarah was dead.

Who would believe what had just happened? He would be arrested for murder. Especially after the row everyone had just witnessed. No question.

Oh fuck!

He ran back to the kitchen.

Sarah lay still.

He knelt again, stretching out his quivering fingers to feel for a pulse in her neck.

Nothing.

He tried to put his ear to her chest, but he could hear only the hammering of his own frantic heart.

He sat back gasping for breath, trying to control the earth-quake which seemed to be going on within his chest.

He re-ran the row which had ended the dinner party. If Sarah was dead—with a huge knife covered in his fingerprints sticking out of her belly—no one would think it had been an accident. How could they?

Martin glanced up at the clock on the oven.

Eleven thirty.

Think. Think. Think.

Oh God!

All those conversations over supper too. Murder, murder, murder and more murder.

Martin froze.

Tess! It wasn't too hard to hear through these walls. Might she have heard anything?

Martin jumped up and paced the kitchen, staring down at Sarah's inert body willing it to move.

His hand rested for an instant on the screw-top of the whisky bottle.

NO!

He had to think clearly.

It was strange. Only a few minutes before he had felt ever so slightly drunk from all that expensive wine. Why on earth people went round spending more than a fiver a bottle he didn't have a clue. It all tasted much the same, and it all got you pissed. Well, except in this case, for all its extortionate price.

Martin felt stone cold sober.

He flopped down onto a stool and sat with his head in his hands.

What was wrong with him? Why was he thinking about fucking wine when his wife was lying dead on the floor with a kitchen knife poking out of her front and he in all probability he would be picked up for murdering her?

He knelt down and listened at her chest. He heard nothing. Then, as he moved his shirt caught the knife handle pulling it. The knife slid to the floor and lay by the body in a pool of blood.

Christ! Christ! Christ!

What to do now?

There were two options. One: He could phone the police and an ambulance and try to explain that, though there had been a fight, Sarah's death was purely accidental...

He groaned.

Who was ever going to fall for that one? And the truth was tonight he had wanted her dead, gone, out of his life—whatever it took to be free again.

And what was it Max had said? The first suspect was always the husband...most murdered wives were killed by their husbands and partners, or something.

Martin thought back through the dinner. Now he considered it, perhaps all that stuff could work in his favour. After all, the minute after the last guest left, Sarah had immediately declared her intention of leaving him. What he must do was follow that through on that. Make everything the same, as though he had walked up those stairs to bed, and he had woken to find her gone. Sarah had left in the night, or at dawn.

A police siren screeched past the front door.

Martin gulped.

It took a fraction of a second for him to realise that they couldn't be coming for him yet—as no one knew anything had happened.

Suddenly he could hear himself.

He was whimpering like a lost dog!

Calm. Calm.

It was pub throwing-out hour. At this time of night there was always police activity on the streets.

Martin edged across to the drawers by the sink and pulled out some bin liners and a roll of parcel tape. As he turned his foot struck the knife, sending it skittering across the floor. He ran after it, picked it up and tossed it in the sink.

It landed with a loud clatter.

Tess would have heard that!

He stood still, petrified, like a waxwork, listening.

Why?

Keep normal, keep normal.

In normal life people dropped knives into sinks. Everyone had seen the knife earlier at dinner. Sarah had used it to cut the pie right in front of them. It would have to be washed up. It was covered in blackcurrant from the pie, wasn't it?

He turned on the hot tap.

It was important to keep up the realistic noises of ordinary life.

He turned the tap off and went to work on Sarah, pulling the plastic bag up, enclosing her legs. He wound the tape round, sticking the bag to her skirt. Averting his eyes, he then pulled another bag down over her head and shoulders.

As he lifted her, Sarah's left arm slumped down, coming to rest on his calf.

He recoiled, only narrowly stopping himself from screaming.

His heart was banging so hard he feared it might smash through his ribcage and go running off across the floor like that thing in *Alien*.

He took a few deep breaths then felt Sarah's chest again for a pulse, a heartbeat, a breath, anything.

After a couple of moments shivering, Martin took Sarah's arms and folded them across her breast. Then, with shaking hands, he unwound the brown tape, and secured the second bag.

After that he rolled a third bag round her waist, and taped that too.

Good.

Now it didn't look like Sarah, it would be easier to leave her while he went out into the darkness and dug a hole.

He rocked back onto his heels.

So?

Was there anything else?

Anything else!

He was thinking like he was going out shopping or something, not about to bury his dead wife in the back garden.

He heard a slamming door, and wondered how much that know-all Yank next door had heard.

Fine. Let her listen.

Keep up the normality.

He went to the stairs and called up: 'Do what you want, Sarah. Women! You're all the same. There are plenty more fish in the sea. I'm going out for some air. At least the roses don't despise me.'

What a useless performance. Even he wasn't convinced. Jesus, if he was this bad at acting, how on earth would he get through the days to come?

He slid open the patio doors.

The garden was dark and quiet, lit only by a moonless orange-tinted London sky.

He paced the length of the lawn. Was this how it felt to be an actor in a stage play? He was utterly conscious of how he looked, his posture, the weight and speed of his tread and gait. At the far end of the garden he turned to face the house, throwing back his head and gulping lungs full of cool night air.

From here Martin could see the houses on either side quite clearly. Presumably anyone looking out of a window would be able to see him too. He briskly walked back towards the house, keeping to the right side, away from the side return. A thicket of jasmine tumbled over the high fence on this side. A few feet from his back window he peered up again.

If he dug here Tess would not be able to watch him.

He spun round and surveyed the houses whose looming backs threw his garden into shadow late every afternoon.

The straggling bush which year after year he had meant to chop back was in full leaf, giving him impenetrable cover.

He took out a spade and started to dig.

He tore out the herbs which covered this part of the border and lay them carefully on the patio, all the while thinking of Max and his ditches. He went over the details of everything Max had said, and realised that the most important thing was to act swiftly, to get as much done tonight as he could. Tomorrow he would try to carry on in as normal a fashion as would any man whose wife had left him the night before.

When the hole was a few feet deep and slightly longer than a large human's height Martin went back inside.

The body in the black bags still lay there. Things within had settled somewhat. The spike heels of Sarah's ludicrous shoes had pierced the plastic.

Lowering himself at the shoulder end of the black plastic package Martin slid his hands under his wife's armpits and tugged the body along the shiny kitchen floor.

The route behind him was painted with a long orange smear of blood.

He would deal with that later.

First get rid of...Martin decided that from now on he must no longer think of it as Sarah. It was just a pile of old stuff in a bin liner. He was getting rid of the unwanted rubbish.

Even better—Compost!

That made him laugh. The roses he would plant on top of her body would bloom like no others. 'What's your system, Martin?' people would ask. 'What is it that makes your roses so very special?'

And he would give a sly shrug and tap his nose with his forefinger.

'State secret,' he'd say. And mean it.

God, but this parcel was heavy. Who'd think that the bloody woman weighed so much. Like an elephant or a manatee.

He recalled nature programmes he had seen. Watching those weird creatures, manatees, so flabby and prehistoric looking, flopping around in tropical seas.

He sniggered, realising how badly Sarah would have taken being likened to such a huge blubbery lumpen animal.

He hauled his parcel onto the lawn and lined it up parallel to the border. Using his foot, he rolled the manatee into the hollow, then stooped to push down odd projecting bits.

Using the spade, he covered the manatee with soil.

Finally he put the herbs back and patted down the rising soil over the whole border.

Now to tackle the kitchen.

Martin knew that the first thing any criminalists would be looking for would be blood. He wasn't going to be a fool and throw away the knife, saying he'd lost it at a barbecue, leaving an empty space in the woodblock.

So he had to get rid of the blood on it.

He watched TV. He'd seen *CSI* and *Trial and Retribution* and *Forensic Files* and all those other morbid programmes about crime scenes. He knew that even when blood wasn't visible you could find it with some kind of ultra violet lights and sprays that revealed the apparently non-existent stains in a vivid shocking pink glow.

So what he needed was a deep clean. It seemed clear to Martin that TV was a great educator. Blood, he knew from the commercials, was a protein—and what got rid of protein?

Why, biological washing powder!

You saw it on the commercials over and over again.

He rooted under the sink, and found a large plastic bottle half full of some washing liquid. 'Enzyme Plus Bio Liquigel' said the label. He filled the sink with water and left the knife and the dishcloth to soak in the cloudy solution.

Tomorrow he would buy one of those huge Euro-packs of Ariel or Persil.

'I'm gonna wash that gal right outta my hair,' he sang under his breath.

It was all going to be all right. He would get through all this stuff. Everyone would believe Sarah had stormed off. Why wouldn't they?

Then time would do its thing.

People would forget.

The body would decompose.

Martin had no intention of moving house for a few years, so when the time came he could always skim away the remaining bones and things—and who would be any the wiser?

As someone (was it Max?) had said at dinner—if there's no manhunt because there's apparently no one missing, there is no search for a murderer. Ergo (that was a word Tess had used earlier and which Martin rather enjoyed repeating) he was in the clear.

With a shrill chirp the phone rang.

Martin leaped six inches from the ground and he slid along the floor, slamming into the wall.

It was midnight.

Who could be phoning at this late hour?

What should he say? Should he pretend Sarah had already gone?

No, he'd say she was upstairs packing, refused to speak to anyone...

His tongue felt as though it was sloughing, his saliva gone, sand in its place. He picked up.

'Hello?' His voice came out a hollow rasp.

A piercing female voice: 'Maureen, is that you?'

'No, it bloody isn't.' Martin slammed down the receiver.

His heart! Surely it could only beat this fast and hard for so long before it packed in altogether and he too keeled over.

How ironic that would be—him lying dead on the kitchen floor when the police broke down the door wondering why neither of them had been seen for days, hadn't answered the phone, paid the paper bill...And who would think then of digging up the garden for her?

It would be a kind of togetherness though.

Not that togetherness with Sarah was what he really wanted.

Only a few months ago Martin thought they would be together forever.

But not lately.

Now, of course, he realised with a shudder, she would always be with him, not just the decomposing remains, but, if he got away with this, even when her body had been eaten by worms, she would always be there in his head.

They would be together for Eternity.

Eternity!

THE RINGS!

Sarah would never have walked off wearing the bloody rings. She'd have left them behind in some small-minded gesture of independence. If he was to give this episode the semblance of truth he needed to have them. And the bloody things were still on her finger. He couldn't leave them there.

Martin swooped out into the garden, and threw himself onto his knees, scooping up the soil with his bare hands.

Everything might well rot in time. But not the rings, not that fucking stupid eternity ring. It wouldn't take a rocket scientist to work out that S-A-R-A-H spelled Sarah.

Once Martin got down to the bag he made a tear in the black plastic, and felt inside for Sarah's hand.

UGH!

It was cold.

He worked at the rings—wedding, engagement and eternity, easing them round and back and forwards. It was easy enough twisting the wretched things off, but as Martin pushed the hand back down into the bin liner, a mound of soil dislodged and spilled down over his arm.

It felt almost as though the body moved and sighed.

Martin leapt back, flinging his arms up, only just stopping himself screeching into the night.

He lay back on the damp grass, gasping for air.

Bugger.

In his fright he had dropped the eternity ring, or rather he had flung it across the garden. Now it lay somewhere on the bloody lawn.

He shoved the other two rings in his trouser pocket, crawled forward and pushed the soil back over the exposed areas of plastic bag. Then he rested back on his haunches, head low, trying to get his breath back. Once he felt more composed he crawled around the lawn on his hands and knees, combing his fingers through the blades of damp grass, inch by inch. He knew this was called "a finger search". He'd seen people in white overalls doing it on the TV news.

Oh god—the news. This silly business mustn't come to that. He'd hate to have his face plastered all over the television.

Martin's heart was breaking the speed limit again. Too much adrenalin.

Calm down. Calm down.

Why the fuck had he given her that horrible ring anyhow? It was disgusting, all those murky purple stones.

He gave a snort.

Well, of course he knew why!

Then the ring was an inexpensive way of buttering her up.

Now it was just a fucking liability.

Just when Martin was on the verge of giving up the search, and returning to more urgent work in the kitchen, he found the eternity ring. It was sticking up, propped by a little stone. He knelt on it and yelped.

It gave his knee a nasty jab.

Tomorrow he'd have a bruise.

He shoved the sodding thing into his pocket and went back inside.

There was mud everywhere.

He was covered in it.

Still, mud was better than blood.

So what?

Who'd think anything of a kitchen floor covered in muddy boot marks? Especially if he had been seen doing a bit of potting. Gardening was a perfectly innocent occupation for a solitary male whose wife had just left him.

In fact, tomorrow after work he would go to the garden centre and buy yards of bedding plants and pretty shrubs.

He'd grow a prize garden, on his newly enriched soil.

Oh god.

He was racked by a dry sob.

How could such a terrible thing have happened to him?

But he knew he must not break down now.

There was work to be done.

Unscrewing the bottle of Bio Liquigel he staggered to the broom cupboard and pulled out a squeegee mop and plastic bucket. He wondered if the action he'd seen on TV, the enzymes eating the protein, needed time to work. Was it like bleach, where you accidentally dropped it on your clothes and pretty much instantly regretted it, or did you need to leave it to soak overnight?

The latter, he decided. That made sense. Give the enzymes some time to munch away at all the protein they were so famous for gobbling up.

He gave the floor a quick once-over. First he must remove all visible traces of blood. Wipe the tops down too, for good measure. Then he'd give the floor another go, only this time he'd make the solution even stronger. Last thing before bed he'd throw the cloth, and the sponge from the mop and the knife into a strong solution in the sink and set the dishwasher off. That would seem a pretty normal thing to do after a dinner party and a row with your wife.

While he sloshed the blood-devouring mixture around the floor Martin tried to work out the exact version of this evening's events.

First there had been the unpleasantness at the dinner table. Then Sarah had stormed off to the bedroom. After that the guests had left. (No wonder, he thought. How embarrassing it had been!) First Max and Lisa, then Tess, then finally KK, his big white hope.

Now Martin had to come up with the creative work: Devastated at his wife's rudeness, he had started unpacking the first dishwasher, which Sarah had set off during the party. And shortly afterwards Sarah came down and started abusing him again and they had fought.

No. Better to leave out any mention of a fight.

Sarah had come downstairs and told him she was leaving. He had begged her to stay, saying it was too dodgy for a woman to go wandering the streets at that time, and that if she was going it would be better to wait till morning.

Why did that sound like rubbish?

It was practically what HAD happened. When you lie, make it close to the truth. They always said that.

Sarah had told him she was going to go, BUT had then asked if he'd mind her staying till morning.

Yes. That was definitely better.

By that time he would have finished the washing up...No. Would he have done the washing up while she just stood there telling him she was leaving?

She had gone upstairs to pack.

That was it.

What had he shouted up the stairs for that stupid next-door bitch to hear? 'Do what you want. Women! You're all the same. I'm going out for some air.'

Yes. Yes. Something like that.

Sarah had gone up to pack. He shouted upstairs after her, then went into the garden for a breather.

That's when he had got the idea to do some gardening. Not then exactly. Tomorrow. He was going to do some gardening tomorrow, after Sarah had gone—plant some new bushes and things. Buy some rose fertiliser.

After that he had come in and finished the washing up, set off the machine for the second time.

Sarah by now was lying on the sofa.

Can you imagine, officer! Lying on the sofa, while he martyred himself in the kitchen.

Good. Good. That's right. Insult to injury.

So now he'd better do all these things he was going to tell people he had done. Leaving the mopping for a bit, Martin quickly unpacked the dishwasher and stacked the dirty pudding bowls and pans inside. The floor was bloody slippery. He almost broke his neck sliding from one end of the room to the other with a stack of plates in his hands. It was like being in some film with Buster Keaton.

Once he had set the washer off for its second time this evening he quickly finished the floor's second coat of the enzyme, blood-eater.

He took his clothes off there and then and put them into the washing machine. He decided it wasn't a good idea to set that off. When the spin sent the house rocking the neighbours would wonder who the hell was doing their washing in the middle of the night, and more to the point, why?

He must remember to turn it on first thing in the morning. Now for bed.

On the stairs he turned back and said in a loudish voice, but he hoped not too stagy: 'If you don't like the situation, Sarah, in the morning I trust you'll be gone.' Then made his way up to the bedroom.

The bed was all tousled where Sarah had obviously lain down earlier.

He took out his pyjamas, still folded under his pillow, and put them on. They felt cold to his skin. He could smell his own sweat, sour and musky.

That was the fear, he knew, the shock, the adrenalin.

He got into bed and turned out the light.

Wait!

Best check the time, so he could say, if asked, 'Oh I went to bed at about...and that was the last time I saw her. In the morning she was gone.'

It was half past midnight.

How odd. It felt much, much later than that.

He curled up and fell into a deep dreamless sleep.

When he woke the sun was shining. He lay basking in the sunlight for a few moments before he remembered what had happened.

He felt momentarily winded. He sprawled out on his back and took deep breaths.

The phone shrieked, sending his heart into hyper-speed again.

Spitless, he answered.

'Martin! Morning. Max!'

Martin tried to part his dry lips, but even his tongue too was dry.

He swallowed and tried again.

'Hello, Max.'

'Have I woken you?'

Best use it.

'Yes.'

'Sorry old man, I was just phoning to thank you for last night and...' Max paused and lowered his voice. '...ask you if everything's OK.'

What could that mean? Martin tried quickly to work out what would be the normal response of a man who hadn't...Oh. His head swum. He feared he would faint. He hauled himself up into a sitting position.

'Yes. Fine.'

'Can't you speak?'

Can't he speak about what? Martin gulped from the water glass by the bed while Max continued.

'Was everything all right after we went? You can just say yes or no, if the dragon's breathing down your neck.'

'No!' Martin suddenly worked out his game, and lowered his voice to a whisper, cupping the receiver with his spare hand. 'We had the most godawful row, Max. She said she was going to leave me, but I've not been downstairs yet to check.'

'Downstairs?'

Martin could feel the panic coming back. But downstairs was right. Of course it was.

His voice was now barely a breath.

'She slept on the sofa. She was going to leave last night, but I persuaded her to wait till morning.' He then added, realising the irony and at the same time seeing that it worked well for him: 'In case anything should happen to her. You know, pubs throwing out, drunks, muggers...'

'Look,' Max said, in an avuncular way. 'If you need any help, Martin, you will let me know, won't you? Go downstairs and check it all out. Then, if you need to, you must phone me back.'

Martin put the phone down.

He got up and pulled on his robe.

Did Max know? What could he mean by all that coded talk about help? Could he have known? Perhaps he had come back, forgotten a glove or something and overheard everything while standing on the front step or peering through the letterbox.

No, that was rubbish. Max had witnessed the initial row at dinner, and was worried that Sarah would have gone on humiliating him after everyone was gone.

The sight that greeted Martin when he reached the kitchen was a shock. For a start he had forgotten about the thick layer of liquigel, and went skating again, this time landing agonisingly on the hard floor, on his arse.

But the mud! It was everywhere. He followed the trail to the garden and, suddenly aware of the neighbours' windows, stepped out, yawning and stretching. His tried to make his thought look like 'Oh what a beautiful morning!'

That was good. He realised that for this thing to work he needed to live the life of a Method actor. Like Marlon Brando, Al Pacino or Robert De Niro. How funny that they all end in O! Methodo Actoro! He smiled.

He must think every thought of the things he wanted others to see in him as the truth.

He did a few arms twirls and put his face up to the sun before casually scanning the borders, starting at the far side, away from...the manatee.

But wait!

Would a man whose wife had just slept on the sofa, and was now gone, leaving him, be out in the garden smiling and flinging his arms around?

Martin scurried inside.

For veracity's sake he went through to the living room and gazed down on the empty sofa, almost expecting to see a pillow and the rug all crumpled, where Sarah had lain.

He wiped his hands, matter of fact, business as usual.

Sarah was gone. She had obviously left the house sometime between half past midnight, when he went to bed, and now—just before eight.

Bitch!

Rather than take his usual leisurely bath, Martin decided to spend a half hour cleaning the kitchen again, giving the floor another once over with the mop, make the place look spick and span, and then he'd make up the lost time by taking a quick shower, rather than his usual bath, before going into work.

The shower wasn't a good idea. He couldn't bear to draw the curtain. *Psycho* came to mind, and poor Janet Leigh, squawking under a rain of knife-blows. Consequently the bathroom floor flooded.

He had just finished mopping that up when the phone rang again.

He was all prepared to deal with Max this time.

But it was Kevin.

The usual pleasantries: thank you for the lovely supper, please thank Sarah for doing all the work, perhaps he should have lent a hand in the washing up?

Martin screwed up his courage. 'I'm afraid I won't be able to do that, Kevin. Last night Sarah decided to leave me. It had been bubbling up for some time, it seems.'

There was an unbearably long silence on the other end of the line.

Martin resisted the inclination to fill it with incriminating babble.

'I'm sorry to hear that, Martin,' said Kevin, his voice sounding suddenly cool. 'It's not looking good for you now.'

Martin's heart started again on its reckless tattoo.

He couldn't think what else to say but 'No.'

'She cooked and cleaned for you, kept house, did the shopping, bookkeeping, VAT etcetera, didn't she?'

'Yes,' Martin was scouring his emotions to work out what was a suitable response. Should he bang on about how much he'd miss her, or play the cool, good riddance line?

He stayed silent.

'Ah well,' said Kevin. 'Just a courtesy call, Martin. I'm sorry to hear your news. Mustn't hold you up. We'll talk soon.'

When, grabbing his coat, Martin looked at the clock, he realised he was going to be late into the office—just what he didn't want.

He shuffled past his employees without a word and holed up in his own office, making himself look important and busy. After that the morning passed in a pretty straightforward way. Justin and Mike, the employees carried on as usual, alternating between making phone calls, and talking between themselves. 'Drawing up strategies' they called it. Martin often wondered whether that translated as: draining his pockets dry while arsing about doing nothing but gossip.

Martin, distracted from the niceties of reading the blurbs of his latest clients, had started writing a list of things he still needed to do about the manatee. Then he wondered about the perils of leaving his ideas anywhere in concrete form. He'd seen detectives on those police shows, using dust and finding imprints of long discarded letters on the lower pages of a notebook.

He got as far as 'pack case' then crumpled up the piece of paper and binned it. A few minutes later he pulled the note from the waste paper basket, smoothed it out and put it into the shredder.

As the last slithers slipped down into the bin beneath, the phone rang.

Kevin again.

'I've been looking at your business plan, Martin, in the light of the news about Sarah.'

What news?

Martin gulped, heart off again, steeple-chasing.

'Sorry to load on the pressure at such a nerve-wracking time but if I go ahead and process this loan, I'm not sure how you're going to manage.'

'Oh, it's been boiling up for some time. I'll get through. Things had been cooling for a while. It's not been that much of a shock, emotionally speaking.'

'Ah!' Kevin paused. 'It wasn't that exactly that I was talking about. It was the other thing...'

What other thing?

Oh god!

What other thing? He could hear papers rustling. Why didn't the bloody man get on with whatever he was about to say.

'Martin, I've looked at it every which way. I really do think...' Kevin lowered his voice. 'Every way I look at it, when you dispose of Sarah you're suddenly in trouble.'

'Dispose of...' What was he talking about?

'Will you get someone in to fill the space?'

Get someone in?

My God!

He knew about the hole in the garden and...

He knew.

Kevin the Czech knew.

'You said yourself that you were on overload, Martin, and that's why you need to take on more staff. So now, I can see, in addition to all that, you'll need a cleaner, someone to do your shopping (though I suppose you could do that yourself, online), a bookkeeper...And as you said, Sarah had her own private income from the inheritance which was there for you to fall back on, and the two of you shared the expenses of the house.'

Martin prickled with relief. 'Yes, we did,' he said. 'But it's not a problem. I'll get by.'

'Will you sell up?'

'Uh, I hadn't thought about it.'

'I'd suggest you should think about it. It's quite a big house for one person. Not to mention the ghosts.'

'Ghosts?'

'I'm sorry. Of course she isn't dead—but you know what I mean. I imagine also she'll fight for some kind of settlement. So selling may be your only option. You've got quite a heavy mortgage. If you downgraded and got a small bachelor pad, then, even after paying Sarah off, that would still give you a bit of equity to play with. I'm worried, you see, about processing this form of yours now that Sarah's no longer part of the equation...well, except in a very negative way. I fear it'll have to be a straight no.'

Martin's mind raced through all the possible replies to this onslaught of negativity. He needed time to work it out, so stayed silent. Why had he told the fucking man all those lies about Sarah's imaginary money and contributions?

DAMN.

'So, I'll put the plan on hold for a little while, shall I, Martin, till you've had a bit of time to think? Perhaps you'll get back to me in the next week and we'll see how it goes.'

Martin took an early lunch and used the time to drive to the garden centre, where he piled a trolley with trays of snapdragons, geraniums and sweet peas. He also chose some pretty roses. The attached photos looked pretty anyhow, the actual bushes looked like feeble leafless stumps. He hoped they grew fast. He wanted results.

While he browsed the rows of bedding plants Martin thought about Mr Bank Manager's bombshell.

Yes. Martin had lied on the form.

Isn't that what everyone did?

It was a known fact that a bank wouldn't lend you money unless they thought you didn't actually need it. So if you wanted to borrow money you had to tell them about private incomes and leave out the fact that your wife works from home and is all but on the payroll, or that you didn't really employ her, officially speaking, so that you'd save on National Insurance contributions.

And as for Sarah's inheritance, for starters, her mother was still very much alive. Martin laughed at the thought of Sarah's mother ever being in a position to leave her daughter anything. The woman's grasp on reality had always been tenuous, and now that she was barking mad all the money would be eaten up paying for the home. The only money Sarah had ever had, and he knew there was none left, was the golden handshake she'd had from that clutch of shrews, termagants and viragos at her old publishing house.

Mind you, who was to say they were really horrible? He only had Sarah's word for it that they were nasty. Martin had always thought they looked rather well turned out, and very fanciable.

But perhaps that was some weirdo thing, because actually they reminded him a bit of his mother—all so stern, practical and elegantly dressed.

Martin tossed a bag of organic fertiliser into the trolley. He didn't like to think about it. But really, after all the time Sarah had spent working in publishing, and then having volunteered for the chop, he felt sure there must be some dosh left over, stashed away in secret premium bonds or a safety-net ISA, or something. Sarah was like that. She always kept private things up her sleeve for a rainy day.

At the checkout there was a problem with Martin's debit card. He suspected it was because the girl on the till was an inept twit. She had wrongly added up the contents of his trolley three times before her debacle with the card machine. Rather than hang about for supervisors to arrive, Martin paid cash and, having seen them stacked up in the car park, at the last minute added a large sack of compost.

If he sprinkled that about all over the place the manatee area wouldn't look so different from the rest of the garden as it did now.

During the afternoon in the office Martin tried working out various scenarios that he could use with KK, regarding the loan and Sarah's disappearance, but it was terribly difficult when you couldn't write anything down. He kept losing track of his thoughts.

If Sarah had got money stashed away, of course, as her next of kin, that would be his anyhow.

Martin slumped back into his typing chair.

Except that she wasn't dead, was she? She'd only run off. Therefore he wasn't next of kin, he was just her ex.

Martin wondered if Sarah had signed up for internet banking or something like that, and that he could get at her savings that way. He might check out her computer when he got home. That would be the thing. She was a methodical old girl and he knew she had a password manager on the laptop. It wouldn't take him two seconds to get into that, after all he knew her date of birth and her mother's maiden name.

Her mother! Oh God!

What would become of the old cow now, without Sarah? Perhaps he should go and visit the barking bag in the home?

No.

He didn't go in before. Why do it now? That was exactly the kind of suspicious behaviour Max was talking about at dinner. Anyhow, as the bloody woman lived on some creepy *C-Beebies Balamory* planet where the only recognised language was *Teletubby*-talk, she wouldn't notice even if he did go in there, ergo, what was the point?

When five o'clock came around Martin only knew because suddenly his two normally reluctant employees started manically packing up their stuff and heading out, no doubt to the pub. It was the fastest he'd seen them move all day.

He realised he himself had done no work at all.

Things couldn't carry on like this or he'd start losing clients and land himself in an even worse mess, if that was possible.

Back home he parked up, then carried all the plant trays from his boot and put them on the front step. He waved gaily at Tess who was peering out from behind a net curtain, no doubt pretending to be working at her computer.

Martin strode up to his front door, hauling the incomprehensibly heavy sack of compost behind him.

His key jammed in the lock.

That was all he needed!

There was no way he was getting a locksmith in today.

He'd rather kick the door in.

He wiggled the key about, shouldering the panels around the stained glass panes.

The door flew open.

The lock was on the catch.

The hallway was strewn with rubbish.

What was going on?

Martin dropped the sack, and tiptoed over the threshold, gingerly pushing doors open before peering inside.

The TV was gone.

And the stereo.

Bollocks!

Oh GOD!

What about the garden?

Gasping for air, Martin rushed through to the back door and gaped down at the flower bed where he had interred Sarah. He stood for a moment panting, his palms pressed against the cool glass, gazing through the mist caused by his breath.

Prat!

What was he thinking about?

Since when did burglars go digging about in the flower-beds? He unlocked the garden door and flung it open, then forced himself back to the front hall to carry the plants through. Wouldn't you know, when he dumped the huge plastic sack of compost down in the middle of the lawn, he looked up and there was that bloody American waving at him again. Who did she think she was, Jessica Fletcher? Snooping on him, front and back.

Martin smiled and returned her wave, then mimed wiping sweat from his brow with the back of his arm.

He was rather pleased with that touch. It seemed very realistic.

Back inside he checked over the whole house. The thieving bastards had taken the bedroom TV and stereo too, and flung stuff from the drawers onto the floor.

He flopped down onto the bed and picked up the phone.

For the second time in 24 hours he started to dial 999.

And for the second time he put down the receiver before the number engaged.

Best think this through before he had invited police to come swarming into the house, poking and snooping about.

Who knows what they might find?

He'd have to bring up the fact that Sarah had 'gone', and he couldn't depend on himself not to blush or lose his spit and do that embarrassing thing where your top lip gets caught on your dry teeth and momentarily you look like Bugs Bunny. Any amateur body language reader knows this means you are stressed and very probably lying.

Martin let out an involuntary sob. He sat for a while on the edge of the bed with his head in his hands.

How long could he keep this charade going?

Why not come clean, tell the police exactly what happened...?

After all he hadn't really killed her. It had been an accident.

Anyway, Sarah herself might have inflicted the fatal wound. It might not have been him at all.

With a shrill jangle, the doorbell broke his thoughts.

Who the fuck was this?

And the place all a mess!

Bugger.

Martin ran down the stairs as quietly as he could. He spent a minute flinging all the stuff from the floor into drawers and cupboards.

'Coming!' He quickly smoothed down his hair, loosened his tie, and opened the door.

Tess was standing on the step, grinning. He thought that if she was a dog she'd have a tail wagging like a windscreen washer on top speed.

'Hi, Martin. Is everything all right?'

Martin swallowed. All right? What did that mean?

'Yeah. Yeah, Tess. Fine.'

'It's just...Well, you know I live in an upstairs apartment. No yard...And I saw you were doing a bit of gardening and thought you could do with an extra hand?'

'Um, I...well...I...'

What did she really want? Martin realised he was stammering like a buffoon and he must pull himself together, pronto.

Tess shuffled from one foot to the other. 'Gore overload.'

Gore overload!

What did she know?

Martin tried to swallow and inadvertently made a hollow gulping sound.

'Bloody crime writing!' Tess was still smiling in that pseudo-innocent Mona Lisa way of hers. 'There are times when you need to get the wind in your hair. You sit for hours in front of the screen, totally stuck. Better to get out.'

Martin took his first breath in what felt like hours. That was the gore she was referring to! Her book! Nothing to do with him at all.

'Writers' block?' he asked, proud that he knew the terminology.

'Writer's block!' Tess gave a scornful snort. 'There's no such thing. I'm just plain stuck. And I thought if I knuckled down on your flower borders and gave them a good turning over, it might free the brain. Comprende?'

Well, no. He didn't understand. So she had writers' block, by another name, but why would that make her suddenly want to dig up his flowerbeds?

Unless...

He grasped the nettle.

'Look, Tess, I don't know if you heard, but Sarah walked out on me this morning. That dinner and everything. Been boiling up for some time, and er...' God, he'd managed to get that bit out convincingly enough. Now to justify his not inviting her to come delving about in his incriminating subsoil. 'Normally I'd love to have someone to help me, but, you see...I'm looking for a bit of hard physical exercise myself, to...'

'Burn off the tension. OK. I get it.' Tess looked disappointed. 'It's the same for you, isn't it? Hours sitting in front of a monitor all day. After that, everything other people do outside the window looks like fun.' She turned to go. 'Oh, by the way...?'

Martin braced himself. Was Tess employing the *Columbo* treatment? Columbo always left the killer question for the last minute, turning back into the scene just when he had walked out of the room.

'Tell me, Martin...' Tess gave another bland smile.

Martin winced, ready for the blow.

'Do you have workmen in?'

'Workmen?' Was this some kind of trap?

Martin realised he was scratching his head with one finger. Who was he trying to impersonate now, Stan Laurel?

'It's, just, I heard a lot of banging going on this afternoon. I was hoping it was carpenters, because I'm looking to have some new bookcases installed.'

'No.' Martin spoke slowly, giving his brain time to run through potential afternoon bangers. 'It wasn't carpenters. The, er, bank manager—well you met him last night, Kevin Kruszynska—thinks perhaps I should sell up. So I, er, had some...surveying people round to check out the electricity and plumbing before I get the estate agents in.'

'Estate agents, meaning realtors, right?'

'Haven't a clue, I'm afraid.' Martin shrugged. 'I don't speak American.'

'Oh Martin!' Tess giggled, holding her hand over her mouth. 'You break me up. Really you do. You're so funny. I can't believe Sarah walked out on you.'

She turned and left, bouncing along the pavement with that smug little walk of hers.

What did she mean by that? "I can't believe Sarah walked out on you."

She did know, didn't she?

Tess knew.

She was a fucking crime writer, after all.

She spent her whole life inventing people like him.

She'd worked it out.

She's heard him through the wall.

Seen him in the garden.

Realised what had happened.

And now she was on the snoop, trying to squeeze the truth out of him.

My god!

What a coup that would be for her.

Think of the publicity she'd get for her dire, commercial, airport books if she unearthed a real life murderer living next door.

Rubbing his face with his hands he went into the kitchen and made himself a cup of instant coffee. He sat at the kitchen table, his eyes mechanically scanning the floor, fascias and skirting board for blood stains.

If he stuck to his story, kept up a normal existence, Martin felt he would be all right.

What could Tess actually do about anything? People's wives left them all the time. That was no reason for the police to come in and start digging up your garden.

But what if she tried to do some of the same amateur sleuthing work she probably wrote about in her lurid novels? If that bloody smirking American hopped over the fence while he was out, then poked about and discovered Sarah's body...

But how could she do that? Unless the little snoop leaped down from her first floor windowsill with the sole intention of probing about in his borders.

No.

It wouldn't happen.

Martin went to turn on the TV, for the evening news, then remembered he didn't have a TV anymore, thanks to those burgling swine. Of course they were the banging "carpenters".

He cursed himself for spinning that idiot story to Tess.

What a bollocking predicament!

What had he done to himself? By not reporting the burglary, and cancelling out Tess as a potential witness he'd let a pair of scumbag criminals get away with robbing him of all his electrical goods, and meanwhile had also thrown away the chance of recouping any of it on the insurance.

Oh well. He could live without TV.

He noticed that, though the sods had nicked his Roberts DAB radio, they had left behind on the kitchen work-top a battered old transistor from the bathroom.

Thanks.

Bastards.

For a moment Martin wondered whether he might be able to use the incident, link it up somehow, make it look as though they, these unknown men who had broken into his house, had also done in Sarah, and buried her in the garden. A kind of burglary gone wrong.

But of course that was useless. He had told Max first thing this morning that Sarah was already gone. And Tess didn't hear the men till this afternoon.

How the hell had the cunts got in?

Cradling his cup, Martin went to inspect the front door. There was no obvious sign of a break-in, but when he thought back to leaving this morning he remembered being in a wild hurry, and couldn't be certain he had double locked. Plus, his Yale lock was not only one of those old ones you could open with a credit card but sometimes it didn't click shut properly.

He frequently came into the hall to find the front door wide open because he hadn't slammed it hard enough behind himself.

Martin spent a half hour wandering slowly round the house a second time, checking what had been taken.

His laptop.

Sarah's laptop.

Dammit.

But perhaps they'd done him a favour by taking that. Now he wouldn't have to dispose of the thing himself. He would certainly have had to offload the laptop. Sarah would never have left home without it. And that would have been no easy thing to do. Not without leaving incriminating trails pointing back to himself.

Martin was glad he hadn't reported the burglary now.

He remembered at dinner Tess had gone on and on about guilty people using too many coincidences. And although this was truly a coincidence, who would believe it?

Best keep things simple. Make sure that as little as possible was out of the ordinary.

Martin rooted through his desk drawer.

His spare bank card, the one he used for foreign holidays, was gone. Well, that was OK. He could phone and block that.

And his passport was missing.

And Sarah's jewellery.

Oh god.

GOD!

Where had he put the rings? Had they taken the bloody rings? He patted down his pockets.

No.

He remembered now. He had put them on the kitchen top in a pudding bowl full of that gel stuff.

Hadn't he?

But they weren't there now.

He'd washed the bowl up.

But the rings were gone.

Damn.

After all that trouble!

Why hadn't he left the sodding things on her fingers, safe under that brown loam which he was about to cover with compost and flowers.

Well, like her laptop, it was probably for the best. After all, these impertinent chancers would be disposing of the things for their own benefit. And, unless they confessed to burgling his house, it would look as though they had somehow taken them from Sarah after she had left home. Martin would simply tell the police that Sarah left with her laptop, and with all three rings on her fingers.

He was sorry now that he had told Max he'd advised Sarah to stay overnight for fear of muggers and that she had taken his advice. If only he had said he had made the offer for Sarah to stay, and she had spurned it, marching out of the front door at 3 am, swinging her laptop like an advertisement for any mugger to jump her.

It was a known fact. Women shouldn't walk about in the darkness, especially when carrying pinchable items and wearing expensive rings.

Then, when the laptop turned up in some police raid, the finger of suspicion would not immediately swing in his direction.

Martin glanced through the window. If he didn't get on with that planting pronto it would grow dark. No point gardening in the Stygian Gloom, as Sarah used to call it, unless he was trying to get everyone to think he was a spooky wife murderer.

Rolling up his sleeves, Martin went outside, realising again that, joking apart, he really was a spooky wife murderer.

He snapped the polystyrene tray and started pulling out small plugs of pansies and snapdragons, ready to arrange in neat rows along the ridge of Sarah's body.

3

Fandango

*Begins slowly, tenderly, the rhythm marked
snapping fingers, and stomping feet. The speed
gradually increases to a whirl of exhilaration.
Towards the end of each figure the dancers
stand rigid, caught by a hiatus in the music,
moving again only when the music is resumed.*

IN THE NIGHT Martin dreamt that Sarah came back and stood
at the end of the bed pointing a finger on him and saying
over and over: 'Eternity?' in a hissy, witchy voice. He tried
to reply but his voice was a garbled scream that wouldn't come
out, as though his lips were sewn together. 'Please stop!' he
had attempted to say. She was frightening him, he had tried
to tell her. She sounded like the girl with green vomit in *The*

Exorcist and if she was to get on in business she needed to take elocution lessons.

He awoke from the dream in a hot sticky sweat.

Elocution lessons?

Where had that come from?

When, a few minutes later, Martin was in the kitchen getting a drink of water, he double checked both the back and front doors. He turned off the lights too, and peered out at the dark flower border.

But the little plants were still there in neat rows stretching the length of the garden.

In the morning light, when he had properly woken, he felt so insecure that, ludicrous as it was, he found himself crawling around on the bedroom floor, searching for footprints or soil traces, just in case the apparition he had seen had not been a mere vision but really had been Sarah, come back from the shallow grave to take her revenge on him.

Of course the carpet was clean.

Martin checked the flowerbed again, then went into work, taking with him a pile of unopened mail and bills. He'd got them from the hall floor and an in-tray on Sarah's desk in the front room. Kevin was right about her importance in the household and the business. She really did deal with all the correspondence, the bill-paying and bookkeeping. Her loss was going to mean much more work for him. It was terrifying. He already felt as though he was on overload.

On the way in Martin stopped the car to pick up some cash from a hole in the wall.

A curt message told him please to refer to his bank.

Damn.

The two lizards he employed were laughing and joking when he came into the office, feet up on the desks, sipping coffee.

'Not got enough to do?' snapped Martin as he walked through their room. He was trying to sound clipped and scary, like Alan Sugar on that *Apprentice* programme, but realised that he sounded more like Mr Humphries in *Are You Being Served*.

As he passed into his own office he could picture them both behind him, pursing their lips, one hand on hip, the other one flapping. He spun round, hoping to catch them, but they were both still sprawled out in the same position as before—immobile, surly, staring.

'Brain-storming session,' said Justin, the slimy one, whom Sarah had dubbed Justin Case. Mike, who was even more of an arsehole, then said something about needing to incentivise enterprise interfaces, but Martin was already shutting the door on them.

He knew he had to phone the bank, but thought he'd better go through the bills and get the full picture before dealing with that next horror.

Using a paper knife, he slit open the envelopes and rapidly sorted the letters into three piles: personal mail, things to be dealt with and bills.

He could feel his heart lurch and his face grow hot as he noted, from the bottom of each page, the figures he owed. For a moment he thought he was going to throw up. He opened a window, trying to get some air while the nausea passed. He wasn't sure what was causing it—the nightmarish worry about money, which had been dogging him for weeks, or the stress of the burglary and his inane mishandling of it, or... that-thing-which-dare-not-speak-its-name-which-had-happened-to-him-the-night-before-yesterday.

The buzzer rang.

It was Mike. 'Kevin Kruschev or someone on the phone for you.'

Martin hesitated. Ah well. This would save him the bother of making the call about the stopped card.

'Put him through.'

'Martin, good morning. How are things?' Kevin spoke in a cheery bright voice which made Martin's skin prickle. 'Had any more chance to think about our little conversation?'

'Do you know, Kevin, I have.' Martin used a deliberate tone, hoping it came over as authoritative. 'And I think that, after all, I'm going to let the loan thing drop.'

Kevin was silent for what felt an age.

'That's the thing to do,' said Martin, uneasy, filling the gap.

'Do you really think that's a good idea, Martin? You said yourself that small operations like yours were going under all over the place, and of course expansion is the only way to keep ahead of the game.'

What? Damn! Martin didn't want to expand. He just wanted to sell up everything and get out, and run away, and lie on a sun lounger on the Costa del Sol, like proper criminals.

'Perhaps for a while I should tighten up the enterprise, and then look again at expanding in a month or two.'

It was all his father's fault. One of the things he'd always said was 'Even when you're up to your neck in shite, my son, especially when you're up top your neck in shite, never, ever let them think you're going down. When your back's against the wall—EXPAND!' Martin ran his fingertips across his brow. Sarah was right. His bloody father was a pompous little popinjay (whatever that meant). Why had he ever thought the old fart was worth quoting?

'You see, I'm running through the paperwork right at this moment, actually, Kevin. Totting up the figures and projecting incentivisations.' [where had that word sprung from? Perhaps he should put Mike on the line, let him deal with the ruddy

Czech] 'Can we take a rain-check, for the moment, and I'll call you back when I have a more commanding view of the broader picture?'

From what dark corner of his brain had he dredged up all that idiotic jargon? Rain check, indeed. What the hell did that mean? He laughed and thought of Sarah. What do you call a bank manager caught in a shower? Rain Czech, she might have said.

The bank manager continued spouting some parting platitudes down the line when Martin's eyes rested on the bill which lay next on the pile: The Robbins—Care Home.

Oh god.

He covered it with his diary then put the phone down.

It was only then that Martin realised he had forgotten to ask Kevin about the hole-in-the-wall bank card message, or indeed, to put a stop on the stolen (he would say lost) card.

Bracing himself, Martin took the diary away from the care home bill and took a closer look.

Oh bugger.

The bloody mother.

What with his father and her mother, he wondered why a person couldn't just sprout from the earth like a flower, with no parents at all. The only thing parents were was a bloody responsibility.

He'd lost Sarah, the only living soul he had ever really cared about, and now he had gained this new obligation—watching out for Sarah's mad mother, whom he detested. Independently Sarah paid fees for her mother's fancy home. If Martin was to keep things looking normal those fees would still have to be paid. Just because Sarah had left him that was no reason she would forget her mother. Martin knew the cost was topped up by some insurance plan, but didn't know the details. The paperwork for that was bound to come through at some point. Meanwhile, if he was to maintain the illusion that Sarah was still around somewhere, not a missing person, but simply no longer living with him, he would have to keep paying the mother's care home bills.

Remember, remember. Everything must stay normal.

So. Normally, if he had just opened this care home bill, what would he do?

Answer: He would take it home and give it to Sarah.

And if Sarah had walked out on him, then what would he do?

Answer: He'd phone her!

That was it.

Phone Sarah.

Phone Sarah's mobile and leave her a message about the care home bill. Brilliant idea. He had no idea where her bloody phone was, probably with the thieves, who would have ripped out the sim-card and sold it on by now. But no doubt his call would go on record in some call centre somewhere...He was always seeing police series where people called for records from "the phone company".

So he would leave a message which was there as proof he had phoned her.

But again, how would that help him exactly? He tried to see the positive and negatives possibilities of this plan.

Perhaps he would do better simply to send cash direct to the home in a plain typed envelope.

While he thought things over, Martin pulled a dictionary from the shelf and looked up the word popinjay. "1. A type of Parrot. 2. Contemptuous term for one who mechanically repeats words and phrases, and perhaps a reference to the parrot's gaudy plumage."

It occurred to him that he was the popinjay, not his father. After all he was constantly repeating things his father had said. That's what parrots did, wasn't it?

Phoning Sarah's mobile was a good idea. He was convinced of it. He'd leave a brusque message saying he had the care home bill, it was for so-and-so pounds, and would she please take care of it to make sure her mother was not to be cast out gibbering into the streets.

He dialled the number and leaned back.

It started to ring.

Christ!

What if the phone had been in Sarah's pocket when he...? His pansy-planted border would at this moment be giving a polyphonic performance of Rondo alla Turca.

Martin slammed down the receiver.

No!

Why had he done that? If he was going to phone, the whole point was that he must leave a message. That call would have been logged somewhere now, and they would know he had dialled her number. But he'd phoned and said nothing, which everyone knew was a creepy thing to do.

Martin sat with his face in his hands. He was beginning to think everything would have been easier if Sarah had killed him, and he was the one now resting under the compost-enriched earth, and a few punnets full of geraniums and snapdragons. Sarah would have known how to cope. She'd always been the cleverer one.

Oh god.

If only she was here now to help him through this bloody mess.

The door opened.

'You all right, boss?' It was Justin. 'It wasn't bad news or anything, just now on the phone?'

Martin tried to keep a blank expression as he looked up.

Justin—Martin's head suddenly went into Sarah-mode and raced through all kinds of names for the self-important boy, Justin Case, Justin Side, Justin Nick O'Time—looked awfully pale. What did he want? Was he about to be about to be sick all over the carpet?

Martin gulped to try and stop himself laughing.

'It's only that...' Justin looked down at his shoes. 'Well, you told Mike and me about Sarah going off yesterday, and, well...' Justin whipped a newspaper from behind his back. 'We weren't sure, boss, whether you'd seen this?'

Justin gently laid the local evening paper down on Martin's desk and turned for the door.

'If you need us, we're only through there.'

Martin looked down at the headline. WOMAN'S BODY DISCOVERED IN DITCH.

His spit turned to dry salt again, his heart sped in a close run thing with Jensen Button. The blood drained from his face. Or had he gone bright scarlet? He could no longer tell anymore whether he was hot or cold.

Even Justin and Mike suspected him.

He read the headline again.

With shaking hands he picked up the newspaper. It rattled like some Latin American Jazz percussionist's maracas solo. Martin never knew mere paper could make such a clattering noise.

The dead woman, in her 30s, was European, of medium build, with dark wavy hair and hazel eyes. She had been stabbed.

Martin read the paragraph through again.

What was going on? Had someone dug Sarah up from his garden border and put her somewhere else to be discovered, as the account informed him, by a man walking his dog?

This body had been found early this morning in a thicket on one of the local commons. Martin got out his A-Z. The place was a mere fifteen minute walk from his house. Three minutes in a car.

Perhaps those burglars were having a laugh. Maybe they had gone digging in his garden. He had heard of weirder places people stashed their money—in fridges and coalbunkers. Why not in a border? Then, what was to stop them from taking Sarah's body and dumping it in a ditch?

Oh god!

What was he thinking?

Why would anyone do such a thing?

Sarah was still there, safe under those fucking snapdragons.

Martin reached out for the phone.

Then remembered. His first instinct, when the crunch came. Call Sarah.

A feeble knock again at the door, and it opened a crack.

Justin.

'Anything you'd like us to do?'

Martin stood up and turned away. He reached for his jacket, which hung from the coat rack behind the desk.

Keep up! If his wife had left him, and then a corpse answering to her description had turned up round the corner from his home, how would he have reacted to that?

He wouldn't stay in the office, would he? He'd leave. Yes. He'd get out.

So that's what he would have to do, then.

He pulled on the jacket, and tumbled a few things from the desk into his briefcase.

'Hold the fort for me, would you please, Justin. I have to go out for a while.'

Justin looked so serious and glum that Martin almost burst out laughing as he passed him.

'Yes, boss. Sure thing.'

'Sorry, Martin.' Head bowed, Mike stood up as he strode through their office. Martin thought Mike looked as though he was going to bob down and pull at his forelock, like someone in a TV Dickens serial.

He felt he had to clamp his lips tight or he might explode with mirth.

Once he was in the car he felt he still daren't let his laughter out in case they were watching from the window. But he was on the edge of hysteria.

Martin steered out into the High Street and sat for ten minutes, in a solid block of stationary traffic, grinning.

Now what?

He had to run the whole scenario through his head once more and then decide how to deal with whatever it presented. When they'd all been talking at that bloody dinner Martin had been thinking how easy it would be to cover up if you'd killed someone. You just assumed an attitude then maintained it. It had never occurred to him how you had to chop and change from moment to moment.

So—the story so far was that his wife had left him after a row. Then a couple of days later he read in the papers that a body, which answered to her description, had turned up very near their home. So what would he do? Would he go to the police? Or would that turn him into one of those ghouls who went on TV and gave themselves away by weeping about the one they had just murdered?

As Martin drove past the Common he couldn't resist taking the road through it, just to see what was going on. The pub on the corner looked the same as it always did on a sunny day, buzzing with people. Martin turned into the single track road lined with parked cars which ran up behind it towards the thicket. He couldn't see any signs of police activity. It wasn't like it was on TV, no blue flashing lights or crowds of people held back by tape reading "Crime Scene—Do Not Cross." Not even a glimpse of those people with clipboards, wearing white space suits and padding about in white paper shoes.

He passed the thicket, glancing over his shoulder to see if there was any more going on the other side. But there seemed to be nothing other than the usual sprawl of sunbathers, and cottaging gays. Martin pulled the car into the dirt and cinder car park, usually only used when a circus or fairground was installed. Spraying dust from his tyres, he span the car's bonnet to face the green sward, switched off the engine and sat looking out at children kicking balls around with their mothers.

He pulled the newspaper from his briefcase and read the whole report through again. Looking at it a second time, without those two reptiles ogling him, Martin believed he should not do anything at all now, but go home. If he presented himself at the police station what would that do except draw attention to himself? The most important rule was to lay low, keep the police out of it. That's how he had dealt with the burglary and that is how he would deal with this new twist.

That's right. He must go home. It was ludicrous, but first he'd check the flower bed. To be sure. Then he would try Sarah's mobile phone again, listening at the back door, just in case the patch of soil did start to ring. He would leave the message he had intended to leave earlier. After all, no one thought Sarah was dead, remember. She had just left him.

So those morons in the office were mere hysterics who had jumped to conclusions, but the fact was, and Martin of all people knew this for sure: that woman they'd found in the ditch had to be someone other than Sarah.

He knew where Sarah was.

And he was the only person who did.

When he let himself into the house Martin found another stack of bills on the mat. He stepped over them, then ambled through to the garden and took a quick look at the flower bed. He stared down at the geraniums in their neat municipal lines, and recalled a nursery rhyme his mother had sung around the house when he was an infant:

Mary, Mary, quite contrary
How does your garden grow?
With cockle shells and silver bells
And pretty maids all in a row.

Only one pretty maid out there though.

After a few hours sitting in the silent living room, Martin felt restless. It seemed all wrong to be there in the house during the day, without even a TV to take his mind off the situation.

And it wasn't just the Sarah situation, it was the money situation too. He was broke. Worse than broke. He was drowning in debt. Before the Sarah incident, finance had been the main worry. Now he had two things giving him hot flushes of panic.

Kevin had had a good idea when he talked about Martin moving house and downsizing. It was certainly one way out of the money problem. But Martin wondered how practical it would be. Obviously he couldn't sell up now, not until the manatee had rotted down and he could take away the loose bits, and put them some place where no one would find them. He'd drop them from the side of a cross channel ferry, or lose them piece by piece in the domestic rubbish.

But how long would it take before the garden "problem" could be...dealt with?

He had no idea.

So there we are. That was something useful he could do now to get him out of the oppressively quiet house.

In fact, he could do two things—get some milk and bread from the supermarket and then swing into the library beside it to find out how long a body took to vanish back to dust.

Martin found a place in the supermarket car park, and spent a quarter of an hour browsing round the shop so that it would look like a decent amount of time to be there. Then he slipped next door to the library.

The bright but stuffy room was packed with pensioners. Martin wondered if it was some special event. He'd never seen so many old people in one room since he attended a matinée performance of some tiresome Alan Ayckbourn play at the National Theatre.

The catalogue readers and online computers were all busy, so Martin browsed along the Non-Fiction corridors. He'd find what he was looking for, he imagined, under True Crime.

After a long stroll past Travel, Motoring and Geography, Martin arrived at Crime. He scanned the shelves, pulling out a couple of books to look at their covers. They seemed to be no more than lurid accounts of serial murderers, like the Yorkshire Ripper, Ted Bundy and Jeffrey Dahmer.

'Could I be of any assistance?' A bossy looking woman in a dowdy tweedy suit and spectacles stood before him. She glanced down at the book in his hand. The cover photo showed the contorted face of a screaming woman, baring her neck to a knife wielded by a gloved hand. It was called *The Murderous Handbook*. Martin crammed it back onto the shelf.

'Just browsing,' he said and walked on. Of course he didn't want her help. A woman like that would surely remember a man who came in asking if there were any books detailing how fast a body decomposed when buried in a bin liner in a London back garden.

He giggled to himself. It was funny really, when you thought about it.

In this strange nether world of drab spinsters, wholesale bus-pass holders and slightly smelly books he felt oddly free, and for the moment he didn't feel in the least frightened or horrified by what he had done.

He wondered if perhaps that was why the tiresome Yank next door always seemed so jolly and cheerful. Maybe the contrapuntal medley of murder and books had some strange calming influence on the soul.

He came to the end of a row. A glance at the adjacent spines showed he was back in Fiction. He turned back and took a saunter down a different stack.

If this type of book wasn't shelved under Crime, where could it be? He tried Medicine next, but those aisles were packed with garishly illustrated volumes about mother and baby, and self help manuals—*How to Keep Supple With Arthritis, You Can Have a Full Life After a Stroke, Coping with Psoriasis, Surviving Death*.

Well there was a comical thought! With the possible exception of Jesus Christ, whoever had ever managed to survive death? Who'd write such a load of tosh? He had pulled the book from the shelf and one glance at the cover made him realise that it was in fact about coping with bereavement. The cover drawing, depicting a lily covered coffin, made him feel edgy, so he put the book back and moved along, ambling through History till he found himself in Social Sciences.

He saw a sub-division marked Police, which was obviously a subject closely allied to Crime, and lo! There was just the book he wanted: *Lecture Notes on Violent Crime Together with an Illustrated Atlas of Forensic Pathology.*

Grabbing the book, Martin dived into the index. When he saw the number of references and the size of the chapter on human decomposition he decided to take the book to a dark corner, where he could study it in detail. There was a tattered armchair by a low Formica table at the end of Transport and Engineering. He sat down under the artificial shade of a dusty plastic palm set in a tin pot full of dry grey stones, and started to read.

There were plenty of case histories, tales of lumps of boiled flesh being pulled out of the Thames, found in sewers or discovered in people's attics. One woman had been fed to pigs. Mind you, like Max said, even there, with no body at all, the police still caught her killers. And that was in the old days before all these ultra-violet lights, computers and DNA. Good lord! There was a woman back in the 1880s who'd gone round trying to sell human dripping to pub landlords. That would make him think twice, if ever he was tempted by a hawker selling packets of those pub-grub home-made pork scratchings. The porkers might have been human-fed, and their piggy remains fried in some other poor person's discarded boiled-down flab.

Some murderers, he read, had tried to speed the process of rotting down the corpse by putting quicklime around the body. Martin skimmed across the page. This stuff could be useful. He'd seen huge plastic sacks of lime piled up near the compost when he bought the snapdragons. He could go back and buy some this afternoon. But when he got to the end of the article he understood that not only did the use of lime sometimes backfire by preserving the corpse, but that anyway garden centres had changed their lime recipe long since, after the days of 10 Rillington Place, so there was no point.

Martin flicked to the appendices to see the section called The Atlas. Eeeugh. The word Atlas was, in his opinion, a sarcastic euphemism for a photo album of horror. After a quick glance at a study of a cadaverous leg complete with shark bite, the close up of a dead man's purple mottled arse with a corkscrew sticking out of his anus, and the blackened tortured face of a dead burns victim, he quickly turned back to plain black and white text.

There he found a basic chart of stages of decomposition. That would be just the thing he needed.

The process of putrefaction started after about 48 hours after death. Martin looked at his watch, as though that would be any help. Around now, he supposed. He read through the description of how bacteria bubbled up within the intestines then spread through the blood vessels, so that technically the body destroyed itself from within. After two to three days the abdomen turned green. Within three weeks everything about the body was swollen and unrecognisable, and a week later it started to liquefy.

With a shudder, Martin realised that one day this would happen to him too.

Unless he chose to be cremated, of course.

He realised he hadn't taken a breath in about a minute and his head started to swim.

After a few deep breaths he felt better.

It was horrible enough reading about it, but too awful to think that it was happening just outside his back window, and to Sarah.

He gulped drily and read on.

The progress from corpse to skeleton took on average a year, warm weather speeding up the process, but it was delayed by things like tight fitting garments.

Damn.

Why had he insisted Sarah wore that outfit for dinner?

DAMN.

Still, a year wasn't too long to wait before he sold up. Financially, he might be able to blag his way through twelve months.

Insects accelerated the stages of decomposition, he read, as did animals, foxes and the like. Well, of course! If a bloody fox took great bites out of you, naturally you'd disappear quicker—down their gullets. But Martin realised he could well do without some urban vulpine vermin digging down to Sarah, and leaving a foot or hand on the topsoil in the next door garden for all to see. That would be all he needed.

Sarah had had a thing about foxes. Like her mother. In fact, the bloody batty old cow was probably at this second sitting in her cell in that ruddy home sending out mental instructions to every fox in Lambeth to come to his back garden and expose Sarah's body to the elements.

Martin flipped the page.

'Professor Glaister's study shows that decomposition times are reduced by the following ratios when the corpse is not in open air: Water x 2. Earth x 8.'

Times Eight? Burying a body slowed down the decomposition times eight. Eight years before he could move!

Why, by then he'd be over forty.

Christ!

He wished now that he'd listened more to that thing they were talking about where the man used a grease gun. What was a grease gun, anyway? He'd never heard of such a thing.

Sarah would have known how to do it.

Oh damn it.

If only she was here to help him in this predicament.

Martin thought again of *The Exorcist* ghost-woman howling at him in the night. How it was Sarah and yet wasn't.

Oh God!

And now, to think that, because of him, the real Sarah was starting to liquefy and rot from within.

Augh.

Shutting his eyes, and inhaling deeply, Martin leaned back in the chair, a finger resting on his place in the book.

A hand landed on his shoulder.

'Gotcha!'

Martin spun round, paralysed with shock, flinging the book to the floor in an effort to distance himself from it.

'Oh heck, Martin, I'm so sorry. Were you asleep?' It was Tess, as ever grinning that Satchmo toothy smile of hers. 'These libraries get very airless, especially when all these old people cram themselves inside. I think someone at the old folks' homes must have told them that the library was doling out free muffins or hip replacements.'

Tess stooped to retrieve the forensic book from the floor, crashing heads with Martin as he went down in an attempt to snatch it first.

'Ouch!' Tess rubbed her scalp. 'Holy Moly, you have one heck of a solid cranium, Martin. What do you keep in there, rocks?' She looked down at the book. 'Hey! Lookit. My favourite book in the whole wide world. Fancy you picking that out. Are you using it for an ad campaign or something?' She flipped the pages back to the plastic sealed dust jacket. 'By the way, I do know why you didn't go to a bookstore and buy it!'

She tapped the side of her nose and gave Martin an elaborate look.

Good god!

Martin sank down into the chair again, gripping the edges of the plastic padded arms with stiff fingers. He tried to swallow but his throat seemed not only to have dried up but utterly constricted. His tongue made an involuntary clicking sound.

This bloody woman. She knew. She'd known all along. She'd heard everything through the wall, watched him dig the grave, seen him roll the manatee into it and cover it with pretty spring flowers.

Tess knew he had killed Sarah.

'Look at that! See!' Tess pointed to the price tag: £85. 'Eighty five of your best English quids. I didn't take you for a library kind of a guy, but, hey, who's got that kind of moola to throw around?'

With a cheery wink Tess handed the book back.

Martin breathed again.

Tess smiled in that Mona Lisa like way of hers.

'Don't worry, Marti. I won't tell anyone your little secret.'

She turned and swaggered off in the direction of True Crime.

What little secret?

My god.

She really did know.

And how enigmatic she'd been about the ruddy horrible book too.

And she had called him Marti! No 'N' on the end. Like the sodding ring. Marti! She'd heard his row with Sarah too.

She really, really did know.

Martin wondered exactly how much more torture Tess was going to put him through before she came out with some demand. It was clear that the fucking annoying woman was toying with him.

What could she want?

Well, if it was money—tough. He didn't have anything to offer but debt.

Mind you...If she really knew, why hadn't she already gone to the police?

Or maybe she had?

Was this all a clever game to make him give himself away, expose himself? A sting, they called it on TV. Perhaps she would come over and give him a peck on the cheek, like Judas Iscariot, and the next thing the room would be swarming with special branch officers, wielding guns and marching him out into a waiting van with a blanket on his head.

Martin stood up. His legs felt quite weak. There was no way he could get out of here now without it looking as though he was avoiding her. That was if he could walk at all.

What a bitch! What a vixen! What a cat! That was it. She was a cat, a feral cat, stalking him. And he was a poor limp, dead sparrow in her fat cat's maw, waiting only for her razor claws to tear him to shreds.

Trying to look casual, Martin crept along the edge of the aisle and slid the revolting forensic book back into its place.

He couldn't see that American bitch at all now. Perhaps she had gone as quietly as she had come. Or maybe she was lurking in some vantage point, perching on a stool on the mezzanine floor, looking down at him, inspecting his body language for tell-tale signs of a psychopath, or schizo, or whatever he was for having done what he had done to his lovely, elegant, funny, clever wife.

Martin stood at the end of the stack, trying to look care-free and business-like. He took another deep breath, checked either side then walked vigorously towards the exit.

His path was blocked by a gaggle of cackling pensioners. He had no idea what was supposed to be so funny but he wanted to kick these babbling dotards into next week, to seize their sticks and zimmer frames and smash them down on their fluffy white heads.

He shouldered his way through them. He had almost reached the door when he noticed that one of the online computers was free. What a brilliant idea. Now that there was no computer at home, why not make use of this one? He took the seat, and logged onto the internet. He could check the bank account and see if he could find out why his card had been refused, without having to exchange words with that arsehole Czech. That would also save him the embarrassment of having to explain away the fact that there was no way he could sell up for another eight years, on account of the fact his wife wouldn't have rotted down sufficiently till then.

He logged into his account and typed in his email address and password.

He waited a few seconds for the screen to change.

"Password Refused."

Password refused? What were they on about? He knew his own password for God's sake. It was his old pet dog's name and his birthday—5Rusty11.

His fingers were shaky today. Perhaps he had mistyped.

He had another go.

"Password Refused."

He tried a third time.

"You have been locked out of this site. If you wish to rein-state this online account please refer directly to your Bank."

So now he was locked out of his own bank account.

Fucking computers.

He tried again, this time using the details for his personal credit card account.

He typed out the password and waited while the little hour glass tipped over and over.

The screen changed.

What?

£5,000.

He rubbed his eyes.

£5,000? Where in god's name had that come from?

Who would have put £5,000 into his account without telling him?

He looked again, this time reading the small print. Then he realised his error.

It wasn't a credit sum. This was his credit card statement after all, not his bank account.

It was what he owed them.

£5,000?

Those bastards had used his credit card and run it up to the maximum limit.

Heart thumping, Martin clicked onto "Recent Transactions" to get the details.

He'd have to phone the police. Not content with taking his TV and computer, those fucking robbing low-lifes who'd broken into his house had cleaned him out. Worse than that, they'd run up debts of £5,000.

And he hadn't reported the burglary, so he was stuffed.

No.

Of course he wasn't.

He needn't tell the bank that the card had been taken from the house. He could say he had lost it. He could say he'd only just noticed that the card was gone. He must have left it in a shop somewhere.

Or maybe it would be better to chuck the whole wallet into a rubbish bin and say the thing had been taken from him, at a bus stop. That was it. People jostled one another at bus stops. It would be easy enough for a thieving hand to slip into his pocket and remove his wallet.

Then Martin remembered that he never actually travelled by bus, and anyhow these days bus-stops had cameras all over the place. You were forever seeing bits of film about missing girls last seen getting on or off a bus. So if something like that actually had happened to him it would be on film somewhere.

He could still report the card missing. He'd be vague. Say he had had it at work, yesterday, or was it the day before, and now he realised it was gone.

He could say it went missing here in the library. Blame one of those sniggering, grey haired Saga-louts. Say they had stolen it while he was dozing under the plastic palm in the fuggy corner. He even had a witness for that. Tess had thought he was asleep, hadn't she?

But of course he was on the website now, after Tess had seen him with that disgusting book. He'd logged on to the bank's site right away. In five or so minutes even a supersonic pensioner wouldn't have had time to have stolen the card, run out into town and ripped off all that dosh.

The next page slowly opened on the screen.

Again it told him please to contact his bank.

He hastily logged off, left the library and bustled along to his car.

Some bastard traffic warden had given him a parking ticket. He was only three minutes over the free 30 minutes, for god's sake. The swine must have been lurking round the corner, poised to stick the fine on his windscreen the second the ruddy ticket went over the allotted time.

Martin sat inside the car, deciding what to do next.

Then he dialled the bank.

After a few moments of irritating muzak Martin was put through to the lost cards department. Trying to keep the rising hysteria from his voice Martin told them that he had lost the card, but couldn't be sure when. He had last used it about three days ago, he claimed. (Best be safe and add an extra day)

A surly sounding girl told him that they would put an instant block on the card. Trouble was, she said, the computers were down at the moment. She'd phone him back, on his home number, once she could get details.

Martin drove home in a frantic fizz of panic.

Once in the house he immediately ran though the house to check the flower bed.

Pretty Maid all in a row.

He looked at the grey undisturbed soil and thought of Sarah's abdomen swelling and turning green, then had to back away, taking deep breaths to quell a rising surge of nausea.

He flopped onto the sofa. Those fucking sods, taking his TV. He wanted to watch the news. To see what was happening with that woman on the common.

He got up, went through to the kitchen, turned on the transistor radio and twiddled the dial, trying to find a news channel. The sound was thin and tinny. Even at full volume Martin had to keep still if he wanted to hear anything at all.

He filled the kettle, but when he switched it on, the noise of the element creaking into action drowned out the radio. Glancing at the clock he flicked the kettle off. It was ten to six.

He would make that call now. Leave the message on Sarah's mobile. Tell her answering machine about the care home bill.

He could tell her about the credit cards, too, while he was about it. He would have done so if she was alive. Of course he would. It was a joint account, for god's sake.

Wow! That was it! A joint account. He would make the most of the loss.

At last he had something in his favour, something he could use.

If that fucking sanctimonious Kevin the Czech was so worried about them sharing out their fortune, now Martin could inform him it was all sorted. Sarah had helped herself. Sarah had used the card. Blame it all on Sarah.

He waited for a second before dialling Sarah's mobile, his mind speeding through the script: Hi Sarah. [Serious, deserted-husband voice] Just to let you know that the bill for the care home has come to me. Oh, and by the way, I do know what you're up to. I know you used the card and ran up £5000 of debt...

His heart was beating with exhilaration as he put his forefinger on the number pad ready to dial.

Wait!

He had still better check the flower bed for sound, just in case. It was very, very unlikely that the cell-phone was buried with her. Even a tech-head like Sarah wouldn't carry her mobile phone around in her pocket during a dinner party, but, as the old girl always used to say: "There are stranger things in Heaven and Earth, Horatio..." Whoever Horatio was, when he was at home. And he didn't want the piping strains of sub-terrestrial polyphonic Mozart bringing his dear American neighbour, Ms Literary-Snoop, to her window.

Martin flung open the back door, ready to listen for Sarah's ring tone. Once he was put through to the answering machine he would shut the door and move right back into the house, to make sure that, even if Ms-Cocky-I'm-a-Best-Selling-Novelist was applying her beer glass to the party wall, she wouldn't hear the call.

He took a breath and dialled the number of Sarah's mobile.

He waited.

And waited.

Then...

The engaged tone.

Engaged?

Stabbing at the off button, Martin backed away from the open back door.

At least the flowerbed wasn't ringing.

But how could it ring when someone was on the line?

Instantly the phone in his hand beeped.

He pressed the on button.

'Hello?'

Silence.

He said 'Hello' again. He knew his voice came out high and shaky.

Silence.

'Who's there?'

Silence.

He turned off and quickly dialled 1471.

'You were called today at 16.58. We do not have the caller's number.'

It was those bastard thieves again, wasn't it? They were taunting him. Taunting him with their stolen goods. He had no doubt in his mind that this last call was a response to his own, and that it had originated from the crooks who were using Sarah's mobile.

The radio time pips set off a harmonic reverberation on the gas hob. Martin rushed over and turned up the sound.

'The time now is five o'clock and this is John Mahoney with the news. The dead woman found on a London Common in the early hours of this morning has been identified...'

With a piercing shriek, the phone in his hand rang again. Martin was so shocked that he dropped it, and had to dive down onto his knees and scramble about under the table to retrieve it.

He stabbed at the green button and put it to his ear.

'Look, you bastards, I know this is you...'

'Mr Martin Beaumont?'

'Yes.'

'You phoned earlier...About your lost debit card?'

'Yes.' Martin flushed with embarrassment as he climbed to his feet, using the table to haul himself up. 'Sorry. I've been having some crank calls.'

'You know that your account has been used up to its limit.'

'Oh!' Martin tried to make it sound like a surprise. 'I see.'

'If you suspect criminal activity you must go to the police.'

'The police?'

'..the woman, in her thirties, had been discovered...'

'To report the criminal activity. You, or your wife.'

'My wife?'

'You have discussed the matter with your wife?'

'Er. No,' Martin stammered. Remember she was gone, not dead. 'Her phone was engaged. I couldn't get through.'

'You'd better talk things through together, and then, if you are assured none of the recent transactions belonged to either of you, you must go to the police and get a crime number.'

'I see.' Martin knew his voice was coming out all floaty, like a girl. What could he do? There was too much information to digest. Too much to work out.

'...The police have announced that the woman's death is being treated as murder...'

Martin strained to listen to the radio, while the bank woman banged on into his ear.

'If you don't get a police log number, of course, you may well both be responsible for a large amount of the expenditure. Can you be sure neither of you have divulged your PIN number to anyone else, or is there any way anyone else could have found it out?'

'What, er, oh, no.'

'I should point out to you Mr Beaumont, that there have been a great many transactions in the last 48 hours. It possible some of these are legal transactions. It would take quite a while to read them to you. Perhaps you would prefer a hard copy?'

'Yes. Yes...' He said vaguely, his concentration still torn. 'Good idea. That would be fine.'

'Would you prefer me to email it, fax it or send it through the mail?'

'...are reluctant to release more details about the librarian's death...'

'Oh, erm...What do you think would be best?'

'Email is obviously quickest.'

'Email?' As Martin hadn't reported the laptops missing he couldn't start down that road now. 'I'm at home—well, you know that. You phoned me! I don't have the computer here with me at this time.' He knew he could not have the patience to wait for the transcript to arrive by the post. It would take at least two days. 'Fax it. That's right. Fax.'

'...a sandwich bar on the High Street. A colleague from the library said this afternoon...'

'...and the number?'

Martin found he couldn't understand either the phone call or the radio news. He walked out of the kitchen into the dining room, trying to concentrate on the phone call. Get that out of the way, then give his full attention to the radio.

He gave the bank the fax number and hung up.

But by time he arrived back in the kitchen, the newsreader had moved on to a story about a double-decker bus getting stuck under a railway bridge and bringing traffic to a stand-still while firemen with welding equipment tried to free the trapped passengers.

Martin flopped down into one of the hard chairs at the kitchen table.

Not content with trashing his house, stealing his bank card and his laptop, the fuckers had broken into the computer and got his bloody PIN. It had never occurred to him when he stored the information that anyone would take both the laptop and the bank card in one fell swoop.

Martin heard the ancient fax machine whoosh into activity in the dining room, where Sarah usually worked. He slung the phone into his pocket and walked though.

With a jolt he realised he had still not left that message on Sarah's mobile. And he had now dialled the number three times, no doubt all three calls logged at 'the phone company'.

While he watched the curl of paper slowly feed through the fax machine he stabbed out Sarah's number for a fourth time.

It was ringing.

The flower bed! He hadn't checked it out. With the hand piece to his ear, he ran back to the back door and listened.

Nothing.

Nothing at all.

Neither from the flower bed nor the phone in his hand.

Someone had picked up!

He could hear them breathing on the other end.

'Hello? Hello?' His voice had shot up into the stratosphere. He could have hit higher notes than Kitty Wacky Tacky or whatever that Kiwi opera singer was called. 'I know you're there, you thieving bastards.' He concentrated on deepening his tone, sounding more manly, more threatening. 'I'll have you know the police are onto you at this moment.'

There was a click on the line.

They had hung up.

Hung up!

Before he had a chance to dial again, the phone in his hand rang.

'Sod you sod you sod you sod you!' he screeched.

'OK, old boy, no need to go on.' It was Max. 'She still playing about with you?'

Martin walked briskly through to the dining room, away from any of Tess's potential listening points. 'Yes, she is,' he said. Now was the time to seize the chance. 'The bitch has been running up bills on the bank card.'

'Joint account?'

'Yep.'

'Good old, Sarah.' Martin heard the sound of Max laughing and thumping his big paw down on his desk. 'I knew she wasn't that clever. Well, my friend, we've got her by the balls. And don't tell me she hasn't got any. She's got bigger balls than Linford Christie. I can see her now,' Max bellowed, 'thinking she's so fucking bright. But we've got her.'

An image came into Martin's mind of Sarah in the darkness, enveloped by dirt, her belly swelling and liquefying from within. He sank down to his knees, overwhelmed with nausea. He realised he had not eaten since breakfast.

At his eye level the pages were still spewing from the fax machine.

'Look Martin. If she phones again, tell her to go fuck herself. Tell her I'm going to help you to sue her for everything under the sun. And you may as well add, when I'm done with her, her life won't be worth living.'

'Yes,' Martin's voice was a mere croak. His stomach heaved. But there was nothing to puke up.

'I'll see you round,' said Max. 'Chin up, my friend.'

The line went dead.

Martin lay flat on the Turkey rug and took deep breaths.

After a few minutes, from his position on the floor he stretched up to the edge of the desk and pulled at the edges of a few sheets of the faxed sheets. They fluttered down upon him, like giant pieces of confetti.

What was he going to do?

He couldn't go on like this.

It was all too hard for him to handle.

He'd go to the police.

That was it.

He'd go to the police and give himself up.

He couldn't cope with anything more.

A tear dribbled down from the corner of his eye and slithered into his ear.

What a mess.

What a bloody mess.

Idly, he picked up one page of the statement. Item after fucking item. The bastards had been everywhere. Electronic shops, shoe shops, clothing shops, bookshops, music shops. Jesus Christ almighty. All his hard-earned money dribbled away on a load of tat. Thirty pounds here, forty there. Nothing big enough to get anyone's suspicions up. He supposed all the stuff those thieving swine had bought, courtesy of him, would be on Ebay or in car boot sales by Sunday.

Martin scooped up a few more pages and glanced down the long columns of transactions. Ha! They'd even treated themselves to groceries from a fancy West End shop, while he was lying here sick from starvation.

Oh God! What would become of him?

He sobbed and picked up another page.

A taxi company. A railway ticket. A care home.

A care home?

He sat up, and peered down at the paper.

The Robins—Care Home. And this transaction was for a huge figure.

Time? Date?—This morning. 11.21 a.m.

Had he done this, inadvertently, from the office, when he was worrying about the situation with her mad mother?

Surely he hadn't.

And the robbers would hardly...

He snatched the phone from where it lay in the centre of the room.

What was the bloody number of the place?

He jumped up and ran through to the kitchen, pulling drawers open until he found the Yellow Pages.

Care Homes...

Care Homes...

He dialled the number and got put through to the Head wardress, as he liked to think of her.

'Just checking,' he said, trying to work out how to word what he needed to say. 'Just checking that the money for dear old Mrs Kavanagh went through into your account today?'

'Ah yes,' said the woman. Martin could almost feel her licking her lips. 'It was all sorted, for the next six months in advance, with extras. Just before Mrs Kavanagh's daughter came in.'

'Mrs Kavanagh's daughter came in?' Martin realised it would have sounded more natural to say my wife, but too late, and anyhow, it amounted to the same thing. His voice too was out of control again. 'Mrs Kavanagh's daughter?'

Martin felt himself reeling and had to grab hold of the kitchen counter to steady himself.

'That's right, Mr Beaumont. About lunchtime. She was showing off her lovely new outfit to her poor mother. Of course the old lady didn't really know who she was, but it was quite moving all the same. It's hard to know whether she'll miss her.'

'Miss her?' Martin wondered in which world anyone would ever miss Sarah's mother.

'But Australia's not so far away these days is it, with jet travel and everything, and she seemed very excited about the new job...'

'I'm sorry? Mrs Kavanagh is going to Australia? I thought...'

'Not Mrs Kavanagh, silly.' The wardress cackled. 'Mrs Kavanagh's daughter...'

Martin put the phone down.

Sarah had been into the home to see her mother?

Sarah was going to Australia?

Sarah was alive?

How could she...?

Martin stood at the back door and looked out.

The flower bed was exactly as he had left it. A neat row of bedding plants.

The phone rang again.

'Martin!' It was Max. 'I've been onto Bill McNamara, a pal at Scotland Yard.'

Martin's throat tightened.

'He'll be onto that bloody wife of yours faster than you can say Maserati.'

Martin unlocked the door and walked out onto the lawn. The sun had set and the garden basked in that eerie twilight before the darkness fell.

'Thank you, Max.' Martin could find no way to put expression in his voice. He realised that he sounded like some computer speech recognition programme. 'Thank you.'

Sarah was alive.

Martin tapped the toe of his shoe into the topsoil.

It was tight. Just as he had left it when he planted those grim little geraniums.

How could Sarah not be down there, rotting away in her three black bin-liners?

'I'll phone you in the morning, Martin. You'll keep out of trouble for me till then I hope?'

'What?' Martin sank down on his haunches and rubbed his fingers along the surface of the flowerbed.

'If you take my advice, old fellow, don't run to the bottle for consolation. It's a poor compensation for sex. Take care now.'

Martin didn't notice Max hang up. He had already started plunging his fingers into the dirt, searching for resistance.

Dropping the phone on the grass, Martin got up and ran to the shed.

He took the spade and placed it on the flowerbed, right over where the edge of the body lay, or rather, where the body should lie.

The doorbell rang.

Martin ignored it.

It would only be Mormons, or kids, or that interfering American cow from next door.

He put his foot on the spade's edge and leaned forward, applying his weight. Calm again now, he watched the blade sink into the soil, just as that other blade had sunk into Sarah's flesh.

He tossed away a mound of dirt, then repeated the action.

The doorbell rang a second time.

Bloody door-steppers. Let them wait. They'd give up eventually.

He dug doggedly on until he reached about three foot down. Still there was no sign of the bin liners.

He felt sure that when he'd gone back to get the rings from her cold fingers the body was not buried as deeply as this.

He plunged the spade further down.

Bloody doorbell again.

He threw himself to his knees and scraped at the soil with his bare hands.

At his side, the phone starting ringing. He ignored it.

How deep down under the surface could Sarah be?

He stood again and smashed the spade into the loam, sending sparks as the blade chipped into stones and pieces of flint.

Distantly, as though through a fog, Martin heard a smashing noise coming from inside the house.

None of that was important.

Where was she gone?

Where was Sarah gone?

Footsteps seemed to be rattling along the wooden hallway towards the kitchen, only the hall sounded miles away, as though heard through a pair of ear muffs.

Unbothered, Martin lay down, thrusting his arms deep into the soil, tumbling the earth away, throwing tiny bedding plants over his shoulder to get them out of his way.

How could this be?

Where was Sarah?

He knew he'd put her here.

Hadn't he?

What was happening?

She wasn't here.

Sarah wasn't here.

Nothing was here.

Not even the bin liners.

Nothing.

From his position, lying splayed out on the lawn, he turned his head and saw a row of police officers peering out at him from the kitchen doorway.

What the bloody hell were they here for? What did they know? How did they know?

He clambered to his feet and started frantically to kick the dirt back into the gaping hole before him.

What would they think?

He looked down at the flowerbed.

Why, it looked just like a grave!

In silence the policemen wormed into the garden then stood in an arc, their arms outstretched, ready to stop him should he make a dash for it.

'Martin Beaumont?' One of them stood next to Martin and looked down at the body-sized hollow before him.

Martin wiped his mud-smeared palms down the sides of his trousers.

What to do?

He gulped and slowly looked up.

'Martin Beaumont?' The officer lay his hand on Martin's forearm.

Martin squirmed. He realised he was making a whimpering sound.

'I think we'll have to take you to the station, sir...'

Panicked, Martin flung the officers hand from his arm and threw himself through the barrier of policemen, heading for the house. But the men surrounded him, and one had grabbed his arm and bent it behind him in a painful wrestling hold.

Martin started to sob.

'I've done nothing. You can't, you can't, you can't...'

Before the constables had managed to grapple him into submission, he glanced up just in time to see the net curtain in Tess's flat fall back into place.

Witness Statement

"If you are unsure of yourself—silence is the best policy" goes a maxim of the French sage Francois de la Rochefoucauld.

But there are times, sure or unsure, when I believe it is wiser to err on the side of caution. And that is why I phoned the police.

Last week, before Jane went missing, the library hosted a "Crime Evening". By this I do not mean that readers were invited to pick one another's pockets, or snatch the handbags of the unsuspecting, but the library invited a group of celebrated crime writers to speak, or, should I say, to put on a display of insincerity unrivalled since O.J. Simpson took the witness stand.

"Crime Fiction," trilled a dark-haired waspish type who has written a string of novels of which no one but her own publishers had heard, "restores Order to a Disturbed World." [The capital letters are how they speak, these people. Everything so Very, Very Important]

How worrying, I thought, if her murky self-righteous books bore any similarity to real life, with bodies turning up every other day, where no killer ever bagged fewer than two corpses before being picked up, and despite being so inept at discovering these annual serial killers in a tiny town, the police never suffered any rebuke from above. You'd think these fictional detectives would be sacked not promoted and turned into TV folk heroes.

These books present a world of banal simplicity, rendered into total chaos by some unlikely villain with an IQ of 150+, and a homespun force of law and order indistinguishable from a school for mental defectives, or even worse some meddling idiot amateur detective who really makes their living as an antiquarian book dealer, a disc jockey, a cook, and in some cases is, in fact, a cat.

'Oh, we are the true successors of Balzac, Dostoevsky and Dickens,' grunted another crime writer on the panel, a grubby little man with bad teeth and boils on his neck. He wore a none too clean Terylene suit from which emanated a nasty smell of greasy hair and goats. Unlike his turgid books, under the warm stage lights, the smell came all too vividly to life. 'Contrary to journalistic opinion,' he smugly told the audience, 'crime writers are not at the bottom of the pile—they at least have someone to look down on: romantic novelists.'

As the sycophants in the audience chuckled, poor Jane prodded me in the ribs and rolled her eyes to heaven.

'Yet we all fall in love, don't we?' she whispered in my ear. 'But how many times have you encountered a murderer?'

I laughed.

Perhaps I would not have done so if I had known that later that night Jane would.

I reported her missing when did not come into work the next day. A week later, on a rubbish

dump in the middle of the Common, they found
her broken body.

How I longed then for the fantastic realms
invented by those complacent crime writers to
be true. What would I have given for a divine
swift restoration of order to my shattered
world?

The police came to the library and took
statements from us all. It turns out that the
policemen in those silly books are positive
euphuists when compared to the grunting
halfwits who came to interview us about Jane.

I fell into deep despair when I realised that
the only way anyone would ever find Jane's
killer was through the plodding endeavours of
these illiterate self-regarding fools.

So, when today I saw him here in the library,
looking sneaky and on edge, the very man who
had shouted abuse at Jane in the car park on
the day she vanished, I kept my eye on him. I
watched him prowling about within the library.
I took his car licence plate number. And later,
after I had inspected the vile books he had
been so furtively studying, I knew I had no
choice but to make the phone call.

4

Single Jig

A solo dance in 6/8 time, performed in soft shoes

TESS LET THE net curtain drop, flopped back into her typing stool and pushed herself away from the desk. Holy shit. Had her writing improvisation come true?

The chair creaked. She winced, fearful the sound would carry to the outside world.

Tess knew exactly what the scene in next door's back yard had looked like, but sometimes what seemed obvious was an illusion. Life was stranger than fiction: the facts leading to a conclusion might be paraded for all to see, but the truth skulked hidden under a piece of withheld knowledge. That was the very basis of all mystery writing. It was also a fact that Truth frequently bore all the hallmarks of a Lie. For instance, back home a few years back, she had decided to do a bit of night gardening by candlelight, planting spring bulbs around the borders of her yard. Her fanatical born-again neighbours had later accused her of being out there to perform midnight satanic rituals.

Tess slid the computer keyboard to the side and moved a jotter into the space on her desk. She unscrewed her fountain pen then slashed a few strokes to get the ink flowing. She pulled the keyboard back. Where were the notes she'd made?

Martin, Martin, Martin!

What had he been burying in the flowerbed?

She scrolled down the list of files on the monitor. Where were her notes about him?

Since that desperately dull dinner Tess had been keeping an eye on Martin. He was just the kind of plain, dull guy who could make a very good character in one of her books. He was almost as effete as a faggot, yet clearly heterosexual, someone dull and ordinary upon whom you could pile the shit and make a killer story. So she'd been watching him. Some people might call it stalking, but she thought of it as research: Watching out for his idiosyncrasies, the little tics of everyday life, those unexpected turns of phrase and actions performed by real people which make a fictional character take off and a narrative soar.

The reason his character would be perfect in a murder mystery was because he was the type of person about whom people might exclaim: "Martin! He wouldn't hurt a fly."

As if flies had anything to do with it.

Tess rifled about in the drawer which was crammed with scraps of paper and tried to find the stuff she had collected. She realised she had been biting hard on the soft inside of her cheek now for almost a minute. Loosening her bite she gazed up again at the list of files on the monitor. She could taste the rusty iron flavour of blood upon her tongue.

Holy fuck! Perhaps this would turn out to be a big story, like Ted Bundy, or Dr Crippen, or Son of Sam, and she could write a personal account of the goings on next door and syndicate it with the newspapers for much more than her usual book advance.

Tess turned off the angle-poise lamp, and, leaving the net in place, slowly moved nearer to the window. She peered through the fabric out into the darkness.

A lone policeman stood in the yard, his arms folded, looking down into the mess of what remained of the flower border.

That was pretty standard behaviour at any potential crime scene. A policeman would guard the spot till scene of crime officers arrived to poke about and bag samples of anything which might help the police to work out the four Ws: When, Where, Why and How (bit of a liberty, that one, as the W came at the end). Inevitably those four Ws equalled the fifth all important Who.

The policeman scratched his neck and slowly looked up. Had his eye been caught by Tess turning the light off?

She ducked down and crawled away on her hands and knees.

Her boots lay in a huddle under the desk. She fumbled with the tangled laces and edged herself across the rug towards the door, where she got to her feet and tiptoed speedily through to the bedroom where she could see out to the street.

A police car was moving away. No blue light. No fuss. Who would think anything serious was happening next door?

Tess supposed this low-key performance was a more likely scenario than the one you saw on TV police shows, where flashing cars screeched off, sirens blaring, into the night.

What would be the point of that? After all, it seemed they had their man.

Tess pressed her cheek against the architrave, her nose touching the window pane, to get a clear view of Sarah and Martin's front door. Her breath formed a patch of mist on the glass.

The street was empty, but for another uniformed officer who stood on the Beaumont's threshold.

He was peering down at his watch. He looked bored.

How perfect! In mystery novels there was barely a police procedural where the detective or police protagonist wasn't suffering from a terminal dose of ennui, and was usually lumbered with a woman who didn't understand him and had a drink or drug problem to boot. But this solitary policeman didn't give off that rank languor. He just looked as though he was longing to go to the pub, or maybe it was the bathroom.

The boy shivered out a yawn and looked up and down the street. No doubt things would get more interesting for him once SOCO arrived.

Tess turned back into the bedroom. Where was her camera? Why hadn't she thought of pulling that out earlier? Dammit. She could have got a shot of Martin's arrest and sold it to a tabloid newspaper.

Fuck!

She pulled out the drawers in the chest next to the bed, rummaging around among her panties and socks. She feared she had left the camera in her locker in the gym club.

How could she get to chat to the constable without it being obvious she was digging for info?

Tea! That was the secret key to the good old British heart. Perhaps if she made a cup of tea and offered it to the kid on the doorstep he might give her a few juicy details in return.

After all Tess didn't want to be chasing around after this story all night only to discover that Martin had been hauled in for tax evasion. Perhaps that was it. Maybe he had a trunkful of English quids buried under the roses.

With some determination, Tess strode through to the kitchen and filled the kettle.

The investigation team were sure to arrive soon.

Dammit!

Why was she wasting time like this? She needed to get down and corner this young pup before a van-load of his superiors rolled up and put him out of bounds. She let herself out of the apartment and crept down the stairs to the front door.

The downstairs tenants' evening paper was lying on the floor in the hall.

She stepped over it and opened the street door. Trying to appear casual, Tess walked outside, wishing for the first time in her life that she smoked. What would look more innocent than a person stepping out for a quick cigarette in the street?

She thrust her hands into her slacks pockets and shambled along towards the Beaumont house.

Feigning mild surprise she looked up at the officer on the step.

'Evening!'

He nodded in her direction, inscrutable.

'Everything all right?' she said, all innocence.

The policeman gave the glimmer of a smile but said nothing.

'Is Martin OK?'

He nodded.

'Only I was quite worried about him these last few days.'

'Worried?'

'He seemed a bit distraught. There was a hell of a lot of banging going on in there yesterday. It sounded like the removal men were in.'

The policeman reaching into his pocket and pulled out a notebook.

'Your name is?'

'Tess—Tess Brandon. I live next door.'

'Then I suggest, Mrs Brandon, that you go back next door and leave us to get on with our job.'

'But I...'

'Someone will probably be along to talk to you within the next few hours.'

'Fine.' Tess hated the way English people went on sometimes. So aloof and snooty. 'So be like that.'

She shrugged and slouched back towards her front door, turning to watch a dark unmarked car pull up. A couple of detectives got out, flashing their badges at the copper on the Beaumont's doorstep.

Picking up the newspaper from the doormat, Tess went back inside. She glanced at the front page: BODY IS MISSING LIBRARIAN.

Jeez!

Where had she last met Martin?

In the library.

What had she caught him rather furtively perusing?

A particularly detailed chapter on decomposition in *The Forensic Atlas*!

Why would a man in advertising want to know how a corpse liquified, or the effects of various temperatures and habitats on a dead body?

Still clutching the newspaper, Tess ran upstairs, her footsteps clattering on the wooden treads.

She read frantically. This librarian was the second woman to have been murdered in the area. Another had disappeared and her corpse had been discovered in similar circumstances a year ago.

Was this what it was all about? Was her neighbour a serial killer?

Tess reached out for a Diet Coke and swigged from the plastic bottle while she considered the facts.

Holy crap, she could sell her story to the international sensation monthlies: My life next door to a serial killer! And then write the whole story up as a novel too, with the guarantee of endless TV interviews.

Eureka! Now her publishers would have to take her seriously.

She slid the mouse and across the desk and scanned the computer for her file on Martin. Dinner party, dinner party, dinner party.

'The dinner party notes'.

She bent nearer the screen and opened the file. Martin had barely uttered once the subject got onto murder. He had just nodded and agreed with everything she and that fat-cat lawyer had said. And Sarah had looked pained and pinched. Perhaps she knew about him. Or suspected. Maybe she was in on it, another Rosemary West. Or had she had just worked out that her husband was a mad murderer and that was why she left in the middle of the night...

Tess scrolled down.

Later in the evening Tess had heard shouting. And Martin had called out:

'Do what you want, Sarah. Women! You're all the same. Plenty more fish in the sea. I'm going out for some air. At least the roses don't despise me.'

Hahahahahahahahaha!

The roses don't despise me!

God, how funny. Drama queen!

Usable though.

She scrolled down.

He had also shouted: 'If you don't like the situation, Sarah, in the morning I trust you'll be gone.'

The situation! What situation might that be? A yard full of dead women, and more in the cellar and under the floorboards?

It would certainly explain why Martin had so adamantly eschewed Tess's offer to help him with the digging.

Tess went again to the window looking down on the yard.

The two detectives were there. She could hear them laughing. Their mood was not very serious, as though they were playing pool in a bar, not looking down into a messed up flower border where, perhaps, a body lay.

One man shook his head. He might have been saying 'this is ridiculous.'

Dammit, there was her camera! Sitting on the window ledge in front of her nose.

She pressed the on button and pulled it up to her face. She might as well get a shot of the detectives and the grave-like hole. But it was dark now. The viewfinder showed nothing but black. She fumbled around with the back of the camera, trying to find the night exposure switch. She didn't want auto-flash on, splashing the garden with light, dragging attention to herself.

When she pressed the shutter release to focus, a red glow filled the LCD screen. With long exposure it was important not to get wobble, so she held her breath while she slowly depressed the button. To her horror flash lit the glass like lightning. At the same moment, with a shriek, her phone rang. Gasping, she steadied herself on the edge of the desk and lifted the receiver.

'Hello?' She found herself whispering, mentally still hiding from the police next door.

The other end of the line was soundless.

'Hello?' She raised her voice to a more normal level. 'I know you're there.'

Nothing.

Tess stood utterly still and listened. She could hear quiet exhalation on the other end of the line.

'Speak up or I'm going to cut you off.'

Silence.

'Okey dokey, smokey. Tata, as you ol' limeys say!'

Tess put down the receiver and hurriedly dialled 1471.

'You were called at 22.30 hours. We do not have the caller's number to return the call.'

We do not have the caller's number! What on earth did that mean? Tess was used to 'The caller withheld their number', but why on earth would the exchange not have the number at all?

She replaced the receiver and dialled the operator for an explanation, but while the number rang out her doorbell buzzed.

After a moment's hesitation Tess replaced the receiver and ran downstairs. Perhaps it was the police.

And about time too.

As she pulled open the street door she heard her cell phone vibrating on the desk upstairs.

A tall dark man in a motorcycle helmet stood on the threshold, looking every bit as sinister as a bogeyman in any teen horror film.

Her heart skipped, and she gave a sideways glance, hoping to see the copper still standing on next door's step.

But no one was there.

'Well?' The man's rasping voice came through his black visor, along with the stench of bad teeth.

'Well, what?'

'Where's the parcel?'

'What parcel?'

He fumbled with a scrap of paper in his hand and read from it.

'A large parcel wrapped in bin-liners, about the size of a woman's body.'

'You won't get something that big on a bike,' Tess said.

'It folds, they told me. Only weighs a few grams.' The man looked down at the paper again. 'Is this number 42A?'

'No,' said Tess, still looking for the policeman. 'This is 44B. 42 is next door and there is no A or B.'

The courier stomped off, his heavy boots squeaking against his leather bike pants.

Tess stood on the step and watched him stop at 42 and hammer his gauntleted fist on the door.

'Miss Brandon?'

Tess spun round. Behind her, emerging from behind a wheelie-bin was a man. It looked like one of the detectives she had watched earlier getting out of the unmarked police car. He flipped open a French steel lighter which gave off a whiff of butane gas. Once the blue flame sprang out he raised the lighter to a cigarette clamped between his teeth, illuminating his face and reminding her of Orson Welles in that film with the zither music.

'Do you have a minute to answer a few questions?' Looking down, he fumbled in the inner pocket of his leather jacket. The lighter dropped to the pavement, while the cigarette looked as though it might burn a hole in the front of his shirt. 'Police,' he said, stooping to retrieve the lighter. 'Detective Stuart Adams.'

'No problems.' Tess could hear her phone ringing again. 'I was expecting you.'

The detective moved nearer and lowered his voice. 'It's about the phone calls.'

'The heavy breather?' Tess was astonished. Even in her books the police weren't this quick off the mark. 'Are you guys psychic or something?'

'Heavy breather, eh?' He gave a wink. 'They don't send detective inspectors out for that kind of thing. I need to talk to you about the little call you made this afternoon.'

Tess's phone stopped. The cell phone started vibrating again.

'I'm sorry?' What on earth could he be talking about? The only phone call she had made today was to her agent back in New York. 'Don't you want to talk about the goings on next door?'

The detective blew a plume of smoke in her direction. Automatically she fanned it away. She hated the smell of tobacco smoke.

The cell stopped and the main phone rang again.

'I thought that's what we were talking about.' The detective smirked. 'All right Ms Brandon, let's take things one step at a time, shall we? Could I come inside?'

'Ok. I er...' Tess fidgeted, darting a look up the stairs, anxious about the ringing phone. 'I...'

'Do you want to run up and get that?' He tilted his head up towards the sound of ringing.

'You'll come up afterwards?' Tess didn't want to lose this opportunity to speak to the police about what she had seen, and also to draw as much as she could out of him.

He nodded.

'I appreciate it,' said Tess, already moving up the stairs.

'Give me a minute or two...' The detective waved his cigarette in the air, '...to finish my fag, and give you a few moments to get whoever it is off the line, then I'll come up and take a few notes. OK?'

Tess took the stairs in threes. Fag! He'd be in for a bit of joshing if he used that kind of language back home.

But by the time she reached her apartment her phone had stopped ringing. She dialled 1471 once again.

With the phone cradled on her shoulder she inspected her cell. She couldn't think of anyone who would phone her at this time of night. Her agent usually called the main phone. This cell was only for the UK contacts. She had hung onto her US cell phone and that was in a pocket somewhere.

She scrolled through the missed calls. Two from an unrecognisable foreign number +33 493 etcetera. Where the hell was that? Holland?

The voice on the main line was repeating the same announcement over and over. 'We do not have the caller's number to return the call.'

It was a while since Tess had had a heavy breather on the line. She wondered whether those vapid blondes like Lisa got them all the time, stalkers too. But perhaps if you really were pretty, it frightened weirdos off—unattainable and all that.

Lisa! She must let them know what was going on. Max was Martin's lawyer after all.

Tess snatched up the phone, while rooting on her desk for the slip of paper where she had exchanged addresses with Lisa to whom she had promised to send a signed copy of her latest book. Lisa had provided her phone number at the bottom of the note, which at the time had amused Tess.

Tess stabbed out the eight digits and waited, glancing at her watch and realising that at 11 o'clock it was probably too late to be calling. But this was urgent, and she needed to do it before the detective came in.

A groggy female voice picked up.

'Hello?'

'Lisa?'

'Yes. Who's that?'

'It's Tess.' During the momentary silence Tess realised that Lisa probably had no idea who she was. 'Is Max there? I need to speak to him urgently.'

Dammit. Now she was on this phone the US cell in her inside pocket had started bleeping, only the cord on this phone was way too short for her to be able to reach her jacket and answer it.

There was a momentary pause before Lisa replied, as though she needed to think hard before replying.

'No. Sorry. Max went out about an hour ago. A bail case at the local nick.'

'...It's just that I need to speak to him urgently. I don't know whether he knows about it yet, but Martin got taken away by the police. And they're digging up the back yard.'

'Back yard? Martin?'

Tess could almost hear the cogs in Lisa's brain grinding into action.

'Martin Beaumont, do you mean? Sarah's husband?'

'That's right. Martin Beaumont. This is Tess, their neighbour. The writer.'

'Oh yes. Tess. You write horror books don't you?'

'Whatever...' This call was even heavier work than she had expected. She enunciated carefully as though talking to a child. 'Look, Lisa, when you speak to Max, you must tell him to call me.'

She could hear the heavy footsteps of the detective thudding up the stairs.

'It's urgent.'

5

Turkey Trot

A face to face dance. Dancers take a step for every beat. Couples move in straight lines, swaying and occasionally pumping the arms like turkeys, or adding a small hop or skip.

M AX TOOK HIS hand away from Lisa's breast as she replaced the receiver, and he hauled himself up to a sitting position. 'What did the ghoulish American harpy want?' He splayed his legs out out on the bed, the crumpled sheets sticking to his sweaty stomach. 'And what's that fool Martin been up to now?'

Lisa had started to explain when the phone rang again.

This time it was the police station telling Max that Martin was being held there, and was calling for a solicitor.

So much for a lazy night in!

Max reluctantly dragged on his clothes.

'You really must give up criminal work,' Lisa whined, from her comfortable position in bed. 'As I see it, the really criminal thing is the way you have to keep getting up in the middle of the night and chasing after these unsavoury characters.'

'It's a job,' said Max, fiddling with his cufflinks. 'I have a reputation.'

Lisa yawned and pulled the duvet round her naked shoulders before snuggling down to sleep.

Women! Max decided not to stoop to her level by reminding her that the luxury Egyptian cotton sheets she lay on, the silk nightdress, not to mention everything else she wore, were paid for by his work with these unsavoury characters.

Within fifteen minutes of the phone call Max was installed inside the bleak grubby interview room at the local nick. In the glare of the strip lighting, he clicked open his briefcase while the dishevelled Martin sat before him and whinged: 'This is a nightmare come true.'

Max's stomach growled. No part of him was in the mood for moronic platitudes.

'I can't believe this is happening to me.' Martin, tonight's version of Lisa's "unsavoury character", employed the high-pitched wail of self pity generally practised by the guilty. 'Why, why, why?'

Max glanced up at the interview room clock. Only eleven thirty.

'You know I didn't do it, Max!'

Blah, blah, blah. Max could see he was in for a long night, when before he even had a chance to sit down Martin had started weeping.

'How long have you known me, Max? You see, I'm the victim here.'

Without speaking Max slapped a clean writing pad on the chipped plastic veneer-topped table. No point engaging. He'd let the imbecile gabble on till he had exhausted his thesaurus of inane platitudes.

'You do believe me, don't you, Max? You know I didn't do it? I wouldn't hurt a fly. Well, perhaps a fly. But I wouldn't kill a woman.'

A sheen of sweat glistened on Martin's brow. Max wondered how it was that once people found themselves in this particular situation they all came out with the same old lines, and used the same cliché intonation, as though they were auditioning for some tatty amateur stage production of I'm Innocent Get Me Out of Here.

'I have to believe you didn't do it, Martin. It's the law.' Max unscrewed the lid of his fountain pen. 'If I even entertained the thought that you might have done it, I am sure you realise that I could not represent you and would have to pass you onto another solicitor.'

Max drew a few short strokes on the blank paper, just to get the pen working, and wished the nick would bring in a nice glass of Port rather than the compulsory cup of pale luke-warm tea. Why had he not left the answering machine on? How much nicer to be nuzzling into the nubile nakedness of Lisa, than sitting in a smelly dank police interview room with a man who had guilt written across his forehead in capitals.

'No. Please. Not another solicitor,' Martin whimpered. 'It has to be you, Max. You understand. I'm so alone.'

Max was appalled to see tears brimming in Martin's eyes.

This level of self pity at this early stage was not just a bad sign. It was a disaster.

'So tell me, Martin...' Max poised his nib over the paper. 'What happened?'

'It's absurd. She was a bitch. You know that.' Martins voice had developed a strange falsetto. 'You saw her. She's not dead anyhow.'

'Enough.' Max held his hands up to stop Martin's diatribe before he incriminated himself. 'The facts, Martin. The facts alone, please.' Max lowered his eyelids halfway down his eyes. He had seen Laurence Oliver do this in a film and thought it a very effective way of looking scary and cool at the same time.

'We fought, with a kitchen knife...' Martin shuddered, briefly grasping around and gulping before continuing, '...and she slumped down. But it was all an act, and I didn't kill her, because she went on to spend all my money, and crawled out of the grave to play with me.'

'Martin!' Max barked like a sergeant major on parade, a tactic which usually worked with hysterics. 'Facts!'

He wished now however that he had not eaten quite so much of the game pie for dinner at the club, nor had the sticky toffee pudding and those glasses of Armagnac to round it all off, before driving home and falling into bed for a quickie with Lisa.

Even more he wished was not working with a client who was not only a friend but also an idiot.

'You don't believe me, do you?' Martin folded his arms and leaned back, sulking. 'I can see it in your face, Max. I know you really think I killed her.'

'Martin!' Max growled, though it was more to do with indigestion and the pain of an impending gout attack than the irritation of dealing with Martin in this hysterical state. Mentally Max had already started toying with ostensibly sensitive ways he might slough Martin off, and thus remove himself from the dilemma of being in the service of a bloody useless defendant who happened to be in possession of his home phone number. 'I'm warning you.' He held up a fat palm, while still looking down at his notepad. 'From this moment, dear boy, you don't say anything to me except in reply to my questions. Not a word.'

Max despised Martin's fearful reaction to the charges. Much better to go at it like a highwayman. If you were guilty, at least lash out, have a try at defending yourself, and if you were innocent, well, even more reason to make some kind of a stand and not sit there snivelling like a teenage girl who'd lost her handbag at a dance. Max hated nothing more than whiny men, with the possible exception of whiny women.

A fly buzzed past his head and landed on the table.

Martin sobbed and wiped the snot away from his nostril with the cuff of his shirt.

Oh god! How many guilty men resorted to these embarrassing tactics, believing it made them appear more innocent. Rather than watch Martin's pathetic amateur theatrics, Max decided to ignore him, fiddle with his pen, check the ink cartridge. Anything.

The fly buzzed off.

'When you have pulled yourself together, Martin, I will ask you some questions and you will reply, telling me only the truth.' Max flicked the tip of the cartridge with a smoke-stained finger nail. 'Do you understand me?' He screwed the pen together again and drew a row of lines across the lines he had already drawn on the top of the paper, creating a grid.

'Martin?'

Martin emitted a little bleat.

'Tell me in detail why you think you are here.'

'I thought you said at dinner that you could get anyone off, Max...whatever they'd done.'

'Martin!' Max threw down the pen and swung his briefcase onto the table. 'I have an aching foot and a rumbling belly, my head throbs and I am tired. If you want me to go back to bed and leave you here to rot, just carry on as you are doing.'

'Please! Don't leave me.' Martin howled like a cartoon dog baying at the moon. 'Please Max. Stay!'

Hoorah.

Three cheers.

Martin had gone to pieces altogether.

Max saw his opportunity to escape.

'I will not represent a frenzied buffoon.' Max stood up, flinging paper and pen back into the briefcase and snapping it shut. 'Friend or otherwise.'

Martin reached out towards him, imploring: Anna Magnani to the life.

Max suppressed a smile. How very touching. Martin's pose reminded him of some penitent woman featured in a Victorian painting with a title like Despair, or The Final Chance.

Or perhaps a new one: The Solicitor Bids His Client Farewell.

'Please, please, please, Max,' Martin whimpered. 'Don't leave me.'

There was something vaguely amusing about this cat and mouse game.

Max suppressed a snigger and sat.

Martin seemed to calm down.

It was like having a pet dog. Max wondered whether if he threw a stick Martin would bound after it.

'You must do as I say. And only as I say.' Max retrieved his pen and paper, and stared Martin in the eye, recalling ancient black and white films about hypnotists.

This case was certainly going to be a challenge. Max wondered whether he would actually be able to get Martin off. If the man had collapsed so quickly here with him, a friend, in private, how fast would he crumble in court under a public inquisition by a top QC?

It didn't bear thinking about. Max opened the top button of his trousers and shuddered. Still, what was the problem? If Martin proved as hopeless as it appeared he would, Max could easily do as he had threatened and pass him off to a junior in his office. Then Max wouldn't have to bear the humiliation of losing a case, but he'd still get the lion's share of the legal fee.

The thought of money always gave Max a warm glow. He was looking forward to an early retirement, a small house with a swimming pool on the French Riviera, or better still in Monaco where he wouldn't have to pay any taxes, with food and wine and Lisa...or some other yielding girl.

'So Martin...' What was the game plan to be? Max held his pen poised over the note pad. 'When did you first meet this woman?'

Martin gave an almost comically quizzical look.

Max returned it followed by a fleeting look of stern warning.

'At university, of course.'

'You've known her that long?' Max scribbled. He kept his eyes on the pad, hoping that, if he didn't connect with Martin, it would keep the man in control. 'I didn't realise. When did you see her last?'

'Just after you left. After the dinner the other night.'

Dinner? Was this "friend" of his losing his marbles?

'You couldn't have seen her then, Martin.' Max looked up and glared into Martin's eyes. 'By then she was already gone. Don't you remember? We discussed the case frequently throughout the meal.'

'But Sarah cooked the meal.'

'What's Sarah got to do with it?'

'This is about me killing Sarah, isn't it?'

Max sucked in air through his teeth and held it at the back of his throat, before slowly exhaling. 'Do you not understand why you are in police custody?'

'Of course I do,' Martin was smiling now, gazing at Max with a face as full of misfortune as a Brueghel simpleton. 'They're questioning me about a murder. But you see, Max, I didn't do it. Sarah ran away, and then she went wild with my credit cards. Taunting me...making me look a fool...She's out there somewhere, teasing, laughing at me. The bitch!'

Max held up his hands again, forbidding Martin to speak. Of course Martin was mad to have got himself hitched to a harpy like Sarah in the first place. What man really wanted to live with a grisly humourless bluestocking? These university females were all very well for a night of hot sex now and then, but there was no point getting yourself tethered up to one for life. That kind of woman seemed to have one motivation in life—cutting off your balls and sucking out your vitals, like an alien in some grisly Hollywood film. No doubt years of being dominated explained why Martin was now sitting before him, a gibbering idiot, lost now that he didn't have his feminist puppeteer to operate him. From the queer ramblings so far this evening it was obvious the fellow had gone stark raving mad, which might be a good thing—useful for the defence case. "My client is insane, m'lud. Married a feminist, wouldn't you know." Judges liked that kind of thing. In the lounge at the club at least.

'I shoved the knife in, yes, Max. I did. I admit it. And I thought she was dead. But she wasn't, you see.' Martin spoke in a shivery voice, as though he was attached to a vibrating machine. 'She can't have been. Despite all the blood. It was just a game to her. You wait, she'll roll in one day, laughing. Either that or we'll find she's been stolen by body snatchers.'

Delusional too! There was his case on a plate: Insanity— mentally ill, as not to know the nature and quality of the act he was doing, or, if he did know it, that he did not know that what he was doing was wrong.

The door opened.

'We can't leave you two alone here much longer, Mr Latham.' The detective, a swarthy man in a red plaid shirt and jeans leaned against the architrave, scratching his crotch. 'We have to get on with our interview.'

Max didn't turn. He held up the back of his pudgy hand, fingers splayed. 'Five minutes.' He glanced up at the whirring electric wall clock. 'Come back in five. Then we're in business.'

'Sorry, mate,' scoffed the detective. 'I'll give you two.'

Bastard.

'As you will.' Max folded his pinkie and his ring finger into his thumb, leaving two fingers up in the traditional Agincourt archers' position. 'Two!'

The detective laughed.

How satisfying to know he could even get a rise out of one of those animals in the police force. Max waited to hear the click of the door shutting before launching his onslaught of questions.

'So what made you do it, Martin? What did you hope to gain? Was it sexual? Did you get your way? Why did you need to murder her?'

Martin just sat there looking vague, and said, almost whispered: 'I didn't.'

'They have strong reasons to suspect you. And it won't take long for them to prove it once the lab starts working on the corpse.'

'What corpse!' Martin gave a sneering snort. 'There is no corpse.'

Max had never in his career seen such a swift mental collapse. The man had an infantile quality. Max had to keep up the pace. After all he only had a few minutes.

'There is a corpse, Martin. They found the body today. On the Common.'

Max noticed that now when Martin tried to speak his top lips caught on his teeth.

'Common?' he rasped. 'They found Sarah on the Common?'

'What's Sarah got to do with it? Max sighed. 'You are here because they think you murdered the librarian.'

'The Librarian?' Martin's grinning face seemed to peel back, exposing an expression of slightly crazed bewilderment. 'They think I killed the librarian? From the library?'

'That's right. The librarian from the library, Martin. Jane Grimshaw was her name. Went missing ten days ago.'

Martin's long fingers gripped the edge of the table. Max noted the whiteness of his knuckles.

'But I don't know any librarians. What librarian are they talking about? I've never met a librarian in my life. How could I have murdered a librarian?'

'You just admitted it to me—the knife, the blood...'

'No. No. That's not what I meant. I've never even met Jane Grimshaw let alone murdered her.'

'You just said you were at university with her.'

'I was never at university with Jane Grimshaw. I know nothing about any Jane Grimshaw, librarian or not. Never. I meant Sarah. I was at university with Sarah. Sarah, my wife. I didn't ever go anywhere with any librarians, not university, not anywhere..' Martin threw his arms up and raised his voice. 'And I certainly didn't kill any Jane Grimshaws.'

'All right, Martin. That's good.' Max folded his arms. At last Martin was responding like a man, even if he was also behaving like an arsehole. 'So what were you doing on the afternoon and evening of the 21st. That's just over a week ago.'

'I know that. I can count.' Martin seemed to perk up. 'And more to the point I can prove it. I know exactly what I was doing, moment by moment on the 21st.' Martin seemed calm again, and spoke with authority. 'It was Sarah's thirtieth birthday. I took her out to dinner and I gave her a ring. An eternity ring as it happens.'

'I see.' Max noted that Martin made a strange dry gulp in the middle of the word eternity. Was that the sign of a lie? 'And Sarah can verify this?'

Max noted that Martin paused just a fraction too long before almost shouting his reply. 'I told you, Max, Sarah walked out on me.' Then he raised his voice a few notes towards the soprano end of the scale. 'And I have had nothing to do with any librarian.'

After the word librarian Martin's teeth started clattering, and he slapped his sides with his hands like some naff actor in a play about the North Pole. Shock, Max supposed. He'd seen it often enough in similar circumstances.

The 'leaving home' incident staged by the ruddy wife had obviously shaken Martin up.

'Help me, Max.' Trembling, Martin reached out, trying to grab Max's hand. 'Oh Christ, Max! Jesus God Almighty, I swear I didn't kill any librarians.'

'And therefore you don't mind, Martin, if I go looking for Sarah to ask her a few questions about you two going out to dinner and her receiving the eternity ring?' Max rubbed his hands together and then turned over to a clean page on his yellow pad. He would very much enjoy paying Sarah a little visit, making her squirm. It was the least he could do in retaliation for that ghastly supper. What on earth gave these non-domesticated females the idea that they could cook? She would have done so much better to have ordered in, like all sensible women did these days. And, anyway, despite all her efforts, the food was grim—much like school dinners, but with pretentious touches. Oh yes. Max would love to put the heat on Sarah.

He sat forward and lowered his voice, trying for the sympathetic avuncular stance.

'Sarah may be a grasping bitch, Martin, but I'm sure even she wouldn't stand by and watch you banged up for a murder you didn't commit.'

Martin shuffled about in his seat, and started whimpering again.

Max once again saw sitting before him a lost cause. Oh god. 'Martin! For Christ's sake will you pull yourself together before the fuzz comes in for the kill.' Although he spoke gruffly, Max had his pen poised, trying to seem logical and businesslike, hoping to pull Martin back to Planet Earth. 'Where might I find Sarah?'

Attempting to lick his dry lips with his even drier tongue, Martin squirmed in his seat and gulped.

'She left me. I told you, Max. After the dinner party.'

Max noticed that Martin's lips quivered as he spoke, and tears filled his eyes. How very touching, thought Max.

'Well, she didn't leave straight after the dinner party. She went the next morning. Early. At about quarter to seven. It could have been earlier. I was asleep you see.'

Who the fuck cared what time she left? 'Any idea where she went?'

Martin's jaw set, and Max could feel the vibration of his legs shaking under the table.

'I was asleep you see. Up in the bedroom. But it was early. It might even have been the middle of the night, for all I know.'

The bloody wife had his knackers in a nutcracker.

'I need to find Sarah, Martin. She is your best hope of a decent defence.'

The fly, which had been crawling across the table for a few minutes now, crept onto Max's notepad. Max slammed his hand down to squash it, but the fly took off and hovered around Martin's head.

Martin flapped his hands in the air and started sobbing.

'Sarah! Sarah! I'm sorry!'

Max could hear the laughter of the cops coming along the echoing corridor of the nick.

'This is no time to pussyfoot about, or to toy with concepts like male pride, Martin. If I am to get you out of this place it is imperative that I contact Sarah. Tell me quickly, did she tell you where she was going?'

Martin looked down, shook his head and swallowed.

'Just out of interest, Martin—the rings, then? Did she take them with her when she left?' Max always thought you got the measure of a woman by whether they took the wedding ring when they walked out on you, or threw it back with fury. 'Rings—wedding, engagement...Did she take them with her?'

'No...Yes...No...She...'

'Well? Did she or didn't she?'

'Yes!' Martin almost shouted. 'She took them, the bitch. She took everything I have.'

'How petty.' Max made a note. These feminists were all the same, greedy, and wanted everything to go their way while giving nothing in return. 'I always thought, Martin, that it was usual to leave the rings if you are the one doing the deserting.' Max made a stab at getting at least some directions to find her. 'I assume she's got another chap? Perhaps you could tell me where I might locate him?'

'The next door neighbour,' sobbed Martin. 'That Yank. She knows I never did anything. She even offered to help me with the gardening. Sarah used to talk to her. Perhaps she knows...' A quivering tear broke loose from Martin's lower lid and tumbled down his cheek. 'Someone has to help me. I've been framed.'

Max rolled his eyes to heaven. This was all he needed. Someone who got his patter from watching TV soaps.

Tapping the table in front of Martin Max said 'There, there,' hoping to hell that Martin would pull himself together pronto. 'Chin up and keep positive. If you're innocent, show them. Be confident, man, not a blubbing teenager.'

The door opened and two detectives gripping plastic mugs of coffee walked in.

'Time up,' said the one in the plaid shirt.

6

Pas De Deux

*A dance for two, usually a woman and a
man. Traditionally it begins with an entree
and adagio, followed by solo variations
for each dancer, and ends in a coda*

'DETECTIVE ADAMS, WHAT a night!' Tess span
her typing chair round and indicated the easy chair.
'Did they find out anything back there?'

'Yes, yes,' he said. 'Very interesting indeed.'

Even though he now sat a good eight feet away, Tess could
still smell the tobacco on the man's breath and clothing. God,
these Brits were like walking chimney stacks. True he'd tried
to cover it up with some vile after-shave but she wasn't sure
if that wasn't worse than the smell of tobacco. She reached

round and opened the window. 'Excuse me, Detective. I'm a little hot.'

'No probs.' He smiled. 'Look, call me Stuart.'

'OK, Stuart.' Tess turned to give him her full attention. 'So, are the Beaumonts turning out to be the new Fred and Rosemary West?' She laughed. 'I suppose what I really mean is, will there be a book in it for me?'

'I ask the questions, miss.' He tapped his nose with a forefinger and leaned forward, looking keenly at her face.

Tess wished she had rigged up something on her computer to record all this stuff, then she could have transcribed it later. How wonderfully authentic to be able to have a genuine conversation, a true-life interrogation with a British copper to use in a novel. She leaned her elbow on the desk and picked up a pen. Perhaps she could surreptitiously make the odd note or two while his head was down writing his own notes and he wouldn't notice.

'Let's go, Stuart' she said. 'Fire away!'

While Tess unwound the cap of the pen Stuart said: 'Tell me everything you know.'

'About Martin? About the night gardening he's been doing? About the phone calls, the library books, the banging? What?'

'Ok, Ok. I get the picture.' Stuart leaned back into the leather chair, his jacket squeaking, leather against leather. 'Let's narrow it down. How well do you know them, next door?'

'I see them around the place. I went to dinner there a couple of days ago.'

'Dinner!' Stuart nodded. 'And what do you think is going on?'

'Search me? Aren't you guys digging up the yard, looking for a body? The missing librarian perhaps?'

Stuart laughed, sniffed and pulled at the septum of his nose with his finger and thumb, still grinning.

'Hey, don't you usually write all this stuff down?' she asked. Tess was disappointed. She had been expecting quite an onslaught of searching questions, like she had seen on *Inspector Morse* and *Rebus*. 'Back in the States our investigating officers...'

'I was getting around to that.' Stuart patted at his pockets with both hands. 'Notebook, notebook...Just trying to be a bit social, you know.' He flung his hands up. 'Damn. I've left it in the squad car.'

Tess tore off a sheet of paper from her pad and handed it to him, along with a pen. She didn't want the man rushing off right now, and maybe getting way-laid by some more pressing business outside, at least not before she had a chance to squeeze some info out of him.

'There was an awful lot of banging in there yesterday,' she said deciding confrontation was the best method. 'Was that Martin chopping someone up?'

'Really? Banging?' Stuart, pen poised over the loose paper, glanced at the wall she had just indicated. 'What kind of banging?'

'The place is usually pretty quiet in the day. Just the wife— that's Sarah—at home. But yesterday I think there were a couple of people and...well...He claimed he was getting it done for the realtors, but it wasn't the right kind of banging for that. There was a thump, thump, thump, as though something heavy was being dragged downstairs.'

Tess looked at him, sitting there, and realised how much better she would do his job. He was looking vacantly around her room, weighing it up, it seemed like. Perhaps he thought she was part of the plot, a murderer's accomplice, a walking red herring.

'I looked out front,' Tess continued despite his lack of questions. 'There was a white van out there in the afternoon. Was that something to do with it?'

Stuart looked vague, leaning over the paper, biting his lip, seemingly on the verge of laughter.

Tess cleared her throat. What a goober! So this was the face of the British Police? How she wished she was in his place. Why hadn't she trained for the FBI rather than going to college to study American Literature?

'Let's start at the top, shall we?' he said. 'Name?'

'Tess Brandon. Lookit, Detective, I'll fire away with all the data. It'll be quicker: I'm an American Citizen. I'm over here for a year, doing research, and a bit of teaching. I'm 30 years old. And I'm a novelist by profession. OK?' After a pause she added, just for completeness, 'Oh—and you know my address as you are sitting in it.' She fumbled into her trouser pocket. 'Here's my card—home address, agent, phone numbers. All that shit.'

She placed her business card on the coffee table before him.

While Stuart silently scribbled, Tess jotted down her own observations about him, noting the slightly shaggy but coiffed hair, the worn leather jacket, the artfully frayed jeans. His chin bore a blondish stubble, though his hair was darker. Oddly, his fingers appeared to be shaking. The paper resting on his knee was quivering, and she could see the tremor at the end of the pen as it scratched away. Maybe he was a drunk, she'd noticed how so many Brits were binge drinkers. Or perhaps he had some kind of RSI.

'Martin next door seems to be one of those quiet, normal guys,' Tess said, trying to keep him writing while she observed. 'But the more you think about it the more he seems, well...a bit creepy.'

'So you're a novelist.' Stuart looked up. Tess quickly leant her elbow on what she'd written and started stagily doodling at the bottom of the notepad.

'Tell me, Tess, can I buy your books in the shops?'

'I don't see why not, as long you hand over the money first.' Stupid fucking question, thought Tess. One degree away from "Where do you get all your ideas?" 'As they say:' she added, putting her fingers up to illustrate quotation marks. '"Available now in all good bookshops."'

He was staring at her now. Looking as though he was trying to remember every detail of her face. Perhaps he knew who she was really, perhaps he had seen her book jacket photo.

'Do you use your own name?'

'Tess Brandon. Yes.'

'I'll look out for you.' He grinned, nodding. 'So tell me, Tess, where do you get all your ideas?'

Oh yawn.

'I buy them in Tesco.'

She waited for him to laugh, but he just went on nodding, sagely, his mind clearly elsewhere.

A cell phone in his jacket rang out a persistent bleep, and he flinched.

'Sorry about this.' He pulled out the phone and bent forward, shielding his face with his hand as he took the call. 'Yeah, yeah. I know. Not so easy...' Tess's heart sank. He was going to leave just when she was starting to get things moving.

'I'll never do it. I'll be right down.' Stuart snapped the phone shut, and sat up again. 'Look, Tess, they need me back at the station...My partner...'

'Don't you want to ask me about the "gardening" I saw Martin doing? The digging of a grave-shaped hole?' Tess grasped about for ways of keeping the man here a little longer.

She wanted at least to get some information out of him. 'You said something about phone calls...'

Stuart stood up, glancing at his watch. 'Tomorrow, maybe.'

'I won't be available tomorrow.' Tess leapt to her feet, racking her brains for a plausible excuse. 'I'm doing a book signing in Leeds.'

'Well...How marvellous...' Stuart hesitated, a finger to his chin, staring at her again in that weird penetrating way. 'Here's an idea. How about you come along with me to HQ and I can get the rest of your statement there?'

'Sure.' Alleluia! Tess was already grabbing her cell phone, pen and small notebook from the desk and stuffing them into her trouser pockets. 'Why not? I just need a jacket.'

Stuart placed his hand on the small of Tess's back, guiding her towards the stairs.

Tess freed herself and pulled a navy blazer from the hook on the back of the door.

'Okeydoke.' She flung the jacket over her shoulder, and went ahead of him. 'Now I'm all yours.'

When they came into the street, Stuart turned up the road, away from all the activity outside the Beaumonts' house.

Tess looked back and saw a gaggle of scene of crime officers in white overalls chatting to men in uniform. One fellow in plain clothes glanced across at them then resumed his conversation, uninterested.

'Aren't you going to wave goodbye to your pals?' said Tess, as Stuart increased his pace in the opposite direction.

'Keep up, if you still want to come with me.' Stuart looked doggedly forward. 'I'm in a bit of a hurry, you see.'

She noticed him nodding towards a shadowy figure of a man sitting in a silver car parked in the gloom beneath a tree on the other side of the road. The man then gave him a thumbs up sign before bending over, as though to pick up something from the car's floor.

'Is he your partner?'

'Hurry up. Er...Yes.' Stuart guided Tess over the road and opened the rear door of the car. 'In you get.'

Tess slid over the back seat and she fastened her belt, as Stuart climbed into the front passenger seat, slamming the door.

The driver sat up, pulling on a woolly hat, the kind builders wore. There was a touch for you! He looked more like a criminal than a policeman.

Tess looked around the car's interior, noting the ripped chair back, the muddy crushed paper cups and fast food wrappers in the foot well.

'This car looks a bit beat up for a police car,' she said.

'All the better for undercover work,' replied Stuart, glancing back over his shoulder. 'Come on, bro. Let's go.'

The car pulled out and Tess turned to watch the police activity around the house next door to her apartment. There was a 'Do Not Cross' tape round the pavement outside Martin and Sarah's place now. Blue and white stripes.

Tess realised it might have been more useful to stay at home and watch all that stuff going on rather than going to the police station.

'Do you know, Stuart, I think I made a mistake,' she said. 'I've just remembered. Leeds is next Tuesday, not tomorrow. Why don't I come in to the station and talk to you tomorrow, like you said?'

'No can do.' Stuart was abrupt now, ignoring her, no longer the smiling man who a few moments ago had sat in her easy chair.

As the car turned the corner out of her street Tess watched as a uniformed policeman clasping a notebook stepped up to her front door and put his finger to the bell. Now she could surely persuade Stuart to bring her back home.

'Don't you want to talk to your colleagues? One of them is knocking on my door. Perhaps they're looking for you.'

'Christ.' Stuart banged his fist on the back of the driver's seat. 'Put your foot down, for Christ's sake.'

The car's tyres screeched as they took the corner. What was the rush?

Tess looked at Stuart in the flicker of passing streetlights. A small muscle in his cheek was bouncing in and out, his lips tight.

The car drove past a traffic cop in a bright yellow jacket, standing in the centre of the road, waving them away from the area. As they came near him both Stuart and the driver held hands up to their faces.

Why did these two not want to communicate with their colleagues? Idiotic as it seemed they actually appeared to be hiding from the police.

What the fuck was going on here?

Tess's chest tightened in a sudden grip of realisation.

Jesus H Christ.

What had she done?

No notebook. No questions. A real policeman was now knocking at her door.

Tess tried to swallow with a dry rigid throat.

It all added up.

She'd been had.

How the fuck had she let this happen?

She was sitting in a moving car with two strange men, and she hadn't even queried that they really were who they said they were.

They could be anyone.

They could be...

Shit.

She looked slyly at them from the side of her eye.

These two assholes were no policemen.

'Can't I get out?' she said, her voice weak. 'I'd like to go back now. I'm very tired.'

'Sorry, love. You stay with us.'

'Oh, you police guys!' Tess knew it was wise to let them think she was still fooled. She tried to keep her voice light, joshing. 'You know it'll all keep till tomorrow. I'm hardly going to jump the country.'

In the dark her hand fumbled for the door handle.

As soon as they hit a red light she would make a run for it.

'So Stuart...' She decided to keep talking, try to pretend things were normal, while trying to work out what was really going on here. 'Where are we going, exactly?'

'I told you,' Stuart replied. 'The station.'

Through the window Tess could see the blue light of the local police station on the corner.

She sensed Stuart watching her so she made a big show of looking in the other direction, pretending not to see it.

The car made no sign of slowing down.

As they sped past the police station, Tess toyed for a moment with asking to see Stuart's ID, or whatever it was that he had flashed before her eyes in the dark street.

But she decided against that. If it was genuine it would make no difference to her situation. But if it was not, they would certainly know she was on to them, and then...

And then...

Tess gripped the door-handle even more firmly and gulped. She could see Stuart's—if that was actually his name—hand on his thigh. The fingers were drumming. He was nervous, or excited, maybe both.

How come she hadn't noticed all these signs before? No note-book, no sense of procedure, the jittery hand...

"Stuart" was no detective. This was no undercover police car. For that matter the man driving it was no police driver.

For some reason Tess did not understand, she realised she was being abducted.

Now all she had to do was keep alert, and get away.

'It's been quite a night,' Tess said, still trying to keep things casual. 'What with one thing and another.'

As the car accelerated into the night she thought she heard the driver snigger.

7

Morris Dance

*An English folk dance that first appeared in the
fifteenth century, in which dancers wear bells
on their legs and characters include a fool, a
boy on a hobby horse, and a man in blackface*

'DON'T LET THEM rattle you,' Max said as the door
opened. 'Brave it out. Remember: Till they prove
you are guilty, you are innocent. Let's see a bit of
the old Martin. Be bold.'

'I can't,' Martin whimpered.

The two detectives slouched in. Max stood, gave a defer-
ential nod and moved round the table to sit beside his client.

'You're in advertising,' Max whispered into Martin's ear.
You know how to stand up and make an impression. Use a bit
of that copywriting flair of yours.'

The detectives sat down, one at the table, the other pulling out his seat so he could lean against the wall. He fiddled with a recorder.

DI Butler, the one in plaid, recited the standard warnings about recording and evidence then took a photo from his file and placed it before Martin.

'Who's that?' he said.

Max peered over. What a fright. The woman was no oil painting, that was for sure.

Max nodded towards Martin, who glanced down, then said with some swagger: 'Some plug ugly woman with one eyebrow and a moustache. Give me a clue? Freda Kahlo's sister?'

Max gave Martin a sideways look. He had intended to inject just a little bravado into him, not turn him into a full blown stand-up comedian.

'That's the woman you murdered.' DI Butler leaned back, folded his arms and gave a challenging leer. 'Don't you remember?'

Max said to Martin, 'You don't have to reply.'

'I know nothing about this woman.' Martin pulled the photo close to his nose and peered at the blurred image. 'Spotty, isn't she? Or is it freckles? She's got dark hair, not unlike my wife's. But I can swear to you on the Bible, or any other book you may have to hand, that I have never seen this woman in my life.'

Where had all this courage come from? Only a few moments before Martin had been wailing like a girl, which actually would have been preferable to this new sassy Martin. Short of knocking him out, Max didn't quite know how to turn off this new flip, glib side.

He watched DI Butler go through his notes and flip forward to a clean sheet. Max could see that unfortunately this detective was not one of those with the brain of a gnat. From the fellow's attitude Max feared there was a coup about to be played out. It seemed clear they had something incriminating up their collective sleeve.

'Don't get enough at home?' sneered DI Butler. 'Is that it? Or perhaps you're bored with your wife and you want to relive the excitement of the chase?'

To Max's surprise, Martin, looking cool as a cucumber, folded his arms and leaned back. He remained silent.

Max smiled. He too knew how to play the Cheshire Cat.

'Strange taste in books, too, haven't you, Martin?' said the detective.

'Books?' said Martin, eyebrows raised. 'What, you mean Salman Rushdie? Well, yes. Everyone bought a copy, you know, but no one finished it. Me included. I do like Ishiguru though. And Amis. And Updike. And of course I can also go low-brow. I read Grisham. Everyone reads Grisham. And PD James, Kathy Reichs, Patricia Cornwell. But I don't stoop to ultra-pop like Dan Brown or JK Rowling or the new tabloid so-called celebrity novelists.'

Reichs! Cornwell! Max suppressed a desire to thump his client. Why admit to reading gory crime books at this juncture? Next thing the bloody man was going to present his collection of driller-killer videos.

'I doubt they actually write the books themselves, all those footballers' wives. I've even read a book by my next door neighbour, Tess Brandon. Pretty run of the mill, as crime fiction goes.'

'I was referring to the books you borrow from your local library, Mr Beaumont.' DI Butler pulled out a list. 'Books you have checked out in the last six months.'

'Not me. I don't take out library books. I buy them.' Martin pulled a face, a cross between a grimace and surprise. 'I thought you must have been checking out my bookshelves at home. Sorry. Wrong man, I'm afraid. I don't even possess a library ticket.'

'So you deny taking out *A History of Torture Through the Ages*, *Mein Kampf* and *120 Days of Sodom?*'

'I told you. I don't have a library ticket.'

DI Butler slid a small plastic card across the table.

'So what's this then?'

Martin glanced at the library card and his jaw fell open.

Max could see it clearly: Martin's name written in a large font. Martin Beaumont.

Max resisted the urge to put his head in his hands and groan. When he had asked Martin to show a bit of chutzpah he wasn't suggesting that he lie through his teeth. Max did not fancy the clean-up operation which was going to be necessary if he was going to get his client out of the hole the fool was indisputably digging for himself.

'You must have presented a utility bill, bank statement, driver's license, Martin. And given them a sample of your signature,' said DI Butler. 'Because, as you see, you certainly do have a ticket—and this ticket proves you have a kinky taste in books.'

'I told you I do not have a ticket.' Martin's voice rose. 'That's a fake. It must be. I don't possess a library ticket.'

'It's not exactly a fake, Martin. It's a repro we got the library to make up in place of the original.'

Max perceived a scornful glint in DI Butler's eye. He wondered what else they had on Martin. He suspected it was rather a lot.

'When did you last visit the library, Martin?'

Max felt Martin stiffen.

Oh no. What was coming now? Max had experienced this kind of thing before. A client could resist the evidence for so long, then suddenly they baulked at one seemingly harmless question.

'I told you—I don't have a library ticket.'

But Max could detect the quiver in Martin's voice.

'Library ticket or no library ticket,' droned DI Butler. 'You don't need to be a member to browse the shelves, and you were in the library yesterday, were you not, Martin?'

Max knew that whatever was coming next was bad news. Martin's body had been the thing which let him know. Max could feel him now, rigid as a board, barely breathing.

'I don't usually go to the library,' said Martin in a higher tone. 'But I wanted to go online. My computer had been stolen.'

Computer stolen! This was news to Max.

'You were recognised, Mr Beaumont. And it was noted you were reading a book about the decomposition of corpses.'

Martin flushed, a deep maroon.

'That bloody Yank, I suppose,' said Martin, aggressive now. 'Her book was crap actually. I was being kind before.' He suddenly clapped his hands and sat forward. 'Of course! She's a novelist. Don't you get it? She writes fiction. She makes a living inventing stories.'

'You were seen reading a book about the decomposition of corpses.'

Max did not like it when detectives started repeating themselves like this. It generally signified they were going in for the kill.

'I might have accidentally picked that book out...' Martin gave a theatrical shrug, but couldn't disguise the trembling of his jaw. 'But that was research for something else. Not for burying the librarian.'

Max had to fight not to close his eyes, slump down and start banging his head on the table.

'You admit to burying her then?'

'I have had nothing at all to do with any librarian whatsoever in my whole life, ever.'

'Jane was her name, you know, Martin. The librarian.'

'Well, I didn't bury Jane...'

'No, you just dumped her on a rubbish tip on the common
and covered her with a pile of debris. But despite having gone
missing ten days she had only been on the common for less
than a day. So naturally, Martin, I was wondering where you
kept her before that? In your garden, was it?'

'No!' shouted Martin

Gauging the eruptive violence of Martin's response, Max
could see that the garden certainly had something to do with it.

Max decided to avoid looking at his client, for despite the
vocal bravado of his responses, Martin now was shuddering
from top to toe. The table was clattering from the tremors
emanating from the man's legs.

Why had he not spilled the beans earlier? How the hell
was Max meant to defend Martin when he was always operating on the rear foot, not to mention in the dark with his
hands tied behind his back? A thought flickered through
Max's mind that perhaps Martin was attempting to challenge
the claim Max had vainly made over dinner that he could get
anyone off, whatever dastardly crime they had committed.
But that was just silly. Max realised he was being an egotist
to even consider it. This librarian woman had already gone
missing by then—Max remembered discussing the case,
while Sarah sulked.

'So who was buried in the garden under that little row of
plug-plants, Martin? Jane Grimshaw wasn't your first victim,
was she?'

Max groaned, then tried to disguise the sound as a burp. He made an elaborate pantomime of patting his pockets, searching for an indigestion pill.

Things were way out of control and Max did not like things being out of control.

'Excuse me detective inspector,' Max stood up and made a little bow to the cocky bastard, Butler. 'I need to have a few private words with my client.'

Neither detective moved.

'No.' DI Butler smirked and shook his head.

Max held on to the man's gaze. It was all a game. And Max had no intention of losing. He always won. He turned to Martin and spoke as firmly as he could without betraying the worry that was flooding his mind.

'You do understand, don't you, Martin, that you don't need to say anything at all. You mustn't let them bully you into making up absurd things which are not true simply to appear clever.' Max turned away from Martin now, and, in the hope of salvaging some of his professional stature, whispered to the detectives. 'Martin's wife left him a couple of days ago. The whole sorry business with that female has distressed him considerably...he has not slept for days. He is naturally on edge.'

At this moment the water jug started to jiggle against the wall, emitting a loud jangle. Max raised his eyebrows in response, indicating the jug with his brow. 'As you can hear.'

Max was relieved when the detectives laughed at his deadpan joke. Martin was now shaking so badly he looked as though he was entering the later stages of malaria.

'It was in the papers.' Martin blurted, without warning. His voice carried the tinny edge of hysteria. 'If it hadn't been in the papers I wouldn't have even known there was a

librarian called Jane or a ditch in that thicket on the Common
or anything. I...I...'

'Talking of the Common...' DI Butler reached into the card-
board folder and pulled out another thin file.

Max felt the juddering emanating from Martin speed up,
rather like the spin on a washing machine. What piece of
incriminating evidence was coming now? He slumped back
into his chair and perched his spectacles on the bridge of his
nose, looking down at the photograph the Detective lay before
them: Martin sitting in a car on the Common, gazing forward.
It was time-date stamped.

'It's a public place. That's why it's called a Common,' whispered Martin through chattering teeth. 'Common land. Since
medieval times. We're all entitled to go there.'

'So you chose to go and park your car in front of the exact
spot where only hours before the body of Jane Grimshaw had
been found. And you sat there staring at the spot for some time
before driving away.'

'I think you will find, Detective Inspector,' said Max, defiant,
'that many men sit in cars in the car park on the Common
during their lunch breaks. There is no crime in that. It's a
way of getting out of the office, and getting some air into their
lungs. I think you'll find it had nothing whatsoever to do with
the young lady's prior disappearance.'

DI Butler slipped another photo out of the folder and
across the table. In it Martin was still in the car, but now
holding up the evening newspaper, seemingly engrossed in
reading about the body just discovered on the Common. His
car was parked next to a sign indicating the facilities available on the common. Martin was clearly oblivious to the
police photographer.

Max exhaled. Then took a long breath in. Bravado, bravado. Keep the façade going even when the earth had cracked open beneath your feet.

'Circumstantial, circumstantial!' Max slid the photos away with a theatrical gesture. 'There is nothing at all here, Detective Inspector, that shows you anything more than the prurient interest of an inhabitant of the area, fascinated by something sensational which had recently taken place in his locale. It's the ghoul instinct. If we are honest with ourselves, we all possess it. Any car crash produces a jam on the other side of the carriageway while onlookers rubber-neck. This is the same thing.' He turned and gripped Martin by the shoulder, hoping it might arrest the shivering fit. 'When you have even one piece of what I would call evidence against my client, Detective Inspector, and I mean something which would stand up in court, give it to us, but for the moment I don't think you have nearly enough.' He rose, indicating that Martin should also get up. 'Look at it! Every single thing you have is circumstantial. You're grasping at straws.' He looked at his watch, worth more probably than either of these grubby gumshoes earned in a year. 'It's late and I am certain you will be wanting to let my client go home now and get a good night's sleep. For one thing is sure, Detective Inspector Butler, you haven't one single thing here which would give you occasion to charge Mr Beaumont.'

Martin gulped, making a loud glugging noise.

Max raised his voice slightly to cover the sound. 'In Great Britain a man may park his car in a public car park on the common. Where's the offence in that? In Great Britain a man may take out any number of nasty library books. If they are so detrimental to a person's psyche, what are they doing in a public lending library in the first place? Some spiteful neighbour makes a phone call telling you that my client is a killer, and then you break into his home and discover him digging at his rose beds. Is there a law against gardening at dusk? Frankly, no case! Charge him, detective. Charge him now, or let him go.'

'I never said it was Mr Beaumont's neighbour who made the call.' DI Butler exchanged a glance at his colleague then looked up at the wall clock. 'And, legally we still have quite a few hours left.'

'Yes, yes, of course,' said Max with a theatrical sigh. 'But you have nothing on my client. Why not let him go home and sleep in a comfortable bed while you grub around for just the teeniest bit of evidence against him?'

As he watched DI Butler slowly put all the photos back into the folder, Max knew that his people had to track down Martin's bloody wife first thing in the morning. She could clear it all up, provide an alibi, whatever...She was obviously the key to the whole thing.

The detectives stood up.

Hoorah.

Max smiled.

With a bit of luck he'd be at home and snuggled up in bed within the hour.

'You'll have to stay at your home address, Mr Beaumont, and Mr...'

'Blah, blah, blah,' said Max, grabbing Martin by the elbow. 'I know the gen.'

As Max marched Martin towards the exit, the door opened and a uniformed policewoman came in.

She was carrying a folder, which she handed to DI Butler.

'Hold your horses.' The Detective Inspector flicked through the pages and ran his eyes quickly up and down the cover sheet.

He thrust out a finger and pointed it towards the graffiti covered plastic chairs. 'I think you might need a seat. Both of you.'

Max's heart sank.

One second too late.

Max could feel Martin's shivering start up again as he shunted him, zombie-like, back towards the table.

DI Butler leaned back, cocky, and folded his arms. A winsome smile rippled on his lips. He addressed Martin as though the man was an infant.

'Any way of explaining all the blood in your kitchen, Martin? All round the edge of the laminate it is, and seeping down the cracks, and on the grouting round the wall tiles, also some smears on the telephone in the hall. And please don't start on about a nosebleed.'

Max's heart lurched.

No bed tonight.

The detective reached inside the folder and pulled out a see-through plastic evidence bag. He threw this down in front of Martin.

The bag contained a ring. He poked at it with a pencil.

'An eternity ring. Perhaps you'd like to tell me who it belongs to?'

'I don't know,' said Martin. 'I've never seen it before in my life.'

Max gazed down at the stones—sapphire, agate, ruby, amethyst and something or other blue, which no doubt started with H. And with that Max realised he had a client who was not only hiding things from him but also lying.

Max watched as Martin stared down at the ring and started to cry.

Although Max had already opened his mouth ready to make an observation, luckily his brain kicked in before he found himself saying aloud: "And what has that ring to do with any murdered librarian? The gems clearly spell out the name of my client's wife, Sarah."

Surreptitiously Max glanced down at Martin's fingers which were fretfully plucking at the fabric of his trouser legs.

His client may or may not have had something to do with the disappearance of a frumpy librarian, but one thing was sure: The fucking idiot had only gone and chosen this week to stand up to his overbearing shrew of a wife, and something very serious was afoot.

Max popped open a blister pack of indigestion tablets, downed two and sat back, ready for a very long night.

8

Czardas

*Hungarian dance which starts slowly and finishes
with kicking out and fast leaps and whirls*

TESS TIGHTENED HER grip on the car's door handle, and
started pressing downwards, ready to make a run for
it. She could see a junction ahead. The light was green.
There was every possibility it would turn red before the car
arrived at it. The best thing to do she decided was to start
up some conversation which would demand an answer just
before the car stopped, so that this "Stuart", or whatever the
hell he was really called, would, for a moment at least, be off
his guard when she jammed the handle down, and leaped out.

Tess waved her hand across at a fast food restaurant she
had never seen before in her life. The neon sign showed a
cartoon man in a huge Stetson.

'Bet you don't know something weird and wonderful about that place, Stuart?' She spoke in as confident a tone as she could manage.

Stuart grunted.

The traffic light ahead duly turned red and the woolly-hatted driver decelerated.

'The folks who ran it were pulled in for serving rat meat. They sold it with fries; rat, deep-fried in savoury crumb.' She laughed and pointed again. 'Right in there. Can you imagine— Southern Fried Rat?'

Instantaneously, as the car stopped, Tess slammed her hand down and shoved at the door.

Nothing.

She pumped away on the handle.

'Child lock,' said Stuart calmly. 'You have to realise that we frequently have to transport some very difficult types. It would never do if they just leapt out every time we hit a red light.' The smell of his tobacco breath, or was it fright, made her gag. 'You can't get out till I let you out. But then why would you want to?'

Tess's heart pumped like a drummer in a heavy metal band. It was all she could do to keep her voice level.

'Who are you, Stuart?' she said. 'Who are you, really?'

'Wouldn't you like to know!' he replied. Then he spoke to the driver. 'Wouldn't they all like to know, the arseholes!'

This made the driver laugh maniacally. As the amber light went out and green came on, he screeched like a witch and the car lurched forward.

Tess looked forward into the rear view mirror. In the strobe of passing streetlights, she caught sight of the driver's eyes— mere slits, lined with tears of laughter. He raised a finger to wipe them away and caught eyes with her in the mirror. His eyes darted back to the road and he pulled out into the fast lane.

So she was right.

She was being abducted.

She knew the most important thing was to keep her head clear.

From her research into true life murders and kidnappings Tess knew all about the types of men who did this kind of thing.

There were those who did it for ransom. The strategists. They usually had some plan which fell apart the second something unforeseen popped up: the wrong weather, a car running out of petrol, the ransom payees refusing to co-operate. But they had a plan and an objective—money.

These two were definitely not from this group.

Neither were they the types who picked up women on the spur of the moment, for rape. This type usually used weapons—knives, guns, a broken bottle and acted out of some sudden lust, easily sated.

The type of abduction she found herself victim to was, she believed, the worst possible scenario. From what she'd seen so far it was obvious that these two were the very nastiest, and least controllable profile imaginable: Tacticians on a spree. They had loose plans which they could easily adapt. They knew ultimately what they wanted, and had things well planned out, but in a twinkling could adjust the methods they used to achieve their goal. But the worst thing was they were doing it for fun, excitement, power.

She ran her mind back over what had happened so far—the way Stuart introduced himself, and then got into her apartment; how he got a call from the driver after a while, worrying things weren't going as smoothly as he wished, and finally how she herself had practically offered herself on a plate, their sacrificial totem.

It was all she could do not to weep at her own stupidity.

She remembered Stuart's signal to the driver that the plan was indeed a live one, and that he should prepare to drive away, and (how this must have multiplied their fun) it was all performed right under the noses of scores of policemen.

Though the driver was obviously the more nervous of the two, this pair were also clearly afflicted by the psychiatric syndrome know as a folie à deux, or shared psychotic disorder. Each of them reassured the other and also spurred the other on. They would operate in a mutual spiral of self-confidence, like Leopold and Loeb, the Menendez brothers, The Hillside Stranglers.

Oh fuck.

Tess's mouth was dry.

The car streamed through a green turning light and onto a large main road.

These two men had her captive; they were essentially boogiemen, unpredictable, unbalanced. When it suited them, she figured, they indubitably intended to kill her.

Tess looked out of the window, trying to seem unperturbed. She knew the only way to play this baby was to keep utterly alert to the pair of them and calmly take opportunities where and when they presented themselves.

She toyed with the idea of making faces at people in passing cars or adjacent buses, but then decided that to do this with Stuart at her side was madness. He would surely shove her down into the footwell and who knows what else. What would it be to them to dispatch her straight away?

The worst thing Tess realised, was that they now knew she was onto them, so they would be on double alert.

She had to make her encyclopaedic knowledge of crime and the criminal mind work for her in a whole new way.

She was amazed at how fast her brain was operating, and how she seemed to be able to carry on three completely comprehensive conversations with herself and never lose the thread.

She was remembering the route as best she could. Marking in her mind memorable buildings and road signs for future use. Though if these men were who she suspected they were, the killers of two women, one more than six months earlier, the other last week, and if she failed to find a method of escape there might be no future in which to use these darned memories.

Meanwhile the other side of her brain was in overdrive. 'If they do murder you, Tess Brandon, it'll be all over the news-papers and TV...' (her professional mind had this maddening way of constantly searching out opportunity) '...imagine the peak in book sales!'

Hahahaha! Pity she wouldn't be alive to see that.

The car was passing into an area of London Tess didn't know at all, currently a divided highway, with signposts to 'Croydon and the M23'. There seemed to be many fewer cars on the road out here. Lots of trees, takeaway restaurants, superstores, industrial parks, sports fields. Where were they taking her?

The driver spoke. His voice was high and quivery.

'She's memorising the route, Stu. I can see her eyes.'

So this gave her some more info: The man beside her quite possibly really was called Stuart, and he was without question the dominant one of the pair.

'Who cares?' Stuart shrugged and replied calmly. 'So what?'

That was a response Tess certainly would not have wished for. It meant that Stuart was confident that Tess would never have the opportunity to use any information she was gathering—i.e. they really did intend to kill her.

The car swerved off the main highway and proceeded along a dimly lit side street lined with pebble-dashed 1930s houses with painted gables and lattice bay windows. After three more turns the driver stretched a hand to his side and fumbled on the passenger seat. He picked up a small remote control and flicked it ahead of the car. Tess watched the infra-red beam flicker. He must be opening a gate.

She knew from the change in the tension of the two men that they were nearing their destination. She could feel Stuart almost holding his breath with anticipation.

When the car had stopped and the men had to open the doors to get out, that would be her biggest, perhaps her last, chance of escape. Whatever happened she would break from them and make a run for it.

She took a deep breath, getting herself mentally prepared.

Ahead stood a semi-circle of houses, each with an adjoining lock-up garage. It was a dead end street so it was obvious that there was only one serious way to head—back to the main highway, with its row of small convenience stores.

The driver was still flicking away at the remote controller till one of the garage doors tilted, and, with a slow lugubrious shuddering movement, started to open.

Tess's hopes crashed. The car mounted a small paved fore-court and slowly drove into the lock-up garage. Shit. Once she was in here she might as well be in outer space—no one could hear you scream.

She knew she had to bolt while the garage door was still open. It had not yet quite hit the top, and presumably would take as long to close.

Tess lunged over the back of the front passenger seat, sprawling out, reaching out for the door. She grabbed the handle and thrust it down. The door sprang open and jarred against the painted brick wall of the garage.

While trying to grip her feet, Stuart yelled at the driver, who was still carefully steering the car into the narrow gap between the garage wall and a battered metal sheeted wall that seemed to stretch the length of the garage.

Kicking out with all her might, Tess writhed, shoving herself forward, slithering over the seat like a seal on ice. Her head was out, one arm stretched ahead to break her fall.

The car spurted forward.

Her knuckles grazed along the oily concrete floor. The garage door was coming down.

The driver swerved wildly and the car came to an abrupt stop, the fender smashing into the blackened rear wall of the garage, rattling the tins and jars on the shelves above. Tess pitched forward, the door jammed back against her neck. She kicked her feet free from Stuart's grip and slid down onto the ground. The driver flung himself over the seat, grabbing at her shoes as she dragged herself along, hauling herself away from the car. There was still a five feet of air beneath the door, she could easily get through.

'Open the bloody room,' wailed Stuart, who was out of the car and marking the open garage door like he was a desperate nickelback and she was the ball. 'Leave hold of her, for fuck's sake, and open the bloody room.'

Tess's knees scraped the uneven concrete as she crawled along towards the decreasing gap. Above the mechanical groan of the garage door, Tess heard a hollow metal sound of bolts being bashed open.

There was still a good three foot before the door hit the deck. If she ducked under she still might make it.

She propelled herself forwards, towards the ever decreasing hope of escape. Stuart had one hand gripping her jacket, the other grabbed her leg.

By rolling onto her stomach, she managed to squeeze through the gap, Stuart all the while hauling her back. She twisted away, freeing herself from his grip, jerking her body towards the pavement.

There was only one foot of the door still open. If only she could get up, and the garage door shut behind her, she would gain a brilliant head start on them.

Once she was up on her feet she could sprint like a deer back to that main road. As she pressed her hands down, and started to thrust herself up, someone grabbed her hair, yanking it hard, dragging her back.

Fuckit.

The garage door shuddered and slammed shut, with her lying inside.

Stuart stood before her. She was being held now from behind, an arm round her waist, the other still tugging her hair.

'You had a mobile phone,' said Stuart, plunging his hand into her trouser pocket. 'I saw you put it in.' He pulled out the phone and slipped the battery pack off, tossing both parts into a dark corner. 'You won't be needing that.'

While the driver shunted Tess towards the back of the garage, Stuart pulled out her apartment keys and slipped them into his own pocket.

Tess took the deepest breath she could manage and hollered for help.

'Save it!' Stuart pressed his gloved hand over her mouth. 'You can scream all you like, once you're in your lovely new lodgings.'

Both men slammed her against the ridged metal side wall and, pressing her into the rusty surface, edged her along in the dark. Her lips brushed the wall, scraping dust into her mouth. The blood-like taste of rust spread over her tongue. The wall ended and with nothing to counter the weight of the men behind her Tess staggered forward. Hands grasped out and spun her round then flung her into total blackness.

She thrust her hands out to soften the fall. Although she expected to hit concrete, when Tess landed it was on a soft shag-pile carpet. She scampered forward, a nocturnal creature hiding from predators. But the men did not follow her now. Instead behind her a heavy iron door slammed and she heard the same metallic ring of the bolts she had heard before, only this time they were being jolted back into position.

The thump of her heart and gushing blood pumping through her body almost deafened her, but in the far distance she thought she heard laughter, footsteps and a slamming door.

9

Spot Dance

A dance in which there is very little
movement along the line of danse

MARTIN PRESSED HIS face to the small square of scratched glass set into the cell door and tried to see out. He had been knocking now for about ten minutes. He had watched the ghostly form of a man in uniform lurking around at the end of the corridor but even shouting didn't affect him. No one came. Then a few minutes ago, the man in uniform left his seat. Martin wasn't sure what time it was. Because the place was artificially lit, for all he knew it might still be the middle of the night. But his inner sensors told him it was morning.

He'd run out of terror now and was filled with the calm which came with accepting the inevitability of what was to some. The police would have found Sarah's body by now. His back garden would be covered in plastic tents with arc lamps and men in white suits putting things into evidence bags.

Imagining it Martin spent a good three hours lying awake on the hard smelly bed, soothing himself by reading the graffiti scratched into the grey gloss walls: "Garry is a cocksucker", "Fuck the police", "Mick Jones luvs Lezzies". All these scratching were interspersed with primitive drawings of genitals and swastikas.

In between alternating bouts of self pity and remorse, Martin mused on how much energy previous detainees must have been expended contributing to the triviality which covered almost every inch of wall space. Who cared so little about being in here that they could spend hours and hours scrawling and scratching such stuff on the walls? He recalled at university someone had spray-painted a huge statement across the front of the library: "Fascist Thatcher must NOT be allowed to speak".

No one had seen the irony.

Maybe all graffitists were naturally illiterate.

His stomach growled. He was starving. The food they served up last night was so disgusting he hadn't eaten it. Now he regretted his fussiness.

He gave another petulant rap on the glass. Surely they must soon bring him something for breakfast. It couldn't be legal to leave him with nothing to eat beyond a certain number of hours. The Howard League would surely have seen to it that police prisoners got fed. There would certainly be regulations. Human Rights. Some legislation from The Hague.

Martin tapped again, knowing that there was no one in the corridor to hear him.

After a few minutes he moved away from the door and threw himself back onto the bed.

CORONER'S INTERIM CERTIFICATE
OF THE FACT OF DEATH
PURSUANT TO THE CORONERS ACT 1988 AND RULE 30 OF THE CORONERS RULES 1984

DEATH	Ref: 000752–200X

Date and Place of Death
Not yet ascertained

Name and Surname	Sex Female
	Maiden Name
Jane Anne Grimshaw	

Date and Place of Birth
20 April 1987

Occupation and Usual Address
Librarian
Flat 3, 47 Sunnyside Gardens, Battersea,
London SW11 7ZX

Date Inquest Opened
Inquest not yet opened
The precise medical cause of death has not
yet been ascertained

I certify that in accordance with my statuary duty, I have opened and inquest into the death of the above named and taken evidence of the facts set out, which stands adjourned for the completion of my enquiries.

Signed Date 27 July 2011

For Inner London Coroner's Office Lambeth

The Registrar of Deaths cannot issue a Death Certificate
until the Inquest has been completed.

He imagined life going on outside. The rush hour. Crammed buses and tubes whisking people to work. What might be going on at his office now, he wondered? Would the police have closed it and stretched that tape across the door, or would Mike and Justin be already in there, rifling through his things, lounging about, feet up, making jokes as per usual? Mind you, once they heard what had happened why should they bother to go on working? He wouldn't be there to give them a pay cheque at the end of the month. They'd hardly come into the office for no money.

All right. Let them stay away. Good! The fewer outgoings the better.

Dammit.

Martin swallowed.

All that wages stuff was on standing order.

They'd get paid anyhow, whether or not they turned up for work.

Even if they lazed around at home the whole time, watching TV and eating kebabs, they would still get their pay-cheques, willy-nilly.

Unless Martin stopped payment.

That's what he'd do, and he'd do it now.

But how?

Perhaps he could get a note to the bank via Max.

He would cut those two lazy lizards off before they bled him dry.

Actually he'd get Max to walk right in there and on the spot, right to their faces Max could give them both the sack.

That would certainly wipe the sneers off their smug, know-all faces.

Oh god.

They'd hardly take it sitting down. They weren't the types.

They'd sue him.

He didn't want them going to some industrial tribunal accusing him of unfair dismissal. After all he was the one languishing in a police cell, not them.

Anyhow, for all he knew they were at work right now and would spend the whole day dutifully sitting at their computers working away like beavers.

Perhaps he should try and get someone to go in and check up on them, crack the whip a bit.

Sarah could do it.

Then his heart again did that thing where it felt like it was plummeting down a bottomless well.

His mind flashed with those hideous photos in that ghastly book. Would Sarah by now be black, and her face slowly sliding off her skull while her stomach erupted into the flower bed. Or was she by now in one of those police fridges that look like drawers, which you see on TV cop shows?

He lay silently retching for a few minutes, cold sweat running down his back.

Even though he was lying down he felt faint at the thought of how out of control he was, and how much worse off he would be when, or, rather, if he ever got out. His wife was rotting somewhere, the firm was falling to bits, all his stuff had been stolen, his bank account was cleared out, and he was looking at spending the rest of his life being gang-raped in Broadmoor or somewhere for kidnapping and murdering two women he'd never set eyes on.

God, how he regretted now having ever had the fucking stupid idea for a bloody dinner party. If he hadn't forced that idiotic evening on Sarah maybe now everything would have been fine. Instead of being banged up in a police cell, he'd have spent last night sitting at home watching TV, while

Sarah cooked one of her fantastic bowls of spaghetti, singing away and dancing round to the music coming from the radio the kitchen.

Sarah! Oh Sarah!

He sobbed and turned in to face the wall.

Who on earth could he turn to? What could he do? What if the police really nobbled him, planted evidence in his house and got him banged up for killing that bloody librarian?

Such things had been known to happen.

How alone he was.

All alone in the world.

Who could he send to?

Who would come here and comfort him?

Not Max, that was certain.

Yesterday he discovered a new hardness in Max, a lack of approachability. Max thought he was guilty as sin.

Mind you, perhaps the old boy needed to distance himself when he was defending you. Once you became a client he would naturally step back and become more detached. In order for the legal case to work it seemed quite probably that Max must necessarily be disinterested, distant even. In these high profile murder cases there was no room for sentimentality.

Max was doing the right thing. Of course he had to stay aloof.

After all, Martin wasn't paying him to be a friend, but a lawyer.

And, by his own admission, Max was the best in the business.

Martin gave another involuntary swallow.

The man earned enough money to speed about all day in a fancy Jag. He lived in a really upmarket house down a posh road, with a front drive big enough for two cars and a huge garden with a lawn big enough to play croquet in. He spent his summers in some exotic holiday home in the Caribbean, plus had another place on the South coast, complete with motor yacht, and also kept that dimwit woman, Lisa, in considerable style.

Max's services wouldn't come cheap.

And whether or not he got Martin off, at the end Max would still present Martin with a bill.

And where was Martin going to find the funds to pay for all this legal action?

He barely had enough to keep himself.

He thought for an instant of trying to contact his father, but the very thought made him squirm. Sarah was right. The man was a pompous little fart. Martin could just picture him coming here, laughing and joking with the policemen, looking down his nose at Martin, telling the cops he always knew his stupid child would come to grief.

Jesus God!

It was a terrible thought, but maybe, now that Sarah was gone, Mike and Justin at the office really were his only friends.

And perhaps those boys would as yet have no idea Martin was in here, so, this morning at least, they might go into work. And, while they were still at work, there was a slight chance they would be bringing in the dosh. Perhaps they'd even start attracting new contracts and pulling money back into the firm.

If Martin could keep them working. But—god forbid—if Martin's mug shot was plastered all over the newspapers, it was as certain as hell they would simply scarper off to find new jobs, leaving the firm to go under.

He wondered how he could contact the lizards if they weren't at work. He'd never been that nosy about where they lived. Tooting or Hackney or somewhere, he presumed. Mind you the way they both swanked about they probably had beautiful Clerkenwell lofts or swish terraced apartments on the river.

He wondered how those two parasites would have coped had they been here in this cell, held by the police under these circumstances, rather than him. No doubt they'd have come up with a great new idea of harnessing the graffiti to get some super new contracts. After all Martin's experience this morning was the very proof that you did read it. Indeed it proved that you read it over and over again. Martin thought he could pass an exam or a memory test on the graffiti on his cell wall.

Question Master: And your specialist subject is...?

Martin: Graffiti on my cell wall.

Question Master: You now have two minutes, Martin, on Graffiti on your cell wall. Question one—In the top left corner who claims the police are all poofs?

Martin (instantaneous): Roger

Question Master: Who is it that loves lezzies?

Martin (faster than a speeding bullet): Mick Jones

Joking apart, it mightn't be a bad idea. Martin could employ spray graffitists to spread advertising campaigns. Of course the clients wouldn't like the idea, but hell, once their prodigious new sales figures came in then they wouldn't be complaining.

Martin felt excited. He wondered whether the policeman, when he eventually rolled in with his breakfast, would allow him to write a note to Mike or Justin, suggesting the idea. Perhaps then Justin might even come in and visit him, and Martin could press on him how important it was to get the business whipped up, while he was temporarily indisposed.

Maybe he could even offer the two boys a share in the company profits, on condition that they could get those profits up by the time he came out.

His thoughts came to a halt.

If he ever came out.

Oh god.

He knew he hadn't killed the librarian or that other woman, maybe not even Sarah. Her body wasn't there, was it? Unless it had been taken by the burglars or he'd been digging in the wrong place.

But proving his innocence was another matter. He wouldn't be the first man to be banged up for a crime he didn't commit. He'd seen it over and over. Thirty years some of those poor wretches served before some do-gooding TV programme proved they had been wrongly convicted. Some poor bastards had even been executed before people worked out they'd got the wrong man.

He started gasping for air.

Calm! Calm!

Be sensible. They couldn't get him for that librarian's death. He hadn't done it. And he had Max for a lawyer, for god's sake! Max, who always boasted about his acquittal rates.

Don't panic, Pike!

Think positive and work towards getting the business on track.

First thing he must get a message to Justin and Mike.

He wondered whether the police would let him have his mobile phone back for a minute. Both of their mobile numbers were on that. He could text them, offer them incentives. Incentivizations even!

He laughed aloud, surprising himself.

Sarah had always laughed so much at all that linguistic guff. He wondered whether she really had managed to escape from her premature grave or whether he was just fooling himself.

He hoped to god she was alive, not body-snatched by mad Burke & Hare burglars.

Sarah understood him.

She was perhaps the only one.

Why had he been so stupid?

Martin rolled over and started to cry.

Oh Sarah, Sarah!

Please let it all have been a bad dream.

Please, please, please.

Meanwhile he must keep up hope.

His business wasn't dead yet. And, look, he had a wonderful lawyer in Max.

The best in the business.

Max was going to save him.

The cell door opened, and a dowdy uniformed policeman entered, bearing a tray.

MAX LATHAM & CO, SOLICITORS

HIGHLY CONFIDENTIAL–INTERNAL

PRELIMINARY REPORT OF MRS MURIEL TEMPLETON ON MARTIN BEAUMONT CASE

Ref ML/MB/X78653- CRIM/12 MT REPORT

CONFIDENTIAL

For the SOLE attention of Mr Latham

BURGLARY

Although Mr Beaumont claimed his house was burgled, the police hold no record that Mr Beaumont reported any burglary at his home on the day after the dinner party.

However according to the police inventory taken after his arrest, the house seems to be lacking many of the items one would expect to find in such a household. There is no computer, nor television, stereo, hi-fi. This seems unusual.

However I have no evidence to show that such things were ever there at all. Perhaps you might recall from personal visits?

TELEPHONE

I have managed to get hold of a list of calls made from the Beaumont family home during the last fortnight (don't ask!).

The emergency services have logged an incomplete 999 call made during the afternoon. The caller hung up before the operator took details, but, as is usual, the call was recorded. It lasted less than 2 seconds. This was the only call made to any police number from this telephone.

The number principally dialled was Mrs Beaumont's cell phone, sometimes at very late hours. No messages were left on her answering service.

LIBRARY TICKET

Mr Beaumont's library ticket was issued over a year ago and granted by the usual visual evidence (utility bill, bank statement etc) displaying Mr Beaumont's home address. The library's paperwork all seems in order and Mr Beaumont had signed the acceptance of terms.

The list of books Mr Beaumont appears to have taken out over the year is largely in the area of violence, in fact there were no books loaned which could not be classified as such:

- A History of Torture throughout the Ages by George Ryley Scott

- 120 Days of Sodom and various other works by the Marquis de Sade

- A guide to Forensic Medicine

- Mein Kampf by Adolf Hitler

- Beyond Good and Evil by Friedrich Nietzsche

- A picture book on Crime Scenes and forensic detection

- An Encyclopaedia of Serial Killers

Innumerable individual accounts of serial killers including biographies and studies of Ted Bundy, David Berkowitz, Charles Manson, The Boston Strangler, The Moors Murderers, Henry Lee Lucas, The Hillside Stranglers, Edmund Kemper, The Yorkshire Ripper, Ed Gein... etcetera. [It is a very long list of books]

The last two withdrawals were a book about Jerry Brudos, a man who murdered and tortured numerous young women in his garage whilst, totally unawares, his wife and children went on with their lives in the adjacent house, and a study of The Chicago Rippers, two men who kidnapped, mutilated and ultimately murdered women in the 1980s. These books were returned to the library the day after Jane Grimshaw went missing. One book remains checked out: Psychopathia Sexualis, by Dr Richard von Krafft-Ebing.

MR BEAUMONT'S CAR

I ran a check on Mr Beaumont's car, a Renault Mégane, and only one thing of relevance came up. Mr Beaumont received a parking ticking at 16.27 on Thursday soon after he was seen in the library by the head librarian, thus strengthening her evidence that she had seen Mr Beaumont in the library that afternoon. Indeed she reported him to the police using his licence plate number.

The car had been parked adjacent to the library in the supermarket car park, and according to the ticket code his time had expired at 16.24.

CELL PHONE

The phone company, TopMob, faxed me a list of calls made from Mr Beaumont's cell phone. [see attachment]

CREDIT CARDS & ACCOUNT

I phoned the bank, having first emailed Mr Kruszynska a copy of your letter explaining the situation and informing him that I am working for you on Mr Beaumont's behalf in this matter. I also let him know that Mr Beaumont was being held by the police on a grave charge and that it was imperative to get clarification as soon as possible in order to aid Mr Beaumont's case. He presented me with the most recent statement of Mr Beaumont's credit card account and bank account statements.

I do not know whether Mr Beaumont had any further accounts or credit cards elsewhere, but this can be ascertained without much bother. I have ordered a credit report, which is due in the office within 24 hours.

It seems that the personal joint bank account Mr Beaumont shared with his wife was systematically emptied between the day after the dinner party and now. Both Mr & Mrs Beaumont possessed debit cards on this account, and both had internet access to it, but all financial transferences were made using Mr Beaumont's card, pin and password. Three online attempts to log on to the account using the wrong password were made between 16.15 and 16.20 on Thursday. Both cards were used at various ATMs in central London to take the full daily allowance i.e. £500 each, thus removing £3000 cash in the last three days. On top of this many charges and payments have been made using the card, emptying the account and running it into overdraft.

During the last few days however, the credit card has also amassed much debt, right to its limit of £5,000. The purchases are all smallish and would not have needed telephone approval from the bank. The maximum cash allowance has also been withdrawn on this account every day [See attachment]

Mr Beaumont reported his card missing at just after 17.00, shortly after returning from the library, but this was clearly a case of locking the stable door...The card was not used at any time after it was reported missing.

The business account, which had contained £20,000 ready to offset against the annual tax bill, has been emptied. The money transferred into Sarah Beaumont's account, and thence to an offshore bank.

WHEREABOUTS OF SARAH BEAUMONT

Following your instructions I have made a number of preliminary investigations in an attempt to ascertain the whereabouts of Mrs Sarah Beaumont.

Mr William McNamara tells me his searches within the data available to the police reveal nothing. Mrs Beaumont's credit card has not been used since last Tuesday morning, when she bought groceries (presumably for the dinner party you attended).

In fact the last verifiable sighting of Mrs Beaumont by anyone appears to have been at the dinner party at the Beaumont home, at which you yourself were present as a witness.

a) The next door neighbour to whom you referred, the novelist Tess Brandon, did not reply when I called last night nor this morning, and has not yet responded to any of my answering machine messages or emails. According to the police report she did offer to talk to one of their constables last evening, right after Mr Beaumont's arrest, but some time later, when they arrived at her door, she had gone out.

I will continue pestering her until I get a response. {I am an enormous fan of her novels so it will be a huge pleasure to get in contact with her}

b) I visited the care home in which Mrs Beaumont's mother is living early this morning. The staff at the home were polite but vague towards me. The girl in the office assured me that, contrary to Mr Beaumont's statement, Mrs Beaumont has not visited her mother since before the night of the dinner party, but that this is not at all unusual. [The care home fees are paid and up to date so I imagine they do not care an ounce who comes and goes to visit the old lady. Security is far from tight in this establishment. I was walking around a good ten minutes before anyone asked me what I was doing there.]

I made a very brief call on Mrs Beaumont's mother, Pauline Kavanagh. She was very keen to tell me that she had indeed seen her daughter only yesterday, but, as she greeted me as a long lost friend, even though I have never set eyes on the woman in my life, and then three times offered to repay five pounds which she was convinced she owed me, I feel that her evidence will not hold much weight.

According to the nurse, Mrs Kavanagh is in the later stages of Alzheimer's disease.

However it is possible that Mrs Beaumont's sister visited the care home, and that Mr Beaumont's account of events has somehow been muddled [see point C, below].

The care home bills, which are the responsibility of Mrs Beaumont, are issued monthly. This month's invoice was settled by the Beaumont's joint account the day after the dinner party, as instructed by an internet banking order from Mr Beaumont's laptop.

c) Mrs Beaumont has one sister, Suzanne Kavanagh, who lives in Sydney, Australia. I am making efforts to contact her. According to the friend who answered the phone at her home number in Sydney, Ms Kavanagh is currently on her way home by air, after a brief business trip to the UK.

RINGS

From the photographs you have provided, the local jeweller, R. Rutherford & Sons, assures me that both the wedding band and engagement ring are pretty standard and could have come from any jewellery shop in the country (and possibly many other places besides)

The eternity ring however he recognised instantly as having been made up specially to order for Mr Beaumont. The semi precious stones are arranged to spell Sarah.

Mr Beaumont picked up this ring on the Tuesday before last.

According to the SOCO report, traces of soil, blood and a proprietary brand of washing liquid have been found on the ring—lodged between the gems.

The blood is the same group as the traces found on the phone, and does not match Martin Beaumont's. DNA testing will presumably ascertain whether or not this blood in fact belongs to Jane Grimshaw (or, perhaps, as I suspect, Sarah Beaumont).

LATE ADDENDUM

After typing out the above I received a phone call from Sarah Beaumont's sister, Suzanne Kavanagh in Australia. I did not tell her the details of Mr Beaumont's arrest, but only used the old lawyers' trick and informed her that we at Max Latham & Co, solicitors, were trying to trace Mrs Sarah Beaumont, with news which may be to her advantage.

Ms Kavanagh at first expressed worry about her mother, and after I had assured her that the old lady was fine (or let's say as fine as could be expected for a women in the throes of Alzheimer's) she told me that she had only flown home from London to Sydney yesterday, arriving this evening. She also said that while she was in London she had indeed visited her mother in the care home.

The trip to the UK was a spur of the minute thing. Ms Kavanagh was only in London for 3 days. Although one of her intentions had been to surprise her sister, Sarah Beaumont, Ms Kavanagh told me had not seen Mrs Beaumont at all while she was in England. She had in fact had no contact whatsoever with her sister, despite leaving several messages on her cell phone and home telephone.

It was unusual for Mrs Beaumont not to respond.

I think we must infer from all this information that the circumstances of Mrs Sarah Beaumont's current whereabouts look extremely grave.

10

Limbo

*Solo dance, in which the dancer leans
backwards and passes under a horizontal
bar which gets lower and lower*

MAX GROANED AS he flicked through the dossier.
Everything he had seen this morning, including the
folder of bank statements and phone bills, made him
more sure he was onto the biggest and most embarrassing
losing case he had ever known. What put the tin lid on the
whole thing was that for many years now he had publicly
socialised with the accused.

How marvellous would it look to potential clients that a
solicitor couldn't spot the symptoms of a dangerous serial
killer within his own social circle?

Not only did all the information the firm had collected since he made a few urgent phone calls from the station last night seem to incriminate Martin for the librarian's murder, but, while he was about it, perhaps he had also done in the bloody wife.

Max pulled out another sheet of paper and ran his fat finger down the list of potential witnesses drawn up for him this morning by a junior. It was supposedly a group who could speak on Martin's behalf: Sarah Beaumont, Tess Brandon, the bloody arsehole of a bank manager, Martin's two slimy employees, Lisa and himself.

Max slammed the folder down. Good god almighty—if that was the case for the defence, who were the prosecution going to come up with? Robespierre? Stalin? Joe McCarthy? The Witchfinder General?

Max snatched a pencil from his desk and once more went through the list of Martin's phone calls. A number of very short calls to his wife's mobile, none long enough to support a conversation. Calls to the bank...That would be Martin cancelling the cards, Max supposed. A silent emergency call had been made from Martin's home at 17.42 on Wednesday.

What was that about?

Who had made it? Ah yes. Martin. The burglary. That could explain dialling 999. But why had Martin not followed through and reported the crime?

Max's stomach rumbled.

What if the call was in fact made for an ambulance, while Martin's wife lay dying on the floor? But, before he had time to speak, he realised it was too late for ambulances...

Max popped another indigestion pill.

He was hungry now, and tired. He had been up practically all fucking night with the police and his whining client, and now his guts were howling for lunch.

He pressed a button on the intercom.

'Muriel! Get me a sandwich. And a glass of red wine.'

Obviously all the evidence was against Martin, but Max had a gnawing suspicion that Martin really was innocent of killing the librarian and that other woman last year, but the complications arising from actually having killed his wife had rotted the man's reason.

Contrary to public expectation, most killers—and Max had met quite a few—were not weird and witty, urbane, wonderful geniuses with IQs in the high 100s, who had impeccable taste in clothes, art and music and were good at cooking.

They were generally an unsightly crew of monosyllabic brutes with BO, bad teeth and an IQ which matched their hat size. They also had egos as big as Buckingham Palace, and an utter indifference to everything in the world, beyond their own pathetic pool of desire.

Martin didn't fit the bill at all.

The library book thing, Max hoped, was a red herring. So what? Yes, Ian Brady had read gory books like that, but who didn't? Crime was the best selling genre in publishing. Walk up any train in the country and you'll see 90% of the commuting noses stuck into books practically dripping with blood.

Anyway—what kind of case was that for the police to toss around? Surely it was only under Fascist regimes you could be condemned for the books you read.

Martin! What a bloody fool.

Max felt slightly warmed to the idea of defending him now. It felt like a ruddy good challenge. Bet a case of Dom Perignon he could get the stupid bugger off.

When Muriel brought the sandwiches Max pocketed them and downed the wine in one before walking out onto the street and hailing a taxi to Martin's agency.

As he walked into the outer office it was clear something had been going on between the two malcontents who worked there, for they flung themselves back into their chairs, barely covering the grins on their faces, while feigning intense interest in the computer monitors on their desks.

But then, Max supposed, while the cat's away...

'Good morning!' He glared at them. 'And you are?'

Max noticed a couple of tabloid newspapers carelessly tumbled between the desks.

So that was it! They were reading about their boss. Max doubted Martin's arrest would have had time to make the dailies, though it was possible there might be something on the internet and TV news. If so he hoped that it was still in the "a 37 year old London man is helping police with their inquiries" stage.

The taller of the two looked up, while dusting the surface of a lay-out pad with a floppy hand. 'Mike Grenville.'

'I'm Justin, but, more to the point, who are you?' The other boy leaned back in his expensive office chair. He was casually rubbing a pencil between his palms.

Max didn't like their attitudes. What if Max had been a potential new client, coming in to offer eternal riches to Martin's agency? Would he not now turn on his heels and head back to the Yellow Pages in search of someone with a keener aspect?

'I am Max Latham,' said Max, striding past them towards Martin's office. 'I am Martin's lawyer and I am here to prepare the company for auditing.'

What a pair! Another case of Martin not having an iota of character judgement.

Max turned back at the door and asked 'Keeping busy?'

Justin looked up from his monitor. 'Well so far this morning's been more fun than work,' he said.

Max barely suppressed a shudder. 'Fun?'

'Answering police questions.'

Of course the bastards would have come here first thing. He hoped these two idle poltroons hadn't given them anything more than they needed to know.

'You didn't let them poke about, I hope.'

'Certainly not,' said Mike with a sneer. 'They didn't have a warrant.'

'Bingo,' Max grunted. 'Glad to hear you've been watching a lot of TV. How long ago were they here?'

'Forty five minutes?' queried Mike in that upward inflection thing so popular in the young.

'Good.' Max looked at his watch. 'That gives me about half an hour. The nearest judges round here are a sluggish lot.'

He moved into the inner sanctum and flicked Martin's computer on. While it whirred to life, with one hand he unwrapped the beef and horseradish sandwich Muriel had fetched for him and stuffed it into his mouth, and with the other he rooted through Martin's drawers, looking for anything which might provide fuel for a decent defence.

When the sandwich was gone Max wiped his mouth and slumped down into Martin's frayed and worn typist's chair. There were a few letters on the desk, laid out in a neat fan.

Max opened a low drawer and pulled out an index card which lay on top of a pile of headed notepaper. In Martin's handwriting it said "Bank Login"—then a sequence of numbers. And then "Password—5Rusty11."

That was clever. Everything a person would need to get into his bank account. Max shook his head. What a twat. This office was about as secure as a split condom. No wonder the man's bank account had been cleared out. It could have been anyone, including either one of the sly fellows in the adjacent room.

There was a set of keys labelled "spare keys—home". He pocketed them. You never knew whether his search might take him there. A diary, too, with entries for the Tuesday before last, the day Jane Grimshaw had gone missing. Rutherford's jewellers—pick up ring 5.30. Dinner 8. La Coupole.

Max grabbed hold of the phone and dialled the restaurant's number.

A sulky girl answered. She eventually confirmed that the dinner booking had been taken by a couple but she couldn't remember anything about them or give descriptions.

An alibi of sorts, thought Max, and it certainly tallied with Martin's account of events.

But, sod it, Sarah was the vital witness. And where was she to be found?

For some reason the police were convinced Martin was the killer of the librarian, but bollocks to that. The charges were nonsense. The very idea of Martin going out and killing women and dumping their bodies on commons under the eagle eye of that virago wife! Absurd.

Max burped. Bloody horseradish.

He thought back to the ghastly interview last night. Martin hadn't handled himself all that well, it was true. Plus, there was a little problem of gore in the kitchen. Max recalled the photo—filmed with black light, the scene sparkled with as much pink as the Christmas decorations on a house in Chingford. Someone's blood had certainly been shed all over Martin's floor.

Damnation! How to get round that one?

No, no, no! Easy.

How stupid of him not to remember.

He himself was witness to the cause of the bloody floor—hadn't Sarah cut herself during the dinner? He wouldn't even have to lie about that. And he'd have Lisa, and that so-called crime writer and the bank manager as witnesses.

Max vividly remembered seeing a big elastoplast wrapped around Sarah's palm when she came back, from the kitchen, wielding a huge Sabatier knife over the pudding. Obviously a cut that size hadn't really been enough to flood the floor with gore, but there were a handful of witnesses who could not deny it had happened, and, well, sometimes didn't silly cuts spurt out so much more blood than was strictly necessary? Max would vouch for a very nasty episode with a knife and a hot pie right out of the oven. Hadn't Sarah gone to the phone at that point too? So, tada! Her cut hand bled badly, leaving traces on the phone before it pumped out all over the kitchen while she struggled to juggle a lethally hot fruit pie, six warm bowls, a hot pan of custard bubbling on the hob and a gigantic sharp knife.

As Max stooped to pick up the folder from his briefcase he looked again at Martin's photo in the file. He didn't look like a serial killer. In fact he was the exact match of any psychiatrist's profile of a battered husband: A clumsy, pathetic, self-pitying New Man, with no balls.

Max let rip a burp as he pulled a large ledger from the top drawer and spread it open at a random page.

He looked more closely.

My oh my!

Max knew enough about accounting to see what it was. The whole thing had been drawn up on a computer spreadsheet. One the recto side was a set of figures called "official", on the verso another set—which carried the same gross total, but differed wildly on the net.

The main gist of the difference between the two sides seemed to be that Martin was claiming all kinds of allowances for Sarah. On the official side she was on a full wage and paying a stamp. She had office expenses and travel costs. On the unofficial side she did not exist.

My God! Martin was cooking the books.

Max raised his eyebrows and chuckled. The little devil!

It was clever, very clever. For months, perhaps years, Martin had been offsetting his profits and thereby exempting his business from oodles of tax.

He was using his wife, Sarah, to swindle the government.

Well now. That threw a whole new light on things.

Max flicked again through the diary's pages.

The dinner party.

Let's say the police were right and that Martin had spent the day before yesterday busily disposing of Jane Grimshaw and dumping her body on the common. Would he have had either the inclination or the insouciance to host a dinner party for his lawyer, bank manager and some crime novelist the evening before?

Max wiped a smear of horseradish from his chin.

A man with Martin's temperament would have crumpled under the pressure, broken out into a cold sweat when the conversation turned to murder, and boy, did it do that. Over and over the subject came up and Martin simply seemed like an eager schoolboy trying to please both Max himself and the idiotic American know-it-all. Crime novelist indeed!

Ah ha!

There was a useful connection that he hadn't thought of heretofore.

The gory library books.

That crackpot American could be the pivot of the story he'd use to explain away Martin's reading preferences.

Naturally Martin was taking books out to impress Tess Brandon. Not for her to read, but because Martin, a polite but competitive man, needed to be able to chat casually with his new neighbour, Ms Brandon, and he wanted to seem to be as casually familiar as she was with serial killers, grease guns, orifices etc.

Hmmm.

Yes.

That one would play.

All Max needed now was a little chat with the adjacent authoress. He would ooze over her novels, and, as surely as Jeffrey Dahmer ate his victims, Max could lasso her into believing this version of that unfortunate episode.

He felt somewhat happier as, with a greasy paw, he grabbed hold of the mouse and went online. He tried logging on to Martin's bank account to see how much, if at all, his accounts tallied with the ledger figures, but the screen announced: "Password details incorrect, please re-enter".

He tried a second time.

Dimly he now recalled Martin wittering on about the same thing happening to him while he was on the computer in the library.

Certainly the 'true' figures in the ledger looked perilous for Martin. Without an injection of cash his business was in desperate trouble.

As the little egg timer on the screen drained away Max idly slit open the letters on the desk with a plastic letter opener.

In his head he ran through the spin:

He would show that Sarah had been diddling Martin, she had been the one who was defrauding her Majesty's Inspector of Taxes, and Martin was the victim. After all he frequently talked about her doing the tax returns.

A devoted husband, Martin had spent all the necessary alibi dates with his wife. ("M'lud, How could Martin have been in a pub kidnapping a librarian at the exact moment he was presenting his wife with a birthday gift on a romantic night out at La Coupole?" etcetera, etcetera...)

But, despite Martin's generosity (the ring, the dinner) Sarah had since walked out on him. And now, sadly for his client, the bitch wife was deliberately not coming forward to assist him, in order to punish her husband (the usual woman scorned stuff).

Yes. This would work.

And, moreover, M'lud, my desolate client has since discovered that his beastly wife has spent the last few years swindling his company. So you see she has every reason to stay away.

Yes, yes. It was thought that Sarah had done the company's accounts. Max remembered that Czech saying something to that effect while they were chatting before dinner.

So...So...

Sarah Beaumont had spent the last year methodically embezzling her husband's business. He had found out, and that is why Martin had gone to pieces in the interview room. The poor man was devastated to discover that not only had his whole marriage been a lie, but now his wife had upped sticks and left him, on top of that, the business he had so carefully nurtured over many years was about to hit the skids. Then in come the police and accuse him of a murder he did not commit.

The burglary was another wonderful thing Max could use to explain Martin's erratic behaviour since his arrest.

"M'lud, The relentless bitch then compounded it all by clearing out Martin's house—stealing his TVs, computers, credit cards: everything."

His unfortunate client now had nothing.

And <wiping away a tear> the wretched man, M'lud, was about to report it to the police, then stopped himself when he realised he would be incriminating the evil woman whom, despite himself, he still loved.

Ha, ha, ha, ha, ha! What fabulous spin!

Not only was it a useful spin, but with it, every day Sarah stayed away it helped Martin's case. The guilty woman, lurking somewhere, ashamed of her actions, who dare not step forward to aid her husband as it would only incriminate herself.

Very effective.

Max was pleased with himself.

As long as Martin's DNA wasn't smeared all over the corpses of the ruddy librarian and the other slut from last year, Max believed he had everything he needed to clear his client of the current charges.

As he opened the next envelope and pulled out yet another flier offering Martin a fabulous loan at a mere 22.9%, Max's mobile phone rang.

It was Bill McNamara, his friend in the police force.

'Bad news, I'm afraid, Max. We've done a bit of digging on the old financial side and it seems that your client, Mr Beaumont, was about to do a runner. For a couple of days he's been moving money around with the dexterity of Penn & Teller. Then, yesterday morning he stashed all his cash in an offshore account. Cayman Islands. The lot. Over 20k.'

But Max was not listening. He had opened another envelope and now his eyes were resting on an invoice. It was to a firm in Wandsworth called "Store It!" There was a handwritten card with two reference numbers, marked FRONT and STORE and a plastic card with holes in it. Some kind of key, Max deduced, like they had in older hotels.

'No problem, Bill.' Max pocketed the key. 'I'm at his office now. Martin had business problems, that's all. But he's no killer.'

Max flipped his phone shut and inspected the card. The references he assumed were the code numbers of the actual storage facility and the lock-up which the key would open.

Great God Almighty.

Max wished he could get hold of a whisky. Instead he lay his head back on the director's chair and took a few breaths.

That stupid little fart, Martin. Fuck him to hell and back.

Max rose, his hand in his pocket, fingering the plastic key inside, hoping to god that he was not about to discover the hidey hole where Jane Grimshaw had been kept for the week before she was killed and her body dumped on the common.

11

The Maxixe

*Samba-like dance with particular
attention paid to the outstretched position
of the arms, and bent over posture*

FROM THE LUMINOUS dial on her watch Tess knew that
it was 10 a.m. She must have been here inside this
container about twelve hours. From about six this
morning she had been huddled into a corner waiting for the
two fuckheads to come back, but not a sign.

She wondered whether this was part of their plan—leaving
her here to starve. Or what?

She puzzled over the identities of these two ass-holes. Was
the guy with the plaid shirt really a policeman? Obviously not.
And the driver. Who was he? What did they do for a living?
They knew each other pretty well. Perhaps they worked

together. You'd have to be very tight with someone to share kidnap and murder. Had one started first and dragged the other into his plan, or had they decided to work together from the start? She thought of couples who killed together. Ian Brady and Myra Hindley lived together. Ditto Fred and Rosemary West. When you thought about it, so many were married or as good as: The Copelands, the Gallegos, Bonnie and Clyde. The *In Cold Blood* killers had met in jail. The Hillside Stranglers were cousins. So she felt pretty sure the profile would indicate that there was a strong link between this pair of assholes as well. Perhaps they were lovers. If only she knew the link, or could work out the relationship between these creeps, she could try to work out a way to save herself. Get the weaker of the two on her side. He had to be the driver. He was most certainly not in control. And yet, when she thought of how they handled her attempt to escape under the garage door, old woollen hat had been the cooler of the two.

All night she had been listening hard trying to work out where she was. From the early morning noise of aircraft the place was under a flight path, but where in London wasn't? But here the planes seemed pretty low, would that indicate she was being held to the west rather than the east, nearer Heathrow. Or how about the south and nearer Gatwick, or the East near the City Airport or Stansted. No the planes meant nothing, except that even without the watch she could pretty well work out when it was 5 a.m. cos that's when the night flying restrictions ended.

She had spent hours examining the inside of the container itself. She wanted to find its weak spots, work out how it locked and opened, discover, if she could, any possible ways of getting out...

The container was small. About ten foot by eight and about six and a half foot high. The thick metal sides where impenetrable, but when she found it had a plywood floor, she was filled with hope that she could escape.

Until she thought about it. Holy crap, if she scraped a hole in that where would it get her but to the concrete floor beneath? Or more likely simply more metal then the concrete floor beneath. A whole lot of work and she'd be back in zero.

The container was quite rusty. She had scratched away with the end of a pencil from her pocket, hoping to find a spot in the metal weak enough to work on.

Amazingly her eyes had adapted remarkably well, and her vision seemed to get better and better the longer she was there. From the stuff left inside the container it was obvious she wasn't the first person who had been imprisoned here.

Shoved in a corner lay a foul smelling mattress and a threadbare blanket. Tess had also found a plastic bottle filled with what she suspected was water, and a bucket which, though empty, reeked of stale urine and faeces.

It wasn't the only smell either. The whole place stank of jism. Holy fuck! Those motherfuckers must have been wanking their tiny heads off in this rusty box.

She dreaded to think what else they may have done in here. She wished now she had taken the time to read in more detail the newspaper report of that librarian's body. Had they done the post mortem yet? How did she die? Tess preferred to be prepared, to know what they had in store for her.

Though she had sat in the darkness, sniffing at the air for hours she couldn't detect the smell of blood at all. But maybe that was cos the stink of shit and cum was so goddamned bad.

Her most marvellous moment had occurred in the early hours of the morning when she took off her jacket to use as a blanket and tumbling from the inside pocket came her US cell phone. She had straightaway tried phoning 911 but the signal was near to nil. After a lot of experimentation she discovered that if she held her hand out and up at its full extent with the phone all but touching the metal ceiling in the corner farthest from the entrance she could get one block of signal power. And much good that would be. What would she do? Screech, hoping her voice would reach the phone? It was a no brainer. She knew she must not do anything to let the assholes who had put her in this shit heap know she still had a phone.

Sure, the calls would be routed via the USA, as it was an American phone, but who cared about the bill at a time like this?

She wondered if 911 was what the English dialled for emergencies anyhow. Wasn't their number 123 or something ridiculous?

Shit, she wished she had concentrated a bit more on those first few pages of her tourist guide book to England.

But anyway, even back in the States, she didn't think you could text the emergency services. She had read about British people shipwrecked in the South China Seas calling the coastguard at Falmouth to get help, but naturally enough she didn't have a number for the coastguard either.

She had fired off a text message to her agent, but realised too late that even counting the five hour difference, New York offices would be shut, and her agent made it a strict rule of taking no client calls outside hours.

All the other numbers in the phone's directory were people back home in the States. People who'd been at high school with her, or old college friends. They'd all think she was having a joke with them if they got a text from her in the middle of the night reading HELP ME. Especially as she had so carefully instructed them not to disturb her till she chose the moment, so she wouldn't lose concentration with surprise social calls.

When she had scrolled through, looking for someone who could help her, she had found a string of missed calls received in the last day from the same British cell phone number. Someone had been repeatedly trying her number, while she stood on the doorstep talking to the real policeman and then the plaid-shirted cocksucker. Who knows maybe it was just someone on a wrong number but hey—what the hell?

So, even though she was unsure whom she was texting, in the wild hope something would happen, Tess sent a message: IN GRAVE DANGER. GIVE POLICE THIS CELL NUMBER. FIND ME. She knew that the police could almost pinpoint a cell phone using the sim card and local masts, but she wasn't sure how accurate all that stuff was. Maybe they could narrow it down to something as half-assed as that the phone she was using was in the London area. But perhaps they might call her and she could...

Damn. What could she do—without yelling her head off?

She fired up the phone again and typed an addendum: HELP HELP HELP TEXT ONLY. Then she balanced on her toes, face scraping the rusty wall, her arm in the air and sent it off to whoever.

Of all the people she could imagine calling her she hoped it had been that ditzy Lisa. She might be an air-head, and that fat-assed boyfriend of hers might be a know-all twat, but at least he was a twat who had contacts in the British police.

Tess curled up on her heels in the corner, balancing her back against the rusty wall. She scrolled down the texts she had sent, the area around her eerily lit by the phone's blue back light.

AM BEING HELD BY KIDNAPPING MURDERERS she fingered in.

Absurd. If she received a text like that what would she do? Fuck all. Just put it down to a drunk or a joker.

Jesus H Christ.

She knew the creepy pieces of shit might come back at any time.

She was going to die.

To stop her heart skipping all over the place, she knelt, huddled over the phone with her head down and composed a text explaining, in as few words as she could and as though to a stranger, exactly what had happened and where she was, and the danger she was in.

If ever there was a writing exercise in being concise and to the point this was it.

When she had finished she read it back.

It was good.

She scrambled to her feet and edged back towards the corner.

Then she heard the footsteps.

Holy shit!

She jammed the phone shut and stuffed it deep down into her trouser packet. Pressing her ear flat against the metal she tried to listen, but she could hear nothing over the sounds of her thundering heart.

She moved backwards along the container wall, towards the spot where the sound seemed to come from.

The footsteps had had a sharp timbre. Hard soled shoes, perhaps wooden or steel tipped. She held her breath as they came closer.

Was the torture, or rape or whatever it was these pieces of shit had in mind for her about to start?

Tess's mouth was dry.

The footsteps stopped.

Tess felt as though she would die from the boom, boom, boom of her heart.

After a few seconds the footsteps clacked away.

The container door had not been opened.

Tess was not sure whether to be thankful or furious.

While the container remained shut she had no hope of making an escape, but at least it meant those two pricks were not yet returning for the orgy or whatever fuck-fest it was they had planned for the moments just before they killed her.

All her life Tess had congratulated herself on being smart. Now look! She'd blindly walked straight into the arms of a pair of psychos. Wow! What a crock. She'd certainly shown those two jack-off dip-shits her ass!

Fuck it!

She gulped and went back to concentrating on the text which asked the recipient, Lisa or whoever it was, to contact Max Latham, the police, her agent...anyone to help her, before they came back, before they killed her.

She took out the phone and flicked it open it, while feeling her way back into the corner where the signal was strongest.

Balancing on tiptoe, Tess raised the phone as high as she could and pressed the send button.

She waited, hand held aloft, for the beep which would tell her that the message had successfully gone off.

But when, after three minutes, despite an aching arm, no sound had come, she lowered it to take a look.

She sank to the ground.

The phone was dead.

Inquisition

AN INQUISITION TAKEN FOR OUR SOVEREIGN LADY THE QUEEN

BEFORE AND BY ME
FOR THE LONDON BOROUGH OF LAMBETH
THE FOLLOWING MATTERS WERE FOUND

1. NAME OF DECEASED

Jane Anne Grimshaw

2. INJURY OR DISEASE CAUSING DEATH

1a. CARDIAC ARREST

b. blood loss

c.

11. malnutrition and dehydration

3. TIME, PLACE AND CIRCUMSTANCES AT OR IN WHICH INJURY WAS SUSTAINED

PM report unable to ascertain place of
death, though it was certainly not where
the partially clothed body was discovered.
Lividity shows the body to have been placed
in position after death. Although the primary
cause of death was cardiac failure, the small
wound in her neck, penetrating the carotid
artery, certainly speeded things along.

4. CONCLUSION OF THE CORONER AS TO THE DEATH

There was old light yellowish bruising to
the upper arms and ankles. The face showed
pallor. Both eyes showed lateral conjunctival
petechial haemorrhages. Signs of recent sexual
activity or vaginal penetration.

As the victim had been missing for a period of
10 days, and the body moved post-mortem, by
person or persons unknown, foul play is highly
probable.

Coroner refers this case to the Crown Court
for further investigation

5.PARTICULARS FOR THE TIME BEING REQUIRED BY THE REGISTRATION ACTS TO
BE REGISTERED CONCERNING THE DEATH

(a) Date and place of birth 20 April 1987, Bolton Lancashire	
(b) Name and Surname of deceased Jane Anne Grimshaw	
(c) Sex female	**(d) maiden surname of woman who has married**
(e) Date and place of death 26th July 2011, between 20:00 - 00:00. Place unknown.	
(f) Occupation and usual address Librarian Flat 3, 47 Sunnyside Gardens, Battersea, London SW11 7AB	

12

Buck & Wing

*A solo tap dance with many leg
flings and sudden leaps*

MAX PRESENTED THE storage firm and a spotty youth in
a brown overall led him to a large automatic glass
entry door.

'You got the code, right?' the boy asked, standing rather too
close for Max's liking. 'You input that when the light bleeps.
The door opens and you go up to your own unit on the second
floor.'

The youth did not wait for a response from Max and by the
time he turned to thank him had already disappeared through
the heavy swing doors at the corner.

Max went inside and took the lift up. He wandered the corridors till he came to a door which bore the second number on

the card. He inserted the key into the slot on the lock. A green light flashed and a persistent beeping sound emanating from the keypad. Max stooped over it to get a closer look. He had noticed the CCTV cameras all over the place and didn't want to look like an idiot or draw undue attention to this bonded room.

He imagined Martin would always stick to the same password, wherever, so he keyed in 5Rusty11. A loud click followed and the light flashed at greater speed.

Max tried the handle.

The door opened, but only a few inches.

Something was jammed up behind it.

Max pushed, but the door was stuck.

He squeezed his face into the gap. The blockage seemed to be something unwieldy lying on the floor just inside the door. Whatever it was, it was heavy and wrapped inside a black bin-liner.

Oh sod.

There was also a rather horrid smell inside the storage unit, redolent with decay, or, worse, decomposition of human matter.

No. No. No!

Don't say that Martin had not only knocked off those two women but had another one banged up here in storage.

Without any acoustic warning the pimply boy appeared at Max's shoulder.

'Need some help?'

Max laughed and pulled at the door, but he couldn't close it properly as his briefcase was in the way.

'Always been a hopeless packer,' he said, blocking the boy's view into the lock-up. 'It's that bloody carpet. I knew it would tumble.'

'No probs,' said the boy, stepping forward, hand stretched towards the door. 'I can handle it.'

'You're quite right,' snapped Max barring his way. 'There are no "probs". I am perfectly able to get into my lock-up unassisted. Thank you so much for your offer.'

'I could get you a broom or something.'

To Max it seemed that the boy was leaning out to get a sneak at whatever was behind the door. Best confront the situation directly.

'Is something in there interesting you at all? You seem to be extraordinarily fascinated by the contents of my inner sanctum.'

'Only trying to be helpful.'

'Yes, yes.' Max considered palming him a tenner, but thought that that might potentially arouse even more suspicion. Stagily Max applied his eye to the open crack. 'Do you know, Mr er...' He turned back. 'What is your name?'

'Dwayne.' The boy pointed to an embossed plastic badge on the lapel of his overall.

Max tried to disguise his horror at realising that anyone could have lumbered a boy, even a half-wit like this one, with such an inane nomenclature.

'Well, Dwayne, do you know, I think that a broom might be just the solution.'

Max waited for the boy to sprint along the corridor and turn the corner, then he applied his shoulder to the door with all the force of a 70s TV cop.

By the time the overalled boy returned Max had squeezed his carcass through the gap and shoved himself right into the storage unit. He popped his head out and waved towards the broom-toting assistant.

'Mission accomplished!' He thrust out a hand. 'A broom could be useful though. Thanks you so much Dwight.'

'Dwayne,' said the boy.

'Of course.' Max grabbed the broom. 'Thanks for all your help. Now I'd better get on. I've got a lot of boxes of paperwork to look through in here!'

'You'll need to turn on the light then.' Dwayne slid his hand through the small opening and flicked a switch on the wall. 'Or once you close the door you'd be in the dark.'

'Ah, yes! Yes. Of course. Light! Jolly good. Thanks again.'

Would the wretched boy just fuck off?

Max gave him a little wave. 'I shall call you if I need you, Dwayne. Thank you so much.'

'Just come out here in the corridor and wave at the camera.' Dwayne pointed up at the CCTV camera in the hallway.

'Will you be filming me?' Max had a horrid thought that there might be cameras inside the units too. 'It must be pretty boring watching people counting their boxes.'

'Don't be stupid,' Dwayne leered. 'We here at "Store It!" believe in total discretion, while at the same time providing total security.'

Max gave him a wan look. What on earth was the idiotic bugger wittering on about?

'Thank you again, Dw...' He decided not to continue with the name in case he got it wrong a second time.

Dwayne slouched away along the corridor and Max heard the swing doors go.

He then closed the unit door and leaned against it in case pimply twerp decided to pop back with any more bright ideas.

A swift glance round the unit showed a square area about the size of a small garden shed. The walls were lined with rows of dexion shelving, upon which was stacked what looked like the valued contents of an average home: a computer, a laptop, a couple of TVs, a hi-fi stereo thingy...In fact, once Max thought about it, all the items in here had an uncanny resemblance to the list of things which Martin seemed to think had been burgled from his home.

Max's heart sank.

Just at his eye-line was a radio with an old paper repair sticker on the back. Upon it was written Martin's name.

What the hell was going on?

Don't say Martin really had gone stark raving bonkers and robbed himself.

Max groaned.

What a bloody mess.

Now it was time to inspect the more serious problem lying at his feet: A bulky bundle, wrapped in bin liners.

It was about the size and shape of a human being.

Max prayed this black plastic clad thing could not be what he feared it was.

He muttered the words: 'Merciful god, do not let this happen to me', then shuffled his foot forward, poking at the bin liner with the toe of his shoe.

He was starting to feel rather queasy, and in a confined space like this he didn't know how well he would keep down his sandwich if, as frequently happened in movies, he managed to cut open the plastic and out flopped a green mouldering human hand.

The shiny toe of his shoe prodded further.

Max couldn't make out anything much except that inside the bin liner there seemed to be yet another bin liner.

What was this, for Christ's sake, a creepy x-rated version of "pass the parcel"?

After fumbling for a few minutes Max realised that there was nothing for it but direct action.

For a nanosecond he toyed with the idea of calling the spotty numskull, Dwayne, and asking for some rubber gloves, but there was no way he could do that without arousing even more suspicion.

Taking a deep breath, Max stooped and ripped at the outer black bag, then staggered back to inspect the contents from a decent distance.

But he was no wiser—all he could see now, through the ragged rip he had created, was the lumpy heavy inner bag. And that inner one was torn, sticky, covered in soil and bound with long strips of wide brown parcel tape.

The tape looked like that stubborn stuff which you could only get through by hours of hacking with a sharp knife. Max scanned the stacked shelves for something to assist— scissors, a Stanley knife, garden shears, anything with a nice quick edge. He knew that stashed among this melee of domestic small electrics there must be something he could use.

But when he saw the thing lying on a shelf right in front of the door, his jaw dropped: it was the huge Sabatier chef's knife. If he was not mistaken it was the one Sarah Beaumont had so ferociously wielded while serving up that revolting pudding during Martin's dinner party.

Max reached out for the knife, then thought better of it.

Better safe than sorry.

It would not be clever for a man of Max's legal standing to smear his own fingerprints all over the handle of something which might turn out to be an item of devastatingly important incriminating evidence. So instead he pulled a grubby handkerchief from his pocket and wrapped it around the handle before picking it up. Once firmly gripped in his paw, Max swiftly stooped again and carefully slashed the package on the floor, hacking outward through the tightly bound bands of tape till sweat dripped from his chin.

He rose again and turned away, leaning against the shelf for a moment, breathing deeply. How stuffy and close it was in this box.

As Max gazed at his own reflection in the screen of a large plasma TV he realised he was feeling dreadfully sick, and looked it. His face was whiter than it ever had been since he was an infant, and his scanty hair was plastered to his scalp with sweat. He repeatedly swallowed, trying to rid his mouth of excess saliva.

Pull yourself together man. This was not time for paroxysms of the effeminate variety. He had to find out what was going on in here, and then promptly take appropriate action.

Get it over with, then to the nearest pub for a drink.

Like a child watching a scary TV programme, Max could not face looking directly at the contents of the bin liners. So, with his back still to the package, he tipped his head forwards and down and sneaked a glance between his underarm and side.

He could see the black bag, and not much else. Slowly he slid his foot back and tried to move the plastic packaging round, further loosening the bin liner with the tip of his toe.

With a clatter something fell out of the package, and tumbled towards his feet.

He flinched, then took a peek.

It was a shoe.

A lady's stiletto-heeled evening shoe.

He had seen the shoe before.

And he remembered where he had seen it.

On Sarah's foot.

Max started to retch.

He grabbed hold of the shelf and, staring into the TV screen, took a long deep breath. He could not possibly vomit on top of all this evidence. It would be unprofessional in the extreme.

He took a second glance at the shoe.

Yes.

It definitely belonged to Sarah Beaumont. Max had last seen her wearing it at that grim dinner.

He spun round, prepared for greater horror.

But the black plastic, still clinging to whatever else was inside, revealed nothing.

Max decided on a new plan of action. Eyes tilted upward, he turned and knelt beside the parcel. Then, averting his face, so that all he could see was a suitcase and a large black stereo speaker, he stretched out a hand to the side and fumbled.

He would feel his way round like this, then when he felt utterly sure it was a corpse—well, then what?

Don't leap ahead.

Don't leap ahead.

Take it one step at a time.

Max tugged at the plastic and this time it fell away, along with a few maggots. In the periphery of his vision Max could make out the shape of the white blouse Sarah had worn at dinner.

And the skirt.

13

Cakewalk

Prancing dance with an occasional backward lilt

'MAX IS ALL very well, but I think I'd really prefer to have a rich grandfather who'd leave me millions.' Lisa tossed the magazine to the side. Much as she enjoyed flicking through all the mags laid out at the hair dressers, even she reached a point when yet another article detailing Paris Hilton's nightlife antics made her want to fling the whole lot onto a bonfire. 'It's just not fair.'

Lisa leaned her head back into the basin as Tony, her hairdresser, lifted the shower head, and tested the water temperature on his palm.

'I think you'll find it was her great-grandfather,' he said.

'You see!' Lisa sighed. 'How lovely. All that money but you'd probably never even meet them so you wouldn't even have to be grateful.'

Since being a child Lisa had always dreamed of being a courtesan, living in some palace where semi-naked eunuchs waved palm-like feather fans in her direction, while a bevy of handmaidens (or preferably tanned, greased-up, six-packed, semi-naked men in shorts) popped chocolates into her mouth.

But no such opportunity had ever presented itself, and unfortunately the days of rich oil sheiks picking up dolly birds in Shepherd Market were long gone before Lisa was even born.

'I sometimes wonder if these mags are only printed to make decent people like us feel jealous.'

'You girls!' Tony laughed and flickered the drizzle of lukewarm water across Lisa's scalp. 'And your whims!'

This comment prickled Lisa. It wasn't a whim, or anything like it. As far as she was concerned the idea of living the high life it was a practical and viable ambition. Look at all those footballers' wives!

Lisa certainly knew what life was like at the bottom of the pile. She had experienced extreme poverty. And now she had a moderate amount of money but nowhere near enough to buy a new pair of Jimmy Choos once a month, or even once a year. And why shouldn't she have that opportunity, if others less bright than her could?

Single handedly, with no education behind her, Lisa had hiked herself out of a childhood in a seedy two room council flat in Bermondsey. Those dilapidated blocks, nestling among the crumbing Victorian dock warehouses had been pulled down now and replaced with fancy apartments for mega-rich people.

Lisa's mother had been a cleaner, and her father, well, what of him? He disappeared when she was three. After that he only made the odd appearance and then only to squeeze some cash out of her mum. Every time her mum stood up to him the horrible man had beaten her till blood spurted out of her head, so more often than not she opened her tatty purse gave him everything she had. For the next few days they didn't eat.

Whenever she heard her father's drunken knock, Lisa had cowered in the corner, hidden behind a big brown armchair, the cushioned arms of which were topped with wooden strips, each with a little circle routed out so it could hold a glass or an ashtray.

One day, when her mother's screams reached a new high, Lisa had reached out, grabbed the ashtray and flung it at her father.

He whipped round, rubbing his head and yanked her out from behind the chair by her ankle, grabbed her arm and tried to whack her. But Lisa had no intention of putting up with this awful man in the same way her mother did. She bit into his arm till she drew blood, then ran for it and hid outside by the bins till she watched him limp off, cursing into the night.

She had made up her mind there and then, as she breathed in the stench of the bins, that no man would ever hit her again, and that she would play all men off for what they were worth.

She never told anyone about her decision. She knew people would disapprove but so what, if they disapproved they could go fuck off and try to live the life her mother had lived, or even the one which society had lined up for her, and which she, through sheer use of her wits, had evaded. Her mother should have got out too. Lisa had never understood why she had put up with it, and hadn't ever tried to escape from all that vile squalor and the violence provided by her Dad.

Lisa knew she had been the only thing in her mother's life which ever brought a smile to those thin blue lips.

'You're a good girl,' her Mum would wheeze when grown-up Lisa had brought her presents. 'You don't have to be so kind to me.'

Though she only worked as a shop assistant Lisa brought her Mum things like a nice cotton blouse or a pair of leather shoes. She had spent her childhood wearing acrylic clothing and plastic shoes. But she wanted only the best for her poor old Mum.

But then her Mum had died, aged 40, hacking her lungs out, looking nearer 60, hair no more than rats' tails, dark lines carved down her pock-marked cheeks. Right up to the moment her heart finally stopped, she was "tired, tired, tired". She always said it three times, her Mum: "I'm tired, tired, tired."

A few months later Lisa met Max in a night-club.

'Day dreaming again?' Tony pulled a swatch of Lisa's hair out of the water. 'Or has the mag brought on a fit of catatonia?'

Lisa didn't like it when people used fancy words on her. She always felt undermined and on edge for the few seconds when she was trying to work out what they meant. Catatonia? Where was that anyhow? And was it a town or a country, or maybe even a ship? The easiest way out, she had learned, was to change the subject.

'I hate TV too,' she said. 'There's never anything to watch. It's all men's things: sport, sport, sport or war, war, war.'

'You're not wrong.' Tony caught eyes with Lisa in the mirror. 'And when it's not it's all those things, it's even worse: politics, politics, politics.'

Lisa watched Tony's firm hand as he used the corner of a hand towel to wipe a tear of shampoo from her neck. She liked a man's hand when it had that soft brown fur on the back, like a teddy bear.

'Mind you,' he confided in a stage whisper. 'I watch cable'

'Movies?'

'Documentaries.'

Lisa couldn't be sure but from the way Tony was looking at her she thought he might be flirting.

'Oh me too,' she said. 'I love those late night things— *Snapped: Women Who Kill* and *Forensic Files*.' Lisa stretched her neck back, showing it to its best advantage by reducing the faint necklace of wrinkles. 'God—some of the women in those cases. But Max says they're really very simplistic.'

Tony bent forward and whispered gently into her ear. 'Aren't we all, dear!'

Lisa shivered.

Secretly she had a bit of a crush on Tony. There was something about the strength of his hairy arms, and the rhythm of his strong fingers as he massaged her scalp which really turned her on.

Of course he was gay. Had to be. Far too handsome to be available.

She pondered what subject she could bring up to test him. Should she hum a show tune and see if he joined in? Or perhaps she'd start a conversation about some gay hunk—mind you, she didn't have a clue who the gay pin-ups were. Elton John was hardly poster material.

Or Stephen Fry!

God!

It didn't bear thinking about.

'What are you smiling about now, Miss? Off in another of your dreams?' Tony indicated to Lisa to move her head over so he could rinse the back of her neck. She turned and his firm fingers massaged the top of her neck. 'I'm starting to wonder whether you're in fact a somnambulist.'

Lisa didn't know how to respond, so she shut her eyes and let out a sigh. Tony had to be doing this on purpose to make her feel stupid. But she wasn't. She might not be educated, but being stupid and being un-educated were two quite different things.

'Going anywhere nice on holiday?' asked Tony.

Oooph!

What a knock-back!

Back to the bored hairdresser's old standby—holidays.

So that was that. He didn't fancy her at all.

He was gay.

'Don't even mention the word holiday to me.' Lisa felt suddenly grumpy and depressed. 'I can't stand the mention of them.'

'Sorry, duck. I thought you'd like holidays, and talking about them. Even if it's just a dream.'

'It's Max,' she countered, feeling embarrassed now for her outburst. 'He doesn't like what I like. I think for him a holiday is sitting at home watching golf on TV.'

Lisa looked up into the mirror as Tony wrapped a towel round her head and started rubbing her hair dry. Tony was still staring right into her eyes with that come hither look all over his handsome face.

'Poor Lisa. I can't believe you never go abroad together. Doesn't he like to show you off.' Tony bent down and whispered conspiratorially. Lisa felt a ripple of excitement as his lip touched her ear. 'After all, it's not as if Max Latham doesn't have the dough.'

'Tell me about it.' Lisa passed a hand over her face, ostensibly to wipe away a splash of water, but in fact to cover her blush.

'So? Come on, Lisa! Let rip, love. I won't tell on you.'

'Well, we did go away once.' Lisa looked Tony right in the eye and mouthed the rest in a conspiratorial whisper . 'It was the most horrible fortnight of my life. Truly ghastly!'

She giggled.

'Where did you go? A business trip?' Tony was now snipping away at the ends of her hair. Lisa watched the damp clumps tumble, forming a semicircular mat on the floor around her feet. 'Don't tell me—a Law conference in Northern Ireland or somewhere.'

'No. It was the Grenade Islands, or something like that.'

'Grenadines. Sounds nice.'

'No, Tony' said Lisa to the man in the mirror. 'Definitely NOT nice. Max owns some shanty on an island you can't even get to unless you take a wind-up plane. Honestly! You'd as well take a journey on one those toy planes men play with out on the Common on Sunday mornings. Then, as if the journey wasn't bad enough, we got there and this beach house he'd been going on about as though it was his own private Centre Parcs turned out to be a garden shed on stilts, with no glass in the windows and rickety home-made ladders to get yourself up and inside.'

'Oh Lisa! You are a one.' Tony guffawed. 'It can't have been that bad.'

'Oh, Tony,' Lisa mocked his tone. 'It was that bad. You may laugh, but I suspect you've read too many Kuoni brochures and not seen enough of those disaster holiday programmes. The Caribbean isn't all rum cocktails and back rubs, you know. For a start, within 500 feet of passport control I had my purse snatched. Then there was the taxi ride in a dilapidated, filthy, stinky, rusty thing which would certainly never have passed its MOT here, with a driver who had never in his life seen a

deodorant stick, let alone applied it. Then there was the pantomime of climbing up the ladder with a suitcase to get into that
spider-infested shack, then I got hives. We had a revolting
dinner—or should I say burnt offering, as Max insisted on
barbecuing some slab of meat he'd picked up on the cheap. I
lay awake all night convinced we were both going to go down
with salmonella, or that a rattlesnake was going to slither in
under the sheets, and then, when Max had finally convinced
me I was safe, I found a scorpion crawling out of my shoe. Oh,
and that was after I had a shower which I think was just a
hose pipe passing cold water through an old baked bean can
he'd previously had a go at with a fork. Never again. Give me
a nice 4 star hotel in France or Italy, with luxury bathroom
and room service any day. If there's one thing I cannot abide,
Tony, it is filth and dirt.'

'That's two things, dearie.'

Glancing in the mirror, Lisa saw the salon manager signal-
ling Tony to the phone.

'Here. Keep busy.' Tony picked up the evening paper and
tossed it into her lap. 'I'll be right back.'

Lisa couldn't work out whether he was being very rude or
simply teasing her. Sometimes with men, especially gay ones,
it was really hard to tell the difference.

She spread out the paper and scoured the front page for an
article about the librarian's murder. She loved to see Max's
name in the papers, "representing the defendant" or whatever.
But the only article relating to the case was a short paragraph
which said nothing except that "a man (35)" was "helping police
with their inquiries." It didn't even mention Martin by name.

A shiver passed through Lisa when she grasped the fact that
only a few days ago she had been sitting next to this very man
(35) who might well really have killed those poor women. Who

knows, perhaps Martin (35) had spent the whole meal thinking about how he might like to finish her off too? Hadn't he spent the entire night talking about horrible things?

Good God.

There was the proof.

Of course he'd done it.

I mean, it wasn't rocket surgery.

What if Max did get him off? Didn't he always boast to all and sundry that he could get anyone off? A drunk motorist nattering on a hand-held mobile phone could mow down a whole crocodile of children and with Max's flair they could be assured they'd never see the inside of a jail. So, if Martin was pronounced innocent, that wouldn't exactly prove that Martin actually was innocent. And if Max got him off and they let Martin go home and she met him in the supermarket or somewhere, she'd better watch out.

Would she and Max still go there for dinner—or, even worse, have to invite Martin (35) and his wife over to their dinner parties? What would she say to him? After this simple small talk like: 'What have you been up to lately?' would have sinister new connotations.

Lisa wondered whether Sarah knew what a freak she was married to. How scary that would be! No wonder the poor woman had walked out on him.

Just think if Max ever turned out to be a killer. How horrid.

Lisa scanned down the rest of the news columns reading about the poor librarian. They kept saying "pretty librarian" but from the photos she'd seen Lisa thought the dead woman looked rather plain, not to mention on the goofy side, with a moustache and a bit of a squint. Her clothes were certainly vile. Lisa wouldn't be seen dead in that horrible outfit. It looked like something that even Oxfam would ship out to the third world cos no one over here with any taste would buy it. Obviously the rule was that once you were murdered no one dared say anything bad about you, and had to flatter you to make up for your being dead.

If only it was that easy in the world of glamour photography!

Lisa had had some pretty nasty scrapes. Even when she was looking perfectly lovely she'd get these photographers talking about her open pores and her "bad" profile and things. Clearly they had never set eyes on anyone who was normal looking— or in their words "a dog".

Lisa was amazed that this was the type of look murderers went out to find. You'd think rapists and those sort of people would want to find pretty people to do it with. Lisa supposed that these rapists and murderers must themselves be rather ugly and that was why they couldn't find a girlfriend through the usual channels.

Perhaps that was just the point. Maybe they were scared of beauty. After all, face it, they'd have to be in really dire straits if they needed to kill poor ugly people just so they could have sex with them.

This unfortunate woman in the paper had been working late at the library, it said, and then she'd gone out to a nearby pub for a drink and was never seen again. Well, not alive anyhow.

God, how awful.

And how desperate too.

Lisa couldn't imagine going to a pub on her own. And now she thought she would never try. Not if that kind of thing happened to you when you went there. There had to be reasons why women didn't go to pubs alone, and this was obviously one of them.

'So where are you now, Dolly Daydream?' Tony tapped Lisa on the shoulder and she jumped. 'What are you reading about?' He stooped and pointed at the newspaper. 'Is your Max anything to do with that case?'

Lisa nodded and put her finger on the paragraph about Martin.

'He's representing "the man, thirty-five".'

'The man who did it?' Tony sighed as he picked up the dryer and tested the heat on his hand. 'Well at least if they've got someone in custody it means you don't have to worry.'

'How come? I would have thought there was plenty to worry about.'

'No, listen—if the bloke's stuck in a police cell he can't go around picking up and murdering women, can he?'

'Oh, I see what you mean.' Lisa laughed. She loved the way Tony was pulling little curls, winding them round his strong fingers, while looking directly ahead at her face in the mirror. 'So how lucky I am. I can go to the library and not be frightened!'

'Lisa, my dear! I wouldn't go that far. Have you seen the types who lurk around all those sinister booky places?' Tony gave a mock shudder. 'Libraries equal creee-peeee."

'Do you ever read books, Tony?'

'Of course. Why?'

'Oh.' Lisa had been hoping he would say he didn't. 'Just wondered.'

Tony looked down at her with such an impudent shrug Lisa felt scolded. At school she had been forced to read, but since then she never had. What was the point? Anything good eventually showed up on TV.

'I prefer magazines really, Tony. Magazines with pictures.'

'Don't get me wrong, Lisa, I don't read anything highbrow.' Tony held up a defensive palm. 'I like to read celebrity biographies, you know. Though I have to say it's clear that not only do the celebs not write them, whoever actually does has a very vivid imagination. And I read thrillers of course. Everyone loves thrillers.'

'Do they?' Lisa was horrified at the conversation and scared that Tony was about to chat to her about some books she'd never heard of, trying to make a fool of her and show her up, thinking she was stupid, as so many people did. 'I did a cover for a book once, actually. When I was still doing modelling.'

Tony laughed and squinted at her through his long lashes. 'Not nude, Miss?'

'Of course not, Tony! I never did Art modelling. No I had to sprawl out on a bed but they told me it was going to be "anti-deconstructionalist". Well naturally I thought that meant it would be on a manual for builders. Imagine my horror when one morning the bloody book turned up in the morning mail.'

'Why?'

Lisa squirmed in her seat. She was sure Tony was laughing up his sleeve. His mouth was all quivery as though he was holding in a great big bellow.

'Well, it was what my old Mum called "a lurid novel". A bonk-buster I think they call them nowadays.'

'What was it called?'

'A bonk-buster. I just said.'

'No, the name of the book, silly.'

'It was years ago. I can't remember.'

'I thought I'd perhaps get hold of a copy,' Tony grinned. 'Get you to sign it.'

'Whatever.' Lisa glanced at her watch and looked out through the plate glass windows which fronted the salon. No sign of Max's car. She hoped he wasn't going to leave her standing outside waiting in the street. Then she remembered that, if Tony really wanted to talk books, not only did she have a book conversation up her sleeve, but that it was much better than anything he could ever come up with.

'I met a writer last week, actually, Tony. American novelist. She's rather successful apparently. She writes thrillers.'

'Name?'

'Tess Brandon.'

'Really!' Tony was plumping up the hair now. 'So anything special this evening?'

Lisa shrugged. She was rather disappointed that he was not more interested in her brief brush with fame. And she didn't believe he wanted to know about her evening.

'What do you mean "anything special"?'

'Hair?' he said, with a goofy expression, pointing down at her head with the pointed end of his styling comb. 'For anything special?'

How utterly boring. He had turned into a hairdresser again. Conversation-wise, all holidays and small talk.

'Well, I'm meant to be going out to dinner with Max.' She sighed. 'But, no, nothing special.'

'Pity,' said Tony. 'If you were free I was going to ask you to join me for a drink later.'

No! What a turn up! She couldn't believe it.

'But isn't he out there, already, waiting?' Lisa picked up her mobile phone and dialled Max. 'I'll see where he's got to.' She let out a heavy sigh. 'Straight to answer-phone.'

She was not really disappointed that Max hadn't answered, but needed Tony to see that she seemed like she was, so he wouldn't think she was the flighty type.

'So either he's turned it off, or he's out of range.'

Tony stared intently at the back of her head while he fiddled about with the fine hairs on her neck.

It made her whole spine tingle.

'He often stands me up. Sometimes I wonder whether he prefers the company of crooks to me.' Lisa realised with a jolt that what she had said could well be true. Sod him. If he could stand her up, for some grubby, stinking, beer-bellied client who'd just robbed a bank, she could stand him up for a handsome hairdresser. She looked at Tony in the mirror, presenting her best naughty schoolgirl expression. 'Perhaps I could play truant and join you for that drink, after all. I mean—it's not as though I haven't tried to get through to him.'

'You know what I think you need,' said Tony, still appraising her hair. 'A nice pretty clip.' He pulled open a drawer. 'Look at this. Swarovski crystals. That'll hold the wave in nicely.' He leaned forward and whispered into her ear, so close she could again smell his musky aftershave. 'A mere £97. I'll disguise it on the bill, so you can charge it to Max.'

Lisa put her fingers up to touch the gorgeous brooch-like clip and smiled.

14

Zoppetto

*A dance from Medieval times,
involving hopping and limping.*

MAX HELD HIS head low, trying not to pass out in the
claustrophobic storage room. He was still turned
away from the black plastic package. The shoe was
all he needed to see. Oh Martin, Martin.

Who would have taken you for a wife slayer!

Max couldn't see Martin luring women away from libraries
to torture them and dump them on the common. It just didn't
compute. But Sarah was another matter.

He felt pretty sure that if he had been trapped inside a relationship with that maenad, sooner or later he too would have
snapped.

Max pulled himself up, wiping a sheen of perspiration from his brow.

The worst was over now, as far as nausea was concerned, but the logistical problems that this grisly discovery threw up had just begun.

How to proceed?

Max could always walk right out of the storage facility and never make an appearance again. After all, he had not had to fill in any forms to get in. He had given them the letter, and flourished the key, and when they had asked his name he had replied Martin Beaumont.

As far as the man at the desk knew Max was Martin Beaumont.

Martin, Martin, Martin!

No wonder the stupid fart had been so wobbly in the police interview room. He was innocent of killing the librarian, but quivering with guilt for his murdered wife. And this also explained the blood on his kitchen floor.

The police were still waiting on the DNA result—thinking the blood would match up with Jane Grimshaw. But voila! The DNA belonged to the parcel on the floor.

But that wasn't such bad news, was it?

It would certainly buy Max a little time, because, temporarily, it would throw the police off the scent.

And Max suspected that Sarah's DNA wouldn't be on file. So who would know the blood was hers?

While his brain was whirring in legal mode, Max felt a whole lot better. He was filled with enough confidence to take a good look at the rest of the contents of the black plastic bin-liners.

He turned.

He looked.

He looked closer.

He knelt down and poked about.

It wasn't Sarah after all.

The thing which lay on the floor, framed in black plastic, was not even a woman's corpse.

It was a woollen rug.

No—not even wool. A nylon carpet, a horrible green and beige affair, which Max recognised from the hall floor of the Beaumonts' house, rolled up and "dressed" in Sarah's blouse and skirt. The blouse was horribly bloodstained. A few desultory maggots crawled about on the stain and amid the folds of black plastic. Another high-heeled shoe, companion to the one which had startled him earlier, was wedged inside the bottom end of the rug. From Max's angle of view it was clear that there was nothing else substantial hidden inside the carpet, as he could see the woollen coils curling right to the centre.

After poking about on the shelves, peering behind the computer monitors and radios, Max knew that nothing further of interest was to be gleaned within this storage unit.

He grabbed a sheaf of official looking papers from his briefcase and clasped it in his hand. He hoped it would look as though this was the important item he had just retrieved from a box within the lock-up, the ostensible purpose of this brief visit.

He kicked the carpet further into the unit and away from the door. If, for any reason, he needed to come back, he didn't want another episode of that pantomime with Dwayne and his broom.

The broom!

He grabbed that with his other hand and left the unit, marching briskly along the CCTV lined corridors till he reached reception.

'Dwayne's, I believe.'

Max plonked the broom on the desk, strode out into the street and hailed a cab to The Adam And Eve by the river, his favourite place for a long contemplative solo drink.

He knew he was due to pick up Lisa quarter of an hour ago, but he wasn't her taxi service. She would have to make her own way back from the hairdressers.

Once at the riverside bar, Max settled himself in a heavy wooden seat by the window with a large gin and tonic.

He looked out at the murky river, the water rippling in the wind, its swift dark swirls indicating the dangerous currents lurking beneath.

What a fuck up!

He wished now that he had never set foot in the storage facility, simply taken the key straight to the river and chucked it in.

Knowledge is power they said. But not in every circumstance.

As Martin's legal representative there were things that he wished he did not know. Apparently Sarah had not run away, as Martin had told him, but rather Martin had killed Sarah, and hidden the body somewhere.

Poor Martin.

Max had seen it over and over again—men, who had been barred from watching a football match on TV, or who had found their wives trawling through the contents of their computers or mobile phones; blokes cracking under the pressure of being taunted drunkenly in public about their lovemaking, the size of their genitals, or something even more meaningless like the colour of their socks.

Then, click! With an uncontrollable rage, the Real Man popped out and smacked the nagging harridan into the next world.

Poor, poor, stupid Martin.

So, if his idiotic client had done in the wife, where the hell had he stashed her corpse?

Max wondered whether or not the police had dug up the whole garden. It wasn't usual unless there was some particular reason—like in the Fred West case, where reports of more missing people led to more digging, like a tumble of dominoes.

And the police had their body—the one they believed themselves to be looking for at any rate—so why dig further? And if they had accidentally stumbled across Sarah's body they would surely have let him know.

So truthfully it looked as though perhaps Sarah was still there. Under Martin's flowerbeds. In the garden.

Maybe Martin had gone into the garden to put in a few more roses to cover up the makeshift grave, but got the wrong spot.

Max snorted.

What fun!

He'd like to ask Martin point blank.

Maybe if Martin knew that Max knew about him killing Sarah he would stop being so evasive and put in a better performance when he was put before the beak.

However he didn't think it would be very clever to confront Martin with his new knowledge quite yet. Not while the silly sod was banged up in a police cell at any rate. Walls have ears. Every imbecile knows that. Whatever they might say about confidentiality, it was a load of piffle. There was always some snoopy copper lurking, his ears out on stalks.

Buggeration.

Max downed the rest of the gin and waved at a waiter for a refill.

What if, however, Martin had in fact killed the two other women, the librarian and that other one...

No.

Martin didn't have the balls to do in strange women.

Clean-shaven sops, like Martin had become, men who lacked the normal male aversion to shopping and housework, who wandered around Waitrose in shorts, wearing babies in papooses, their nicely shampooed and cropped hair setting off nicely the ugly little spectacles which perched on the bridge of their well scrubbed noses, didn't do things like that.

They were all too anxiously pleasing strange women to go round slaying them. It was a different mentality.

But for argument's sake, let's say he had.

Could it be possible that Martin had found the time to kill his wife and deal with her body on the same day that he was depositing Miss Grimshaw's cadaver on the Common?

To dispatch one corpse in a day might be seen as burdensome, to dispose of two utterly incredible. Could a man like Martin be that efficient in body dumping?

Dead bodies are big clumsy things which weigh a ton and are hard to disguise.

If Martin had killed and hidden the body of Sarah, he could not possibly have killed and dumped the librarian within the same twenty four hours.

But that would hardly play as a defence. "Sorry, M'lud, my client could not have killed this librarian, he was occupied at the time, you see, murdering and disposing of his wife."

Max wondered what other practical jokes his client had left for him to find.

Now that he thought about it, right from the start it was plain as a pikestaff Martin had knocked off Sarah.

Even New Men had to have a breaking point. In fact Max suspected it was probably lower than those of the hell-raising types of yesteryear. Suppressing all that male energy must be very exhausting. The unreconstructed man of yesteryear could at least get things out of his system by fucking around or giving the wife the odd slap. For New Men the hormones must still be seething beneath, hidden resentment smouldering away, then, when they were provoked too far, or sexually challenged which amounted to much the same thing, the whole thing reached combustion point.

And that Sarah was a virago.

Max felt lucky that he had the willing and grateful Lisa, a woman who was only too happy to get her housing, clothing and dinners paid for in exchange for nightly sex.

Max reached down and opened his briefcase. The letter and envelope from the storage company were still there. He had the plastic key in his pocket. What other evidence was there of the lock-up existing at all?

His phone rang.

'Max?' It was Lisa. Bugger it. He glanced at his watch. He'd stood her up. 'Where on earth are you? I've been waiting hours.'

Max sighed. 'You know how it gets. Things pop up...'

Lisa's tone increased a pitch. 'You could have rung me.'

What was this? Lisa shouting at him? A revolution!

Max was not in the mood. 'It was inconvenient, Lisa. Work took a strange turn.' Max gulped down the remains of the second gin. 'Take a cab.'

'What time will you be home?'

'When I get there,' Max snapped down the line. 'Don't wait in for me. I still have a few more inquiries to make.'

Lisa emitted a long feminine whine. 'So I suppose there's no dinner at La Coupole either?'

'I will have to eat, Lisa. So why don't we meet up there? Say 8.30.'

'And what are you doing till then?'

Max pictured himself with a garden fork prodding about in the Beaumont's flowerbeds.

'I'm going to Martin's. I have to pick something up. I also need to pop next door for a little chat with our crime-writing friend. See what she might have seen or heard.'

'Are you two having an affair?'

'Me and Tess Brandon?' Max laughed so loud that the other people in the pub turned and stared. 'I rather suspect you're more her type than I am, my dear.'

Lisa emitted a strange squeak and said goodbye.

What was that all about? Unlike Lisa to come over demanding like that. Ah well. Probably nothing that a little present of a bracelet or something wouldn't fix.

But to business...

Max knew what he knew but did not intend to share it.

The police did not yet suspect that there was anything odd about Sarah Beaumont's absence. They were so busy trying to tie Martin into charges of murdering the two strangers, that they hadn't noticed the glaring domestic discrepancy.

Sarah's blood was all over the kitchen floor, but that was because, in front of several people including himself, she had badly cut her hand.

Then the following day she had done a runner. Reason: She knew that Martin had discovered that she had fiddled the company books and stashed his money in an offshore account.

Knowing the trouble she would face if she returned she was not likely to come back, even to affirm Martin's alibis.

Max still had a case.

And Sarah Beaumont was the key.

There was only thing Max needed to be sure of, and that was that her corpse wasn't going pop up in a ditch somewhere, for he was as sure as hell the actual live Sarah Beaumont was in no position to make an appearance.

15

Slip Jig

*An Irish solo dance performed
by a woman in soft shoes*

S ARAH BEAUMONT LAY back on the huge hotel bed and
kicked off her shoes. From her viewpoint through
ceiling-high picture windows she could see the turquoise
band of sea sparkling below her, and the heat haze shimmering
up to an azure sky.

In a few moments she hoped that she would get a knock on
the door and room service would wheel in one of those lovely
trolleys with cut glass, silver, good china, a crisp white tablecloth and a meal to die for.

It was early for lunch. Barely eleven a.m. But she was
starving, having for more than two days lived on train

sandwiches and the little picnic of salad she had bought at Fortnum's before she caught the train.

She'd ordered champagne with her brunch. A half bottle of the best. None of your supermarket "special buys" that Martin went for. Why not champagne? Especially after the hideous events of these last few days.

Reaching over for the TV controller, Sarah crumpled up in agony. She kept forgetting about the stitches in her abdomen. The analgesics they had given her at the hospital were very effective, till she moved about too violently.

While the wave of pain spread over her she lay back on the bed and took a few deep breaths.

Bravo! Viva Life!

Who gave a sod about the silly pain when you know it could have been so much worse?

Inconceivably worse.

Here she was—alive!

And to reward herself for surviving she had taken herself to an earthly paradise—the beautiful, sunny French Riviera.

That arsehole, Martin.

His insufferable behaviour throughout dinner had been one thing. But, after the fight, when she had blacked out, that idiot bastard had wrapped her in bin-liners and buried her without ever actually checking whether or not she was alive and breathing.

Which she had been.

And then, having buried her in the garden, he had had the nerve to come back and dig her up to pull the fucking rings off her fingers.

Jesus God Almighty!

What could they be worth? Fifty quid max.

Mind you, she thanked god for the rings episode. For if Martin hadn't been so greedy she doubted she would be here today in a beautiful seafront hotel in Nice. For, by digging down, loosening the soil, jabbing at her with the spade, he had stirred her into consciousness. Then, while he fumbled around in the soil for her hands, he had torn a huge hole in the bin bag which covered her face, and manhandled her arms and tugged at her hands, bringing her back to consciousness with a vengeance.

At the time she had been so horrified she almost cried aloud, begging him to help her out, but, fearful that, if he realised he had not in fact killed her, he would want to finish her off and maybe smash in her skull with the spade, she held back from making a sound.

Sarah wanted to live. So she took no chances. She lay still in her damp bed of soil and continued to play dead.

With a crack of wings, a huge seagull landed on the cross bar of the room's balcony, snapping Sarah's attention away from the past. She hauled herself from the bed and moved over to the window. The gull took off, screeching into the shimmering air.

For a minute or two she leaned on the rail, watching the roller-bladers and bikers skimming along the red pavement of the Promenade des Anglais. A gaggle of elderly American tourists wearing shell suits, trainers and visors, dutifully followed their team leader, furled scarlet umbrella held aloft.

Gripping her side Sarah chuckled at the mental image of that American neighbour of theirs in London, Tess Brandon, peering out of the next door window, as she so often did, like the nosy neighbour in *Bewitched,* while Martin dug a grave in the flowerbed.

Mind you, she wouldn't have seen much, as the whole dismal episode happened around midnight. But had Tess been wearing infra-red spectacles (which frankly Sarah would not have put past her) what would she have made of it? Particularly if she had later seen the soil erupt immediately after Martin went back inside with the rings and watched Sarah dragging herself from the flower bed, clad in black bin-liners and stilettos, like some middle-aged Chelsea punk in a remake of *Plague Of The Zombies?*

For Sarah herself the picture was so vivid she doubted it would ever dim. She remembered clearly the terror when she came to, gasping for breath as she tried to work out why she could not see, wondering what was bearing down on her body. Then the stink of black plastic against her face, the gritty taste of the soil; finally, when Martin had left her and gone inside, the triumph of bursting out, thrusting her arms up through the earth to get air, and hauling herself from her sodden premature grave.

After that she recalled the cold, sharp feel of tearing plastic and parcel tape, as she ripped apart her filthy black mermaid's tail; the pumping of her heart and the throbbing shriek of pain in her side as she sat shivering, huddled against the garden fence, watching Martin move about in the brightly lit kitchen, observing him coolly mopping the kitchen floor then unpacking the dishwasher as though it was any normal night.

When finally he put out the downstairs light, Sarah had edged herself towards the back door, and overheard Martin call out in a stagy voice: "If you don't like the situation, Sarah, in the morning I trust you'll be gone."

If Sarah had needed a final straw that had been it.

She would be gone all right, but not quite in the way Martin was expecting.

And she would make sure that that fucker Martin paid for his gross indifference and wilful negligence.

All he had had to do was call a bloody ambulance, for fuck's sake!

And what had he done instead?

It didn't bear thinking about.

Once Martin was safely upstairs in the bathroom, Sarah let herself in to the kitchen, picked up the case she had left under the table and went out into the street, leaving only a trail of mud.

A knock on the hotel room door startled Sarah out of her daydream.

A handsome young waiter wheeled in the lunch trolley.

'Chargeur, aussi!' He pulled a mobile phone charger from his pocket and stooped to plug it into a socket near the window. Her phone battery had died sometime before she got into the sleeper in Paris last night.

He reached out for her phone and connected it to the charger.

As Sarah rose, to get her purse for a tip, she winced.

'Vous êtes blessé, Madame?'

'Oui.' Sarah nodded as she palmed coins into his hand. 'Mais ce n'est pas grave.'

The boy held out the chair as she sank down.

He folded out the wings of the trolley and spread out the dishes and cutlery. Then he screwed the cork out of the bottle and poured champagne into a tall flute.

'You are English?' he asked in a heavy French accent as he wiped the neck of the bottle with a linen napkin.

'Irish,' she said, holding up her passport as she made space for the ice bucket. 'Irlandais.' Sarah raised her glass.

'Bon appetit, madame.' He grinned. 'Ca, c'est un medecin superior!'

The waiter left with a wink.

Apart from wilful determination, her Irish mother had given her a second great advantage, dual nationality. When, some years earlier, Sarah had seen how much better the Irish were received abroad than the English (and with good reason) she had applied for a second passport, which she kept at all times in her computer case, just in case she ever felt an irresistible desire to flee the country—another typically Irish trait.

Sarah pulled the lids from the dishes. A truffled mushroom macaroni, garlic spinach, salade du tomates and a bowl of niçoise olives—perfection.

She ate greedily, keeping her eye on the glittering horizon.

How lucky she had been that that taxi had stopped. Black cabs were notorious for turning off their lights after pub closing time when the punters looked like drunks or lunatics, and she must have resembled both. But Sarah supposed most drunks wouldn't have been running along, bloody and barefoot, with a wheely case.

'Help me, please. I've been stabbed,' she said to him, waving a bloody hand. 'Take me to Accident & Emergency.'

The cabbie had driven as furiously as a coachman in a Dracula film, crashing red lights and ignoring the speed limit, and, when they reached St Thomas's, the midnight Jehu had carried her inside, cradled in his arms like the dead Christ in Michelangelo's Pietà.

In reception Sarah had been lifted onto a trolley and wheeled at speed into a resuscitation cubicle where a team of doctors flapped about her, assuring her she was not going to die, because the wound, however gaping and bloody, was superficial. She had been very lucky.

She cried, lying there in the dark operating theatre as they injected her with painkillers and anaesthetic, then stitched her wound. When it was all done the nurses gently dressed her in a hospital nightgown, all the while trying to get further details of the stabbing incident out of her.

'I was stupid,' she told them. 'I went for a walk after dark in Battersea Park.'

When they asked for her name and details she made them up. Her name, she said, was Laura. Laura Fairlie. Her address 46 Limmeradge Road, Hampstead. Not a flicker of recognition. Clearly the hospital staff were not fans of Wilkie Collins.

She told them she hadn't seen her attacker, but he smelled of urine, like a tramp and, no, she didn't want to talk to the police.

'We will be obliged to report it,' said a keen young registrar. 'For all you know it might have been the same man who killed that woman, Marina Sutton, last year.'

'Or the librarian,' said the nurse. 'They haven't found her body yet, but she's been missing a week.'

This brought to Sarah's mind memories of the dreadful dinner earlier, before Martin had flipped.

'Well, in that case,' said Sarah, 'I'll come clean. It was a domestic. My boyfriend is a nutter. He did it.'

'What's his name?' asked the registrar.

'Fosco,' said Sarah. 'Martin Fosco.'

'The bastard,' muttered the nurse.

'I presume this Fosco fellow of yours never made the darts team,' said the registrar as he surveyed the patient file at the end of Sarah's bed. 'He missed more organs and blood vessels with that blade than is humanly possible. I cannot believe that a knife can get that deep into the human body and not manage to pierce one vital organ.'

'Yes.' Sarah sighed. 'I am very lucky that Martin is inept in all departments requiring hand/eye co-ordination.'

'You should report him,' repeated the nurse. 'Before he finds another girlfriend to practice his circus act on.'

'I don't have time for all this,' said Sarah, hoping there was no such address as Limmeradge Road in Hampstead in case the nurse started looking things up in the A-Z. 'Please just leave me alone now. I am so tired.'

They put her in a public ward, where she slept fitfully, waking often, comforted by the sight of the night nurse busily scribbling notes in the halo of an angle-poise lamp.

Sarah woke fully at dawn, and watched the sun's first pink light hit the clock tower of the Houses of Parliament. She lay awake, going though over and over again the events of the previous night.

Having decided to take revenge on Martin, she formulated further plans. She would oblige him by disappearing and, at the same time, get her own back.

Shortly after the rush hour traffic on Westminster Bridge had died down, Sarah discharged herself. The ward sister argued with her, but eventually relented. She was prescribed painkillers and anti-inflammatories, and given a bundle of dressings for the wound. If the wound hadn't properly closed up within a fortnight, they told her, or if there was any sign of infection she was to come straight back to St Thomas's, other-wise go to her GP. If she banged the scar it was possible that the wound might bleed quite heavily. And if the bleeding hadn't stopped within quarter of an hour she should report at once to the emergency department. The stitches should dissolve in their own time.

Sarah went straight across the road from the hospital to a huge impersonal hotel near the London Eye. Keeping up *The Woman in White* theme, she checked herself in as Laura Fairlie.

Sarah took another mouthful of the delicious pasta while soothing the hot pain by running her hand smoothly around the wound. She pulled the dripping bottle from the ice bucket and poured herself another flute of champagne. It was a painful move.

She leaned back and took a few deep breaths, then flicked on the TV. She was tired of thinking about the last few days.

Sky News was, as usual, all sport, business and world markets, so, while she finished her meal, she tuned to a French station which was transmitting a concert of tango music and apaché dancing.

The male dancer flung his partner around on the floor. The female flinched and recoiled from his attack in time to the music.

Most fitting.

Sarah rooted about in her purse for Tess's business card. She wanted to know how Martin was now, and if he was coping with the onslaught of incidents she had devised for him: the burglary, the removal of all the money from their bank account, and his credit card being used up to the limit. How had he reacted when the evening courier arrived to pick up "a large parcel wrapped in bin-liners, about the size of a human body"?

Sarah had already tried to phone Tess a number of times, but with no joy. She'd even tried a few times from a pay phone booth on Gare d'Austerlitz last night before she got on the sleeper. Did the woman never pick up her calls?

She thought of Martin's face and laughed, sending a dart of pain up her side.

Oddly Martin had phoned Sarah's mobile a few times, when presumably he thought she was lying dead in the flowerbed.

He had never left a message. What on earth had that been about?

Maybe he was trying to find her cell phone, in order to dispose of it. But the calls had stopped. Perhaps he thought the "burglars" had taken the phone.

Once her phone rang while she was on the train, speeding through Northern France, and his number came up. Sarah had been worried that something must have happened to her mother, so, without thinking she instantly phoned him back. When she heard his weaselly voice she had thought better of it, hung up and phoned the care home instead.

That reminded her. She must also phone her sister. While Sarah was busily getting things sorted and making her escape, Suzanne had left a number of messages.

Sarah pushed the empty plates to one side and started on dessert, a luscious fruit tart.

She wondered how long she should leave it before putting Martin out of his misery and letting him know that he was not actually a wife murderer.

How would he feel once he knew that all his precious possessions were safe in a storage warehouse in Battersea, (along with her little bin-liner and carpet joke to give him a bit of a fright when he went to retrieve it all) fees paid for with his own credit card, and that all his money was in fact safely making tons of interest in a premium investment account in the Cayman Islands? Internet banking was a marvellous invention. Once Sarah had removed her own share of the cash, plus a little for clothes and travel, she had locked him out of the account, changed his password from 5Rusty11 to 8Sarah12.

It was fair game, she believed, to have used his credit and debit card to buy clothes and food and get cash to buy her little trip to the South of France. After all—she would never have needed to recuperate from the shock of being buried alive if he had simply picked up the fucking phone and called an ambulance that night.

God, she was tired.

The night after hospital Sarah had been unable to sleep in the hotel so took a cab home. She directed the driver to wait for her while she picked something up from inside. The house was in darkness. Sarah wondered whether Martin might be out. But she tiptoed up the stairs to the bedroom and found him curled up, fast asleep. She had stood for a moment at the foot of the bed and watched him squeaking and squirming in his sleep. At one point he seemed to open his eyes and stare at her.

'Martin?' she whispered. 'What have you done?'

He seemed to spit at her and said something about elocution lessons.

Revolted, she had turned away, and left him to his nightmare.

She looked around the house. She was very impressed by the work of the removal firm. They really had cleared the place of all the valuables, as she had instructed. Sarah had planned to leave the key to the storage space on the kitchen table for Martin to find in the morning. It wouldn't take him long to work out his password at the warehouse as she had used his usual, 5Rusty11. But when she peeked out into the garden and seen how efficiently he had covered that spot with a neat row of snapdragons and pansies (of all things!) she decided to let him stew for a few days more.

If he was that methodical about getting rid of her, he could live without TV and radio for another day, and as for the computer—well, he could always use the one at work. She posted the key and relevant numbers to him at his office.

Before she left for France, Sarah visited her mother at the care home.

Sitting in the tiny room, Sarah held both of her Ma's hands in her own as the darling sat opposite her, dribbling into her lap. Her mother had at one point looked up at her and winked, like she used to do in the old days. It was all Sarah could do to hold back howls of misery. As she left her she stroked her mother's cheek. Her mother had put her hand up and held it in place.

For a sparkling moment Sarah believed her mother had known her again.

'I'll send you a post card,' Sarah said from the door.

'From Ireland?' Her mother's voice was a mere breath.

'No,' Sarah smiled. 'It's exotic places I am after. The Riviera, that's what takes my fancy.'

'Nice,' said her mother. 'Nice. Nice.'

So Nice it was.

She went straight to Charing Cross station, where she posted the storage key to Martin's office, before taking a train to Dover. She enjoyed a bright ferry crossing to Calais, where she started the long train journey via Paris which brought her here.

Sarah's phone emitted the unpleasant high pitched beep of an incoming text.

Probably her sister again.

She glanced at her watch.

In Australia it would be the middle of the night. Please god, not bad news of her mother...

She grabbed the phone, still wired up to the charger, and stabbed at the buttons.

The message was weird, with no sender's name attached.

IN GRAVE DANGER. GIVE POLICE THIS CELL NUMBER.

What was this? Martin fighting back? Perhaps he had worked it all out and was now reversing the tables on her.

She scrolled down.

The caller was +1. An American phone number.

But Sarah didn't know anyone in America. And, anyhow, how could she, here in France, alert the American FBI or whatever it was, and to what, where?

Perhaps it was some marketing ploy. She'd heard about these phishing scams where you receive a call and when you phone back your call is diverted to Somalia or somewhere, on a premium rate line.

Sarah dropped the phone back onto the table, and sipped her drink.

After lunch she would take a short stroll along the promenade, perhaps sit in a café on the beach for a while with a coffee. Then, this afternoon she'd have another try at calling Tess.

The phone rang again.

Her sister.

Sarah picked up.

'Suzanne?'

'Where the fucking hell have you been?' Suzanne screamed down the phone.

Before Sarah had a chance to reply her sister delivered the bad news:

'Mum's had a fall. It's serious. You'd better get there fast.'

16

Stomp

Jazz dance featuring much heavy foot stamping

WHILE SHE PHONED Max, Lisa stood in the street outside the salon having a furtive cigarette. For some reason he was being really stand-offish and strange. Then suddenly, while she was talking, Tony came up from behind and goosed her. Had it been anyone else, Lisa would have turned and given him a good slap. But there was something about Tony. Was it that hint of gayness, or perhaps it was simply because he was so dishy looking, with those butch hairy arms? Anyhow, whatever he was, it was obvious the man was really sensitive—he had instantly seen she was upset and, after she said goodbye to Max on that chopped off phone call, he had reiterated his offer of a drink.

'In fact,' Tony said turning back into the salon with a quite unmanly swish, 'we're going to go right now.'

'But work, Tony!' Lisa cried. She was unused to spontaneity, especially after living with Max for a few years. 'You're meant to be working.'

'Give me five, and I'm yours,' he said, disappearing back inside the sepia tinted glass doors.

Once he was gone Lisa was unsure what to do. Should she wait outside on the pavement, like a hooker with her newly cut and blow-dried hair and a fag in her mouth? Or should she stub out, then go inside and hang about in the waiting area.

It was rather nippy out, with a strong wind, but she decided the pavement was the less desperate choice. She walked up and down, puffing the cigarette down to the filter tip, while gazing into the adjacent shop window which was stacked with indecently shaped perfume bottles, some of which contained flecks of real gold, or pearls. Honestly, it was like being back in those decadent days of history where people got hung, drawn and quartered for stealing a handkerchief, while others feasted on peacocks hearts and larks tongues and stuffed swans, and dissolved pearls in glasses of wine, and lived in palaces where the walls were decorated with real gold and diamonds.

Lisa wondered if someday soon there might be a revolution and all the smelly people who live in boxes near railways stations would rise up and kill all the people driving round in Lamborghinis and Porsches and spending £4000 on a single bottle of wine. Really if there was any fairness, one night those paupers might well set upon the over-stuffed people staggering out of The Ivy or The Wolseley, half-cut and three sails to the wind as her mother used to say, then stick their fat heads on poles and march, spattered with fat rich blood, to Buckingham Palace where they would demand Equality for All.

There was such a difference between having comfort and nice things and this extravagance, which to Lisa was beyond belief, especially when every night the TV was crammed with heart rendering images of poor black people with flies crawling on their eyes, starving to death.

When Lisa first met Max she feared he was going to be one of those types who spent thousands on new suits and expensive pomades and after-shaves, which she would not have liked at all, but it turned out he was actually quite a miser. He had always been very generous to her, bought her little trinkets from time to time, and his only real extravagance was that most nights he preferred to eat in a restaurant. Lisa wondered whether he just hated her cooking. If he wanted, Lisa would have been quite willing to make Max daily plates of spaghetti bol, or shepherd's pie. But he'd never let her.

At first, when they had gone out a few times, Lisa hadn't been looking for a permanent relationship or anything like it, but when Max had asked her to move in with him, she had decided that his house was certainly a lot nicer than the little studio flat she was renting in Peckham.

The deal, laid down by Max at the outset, was that when she became his live-in partner Lisa had to give up her job behind the perfume counter at Harvey Nicks, because he didn't want her going out working. It meant in many ways she gave up her independence for him, but really it was just as well that she didn't have to go into Sloane Street every morning. The girls in that place were such snobs. Lisa had had quite some difficulty hiding her working class background from them, and when they lolled around the staff room discussing Bedales and the Lycée, she hadn't a clue what they were on about. Eventually she worked out that they were just names of schools. In the first one it seemed you didn't have to do any

lessons, and in the other you had to do them all in French—
which was a lot of good if you lived in South London. One girl
had gone on and on about some place in Switzerland where
she was "finished". For many months Lisa had understood
"finished" to be a euphemism for having an abortion, and felt
quite sorry for the girl. But then she found out it was just a
place where you went and learned to write shorthand and ski,
two even more totally useless qualifications to have under your
belt, so she quickly withdrew her pity.

But Lisa felt she had learned quite a lot all in all from those
years smearing on dark brown make up in the morning and
spending her days squirting unsuspecting customers with
sickly perfumes with names like "Opium" and "Poison", which
in Lisa's opinion was aptly named. There was another scent
called "Oui" and when Lisa was told how it was pronounced
she thought the girl was winding her up. She had to control
herself and remember not to ask passing women 'Can I spray
you with Oui?'

Anyhow Max had taken her away from that world, and
replaced it with...what exactly? Living in his house and eating
out in nice restaurants and never having to get the bill, and in
exchange she had to let him do it with her whenever he fancied,
and publicly to agree with everything he said. It seemed a
simple enough contract, but lately she was getting bored and
even irritated by the way Max seemed to think she wasn't
even a real person. Take that dinner party the other night
with the nutter who had killed that librarian. When Lisa had
tried to stick up for the wife (who had, after all, made all
the food and served it as though she was a waitress, even
though the woman had a posh accent and a university education and everything) Max had rudely slapped her down. But
Lisa really thought Sarah was quite nice. And no one at that

table had complimented the poor woman the whole evening, which seemed to Lisa like the very soul of bad manners. And, to add insult to injury, they all went on having that beastly conversation about murdering people with grease guns, and all Sarah had seemed to want was for everything to be nice, like the pretty table decorations.

And that was just what Lisa herself would have wanted if she had thrown a dinner party for her friends. She hated to see women taken advantage of like that.

It would be fun to have a change of scenery and take a drink with Tony before she met up with Max for dinner.

She wondered if perhaps it would go further. Maybe they would start up a little romance. It couldn't be so bad having a thing with a hairdresser, perhaps moving in with him, even.

If she threw it all in and left Max, she could always go back and work in a shop so that she could pay her way again. Maybe she'd try Selfridges this time, or Peter Jones, or the one that people pronounced in a funny way which apparently made it funny—zhon looey, it sounded like—but they really meant John Lewis. Perhaps the girls there would be a bit nicer. And it would certainly be more fun than sitting at home every day, watching those bitchy women on lunchtime TV, and people going round houses they had no intention of buying.

'Going to wangle Max into buying you those rocks?' Tony had crept up behind her and was standing really close to her shoulder. Lisa could feel the warmth of his breath on her ear and it felt good.

He pointed towards a huge but vulgar set of earrings with matching wrist band.

'Not for me, thanks.'

Tony looked at his watch. Lisa noticed it was a good one. 'Look, they need me for about half an hour more.'

Lisa's heart dipped. He was going to call it off just as she was starting to want it to happen.

'But if you fancy going on to the bar on the common and getting us a nice seat, I'll join you. That OK?'

Lisa hadn't time to reply before he continued.

'You haven't gone off the idea, have you? I understand if you just want to go home. I won't mind. But I thought we could have some fun.'

Lisa smiled. What the hell.

'Is it far, this here bar?' She burst out laughing. 'I made a poem. I'm always doing that.'

'It's on the Common, by the bus stop. You can almost see it from here.' He pointed in the direction. 'Just past the tube station. About a five minute walk.'

Lisa strolled across the grass, watching mothers and children playing ball on the green in the evening sunshine.

The pub was quite bright, with lots of glass panels in the ceiling. She ordered herself a spritzer. She didn't really like the taste much, but it was cool and fizzy, and from her time at Harvey Nicks she knew it was what posh girls drank on sunny evenings.

She perched on a small bar-side stool near a table where it was clear the people were about to leave.

So, how about this! Here she was making the ultimate trip, conquering new frontiers—going into a pub on her own! She felt rather self-conscious but, apart from that, it wasn't so bad. Lots of people were here, most of them were laughing, or chatting earnestly. She didn't sense any hovering men about to loom over her and make suggestive remarks, which is what she had always supposed would happen.

Just then something lightly hit her head. She raised a hand to stroke her hair, hoping there wasn't a wasp or a bee lodged there.

A peanut fell to the wooden floor.

Behind her she heard a man laughing. When she turned to look she saw that there were in fact two men, sitting opposite one another, both pursing their lips, hiding their mirth and looking down guiltily at the table where there was an open packet of peanuts.

Bloody jokers!

Lisa had come across these types before. Young boys, probably worked in some office in the City, in finance or advertising, with more money than brains, flashy suits and cars, and thought they could pick you up and get a shag just by winking at you.

She gave them a flinty look and turned back to watch a group of people at a nearby table draining their glasses. She gathered her drink, coat and bag ready to pounce on the table for her and Tony.

Another nut hit her, bouncing off her cheek and falling into her glass. It floated on the sparkling surface of the drink. She gazed at it for a moment before spinning round on them in fury.

'Look, you pair of half-wit morons, keep your nuts to yourself!'

The two men fell back upon their banquette, howling with laughter. The taller of the two poked a finger towards his friend. 'You heard the woman, Justin. She has no desire to see your nuts.'

Lisa felt a fool now. She had handed it to them on a plate. Was this how men picked you up in bars, throwing nuts cos they knew that any repost would always have a sleazy double meaning?

She turned away and saw other people had taken the table she was waiting for. On top of that someone had swiped the stool she had been perching on before, so she'd have to remain standing, which was awkward and embarrassing.

She waited in the middle of the pub, clutching her glass, bag and coat, trying to smile and in fact feeling a total prat.

She made up her mind. She'd phone Tony at the salon to apologise.

She moved towards the bar to put down the glass and get her phone.

A hand slid round her waist. She felt so cross and humiliated, Lisa was ready to land the bloke a good upper cut.

'You weren't going to stand me up, were you, Miss Lisa?'

Tony stood beside her, smiling and holding out a hand to help her.

'Come on.' He took her coat and slung it over one arm. 'There's a little corner over there where we can have a nice quiet time together.'

As they walked past the table where the peanut boys sat, Lisa said loudly to Tony. 'You see that fellow there, with the brown hair. My friend went out with him once. He's called Justin and he's got pubic crabs.'

Tony exploded with laughter in a way that made Lisa again swing towards her original idea that he was gay.

'You've never seen him before in your life, have you?' Tony stuck his tongue into his cheek and gave her an old fashioned look.

Lisa giggled.

'He was throwing peanuts at me.' She slid along the leatherette bench. 'I owed him one.'

'Oooooh!' Tony winced. 'I certainly hope I never accidentally cross your path when you're in a mood.'

'I'm not in a mood. I just don't like people taking the mick.'

'You're not all you seem, are you Miss Lisa?'

Lisa shifted in her seat. What was he getting at? Did he recognise her from when she was a kid? Could he spot that she was a fake?

'I am what I am, Tony,' she said, sipping her drink. 'As Shirley Bassey says.'

'Donna Summer, actually. It's originally from *La Cage Aux Folles.*'

Gotcha, bang to rights, thought Lisa. Queer as a plaid rabbit. What straight men knew which songs came from which musicals, or were intimate with the oeuvre of Donna Summer?

'Talking of French, Tony, can you tell me exactly what oeuvre means? I know people use it on the radio for a group of songs, but I always thought it meant an egg.'

'Not egg.' Tony did his queeny laughing thing again. 'It means work. Or in this context, a body of work, Miss Ditz.'

Miss Ditz, indeed! So there it was, Lisa had been lured here by Tony just so he could have a camp evening. She supposed he thought of her as some kind of hilarious fag-hag. How very disappointing.

'You always been a hair-dresser then, Tony?'

'No.' Tony looked at her with a curiously suspicious look. 'Why do you ask?'

'Just wondering. Seems quite an effeminate job for a man with such a physique.'

'I used to be an actor.'

'You joking me?' Lisa had always wanted to meet actors. 'Were you ever in anything?'

'No. I just sat at home doing nothing for several years while I called myself an actor.'

Lisa was astonished at how cross Tony seemed. But then he laughed and it was suddenly all right again. 'Of course I was in things. Otherwise why say I was an actor?'

'I thought that's what most actors did,' she said. 'Sit at home doing nothing and call themselves actors.'

Tony didn't seem to get Lisa's joke, so she tried to explain it a bit.

'...Waiting for the phone to ring and all that.'

Lisa really regretted coming here. Tony seemed so different once out of the salon. He was all tricky and edgy.

'So, Tony, were you ever in a soap or anything famous?'

He seemed to relax a bit as he replied: 'I played some spies and things like that. I was in *The Bill* a couple of times. And *Casualty*. The usual suspects.'

'*The Usual Suspects*?' How thrilling, thought Lisa, to meet someone who had worked with Kevin Spacey. 'You were in a Hollywood film?'

'It's just a phrase love—the usual suspects. In acting that means bread and butter stuff like *The Bill* and *Casualty*.'

Lisa felt stupid again. She had no idea what he meant by bread and butter stuff. Did that mean chefs programmes or something? But *Casualty* she knew, and that was a popular enough show.

'Were you a doctor or did you die? Or were you one of those people who fall off a ladder in the first scene and get covered in blood and stuff?'

'The latter. I played a middle European immigrant who had an industrial accident, but no one could understand me as I couldn't speak English, so they got the diagnosis wrong cos they didn't know I was a haemophiliac.'

Lisa buckled. Tony had given her just the opening she was waiting for.

'And are you?' she said with as much suggestion as she could muster.

'Am I what?'

'That word you just said.'

'A haemophiliac? No? I was acting a role. Why would you think I was a haemophiliac just cos I played one?'

'Cos of the way you like Donna Summer and know about musicals and things.'

Tony sat there blinking for a few seconds, then gave another roar of laughter.

'Haemophiliac does not mean the same thing as homosexual, any more than a garrotte resembles a carrot.'

'Whatever,' said Lisa, knowing that Tony was making a joke against her now but not being able to get it. 'Well? Are you?'

'No, Lisa. I am neither a haemophiliac, nor a homosexual.'

'Silly!' Feeling a total fool, Lisa tried to make light of her mistake. 'What I meant, Tony, was are you a carrot?'

Lisa could hear that the nasty raucous boys at the adjacent table had shut up. She knew they had to be listening to her conversation with Tony. At any moment she expected that the peanuts would again start flying.

Perhaps Tony really was straight, single and available. Maybe he really was making a pass at her by inviting her for this drink. The more she thought about it the more she truly liked the idea of leaving Max and getting a proper boyfriend, a handsome one this time. And not having to pretend all the time, and say supportive things and agree with everything he said, and being able to go out and work again and be with people and have tea breaks and sometimes go to the local Thai restaurant for girly nights out.

In fact her heart leaped with joy at the thought.

So she pressed on, trying to work out why exactly Tony had asked her here, trying to close the loopholes, trying to make it all happen the way she wanted. 'Do you live on your own then, Tony?'

'I do, actually. If it's any of your business, Miss.'

'I'm not being nosey, Tony, I promise. I just wanted to know. It makes a difference, doesn't it? I don't want some irate girlfriend or boyfriend or wife coming after me with a hatchet for going out with you like this.'

'And yet, Miss Lisa, you'd think nothing of putting me at the mercy of an irate Max Latham?'

Before she could reply, Tony's phone rang. It emitted an urgent bleeping noise, like some emergency call for a doctor to rush into the resuscitation unit or something. Lisa noticed that quite a few people looked round.

'Now?' Tony spoke quietly into the phone, as though begging for privacy. 'But Carol...'

Carol! Who was Carol? A wife? A girlfriend?

Lisa took the opportunity to glance round and glare at Justin and his peanut throwing friend, but they were gone.

When she turned back, Tony was snapping his phone shut.

'Look, Lisa, I'm awfully sorry but something has popped up and I'm going to have to love you and leave you.'

Lisa bridled.

So that was that.

There was someone, and she was called Carol.

This whole episode had been a bad idea. Beneath her serene smile and perfectly drawn make-up, she was seething. To think she had almost endangered her comfy domestic set-up for this!

And the horrid queeny man was sneaking in here behind the back of some poor girlfriend called Carol who, for all Lisa knew, was sitting at home over a rapidly drying-out burnt supper which she had lovingly prepared for Tony's return home.

Lisa toyed with her drink. She would play it cool. Show him she didn't care one way or another about his awful lying life.

'Well, you can leave me, all right, Tony, but I don't know about love me.' She raised her glass and shot a lethally cold smile in his direction. 'As you well know, if you so much as tried anything like that, Max would have your bollocks for a pair of clackers.'

'Don't be like that,' said Tony, displaying a hang-dog expression. 'You know I adore you, duck. But you see...' He hesitated before continuing. 'It's my dog. He's not well. That was my neighbour phoning to say he's been sick all over the landing. So I REALLY have to go.' He stood up, stooping to print a tender kiss on her cheek. 'I really do hope we can do this again, soon. Truly.'

Oh God! He really did want to be with her. There she was with her silly old suspicious mind.

'If you really mean that, Tony,' said Lisa, feeling dizzy from the way his slightly rough chin scuffed her cheek, 'you'll invite me round for a drink at your place one evening.' Embarrassed by the blush rising up her throat, Lisa reached down into her handbag and pulled out her packet of cigarettes.

Tony reached down and gripped her wrist. 'You can't do that in here, you know.'

He took the cigarette packet from her.

'Oh,' she gasped, mithered by his attention. 'I'm going doolally. I meant to get out my mobile phone.'

'I'll have a fag, anyhow.' Tony pulled a couple of cigarettes from the packet and slid them into his jacket pocket before dropping it back into her open bag. He did that thing people did, miming with their finger and thumb. 'Phone me.'

He announced his phone number, while Lisa keyed it into her phone.

'Call me tomorrow, Missy, won't you? About 11. Tea break time.'

When he was gone, she wasn't sure if the agitation she felt was disappointment, anger or excitement. She wondered too about the odd set-up where his neighbour knew so much about his dog. Could Tony be lying? Was this Carol really refusing to mop up the sick or was she a girlfriend, bored and lonely and wondering why her fellah was late home?

Lisa drained her glass. There was a first! Being deserted by a man who preferred to go home and wipe up dog vomit.

She looked at her watch. Not enough time to go home to Max's and come out again to meet him at the restaurant, but just too long to walk there and sit waiting for him. Nor was she going to sit here on her own in the pub like a twit.

She visited the ladies room first and touched up her make-up. There was a slightly pink area where Tony's rough skin had scraped some of her foundation. She ran her fingers over it, oddly excited.

When she got outside into the street, London was going through that moment of twilight when the streetlights are on, but there was still some light in the sky and a slight mist hung around the trees, so that visibility was murky.

She crossed a small stretch of the common, heading for the main road. She was glad that it was not any darker. This walk would have been terrifying alone at night, despite the rows of jaunty coloured lights hung in the trees around the pub, and their cheerful bobbing reflections in the nearby paddling pool.

She phoned Max's number as she walked, but he must have turned his phone off again, for it went straight to machine. She remembered he had said he was going to visit that American writer, Tess Brandon. Lisa knew Tess's flat was next door to Martin and Sarah's, and therefore it wasn't so far from here. On the night of the awful dinner she remembered sitting in Max's Jag and coming along the very road she was walking on, before swinging down the tree lined avenue opposite, making two turns and then they were there.

Well, it couldn't be that hard to find. With any luck Max would be inside, his car outside, and she could wait and accompany him up to La Coupole.

If Max wasn't there, Lisa felt sure Tess wouldn't turn her away. Though she remembered that Max had said Lisa was Tess's type or something to that effect, implying the American was a bit on the butch side. But then Max thought Hillary Clinton was on the butch side, and everyone knew she was married with children.

Lisa turned into a curving road, where the lighting was slightly more subdued, and increased her pace. She had read in a mag once that your chances of being sprung upon by muggers were so much less if you walked in a positive, determined way.

After a few hundred yards she heard footsteps behind her and walked faster again. As the footsteps closed on in on her Lisa's heart started to pump so violently that she could barely hear. When the person was almost touching her, Lisa flung herself backwards into someone's garden hedge, ready to fight for her life.

A woman, laden with shopping bags, overtook her, and gave a strange look as she turned in through a front gate a few houses ahead.

Stupid, thought Lisa. Of course people walk home quickly when they have shopping. She herself had practically sprinted home when the plastic straps of the bags had started cutting into her fingers, back in those good old days when she had her own flat. She took a few deep breaths as she wiped down the back of her clothes, making sure she was not covered with dust and cobwebs from the bush. She was about to walk on when her eye caught sight of movement a few yards away.

It was a couple of men talking earnestly in the front seats of a car.

Oh god, no.

This was all she needed.

The peanut throwers.

Momentarily the man who wasn't Justin turned and caught Lisa's eye. Before she had a chance to turn away she saw him say something. Then both men laughed.

Lisa clutched her bag tight to her front and walked on.

She knew where Tess lived. It could only be a few minutes' walk away.

As she strode along she heard the car's engine rev up.

Those bastards were trailing her.

She walked faster.

She turned the corner and started to run, but the car turned after her.

After a minute or two the driver pulled level and slowed down, curb-crawling her.

Lisa turned her face forward, tilting her chin up. She did everything to look as assured as if she was on a fashion runway, never once letting them catch her eye.

Justin, in the driver's seat, wound down the window and stuck out his head, making lewd gestures at her with his tongue.

Lisa stopped and with her hands on her hips said firmly: 'Shove off, you pair of wankers.'

The other man was laughing, his lips peeled back tight over a leering mouth. His eyes were mere slits, but Lisa could see they were looking right at her.

But she could also see that she was now in the right road and was very near the safety of Tess's flat. Plus, halleluiah, she could see Max's Jag parked outside.

Hoorah! Hoorah! Hoorah! He was already inside with Tess.

All Lisa needed to do was bring Max out and set him on them and they'd soon stop this horrible behaviour.

She started to run, the car keeping up with her. They were so near her, that, as she ran, Lisa could hear the slurping noises the men were making. When she reached the door to Tess's flat she stopped and scanned for the bell-push.

A car door opened behind her.

She grabbed the post box flap, ready to call up, but to her amazement the front door was on the latch and opened with no effort.

She came into the hall, slammed the door behind her and turned down the snib.

The hall floor was strewn with junk mail. Lisa remembered that used to happen to her hall in Peckham too, whenever the downstairs neighbour went off on holiday.

She peered up the steep stairs.

Someone was certainly there.

'Come on up!' A man's voice.

Not Max's she thought, but from the proximity of his car Max was either up there or had popped next door to pick up whatever he was picking up.

She was glad anyhow to be off the street and away from those nasty men.

Lisa ran up the stairs and into Tess's flat.

INTERNAL ONLY–personal note

Attn: D. I. GEOFF BUTLER

REF Jane Grimshaw Murder

Geoff,

Just knocking off for the night and need to bring you up to speed with
what gives re the Grimshaw investigation.

As we discussed in the canteen it's obvious there's more than one
perp on this case: 1. The methods of picking the women up, the holding and dumping. 2. Indications within the PM results, the finger
mark bruising round the face etc, clear evidence that she was being
held by one person, while another worked on pressing the carotid,
(presumably they'd read too many murder mysteries "Death by pressure point–The Perfect Murder Method" and all that bollocks. Christ,
if you don't have medical or martial arts training, we all know that
that one is harder to pull off than boring someone to death, and probably takes as long) They obviously discovered this for themselves and
eventually resorted to using the penknife or whatever it was which
caused the fatal nick in the artery. I reckon when we get hold of the
car which brought her to the Common we're going to find blood. Don't
know about you, Geoff, but I'd bet they thought they'd worked the carotid trick, but the woman stirred back to life while they were taking
her off to unload her into the makeshift grave.

We've still got nothing on the location or type of place where they've
been keeping these women before they kill and dump. As you know the
PM only gave us that the hygiene wasn't up to much, and that there
were rust particles on the skin and clothing, indicating they were kept
somewhere with lots of rust. Could be an old lock up or shed with
rusty sides, Nissan hut, garden shed made from old corrugated iron–
something like that. Perhaps an ancient shipping container, though in
this country we tend only to find these in pretty good nick with pre-
painted interiors. Maybe they used some windowless off-the-road dead

vehicle, which hasn't passed an MOT since forever, a van, a pick-up, a lorry?

Nothing we can find attached to Martin Beaumont in any way comes anywhere close to this description.

It's interesting that Jane Grimshaw was last seen alive in the pub on the Common, and a week later her body was dumped within 500 metres of where she was last seen. There was a similar pattern with Marina Sutton, last year, but on a different common. Does this mean the rusty place is somewhere near, or maybe somewhere between the two commons? Or is this all a red herring because, as we know, commons are notorious for this kind of crime, along with gay cottaging, vagrancy, etcetera, purely because there are so many quiet nooks and crannies, with bushes, thickets etc obscuring the view?

NEW STUFF IN TODAY

First we've checked out the keys which were found in the ditch under Grimshaw's body. These did not belong to the flat where Jane Grimshaw lived, nor to any locks within the library where she worked. Possible that they could be the keys to a boyfriend's flat but "Miss Stern Librarian" poo-pooed this theory with a flustered blush which means, I think, that Grimshaw was not a man-loving kind of gal. Mind you, that's not to say the keys couldn't belong to a lover of the female gender, but the old bat seemed to think that Miss Grimshaw definitely lived alone and had no current romantic connections.

Whatever, there is a strong possibility that the keys fell out of the pocket of one of the perps during the corpse dumping exercise. That's where my money is, anyhow, mate.

Once we get hold of the perp, I reckon the keys will slip into his front door like fingers into a glove (and I am nor referring to the OJ Simpson pantomime)

Bigger turn-ups for us came today from forensic investigation of Martin Beaumont's bank accounts and credit cards.

One debit card showed up a payment on a self storage lock- up in Battersea. There is a deposit plus a month in advance. This immediately caught my eye and I sent Jim over to investigate. To his astonishment the actual lock-up paid for by MB's bank card was activated while Jim was sitting chatting to the Self Storage Warehouse manager in the warehouse office. The manager was alerted by some kid who showed the key-holder round, and thus Jim was able to watch the whole fucking thing live on the head honcho's office CCVT.

A person in possession of the key to the Beaumont lock-up came to the desk, and was taken to the unit. There was a momentary hiatus with the password pin code or something, but then the confident fellow let himself into the unit paid for by Martin Beaumont, and stayed inside it for quite a lengthy while. When he came out he appeared flustered, and left the building in a marked manner.

But Geoff—You'll never guess who it was!

It's too fucking marvellous to be true.

It was ~ ~ ~

one moment for you to have a try at guessing ~ ~ ~

Any ideas?

Cue Cilla Black to pop out and shout: Surprise, Surprise!

It was that bloody pompous old fart, Max Latham!

How about that for a fucking turn up!

The number of times that wheezing fat fuck has wrecked our cases in court, Geoff, or had us stuffed over a barrel due to some ruddy legal technicality, makes me lose it so badly. I have to say I could not be happier that after all these years of him stuffing US, we've actually finally got something on HIM!

Anyhow, for all the old bugger's legal know-how and his savoir fair of the laxities and loopholes of the Law, the stupid fat arsehole actually told the boy his name was Martin Beaumont, right there on camera! We've got the video on file here at the station. So, even if nothing else comes out of this case, we've got Max Latham on the rack over a little episode of fraud and impersonation.

You thought THAT was good! ~ ~ ~

~ So now, Here comes the really interesting stuff.

Once Latham had left the warehouse, Jim took a look round the actual storage room, and found that all the contents of the Beaumont house, which Martin Beaumont had told us were stolen by burglars, are in there—the TVs, the computers, radios—the lot.

But bingo—Geoff!

What the fuck did he find lying on the floor but some blood-stained clothing and an old carpet with bloody, mud-covered torn bin liners. And to round the picture off—the whole scene was crawling with larvae. So that gives us DNA and, from the maggot department, a pretty good chance of dating the blood spill.

The SOCO team are down there now, photographing, bagging and sifting through it all.

One thing that occurred to me was that both Jane Grimshaw and Marina Sutton had their flats burgled during the days after they went missing. I don't know—could there be a link here? I've got the SOCO boys looking out for other things which may have come from either woman's place.

I really think we're onto something here, Geoff, and for my money I KNOW that somehow or other Latham is in on it. It's obvious to me now why Beaumont went to pieces in the interview room in front of us, and only too clear now why Latham couldn't pull him together.

What if the pair of them are in this thing together???

What do you think?

After Jim phoned us through all the details from the storage I thought it all through and acted fast.

So we managed to put a tail on Latham.

Last heard of (if you'd "Adam and Eve" it!) taking a solitary drink down at the Adam and Eve by the river. But from now on they're going to keep in touch with the Murder Room and let you all know where he is every second of the day—even if he's just taking a dump in a public convenience.

Keep me informed, Geoff, won't you.

If you find yourself in a position where you have enough to pull in that fat bastard I want to be there in person to watch his smug pompous face when the sweat breaks out.

Anyhow as you know we got onto this lock-up because it was paid for by Beaumont bank debit card.

Now— While Mr Latham was rifling this storage unit, after two dead days, the same fucking bank account came alive again in of all places the South of bloody France.

Now, of course we have Mr Beaumont in custody so we're sure as fuck it ain't him.

Trouble with these sodding chip and pin cards means that anyone who knows the pin can use the ruddy card. So it doesn't really get us much further. But it does appear that this time the card was used by Beaumont's wife—who we have tracked to a hotel in Nice, and who must have missed the whole bloody farrago of her husband's little activities during the last 48 hours.

The money was spent on a flight from Nice to London today, booked in the name of Mrs Sarah Beaumont. She'll be arriving at Heathrow any minute.

Poor bloody bitch—probably has no idea what her husband and his fat friend have been up to while she was away soaking up the sun.

PS—As I write this I just got news in that not only our lot, but also Mrs B's sister, who was over from Australia, had earlier this week been trying to contact Mrs B for days with no luck—but Mrs B has come back to the UK today because her mother is dying.

Phone me.

Bill

17

Pavane

*Slow sequential dance in varying
measures and different sections*

SARAH HAD FLOWN to Heathrow on the first available flight
and gone straight to the hospital. But it was too late.
Her mother had died while she was in mid air.

She had sat for a while in the curtained cubicle with her
mother's body, holding her hand and chatting, but choosing
not to look at the grey, serene visage which only dimly resembled the active living woman.

When her mother's arm was cold she left her and went to
face the nurses.

She hated the way they stood in a gaggle round the desk,
chatting about the mascara bargains to be had at Boots. When
they saw Sarah approach they put on sanctimonious faces,

and spoke to her slowly in quiet sympathetic voices as though she was simpleton rather than a person who had just lost the great love of her life.

'Come this way,' cooed the ward sister, guiding Sarah by the elbow into the neon-lit office. 'Would you like me to get you a glass of water?'

So there were the NHS cuts for you! In the old days it would have been a cup of tea.

'I'll leave you on your own with this for a while, shall I?'

Sarah bit her tongue and prevented herself replying: 'I don't know, sister, shall you, or shall you not?'

'Will you be all right on your own, or should I phone someone?' Again the cloying tone. 'Your husband perhaps.'

Martin! It was all Sarah could do to stop herself laughing aloud. How could she explain that one away? "Well, sister, my husband currently thinks he murdered me and buried me under the patio, so probably best not"?

'Thank you.' Sarah shook her head. 'I prefer to be alone.'

The hospital management had ways of dealing with grief. They set you forms to fill and gave you a handful of "important" leaflets to read. One of these was for grief counselling, but Sarah could not imagine going to some total stranger and trying to explain her terrible loss.

Breaking the rules and using her mobile, she phoned her sister in Sydney to deliver the bad news. Suzanne burst into loud sobs.

Sarah marvelled. How did her sister manage to do this to order? For Sarah crying now would be impossible. What she felt, sitting in this dismal room was another emotion altogether, with an altogether different physiology. At first she was numb. Then another sensation took over, rather as though she had been kicked in the stomach and winded, and that she was having to struggle to keep breathing. There were no tears, though somewhere, deep inside, a dark quivering feeling like fury rumbled.

When, an hour later, the form filling was complete and she had contacted the funeral directors, Sarah was informed by a hard-faced nurse, wearing the usual sympathetic mask, that she would have to leave smartish, as they needed the bed her mother was "occupying", and the porters were already here to take "the body" down to the morgue.

Exhausted and stunned, Sarah said one last goodbye and made for the lift.

Once inside she leaned back against the shiny aluminium wall, gazing up at the numbers above the doors lighting up as the lift plunged downwards.

She felt dizzy, almost drunk from the events of the last week.

The lift stopped at 3.

The doors opened and closed.

'Are you feeling all right?'

A nurse had come in and was looking hard at Sarah.

'It's just that you look rather pale.'

'I'm very tired.'

'Understandably.' The nurse gave her a sympathetic look. 'Did you report him in the end? Fosco, wasn't it?'

Sarah looked at the nurse blankly. What on earth was she talking about? Count Fosco? *The Woman in White?*

'You'd better get home, I think.' The nurse spoke guardedly. 'And take it easy.'

Well of course that was what she was going to do! What did the woman expect her to do when her mother had just died— spend the night line-dancing?

'Take care. Don't let anyone bang into you, will you?' the nurse called as Sarah walked out of the lift into the bustling hospital entrance hall. Then she remembered that the nurse was the same one who had attended her in the emergency cubicle after Martin had stabbed her, and who had tenderly cleaned the mud and blood from her skin, before applying a dressing to her wound.

Sarah hesitated, wondering whether to go back and thank the nurse, explain about her mother and why she had been confused.

But she realised, too, that that could only lead to mischief, so instead she made hastily for the exit, desperate to get home and lie down.

Home?

Where was home exactly?

Could she really count the house in Clapham which she had once shared with Martin? Or had she relinquished ownership when she walked out on him? Although the desertion hadn't taken quite the course she had originally intended.

No, she couldn't go there.

Actually—Sarah owned half of the damned house, didn't she? She had paid the mortgage, just as he had. Really, as Sarah perceived it, Martin was in no position to take umbrage if she walked back into the front door and presented herself as a living breathing wife, sans mud and bin-liners. If anything, he ought to be utterly delighted to find that he was not in fact a murderer.

Plus there was her current cash situation. Sarah had used up all of her cash now, first on travelling to the Riviera, then on the un-slept in hotel room. Also she owed the credit card for the exceedingly expensive flight home, and the taxi ride to the hospital.

There was no question of trudging round in the gloaming searching for a cheap dingy hotel in which to spend the grim week preparing for her mother's funeral. Sarah knew she couldn't cope with that, either financially or emotionally.

Sarah made her way to the nearest stop and took the bus home.

The light was fading as she alighted at the stop beside the Common. Darkness loomed along the avenues of trees, while flicks of colour danced like windblown confetti in the black water of the rippling paddling pool.

To be sure of some comfort food, Sarah walked briskly through the small mini-market on the corner and bought herself a pint of milk and some tea, with a packet of biscuits and some chocolate, plus a loaf for the morning toast.

When she reached the front door of her home, as she took the key from her pocket she thought again.

Perhaps this was a really bad idea. She felt weak and vulnerable and couldn't cope with an emotional scene.

But all the lights were out, so it did look as though Martin wasn't home.

Quietly she turned the key in the door.

She stepped inside, and flicked the light in the hall. The bulb had gone.

She was momentarily shocked by the murky emptiness of the place, then remembered that she herself had paid the removal men to take out all the valuables and electronics.

She stood and listened. It didn't sound as though there was anyone in.

Somehow the darkness seemed appropriate for her current sadness, the numbness and that tumbling feeling in her gut.

She did not want to give Martin, if he was in, warning of her arrival. So, without turning on any other lights, Sarah quietly dropped the shopping in the kitchen and made her way straight up the stairs.

She was relieved to find the bedroom was empty.

The only things the removal people had taken from the bedroom were the clock radio, and a small TV but it too seemed oddly bare.

With a sigh Sarah flopped down onto the bed and kicked off her shoes.

How petty and ludicrous her row with Martin seemed now, under the lowering shadow of her mother's death.

She shut her eyes, longing for sleep to dull the pain—physical and mental.

Through the wall she could hear voices coming from the next door flat.

A woman and a man, murmuring.

In fact she supposed they were probably talking perfectly loudly, but the muffling effect of the cavity wall insulated the sound and made it seem as though they were only whispering.

Tess must have a visitor.

Sarah turned over. She yearned for true silence, but wondered whether such a state was possible. Wasn't that what John Cage had tried to show in his 4 minutes 33 seconds for silent piano? Even "silence" always consisted of a medley of sounds. No such thing as silence.

Not for the living, at any rate.

Ironically, now that she was away from the hospital and all the nurses with their phoney empathy, the physical pain of the stab wound in her side had returned with a vengeance. On the plane and in the hospital she had been quite unaware of it.

She rolled over in the other direction, taking the pressure off her side, and reached down into her bag to get a pain-killer.

Again she was filled with outrage that, after she had been stabbed, Martin had done nothing to help her or to get medical assistance. The little spineless bastard. She hoped he would be sorry when he saw what he had done to her.

Sarah shut her eyes and tried to relax.

The conversation next door seemed to have stopped. Sarah wondered whether she should phone Tess now to ask her what had been going on in her absence, but considered that perhaps things next door had gone silent because Tess and whoever the bloke was were kissing, or something equally embarrassing to interrupt with an unexpected phone call.

She closed her eyes.

What was it the Beatles had sung? "Lay down all thought, surrender to the void"?

But the fleeting silence was filled with yet another annoying noise. It sounded like a kind of metallic scraping but had a regular rhythm behind it. It seemed to be coming from the back garden.

Hauling herself up from the bed Sarah made her way to the window and looked out.

There was someone out there in the dark, in her back garden, digging.

And it was not Martin. Far too fat for him.

In the gloaming Sarah could not make out the man's features but from the shape of his rear end it looked a lot like Max Latham!

She stepped to the side, watching him through the net curtain.

The man certainly had been hard at it. He had turned over nearly all of the flower beds.

What on earth was going on?

Was he looking for her body?

Had Martin confessed to Max, his lawyer, and sent him to find her and then to dispose of her corpse?

How very rum!

Sarah pondered. Should she let him carry on digging right through to Australia in his quest to find her? Or simply walk out into the garden and go "Boo!"?

Max stood up, rubbed the base of his spine and wiped the sweat from his face.

Sarah heard him curse.

She dropped the curtain as he looked up. She felt sure that momentarily they caught eyes. She ducked back behind the window frame.

Where was Martin, anyhow, that he'd just sent Max here like this? Had Martin been here earlier to let him in, or did Max have his own key?

With one eye to the edge of the window she now watched as Max flung down the spade and walked speedily towards the house. He was looking up at the window, heading towards her.

Sarah moved back towards the centre of the bedroom.

The game was up.

She sat on the end of the bed, facing the door, waiting for the trudge of Max's footfall on the stairs, ready to face the music.

But instead she heard Max's footsteps hurry across the kitchen, then shuffle briskly along the hall.

Then the front door slammed.

She crept to the front window and looked down.

Max trotted swiftly across the road, and brushing his suit down with both hands. Looking almost panicked, he pulled his car keys from his pocket and dropped them on the pavement, with a jangle. He stooped, again rubbing the small of his back, and quickly snatched the keys from the gutter. After clambering into his car and starting the engine, Max looked up at the front of the house.

Sarah ducked back behind the curtain.

She heard the car drive off at speed.

How mysterious!

Sarah dialled Martin's mobile number, ready to have it out with him.

It switched straight to machine.

Sarah looked at her watch. Much too late to phone the office. No one would be there. Certainly those two lazy slime-balls would be down at the pub by now, knocking back the tequila or Pimms, or whatever it was they deemed to be the "in" drink.

Too late also to try Max's office. She knew he had a very efficient woman who worked for him, but by this time surely she too would have packed up and gone home.

Despite the silence, Sarah was again tempted to phone next door and ask Tess what she had heard from Martin over the last few days, and also whether she had noticed how often Max had been here. She knew she certainly wasn't going to be able to sleep until she had a few answers, in particular would the big greasy pompous porpoise be coming back here later tonight?

She had to phone Tess. And if Tess picked up, Sarah would suggest nipping round. If not she would have to leave it till morning.

Sarah went downstairs and found the desk diary, and out fell another of Tess's ubiquitous business cards. That woman handed these things out right left and centre.

She stood by the phone and dialled.

While she stood there listening to the phone ringing out— with the ever so faint echo coming through the wall from next door, Sarah studied the card.

The other phone numbers on the card were mobile numbers. Fancy having two mobiles! But when Sarah looked at them it made sense. One number was local, the other Tess's American 'cell', as they called them.

Sarah looked hard at the cell number. Wasn't that the same one that had come up on her own phone attached to the weird text message?

Sarah ran upstairs to get her mobile from her handbag.

Just then she heard the clatter of footsteps going down the stairs from Tess's flat.

She looked out of the window and waited.

She heard the door open.

If it was Tess, Sarah decided she would open the window and call out, invite her in for a quick drink.

But it was not her at all.

It was Lisa.

Max's Lisa!

Sarah watched as the half-witted girl looked across the road. When she realised that Max's car had gone, Lisa threw her arms up in a dramatic gesture, then stood for a while with her hands on her hips, dramatically shaking her head. You could almost hear the gears grinding in the poor girl's brain.

Although she felt rather sorry for her, Sarah decided against asking Lisa in. She couldn't face all the explaining—why the house was stripped of the TV etc, where she had been, why she had come back—her heart thumped—the death of her mother.

She took a deep breath and perched on the window sill.

What a mess.

She wished Martin would come home.

Where was he?

What was going on?

Even though she might well get some answers from Lisa, Tess would be much easier to deal with, and not be a direct conduit of information to that ghastly Max Latham.

While still watching the street, Sarah pulled out her mobile phone and switched to the text message.

At the same moment Lisa stepped back onto the pavement and caught her heel in the drain cover.

Sarah heard the crack. She also heard Lisa curse.

The stiletto heel lay jammed in the grate.

Lisa screwed the heelless shoe back onto her foot. After yanking the heel from the gutter she limped along, all the while stabbing at her mobile phone.

The sharp tone of Lisa's whining echoed along the street. Sarah could imagine the earful Max was getting.

She returned to inspect her own phone and scrolled through the recently received texts: IN GRAVE DANGER. GIVE POLICE THIS CELL NUMBER. FIND ME. Sarah held the card next to the phone and compared the number, digit by digit.

It was the one.

The text had come from Tess's US cell-phone.

Tess? Why?

She scrolled down to the next text: HELP HELP HELP TEXT ONLY.

How bizarre.

What was all this about? Some outlandish method of getting a story moving, perhaps?

Sarah would certainly need to follow this up.

Or might Tess be playing some mad game with her, perhaps on behalf of Martin?

She could still hear someone moving around next door. She presumed this would be Tess herself. No need to text or phone. She would simply arrive at the door, present the text message and demand an explanation.

Sarah saw Lisa, still limping along, slip her phone into her pocket. Instantly it rang and Lisa answered.

Simultaneously Sarah noticed, further back along the road, a car pull out, heading in the same direction that Lisa was walking. The car was travelling unusually slowly. A kerb crawler?

Although it might seem mad, to Sarah it appeared that the car was tailing Lisa, who, at the same moment put her mobile back into her pocket and glanced back.

She had almost reached the end of the street.

At the same moment the car shot forward, and sped a few hundred yards past Lisa. Then suddenly the driver slammed on the brakes and the car reversed in her direction.

Sarah watched the dumb-show.

Lisa threw her hands into the air and shouted at the driver. She was too far away now for Sarah to be able to hear exactly what was being said.

Lisa took a step forward off the kerb.

A hand shot out of the driver's window, grabbing Lisa by the wrist.

Lisa violently shook her head and pulled her hand away.

Sarah didn't like what she was seeing. Lisa might be a half-wit but she was being harassed by someone with a lot more strength than her.

Sarah grabbed her shoes. She would stop this, scare away the man in the car, then ask Lisa if she needed any help, before calling on Tess.

Shoes in her hand, Sarah ran down stairs and out into the street.

But by the time she reached the pavement, both the car and Lisa were gone.

18

Lindy-Hop

Improvised American dance featuring elements of
jazz, Charleston, tap, swingout and breakaway.

TESS HAD BEEN debating for hours whether or not to drink from the bottle of water. It was a 2 litre pale plastic bottle with a shop label announcing it to be Scottish Mineral Water, and seemed authentic. But what if it was something else? Piss for example. Or perhaps it really was bona fide water but they had put a few tabs of a date rape drug into it.

Tess knew all about date rape drugs—GHB, roofies, Halcion, special K and the rest. She'd used them, in a fictional way naturally, in her books. And the research she had done meant she knew all there was to know about all the effects of the Benzodiazepines. They'd knock her out. First she'd lose the control of her muscles, then pass out. When she was unconscious, it would be exactly as though she was under anaesthetic, after all that's what most of these drugs were actually intended for—knocking people out for an operation, or as a pre-med. Special K was an anaesthetic for animals, for fuck's sake. If there was anything like that in the water, while she was out cold anybody could do whatever they liked with her apparently lifeless body, and she'd know nothing about it.

Afterwards she'd suffer anterograde amnesia, meaning she wouldn't remember anything that had happened while she was under. But Tess supposed not being able to remember something wouldn't be such a problem if you became dead before you were revived.

Holy shit, at this rate she'd die of dehydration before they came back to rape and kill her.

She picked up the bottle again, and inspected the lid. In the darkness it was impossible to see whether the plastic lid was intact, and therefore it was safe. She twisted. There was no fizz, but then, duh, it was a still water, so any fizzing sound would be a contra indication.

She sniffed.

No smell.

But again that didn't mean anything.

Tess knew the manufacturers of Rohypnol were now obliged to put in a blue dye so that unwary girls in bars would get a bit suspicious when their glass of chardonnay turned green, but who'd be able to see it in this light and anyhow even if it was broad daylight in here the water was in a green bottle.

She dipped a finger in and pulled it out. Gingerly she licked her fingertip.

Holy crap, who would think the feeling of liquid on her lips could be so wonderful? Deprivation obviously did a lot for your senses. She marked this down in her mind. When she got out of this goddamed box and was writing her next book she would use it, that was for sure.

She'd use the lot—the phony detective, the car ride, the garage...

And hey, wouldn't the marketing people be impressed! What a publicity campaign they would be able to mount after this. Her sales would rocket!

Slowly Tess wiped her lips with her tongue, then applied the wet finger again.

When she had finished she screwed the bottle tight shut and put it safely in the corner where she could find it later. Maybe if she did this water/finger routine over a length of time she could put off dehydration and not suffer any evil effects from the water even if that pair of fucks had put some type of incapacitating drug into it.

After almost a day in the murky darkness of the container Tess was hungry too. She rooted about in her clothing. Luckily she was a candy addict and found, squashed behind a wad of business cards at the bottom of a pocket, three pieces of sour apple candy and a wrapped toffee. Like the water, she would refrain from eating them all right now. Instead she sucked slowly on one of them, and then later she could take small licks whenever the hunger pangs became too unbearable.

Tess thoroughly intended to survive this ordeal.

That pair of butt-heads were not going to demoralize her or kill her.

She made mental notes of every sound she heard. Even if she had been unable to see the dial on her watch she knew the time by the sounds which penetrated the container walls.

Between half seven and half eight she heard children chattering, and laughing on their way to school. A lull then till nine, when a spate of cars started up and drove away. She presumed these were housewife/mothers going to the stores and office people, who didn't start till ten, going to work.

Just after ten there had been the fright when she had heard footsteps within the garage come very near the container and she had thought her time was up.

At around one there was another flurry of car activity in the street. People coming home for lunch perhaps, or people on morning shifts finishing and the afternoon shift people leaving.

Tess now presumed that the next visitation by the two fuckheads would occur when they came home from work. Presumably they worked for a living and that was why they weren't in here now, sodomising or slashing her. But she was forced to revise her understanding of the situation when six and seven o'clock had gone by without a hint of anyone coming near the container.

Perhaps it was all part of the clever mental game they were playing. For as the hours went by the dread of their return transformed into something akin to hope. And although she was certainly not looking forward to the men returning to the container, deep inside herself Tess yearned for action, for change, for something which would give her an opportunity to act rather than just sit and think. Thinking she was pretty good at, that was an indisputable fact, but when it came to this murder stuff her imagination was a bit too good.

Tess knew all about the horrible things that were done to the poor victims of psychopaths prior to their deaths, and afterwards too, but she suspected that what happened to her after death wouldn't be of such pressing concern as the stuff she'd know about.

She needed her own game plan. So what were the facts?

There were two people in this kidnapping crap together. One was a very confident, slimy operator. She didn't know very much about the other except for his use of a woollen hat and that he/she could drive. Yes, it had seemed to have been a man, but Tess hadn't got a close up look, like she had got of that goddamned chimney-stack of a fake detective. For all she knew it was some freak woman in the driver's seat.

So the given information was only that they were a pair.

She ran through all the cases she knew where killers worked in tandem. It was not good news: The Hillside Stranglers, The Chicago Rippers, Hindley and Brady, The Wests, Truman Capote's pair of hicks...

It was almost as though when the folie à deux principle kicked in there was no fear, as though a swaggering need to impress one another ratcheted up not only the horror level, but their audacity too.

Henry Lee Lucas killed with a sidekick. Hell, there were even those two old biddies Ray and Faye Copeland, ancient pensioners who killed five men or more and strew their muti-lated bodies over their farm in the wilds of rural Missouri. Even when it was mere murderous kids, or teens, they committed pretty effective killing sprees in pairs: Look at Leopold and Loeb, The Menendez Brothers, those two girls in New Zealand they made the film about, the Columbine High boys, even that Bulger child had been killed by two tiny rug rats who, though their voices weren't even broken, had worked one another up to commit indescribable atrocities on an even smaller infant.

That was the way it happened. When two people had murder in common, the whole operation seemed to escalate as each killer tried to impress the other by outdoing them in revulsion.

So who knew what terrors the two fucks who had trapped her in this container were capable of? They both seemed fit and strong. They also were cool and confident. Well spoken, too, which probably showed an element of education behind them. Not that education ever watered down the creepiness. Lookit, the worst of all serial killers, handsome and audacious Ted Bundy, had got good grades all through high school, been a boy scout, regularly gone to church and attended the University of Washington studying psychology, of all things.

However hard she dug, Tess couldn't think of anything which mitigated the predicament she was in. Nor could she find anything even resembling an Achilles heel within them (or even the container) she could work on to save herself.

Tess feared that this long period of inactivity would dull her senses, and by the time the two bastards arrived to start chapter two of their hi-jinks she would be all in.

Tess looked at the faint glimmer of her watch. The luminosity wasn't going to last much longer. Ten minutes before eight.

She pulled the bottle from the corner and unscrewed the top to have another lip smear before settling down for forty winks.

It was at that moment she heard a noise.

This was not outside in the street.

A door slammed.

Then the clatter of footsteps, coming nearer to the container.

Tess jumped to her feet, stooping instantly to save the water bottle which had toppling on the uneven surface. Dammit. Quite a lot had spilled. If it was good water she had just truly fucked herself.

She applied her ear to the metal wall.

The feet clattered about, coming nearer and stopping, then going and stopping again. It was as though someone was in the garage walking about doing something like hanging washing or putting things into drawers. The noise continued for about three minutes. Then the footsteps stopped and a door closed.

So what was going on?

Was it one of her captors simply coming out here to gloat or to check the locks were still intact?

Or was it someone else? A person maybe fetching something, like a fuse or electric light bulb or a wrench. After all most people kept their tools in the garage. Or maybe they were leaving something in the garage.

Perhaps they were on their way out, going to the cinema, or on their way out because they worked nights? Obviously you could only get into the garage with the correct car sensor, and once inside the person with the car could maybe pick up a key and let themselves into the side door to the house.

Mind you—why would they only have one key between them?

No.

She was barking up the wrong alley here.

Then Tess heard a more distant sound of a heavy door slamming, and footsteps going away along the street. She also heard a squeaky wheel, like you'd get on a stroller.

Tess hastily tried to calculate what time it had been when she had been brought here last night.

About ten, she estimated. Twenty two hours, military time.

That could be relevant.

The librarian, she remembered, had last been seen leaving the pub at around nine thirty.

So, as a potential scenario, that would sure figure.

If she was still here tomorrow morning, Tess decided that she would holler when those daytime footsteps were around. If it was one of her captors, what would be the bother? After all, they already knew she was here. But if it was someone else, someone else who did not know anything about women being held locked up in this rusty old shipping container in their garage...

A loud bang stopped her thoughts. Then another. And another. The sound was metallic. A booming noise.

She listened harder, straining to define the noise. It sounded like the garage door. Perhaps someone was hammering on it, or kicking it.

No.

It was kids playing. Maybe with a soccer ball or something. A ball bouncing against the garage door.

Could she yell loud enough to get their attention?

She moved hastily to the end of the container which stood nearest to the garage door.

'Hey!' she yelled. 'You kids. Call the police. Do you hear me?'

The ball bouncing stopped.

'CALL...' she gathered her breath to let rip, 'THE POLICE! NOW!'

There was a sound of running feet. They were going away.

Much as Tess loathed snotty soccer-playing kids, she prayed that these ones would come up trumps for her.

With any luck they'd be heading for home now, to tell their Moms that some lady in a lock-up wanted them to call the police.

Then she imagined writing the story from their point of view.

They were casually popping a ball against a garage door, when they hear a voice inside crying for help. It would be like being in an adventure film, wouldn't it? 'Call the police!' So they'd run home and...

Then it occurred to Tess, that what they might have heard was just 'Call the police' and the stupid kids would assume that there was someone inside the house telling them that if they didn't stop kicking their goddamned ball against her wall SHE would call the police to them.

Oh Jeez.

That would explain the swiftness of their departure.

Dammit!

Tess sank down onto the floor, her butt bone landing on a hard lump on the floor. She scraped around with the palm of her hand and found that it was her cell phone. It was off, naturally, as it had died on her.

She thought there was no harm in giving it another go. There had certainly been times when the thing had apparently run out of juice but if you switched it off for a while you could get another tiny twinkling of life out of it.

She flipped open and pressed the red "on" button. To her delight the light came on and the phone started going through its start-up regime.

The first thing she saw was that the time was 20:57.

She knew from habit that if the phone made it to 20:58, the minute change, any new messages or texts would register. She stared at the tiny screen, watching the pulsating colon between the numbers, barely daring to breathe.

As the number 7 flipped to 8, three things happened—the phone bleeped, the phone turned off (dead again) and she heard a high pitched electronic whine as the garage door lurched into action.

The groaning of the metal as it swung open, was almost deafening. It was followed by the rev of a car engine, the wheels swinging over the pavement and into the garage.

Holy shit.

They were back.

This was it.

This was really it.

Her moment had come.

She gulped and found she was unable to swallow and her heart thundered like Keith Moon on a drugged-up drum solo.

Fuck, fuck, fuck.

Where was the best place to be when the door opened.

Jesus H Christ almighty.

What could she use?

She would line up beside the door opening and gripping the mobile phone in her palm, slam it down onto the head of...one of them.

Holy fuck.

If she did that it still left her the other one to deal with.

Holy mother fuck.

The car edged into the garage and stopped.

Then came the slow growl of the garage door shutting.

Then nothing.

Nothing at all.

The car doors did not open.

Fuck.

Why not?

They'd have to come out of the car eventually, wouldn't they, those two fucks? They weren't planning to just sit in a fucking car in a garage all night.

Fuck.

Nothing.

Nothing but her heart beating and beating and the blood pumping in her ears till she was almost deaf.

Use the time.

Use the time.

She took a breath, a deep one, then let it out slowly, slowly.

And then another.

Calm, calm, calm.

Get ready.

Get ready.

Still nothing.

What the fuck?

What the holy fuck was going on here?

She pressed her ear hard against the rusting container wall.

She could hear muffled murmuring.

They were planning something.

Shit.

They were sitting inside the car and discussing what they were about to do to her.

Maybe they were jacking off in anticipation of the delights they had planned for her.

Oh fuck.

Holy shit.

Mother-fucking fuck.

What were they doing?

How long was this going to last before they got out of the fucking car?

Then she heard a click as the car locks undid themselves. Then one car door opened.

A footstep on the concrete garage floor. More cushioned than the ones earlier. It sounded like a trainer.

Next the other door opened.

Oh god.

It was going to happen.

They were coming to kill her.

The time had come.

Keep calm, keep calm. Keep your wits. Keep your brain going, keep your humour up, don't let them win. Chances will come.

Tess knew she only had hope if she kept her mind on top of it all.

She could hear more muttering, then a thump against the container, and a sound like a giggle.

High pitched for a guy, but hey, look at Jack Nicholson in *The Shining*, and the Yorkshire Ripper, and the two creeps in *Scream*. Perhaps it was de rigeur for psychopaths to talk soprano these days.

Maybe it was a woman who happened to be part of the gang. It wouldn't be the first time that some jack-off asshole of a bimbo got turned on by murder and other horrible shit. How about Myra Hindley or Rosemary West, or that Canadian bitch, Karla Homolka, who not only joined in with her husband's killing games, but even served up her own sister to him to rape and murder.

Tess shuddered. Just because there was a woman out there it didn't make her feel any safer.

She edged along the container until she knew she was standing parallel to the area where she suspected one of them was leaning with his back against the outside of the container wall.

Her ear right up close to the metal she really could hear a male voice.

He was talking very quietly, so quietly Tess couldn't make out words, just a deep bumble-bee hum.

She moved her ear higher, still barely breathing.

Perhaps they weren't talking. It didn't sound like speech. It was more like they were both humming, a man and a woman together.

Then came a sound which surprised her, like a woman making a kind of sex noise.

What the fuck?

This could not be happening.

There were two people making out only two metal inches from her ear.

Now for the debate...to holler or not to holler?

Unless he was some kind of stage performer there was no way that that sex squeal had come out of a man.

Tess pressed her ear again to the rusty metal. All she could hear was the moist simpering of sexual foreplay.

But then—what if this groaning female was another victim? Could that be possible?

It certainly didn't go to the pattern. Usually killers needed to dispose of one before they got another one in—unless they were collectors, and collectors rarely worked in pairs. Plus they'd have had to make lampshades and bedside tables and masks and things out of the previous carcasses before hauling a new one in. No. From the fact that they had dumped the librarian on the Common, they had shown themselves not to be collectors.

So let's assume one kidnapper, plus a girlfriend. Hey, it took all kinds of things to turn a person on. So where was the other motherfucker? From what Tess could make out there were only two voices in the garage.

Dammit. The other one was still in the car.

For all she knew, the joker in the hat was sitting in the driver's seat jacking off, as he watched his handsome friend make out with a girl while leaning against the container where they held all their potential murder victims. Like some real-life pervy twist on drive-in movies.

Clothing scratched against the metal as the lovers changed position, and a hand slammed against her ear.

Jeez, how disgusting. She could hear them wriggling about and slurping, eating each other's faces off.

Tess made her mind up.

If it was the two monsters, what the fuck? They knew she was in here, so where was the surprise if she started calling for help? If there was only one of them with someone else who perhaps knew nothing, that other someone may be able to do something to help free her.

So finally Tess hollered, hollered like she was yodelling down the Grand Canyon.

When she finished she pressed her ear hard against the container wall to listen out for the reaction.

'What was that?' Definitely a female voice. 'Is someone stuck inside this thing? Hello? Is someone in there?'

'Don't bother,' said the male voice, which Tess instantly recognised as her mock-detective kidnapper, so-called Stuart Adams. 'Ignore it. It's just kids mucking about.'

He clearly dived in for another snog, but the woman pushed him off. Tess could make out the woman's words now as, alarmed by Tess's scream, her tone had utterly changed and acquired a brittle edge.

'No. Seriously. If someone is stuck in there, it could be dangerous.' Tess could hear sounds like a scuffle. 'Look, they could suffocate or something. We should investigate.'

For good measure Tess yelled: 'Help me, please, lady. I'm trapped inside here.'

Some muffled banging against the container wall indicated a more violent struggle.

'Leave it!' An order from the man.

'Help me!' Tess cried out with all her might. 'I'm locked in here. I've been here all day. Help!'

'Come on!' said the woman. 'We have to help her.'

'I said leave it!' The man's voice seemed to lose power and depth when the woman disobeyed him. Tess could hear fumbling hands on the lock at the end. She moved quickly up so that when the door opened she could make a run for it.

Tess heard a thudding noise and a whimper.

'Fuck you bitch!'

It was the male voice.

Jeez.

Splaying out her hands in the darkness Tess reached out for the plastic bucket—the only weapon she had.

She could hear the container handle being drawn back and the high bolts sliding out of their locking positions.

She remembered that they when they shoved her in they had opened the right door first, so she stood pressed against the left, urine-filled bucket poised.

For a moment Tess wondered whether she should storm the door, pushing it outwards as he opened it. Perhaps that would be better than throwing the bucket.

She stooped to put the bucket down, but tripped against the edge of the mattress. In her effort to steady herself she knocked the bucket over, drenching herself with her own urine and falling to her knees, just as the door started to open.

Seeing the opening crack of dim light, Tess lurched forward on all fours, throwing her body with full force against the opening door. As she hit the metal something heavy landed on her back. She thought it was him, "detective" Adams, trying to incapacitate her. Now, as she crumpled down to the floor, she could clearly see his feet a few inches from her face. He was stooping, his hairy hands shoving at her shoulders, pushing her back into the container. But at the same time she was still being held down by this indistinguishable weight. She humped her back and the weight fell to her right.

In the split second that she was distracted the fucker had slammed the door shut again.

Fuck, fuck, fuck.

While he worked at throwing the bolts, Tess staggered to her feet and again heaved her whole weight against the door. She could feel that his body was pressing back on the other side.

Tess managed to force the door open a couple of inches, and briskly she jammed her boot into the space and rammed her full weight against his.

Behind her she could hear a faint whimpering. A woman's voice, high and reedy.

Tess shuffled forward, levering the door by pressing her feet hard against the side of the container. She managed to get the gap a few inches wider. But it was still not enough for her to squeeze through.

Then she noticed that the man's fingers were curled around the edge of the metal door and another idea came to her. Instead of pushing, she released all pressure, leaving him to shunt all his weight onto the door, and slamming his own fingers between the closing metal.

He let out an animal shriek and jerked backwards.

As he did so, Tess again pitched herself forwards, kicking out as she smashed herself past him, leaving him cradling his fist and leaping from foot to foot, cursing under his breath.

She shoved him back against the car, hoping to fuck that the perverted bastard had broken every single one of the twenty seven bones in his hand.

Now to make a run for it.

But before her was only the solid barrier of the closed garage door.

She banged and called, fumbling about on the side wall for a switch or lever.

There was nothing.

She span round, peering into the darkness, looking for another way out.

There was certainly a door in the far corner, which must lead into the adjacent house.

Tess ran back round the front of the car, heading towards that door.

The man must have slipped down to hide in the gap between the container and the other side of the car, for she could not see him.

Feeling her way with her fingertips, Tess edged briskly sideways between the wall and the car, aiming for that corner door.

Heat rose from the car hood.

Still she could not see him.

Holy shit.

Where had the asshole vanished to?

She reached the door and slammed her hand down on the handle.

Fuck.

The freaking thing was locked.

She whirled round, looking frantically along the shelves and cubby-holes on the back wall, with their rows of hooks bearing ropes and clamps and power tools, hoping to hell she could find a set of keys.

Then she saw him.

He was a few feet away, running right at her. And he was holding an axe.

Tess flung herself down on the garage floor as the axe swung above her head.

The door shuddered as the blade hit it, sending sparks into the air.

Tess wiggled round and grabbed onto the man's ankles. With all her might Tess bit into his calf. He tried to kick her off, but the effort merely unbalanced him. He staggered backwards.

Tess crawled away and rolled under the car.

When she heard a flurry of movement behind her Tess turned her head to see what he was up to. She could see his feet edging along past the hood of the car. What was that about? It was almost as though he had forgotten she was there.

Tess heard a rattling sound, like coins in a bottle, then the man moved swiftly backwards towards the door.

He had found the key and was about to let himself into the adjacent house.

Hauling herself out, and leaping to her feet, Tess charged him from behind, flinging him into the wall with some force. She heard the metallic jangle as the key hit the concrete floor. She darted out her hand to grab it.

His foot came down hard on the back of her fist.

She yelled out in pain.

He stooped and yanked her hair up, twisting it ferociously. Instinctively Tess reached up and grabbed at his wrists, trying to loosen his grip.

In an instant he swung his hands down to her waist, lifted her and flung her over his shoulder, like a fireman on a rescue mission.

Tess slithered about trying to get down.

Inside one of his pockets a cell phone was ringing—the same alarming persistent tone it had had when he was seated "interviewing" her in her apartment.

As he reached the open container he staggered.

Tess grabbed out hoping to cling to the doorframe, but the man's loss of balance only made it easier for him to toss Tess over the threshold, back inside the container.

Tess landed heavily, hurting her shoulder. As she rolled over, trying to stop him shutting the door, her foot slid along the damp blanket. She only managed to get to her knees, but too late. Before she could get anything in the way, he had slammed the metallic door and thumped the bolt home.

His mobile phone stopped ringing.

She heard him curse as he opened the car door.

Then the phone started up again.

He slammed the car door shut as he answered the call, then, with a cloud of fumes, he started the engine and put the clanking garage door into operation before reversing out.

Tess fell backwards in the dark and landed on something which was warm and moving, squirming around beneath her.

19

The Shag

*Uptempo dance recognisable by the backward
flips of the feet and a pronounced hopping action*

MARTIN SHIVERED AS he was led into the interview room.
Having spent the last day huddled on his small bed
analysing the graffiti on his cell walls, a change of
scenery was welcome. He hoped they were having second
thoughts about him having killed the librarian. Or maybe they
were simply running out of time. He had heard this over and
over on TV programmes, how the police only had a certain
number of hours and then they had to charge you and commit
you to trial or let you go. So perhaps his time was up, and
they were going to squeeze in a final bit of persecution before
they sent him home.

Then he jolted to a stop.

Perhaps this wasn't about the librarian. Perhaps it was Sarah this time.

Christ.

They'd certainly have something to charge him with then.

Old tartan shirt was standing in front of the table with a sly grin on his face.

'Nice to see you, Martin.' DI Butler screwed up his mouth. It was the look of a person who had just won a trophy.

Martin gulped. This was the high jump for sure. As the detective stood aside with a flourish Martin looked down. The mat from his front hall lay at on the table.

'Tada!' The detective gave him a wink as he stepped away, exposing torn, muddy black bin-liners, complete with brown parcel tape. 'So how would you like to explain this lot then, Martin?'

Martin gulped, but found he had no saliva. His throat made a weird grating sound.

'So who is she, Martin?'

Martin gulped. Better to admit the truth, he thought. Like that old song, perhaps the "Truth would set him Free".

'It's my wife.'

'Really.' Detective Inspector Butler raised his eyebrows. 'Your wife was one of your victims, was she, Martin? Where is she now then?'

'You must know where my wife is,' Martin challenged. 'Otherwise how did you get the bin-liners?'

'She at home now, Martin? After her trip to the South of France?'

'She's in the garden. Under the pansies.'

The detective smirked, and nodded, as though he was going to play along with something clever that Martin was doing.

Only Martin knew that, finally, he was simply telling them the truth.

'So you rolled "your wife" up in this carpet, right?' The detective pointed at the runner from the front hall, which lay next to the bin liners with a luggage tag attached to the stringy fronds at the end. 'Then what did you do with "your wife"?'

Martin thought it strange the way he said "your wife" in that cynical tone, almost as though it was in quotation marks, and meaning your mistress or something else—anything, but not your wife.

'I didn't wrap her in that carpet. Just the bin liners and tape.'

'And who helped you carry "your wife"? A body is heavier than anyone imagines. I don't think you did that all alone, did you, Martin?'

'I did it. I dragged her out there myself.'

DI Butler let out a slow sneery laugh. 'Really Martin! Dragged her all on your own, did you, all the way to the middle of the common, eh? You must be stronger than you look.'

'Did you find those bin-liners on the common?' Martin looked at the table again.

Fuck.

They had led him on and he had almost played into their hands.

'In that case they'd be different bin liners. Not my ones.' Martin started to shake when he thought how near he had come to giving the game away. 'You know, all bin liners look the same, don't they? And parcel tape. If they came from the Common they can't be mine. Mine are in my garden.'

'Ever the joker, eh, Martin. Perhaps you'd like to tell us about Max Latham's part in all this?'

'He's my lawyer.'

'Mmmm?' The detective smirked. 'Your lawyer. And...?'

Martin was mystified. What did they want him to say?

'My friend?'

'Ah. He's very much your friend. Or not.' The detective wiped his hands together. Martin thought he looked as though he was about to pull a rabbit from a top hat. 'Might as well tell you now, Martin, that your colleague in crime, Mr Max Latham, was picked up about an hour ago.'

'Picked up?'

'And at this minute, Martin, he's down the corridor in another interview room, helping us with our inquiries.'

'Inquiries?'

'He's telling us about your little storage centre in Wandsworth, Martin. I suppose if he wasn't actually involved in the slayings...'

'Slayings?'

'...he must have just been checking things out for you, is that right?'

'Storage centre?'

'You on echo, Martin? Why are you repeating everything?'

'I'm confused.'

'Don't you have anything you'd like to tell me, Martin?'

'I'm mystified.' Martin knew some game was going on, but he hadn't a clue what it could be. 'Max is my lawyer.'

'Yes, Martin, and Max was round at your place this evening with a spade. Doing a spot of gardening for you, eh?'

'Max? My place?'

'Your home, Martin. Where you live with your wife, Sarah.'

Martin lost his spit. All this *was* about Sarah. So Max had worked it out and spilled the beans on him? Were solicitors allowed to do that? Surely they couldn't grass on their own clients? What on earth was going on?

'I need to see Max now,' said Martin. 'I demand to see my solicitor.'

'It'll have to be a duty solicitor, I'm afraid, Martin.' Geoff Butler gave Martin a knowing wink. 'We can't have you two conspirators colluding again, can we, eh? Not when that conspiracy involves murder.'

Martin tried to gulp, but his throat just made a painful contraction.

'And, Martin, tell me about your wife. How exactly does she fit in to all this?'

Martin decided not to reply to this one.

If they were asking questions he felt sure they must simply be fishing and therefore actually knew nothing.

Nil desperandum. He would play innocent right up till they presented him with incontrovertible evidence that they really knew something.

'Do what you like with me, Detective Inspector.' Martin leaned back, arms folded. 'I will say nothing more until I have a solicitor present.'

'So Martin,' The detective leaned back in imitation. 'What else would you like, besides a solicitor?'

Martin jammed his lips together.

'A three course dinner—langoustine, caviar, champagne, perhaps?' The detective raised his eyebrows. 'No? Not interested in food? How about a conjugal visit? Would you like that? Be nice to see your wife again?'

Martin's heart thudded. What was the man playing at?

'I want my solicitor.'

The detective laughed.

Where was Max? What was this game they were playing? Martin had always had a sneaking fear that Max was a deceitful turncoat and that he was available to the highest bidder. Was he now colluding with the police to frame him?

'So what was this thing between you and Max Latham then, Martin? You both get off on killing young women?'

'I don't know how many times I have to tell you I did not kill any young women.'

'I see—but you did fiddle the books, stash your money in the Cayman Islands and burgle yourself? What was the idea behind the burglary, then, to give yourself an excuse to get the woman's body into the storage facility, wrapped up in a carpet? Or was it only a smoke screen so we'd look there while you stashed her away elsewhere?'

'I was burgled by persons unknown. I can't help it if some local scum came into my house and cleaned the place out. It was hardly convenient for me to lose my computer and TV and everything.'

'You have a fascination with violent death, that's clear from the books you read. And we know that both of the dead girls were burgled after they went missing. And we also know there were two people involved in the murders, and I think that was you and Max Latham.'

'Max is my lawyer, that's all. And a family friend.'

'Some friend.' The detective chortled. 'You two must be pretty close. Spends a lot of time at your place, does he?'

'Not really. My wife detested him.'

Past tense!

Martin gulped.

They were tricking him into giving himself away. He gritted his teeth determined to concentrate harder.

'So tell me Martin, why would Max Latham have keys to come and go in your private lockup?'

'How many times must I tell you—I do not have a lock-up.' Stay cool. Stay cool. Martin realised he had to avoid all the cunning traps designed to make him slip up. He hoped he would be on safer ground if he slowed down. 'I have never in my life had a lock-up. I have never even visited a lock-up. Scouts honour.'

'Come, come, Martin. Let's not be glib. Your "storage facility" then. You certainly have one of those. Here's the bill, look—paid for with your own debit card.' The detective slammed a printed piece of paper onto the table before him. 'And this non-existent lock-up, why, it's fucking chocker, mate. Filled to the brim with all your "stolen" stuff. Plus some nice blood-stained bin liners, and who knows what else.'

While Martin, agog, scanned the incriminating piece of paper, the detective continued.

'And Max Latham knows your passwords, and he has keys to your home. What's that about then, Martin? Pretty cosy set up to have with your lawyer, I'd say.'

Martin's head whirled. Max didn't have those things, surely. And Martin knew nothing of any storage facility. But there it was, the proof of ownership, lying before him in black and white.

'Do you go on these murder sprees whenever your wife goes away to the Riviera, Martin? Or is it simply a coincidence that she was away sunning herself in Nice?'

'Nice?'

'You're on repeats again, Martin.' The detective leaned back in his chair. 'So tell us a little about Sarah. You know her mother died this morning?'

'Not before time.' Martin wanted to get off the subject of Sarah right away. 'Ghastly old cow. She never liked me.'

'Your wife or her mother.'

'Her mother, of course.' Martin started involuntarily to shiver. 'My wife loved me.'

'Maybe your mother-in-law was on to you Martin, you and your little ways. What woman wants a son in law who spends his time fiddling the books, burgling himself and murdering young women?'

Martin remained silent.

'She's pretty cut up, your wife.'

Oh god, oh god, oh god! They did know. Despite himself Martin burst into uncontrollable sobs.

'I don't want to say anything else, please.' Martin gasped, wiping the tears from his cheek. 'Not till I have a solicitor present. Please. I need to talk to Max Latham.'

Detective Inspector Butler pressed a button and spoke into an intercom. 'Get one of the duty boys in would you, Phil. Little cry-baby wants a new solicitor.'

Despite an uncontrollably wobbling chin, Martin sat back and folded his arms. He was resolute in his determination not to talk till he had some legal representation.

After a few minutes sitting opposite him in silence the detective leaned forward, spoke the official rigmarole and flipped off the voice recorder.

'Let's go walkies.' He stood up and the policeman by the door stepped forward to lead Martin out of the room.

They branched off halfway along the corridor and stopped outside another room with a peephole window.

The detective pushed Martin forward so he could take a look through the glass.

There was Max, sitting opposite a police detective, his jacket off, sweating and purple faced. His hands were muddy.

The detective was apparently giving him a good grilling.

'If we were in one of those black and white films, Martin, I'd turn to you now and say "He's singing like a canary". Know what that means? It means he's trying to save his own skin by dumping you in it.'

Martin could see that they were not lying to him. The Max they were presenting was not a man bursting with pompous confidence, but a cowering finger-pointer. Suddenly Max's eyes swivelled up to the door and he caught Martin's eye.

The detective pushed Martin along, out of Max's vision. They turned the corner, heading back towards the holding cells.

'We've another surprise lined up for you later.' The detective stopped at the cell door. 'We're taking you to see your wife, Sarah. Back at your house.'

Martin grasped the architrave and was sick all over the threshold.

'All right.' He said wiping the vomit from his lips. 'I confess. I did it. I killed her.'

20

Galop

*Hungarian springy dance including
a glissade and a chasse*

SARAH PRESSED HARD on the bell to Tess's apartment. She heard a man's voice, bidding her rather impatiently to 'come on up.'

How odd. Perhaps it was an editor or agent or someone from work, up there with her. Maybe a friend over from the States, needing a place to lay his head.

As she climbed the stairs Sarah flipped the phone open again, ready to show Tess the text message she appeared to have sent her, and to get an explanation.

'You took your time,' said the man as Sarah reached the top of the stairs and pushed the door open.

She found herself face to face with that awful bank manager of Martin's, Kevin the Czech.

He blushed thoroughly.

Sarah noted the polyhedron of his Adam's apple bounce in his gullet.

'Sorry, Sarah.' His lips parted into a thin, tight smile. 'I was expecting someone else.'

Sarah flipped the phone shut, her mind racing through the computations of what the hell this could mean. Over dinner on that ghastly knife-wielding night had Tess struck up a close relationship with the humourless bank manager? How bizarre! And even if that was true why was he here alone in Tess's flat at nine o'clock at night, holding court with Lisa?

'I was looking for Tess,' Sarah said glancing round. 'Is she in?'

Sarah noted that the TV was unplugged and standing in the middle of the carpet, next to it was Tess's laptop computer and a bedside clock radio.

'Looking for Tess?' Kevin shrugged and presented Sarah his open palms. 'Aren't we all. No one seems to have heard a squeak out of her for two days.'

Sarah glanced back towards the door.

If Tess wasn't here how had Mr Kruszynska got in? You'd need three keys to get into this flat, two for the front and one for the inner door. Did he have keys to Tess's flat? If so, why?

Before she could utter her concern, Kevin spoke.

'I found the door open,' he said. 'So I came on up.'

Again Sarah put her lips together ready to ask him how Lisa had come to be in here with him a few minutes ago. But before she had a chance to form the words he had pre-empted her again.

'Lisa too,' he said. 'She came here because she was worried when Tess hadn't answered her calls.'

Lisa phoning Tess! What an extraordinary idea. How many more of these outlandish friendships had been created during that ghastly dinner?

'I suppose, Mr Kruszynska, that I must be the third in the Check-up-on-Tess Club.'

'Are there others?' Kevin looked nervously towards the door. 'I wonder who else will be joining us?'

'Peter Gurney, Peter Davy, Daniel Whiddon, Harry Hawke and Uncle Tom Cobley by the look of it.'

Kevin's face creased with worry.

'Who are they?'

Sarah recalled that, despite his impeccable English, Kevin of the unpronounceable Eastern European surname had not been brought up in England, and therefore was unlikely, as a child, to have learned the words of whimsical English folk songs.

'So Sarah...' He frowned in a patronising way which Sarah supposed was his method of showing concern. 'Have you heard from Tess at all?'

'Yes, actually.' Sarah flipped open her mobile phone and scrolled down through the texts.

'Not that it's any business of mine,' said Kevin. 'Just concern for a client you understand.'

She noted that the frantic anxiety he had displayed over Uncle Tom Cobley, had turned about. He queried her now with an insouciant "I couldn't care less" air which Sarah interpreted as truly serious interest.

There were various ways of looking at this, possibly Kevin of the bouncing cheques was having an illicit affair with the American writer behind his poor baby-laden wife's back. Perhaps he had really come here because Tess wasn't answering his calls.

But whatever was going on there was something about his quivering, cold energy which frightened Sarah.

She decided not to show him the text.

'Sorry I got a bit confused. No, Kevin, I've not heard from Tess since the dinner party.' Sarah closed the phone and dropped it into her pocket. 'I've been away.'

'Yes, I know,' said the Czech. 'Quite a bit of trouble your husband has got himself into while you were missing, hasn't he? Have you come back to give evidence?'

Sarah tried to decipher what he was saying. Her mind whirled back over all she knew. They couldn't have arrested Martin for murdering her, as here she was, alive and well. And on top of that she had never told a soul the true facts about the episode with the knife, so who else knew?

If this creepy bank manager was standing before her asking if she was back to "give evidence" it would have to be a very weird investigation indeed. She had never heard of the suspect in a murder case being held when the "victim" was seen to be alive and well, or even more hilariously, the corpse was coming back to give evidence on behalf of their killer. He couldn't possibly mean that. Could he?

'This is all very peculiar, Kevin.'

'Haven't you heard?' Kevin Kruszynska knotted his eyebrows and seemed to scrutinize her whole body with his remote shark-like eyes. 'Martin has been arrested and is being held for the murder of that librarian.'

'The librarian? Martin's being held?' Sarah contemplated these fantastic statements. 'I'm sorry I don't understand you. Are you saying that my husband, Martin is being held for killing the librarian who went missing last week?'

Kevin stood before her, sanctimonious smile smeared across his face, nodding like a dog in a car's rear window.

'Let's get this straight, Kevin.' Sarah was sure she must have misheard, or that this idiotic number cruncher from Transylvania, or wherever he came from, had got his facts in a muddle. Hadn't they all been talking about that case throughout the dinner party? Perhaps he was referring to some conversation they had had while she was in the kitchen. 'Are you seriously trying to tell me that my husband Martin is being held by the police for murdering some strange woman that he did not know?'

'That's exactly what I am saying.'

'This is not a practical joke?'

'Absolutely not.'

Kevin's phone rang. An annoying sharp repetitive beep.

Sarah turned for the stairs.

'I'm sorry, Kevin. I have to go.' She clattered down the stairs, calling up before she went out into the street. 'If you hear from Tess let me know.'

She could hear Kevin on the phone. '...Now. Same as before.'

Even though she was on the street threshold she heard also the change in the tone of his voice as it took on a very hard, slightly panicked tone and he said harshly: 'You've done what?'

Sarah walked towards her home.

A silver car turned into the road and pulled over.

Sarah's toe flipped against something lying on the pavement which went skittering into the gutter. She stooped to look.

It was the heel of Lisa's shoe.

That was weird too. No woman simply left the heel of their shoe behind on the pavement, even if it did look un-repairable.

Sarah picked up the heel, then thought perhaps Lisa might come back looking for it, and so placed it carefully on the kerb, where it would be easy to find.

As she rose, Sarah caught eyes with a man sitting in the silver car, talking on a mobile phone. He turned away.

Sarah turned into her own front gate.

There was something wrong with Kevin and his story concerning Tess. It didn't add up. Not only that, but the man was positively creepy. Those dead fish-like eyes seemed to have no connection to the soul. His icy demeanour, and the tension in the room had scared Sarah. She feared for Tess.

She pulled out her mobile phone and scrolled down through the received texts. She would try to phone Tess again then call the police to report her missing. She'd have to phone the police anyway, to help poor Martin.

As she put her finger to the keyboard, her phone vibrated in her hand. An incoming call from some mobile number.

'Hello? Is that you Tess?'

'Sarah?'

Sarah did not recognise the male voice.

'It's Peter.'

'Peter?'

'Peter Beaumont. Marti's dad.'

Oh god—the pompous popinjay.

'I've been having a bit of trouble rousing that prodigal son of mine, and wondered if everything was AOK down at Beaumont Towers?'

Sarah turned into her front gate.

'Yes, yes. I was just about to phone him actually.'

'Phone him? He told me you'd had a bit of a squabble over a dinner party or something. Are you living apart, is that it? Trial separation?'

As Sarah didn't really know what was going on, she decided that for the moment she could not give Martin's father the bad news over the phone that his son had been arrested for murder. Just because Kevin had told her it had happened did not mean it was true. And even if it was true, the old boy was in his 80s. Who knew what effect news like that would have on an ancient heart? With a pang, which felt somewhere between a sigh and a blow to the stomach, she thought of her dead mother, not yet buried. 'Look, Peter, I am just going into our house now. I'll phone you from the landline when I get inside. OK?'

She slammed the phone shut and re-opened at Tess's text.

She pressed the button to dial the number. But Tess's number cut straight to answering service. This time she left a message. 'Tess. Hello. This is Sarah Beaumont. I'm worried about you, and not sure whether you know that Kevin Kruszynska is in your flat.' She paused, unsure whether an American understood the word flat. '...Your apartment. He was in there with Lisa Pope. You know, Max Latham's girlfriend. And all your things were piled up in the centre of the room.'

Sarah stood at her front door, holding the phone with one hand and groping in her pocket, searching for the keys with the other.

'Also, Tess, I had some strange texts from what appeared to be your number.'

Sarah slipped the key into the lock and shoved the front door open with her foot.

'Is everything all right? I'm seriously worried about you, Tess. Please call me. In the meantime I will call the police and see if they can trace you.'

Still holding the phone to her ear, Sarah stepped into the hall, kicking the door shut behind her. She did not hear the slam, so turned round to close it.

A man she had never seen before was standing on the threshold, his foot in the gap.

He whirled his hand, waving his finger in a circle, instructing her to wind up the call.

Sarah wasn't sure whether to yell for help or obey him.

'Mrs Sarah Beaumont?' asked the man, reaching into his jacket pocket.

For an instant Sarah thought he was going to pull out a gun. But he took out something like a wallet, held it up and flipped it open.

It was a police badge.

'Detective Stuart Adams,' said the man, walking into the hall. 'I think we need to talk.'

'I have to go,' said Sarah into the phone. 'Someone from the police has arrived. I'll tell him my worries.'

21

Sarabande

*A stately dance in which the dancers continuously
move four steps forward and four steps back*

B
EFORE TESS COULD find her equilibrium, the person
beneath her started shrieking, pulling at her hair,
scratching at her eyes. They wrestled for a second or
two, with Tess trying to out-yell the other woman, begging
her to calm down. 'What's going on?' shrieked the woman.
'Let me out of this stinking box.'

She pulled away from Tess and flung herself against the
door, beating on the metal with her fists, shouting: 'Open up,
you bastard. It's not funny.'

'He's gone.' Tess spoke levelly. 'Didn't you hear the car rev
up, and the garage door open?'

'Who are you?' asked the woman. 'The joke's over, lady. Come on, whoever you are. Let me out.'

'I am an American citizen and I am being held here against my will by two men who, I believe, plan to kill us.' Tess did her best to sound level and calm. 'My name is Tess Brandon.'

The newly arrived woman turned and peered in Tess's direction.

'Tess Brandon? The crime writer?'

'That's me.' In the dark Tess blushed. She could barely believe how it still felt great, even in these circumstances, to be recognised by a fan.

The other woman lurched forwards in the dark, stretching out her arms like a child playing Blind Man's Buff. She stooped to cradled Tess's face in her hands, then pulled one hand back and gave her a sharp slap across the cheek.

'Hey!' cried Tess. 'What's that about? Lookit, if you don't like my books...'

'I've had enough of this. It's not funny. Max is meant to be meeting me for dinner. Let me out at once.'

'Max?' Tess reeled. 'Is that...Lisa? Holy shit.'

'Yes, Tess, as you well know, it is me, Lisa, and I am ordering you to open that door and let me out. The joke's gone far enough.'

'Holy fuck!' Tess said. 'What in crap's name is going on?'

'You tell me. And if it's supposed to be a sort of American prank, it just isn't funny.'

Tess grabbed Lisa's hands.

'This is no joke, Lisa. You know the librarian who was killed...'

'Oh for GOD'S SAKE, Tess, not again.' Lisa freed herself and flopped down into a sitting position. 'We all had quite enough of that kind of talk during Sarah and Martin's dinner party.'

'Lisa, please, please listen. Those two men who put us in here...' Tess tried to continue in an earnest and level voice. She knew she had to make Lisa grasp the truth. 'You realise, I hope, that they're the mad fuckers who killed that librarian, right—the bodies dumped on the Commons. Well, they're going to kill us just the same way. We're going to be next.'

'Stop being absurd, Tess.' Lisa sat up and shouted into the darkness. 'You've got too vivid an imagination. And anyhow, I wasn't brought here, as you put it, by two "mad fuckers". There was only one.'

'OK, so how did that one mad fucker get you into the car?' Tess asked quietly. 'Did he pretend to be a detective?'

'He was taking me on a date.' Lisa's voice started to quiver. Tess couldn't work out if she was frightened or on the verge of tears. 'Max stood me up. Then he stopped and offered me a lift.'

'Max brought you here?'

'No. This other bloke. I only got in the car cos he seemed so sweet.'

'You got into a car with a total stranger?'

'Of course not, Tess. I'm not a total fool. I've known him a while.'

'Woh! Holy fuck, Lisa!' Tess slammed her fist down on the damp mattress. 'You mean to say you actually know the jerk?'

Lisa lifted her head, nodded and said quietly. 'Kind of.'

'Leather jacket, dark hair, shiny white teeth, hairy arms and hands?' Tess had to make sure it was the same guy who had brought her here. 'Smells of after-shave and cigarettes?'

'Yeah. That's Tony.'

'Tony? He told you he was called Tony? He told me he was called Stuart Adams.'

'Tony's done my hair for about a year. You must be talking about someone else.'

'He's a hairdresser?' Tess flung herself back against the door. This was one occupation she'd, so far, never found in serial killer profiles. 'Holy shit. That's all we need. A fucking psycho fairy. So who's the other one?' she asked.

'What other one?' replied Lisa.

'His partner in crime. Who's his friend?'

'I don't know about anyone else.'

'You got brought here by one man on his own...' Tess knew that it was most unusual for a pair of spree killers to break a pattern and work individually. '...But you do know that there's two of those bastards, right, and I'm not joking or exaggerating when I tell you that they're going to kill us?'

'Why would Tony want to kill me? He's nice.'

'No. Not nice, Lisa. You really do have to get that shit detector working you know.'

There was a momentary silence.

'I broke my shoe.' Lisa tugged off her shoes and sat squeezing them together. 'I've lost the heel. I dropped it while I was getting into the car.'

Tess gave the shoes a cursory glance, and muttered: 'The car was silver, right? Small sedan?'

'I don't know anything about cars,' Lisa said. 'But, yes. It was silver.'

Tess began to wonder whether the arrival of Lisa might also bring some advantages. 'Listen up, gal. D'yall have a cell?'

'Very funny,' said Lisa with a sneer. 'Apart from this one we're sitting in, you mean?'

'No—a cell phone. Vodaphone kinda thing?'

'Yes. It's in my...' Lisa scrambled to her bare feet, then stopped still and groaned. 'In my handbag, which is out there on the garage floor.' She pressed her hands against the rusty walls. 'Why are we wasting time chatting, Tess? We should be trying to break that door open, or scrape our way out, or something.'

'You think I haven't spent the last twenty four hours trying?'

'You've been here a whole day?' said Lisa, her voice high with panic. 'Oh no! God, Tess! You're serious, aren't you?'

'Sure. Now we got to work out what the hell is going on with these two men.'

'I keep telling you, Tess. There was only one.'

'Okay. Okay. So first—What do you know about Tony? Quick as you can.'

'The thing with people like hairdressers,' said Lisa, 'is that you feel you know them cos they chat away with you, but when you think about it, you don't really know anything at all.'

'He must have said something. Does he go out dancing? Is he married?'

'It was strange though that you said he was gay. That's what I thought too, until tonight, when he picked me up in the car. He seemed to be laughing inwardly, then, and as though he had turned into another person. I could almost smell his feral hormones or whatever they're called.'

'Pheromones.'

'Anyway, he'd got that really leathery, manly smell about him. And he kept saying he was going to take me somewhere very special. So naturally I imagined we were going to The Met Bar or Bouji's or some really cool place full of celebrities and everything.'

'Come on, Lisa,' Tess snapped. 'Tony!'

'You know I was pretty pissed off when I came out of your flat only to find that Max's car was gone, and then, when my bloody shoe collapsed on me...'

'Whoa! Hold it right there. My flat? You were in my apartment today?'

'I had arranged to see Max later for dinner, but he said he'd arranged to go to your flat and talk to you first, and...'

Tess flicked her palms up to stop Lisa again.

'Max Latham told you he was visiting me?'

'That's what he said.' Lisa shrugged. 'But he wasn't there. Maybe he was lying. But then why was his car was parked outside your door? But anyway the door was open so naturally I went up to your place and the man said to come on in...'

'The man? Holy fuck!' Again Tess raised her hands. 'My apartment was open and there was a man in there?'

'Your bank manager...'

'My bank manager? My bank manager from Knoxville, Tennessee, the "underwear capital of the world" was standing in my apartment in Clapham, England?' asked Tess.

'No, silly,' Lisa laughed. 'That Czechish man with the pale blue eyes who was at Sarah and Martin's dinner.'

'Kevin Kruszynska was there? What the fuck? That creep was in my apartment?'

'Yes. I think he and Max were there trying to help Martin from next door, since Martin was being held for the murders and everything.'

'Holy fuck! The police have Martin for this?' Tess put her head in her hands. 'You realise that while they think it's Martin, they ain't gonna be looking very hard for anyone else, right? So, basically, we're up the creek.'

A door slammed.

'Oh god!' Tess clambered to her feet. 'They've come for us....'

Outside the box, footsteps clacked around in the garage.

Lisa grabbed Tess. 'Come on, we've got to let them know we're in here!'

'No!' Tess clamped her hand round Lisa's mouth and whispered urgently into her ear. 'Look what happened when I tried that earlier. But, they may open up anyhow. And when that door opens, we're gonna making a break for it. OK?'

Tess pressed herself back against the wall, beside the container door. Lisa did the same.

'Ready?'

Lisa nodded.

Both women stood braced, quivering with anticipation of action.

The footsteps clacked away. The corner door slammed again.

Silence.

'Where have they gone?' Lisa turned to Tess, crying. 'You let them go! It wasn't Tony. We should have shouted. It was someone else.' She threw herself against the container door and beat on it with her fists. 'We're in here. Whoever you are, help us. Help us, please!'

'Lisa, do you have a watch,' asked Tess. 'I'd say it was ten before eight.'

Lisa raised her wrist.

'How did you know?'

'It was the same time yesterday someone was in the garage. You were right. There must be someone else around, and that someone comes in here each night around eight and may know nothing about it. Lookit, this time tomorrow...'

'Tomorrow?' squealed Lisa. 'We've got to get out of here before then.'

'They kept that librarian a week, didn't they, before dumping her body on the common?'

'Have they brought you anything to eat?'

'You gotta be kidding. That's the whole point. They try to put you in a position where you want them to come back, and at the same time they leave you utterly weak so you can't do anything. It's classic.'

Tess searched around on the blanket for the water bottle. 'They did leave this. I think it's water, but I can't be sure.'

'Oh Tess!' Lisa held her broken shoes up to her face and wept. 'What's going to happen to us?'

Tess sighed. She wished she could give a credible answer which involved at least an iota of hope.

Suddenly Lisa flung the shoes into the corner and started wiping the tears from her cheeks with the back of her hand.

'I hate men,' she sobbed. 'How could I have been so stupid?'

'Lookit, Lisa, I made the same mistake myself. I am in here too.' Tess stretched out a hand in the darkness and ruffled Lisa's hair. 'Come on, kid. Did the jerk say anything while he was driving you here?'

'He talked about how the leaves were looking lovely on the trees on the common, and how he loved listening to jazz on the radio.'

'Yeah, yeah,' Tess tried to speed Lisa on. 'And what about towards the end. When you could see you were heading out of town, and not to a club?'

'I asked where we were and said we were going to his brother's house to pick something up and we could have a bit of a cuddle, and then we'd go on out and have some fun.'

'You could see out of the car, right? So do you know where we are?'

'I wasn't really looking. It was away from town.'

'His brother?' said Tess, still the bloodhound on the scent. 'What do you know about him?'

'Nothing. I didn't even know he had a brother till he said "my brother's place".'

'So why didn't he take you back to his own place for a "cuddle"?'

'He told me he had a dog which had been sick, but there was some woman called Carol, and, oh...I don't think anything he told me was true.'

'But his name is Tony, you said? Tony what?'

'Hairdressers only use their first names.'

'And he's never been known as Stuart Adams, or been a detective, or in the police, that you know about?'

'He used to be an actor. But that was probably a lie too. He was all very sweet in the car, right up to when we pulled into this garage. I let him know I was a bit disappointed that we had had our first kiss in a car in a horrible garage, but he was so tender. Then he got very hot and bothered. He could barely control himself.'

'That's because he knew he had me locked up inside the box here, ready to kill. It's classic.'

Lisa sobbed.

'D'you see how they're starting to go wrong now.' Tess gnawed at her lower lip, her eyes flashing in the darkness. 'I think this Tony of yours was acting alone tonight, and I'll bet you his partner in crime had no idea he brought you here. But, really, he's scared of Mr X. That's what it is. I was wrong. I thought my Stuart—your Tony—was the top dog. But no. Mr X is the dominant one, the hard one. Dammit.' Tess slammed her hands together again. 'I got it all wrong in the car. Your Tony is like the naughty second in command trying to prove to himself that he is as good as his "brother", the jerk in the woolly hat.'

Tess leaned back.

'I'm so sorry, Lisa. I bet if I hadn't yelled out tonight, Tony might simply have laid you, standing up against the container wall, then shoved you back in the car and driven away with you, and now at least you'd be out with Max, feeling shitty... but you'd be safe. Tony hadn't planned to put you in here, and starve you and eventually kill you. Those delights were intended only for me.'

Suddenly from the garage there was music.

'What the...?'

'That's my phone,' said Lisa. 'Someone's trying to call me.' She pressed herself against the wall listening to the ringing till it stopped. 'Last person to phone me on that thing was Tony, just when I came out of your flat.'

Tess sat up. A link!

'Lisa, as you came down the stairs and into the street, what was the bank manager doing?'

'Making a phone call.'

'And Tony phoned you how long after you came out of my door?'

'I don't know. A minute? Less?'

'And then his car was suddenly there, right alongside you?' Tess tilted her head in Lisa's direction. 'So, tell me, how did Tony know where to find you?'

'He didn't,' said Lisa, remembering looking up at Tess's window and seeing creepy Kevin standing at the window, holding his phone. 'He said it was just chance.'

'Yeah right!' Tess buzzed with a whole new energy. 'We may be fucked, stuck inside this box with no hope of getting out, but finally we worked out who we're up against.'

Lisa nodded. She had worked it out too.

Tess asked 'So, Mr X is...?'

'I thought it was spelled with a K, but anyway...' Lisa had no idea how to pronounce it, but had a jolly good go. 'Kevin Krushpinky?'

22

Alegrías

Spanish gypsy dance, suggesting the movements of a bullfight. Usually danced by a lone woman

SARAH PERCHED ON a stool in the kitchen, while Detective Adams took a seat at the table opposite. He looked sweaty and his hair was tousled. To Sarah it looked as though he'd just been in a fight. But she supposed that was what being in the police was all about. In police dramas on TV they were always running up and down tiny lanes and leaping over fences onto shed roofs. Maybe this fellow had come hot-foot from chasing some burglar up an alley.

'OK,' said Sarah. 'I can guess why you are here, but I tell you it can't be true. I can vouch...'

The man raised his hand to stop her.

'It's OK, madam. All under control. I just need to ask you a few questions.'

'I've only just got back into the country.' Sarah went to the counter and opened her handbag, looking for the plane tickets. 'I had no idea. And I have a lot to do. My mother died, you see. I have to arrange the funeral and make phone calls and get certificates and all that stuff.'

Sarah's heart made that dip again, and she took a deep breath.

'I won't keep you long,' said the detective. Then, as though remembering something, he reached into his pocket and pulled out a notebook and pencil. 'So I gather you were making inquiries about the American lady who lives next door?'

'I thought you were here to talk about my husband?'

'Yeah. Of course. But first I need to ask you a few questions about your neighbour.'

'He didn't do it, you know. If he's acting guilty, it's all because of me. We had a bit of a fight. He thought he'd killed me.'

Sarah noticed that the man's fingers seemed to be trembling as he poised the pencil over the notebook.

'In fact,' Sarah laughed. 'I know it all sounds mad, but you see, Detective, my husband honestly thinks he buried me out in the garden. We had a terrible fight. He thought he'd killed me and he put me there. But, as you see, I am OK. So any crime you might believe he committed is much more minor than whatever you're holding him for.'

'So when did you report Tess Brandon missing?'

'I didn't.' Sarah could see that the detective was doodling on his notepad, not taking notes at all. 'I didn't realise that Tess was missing at all till a few minutes ago. I have to say, though, that I do think there is something rather fishy going on, don't you? That weird bank manager being in there...I mean, he says the door was wide open...but...I think perhaps someone should look into that...'

The detective seemed to Sarah as though he was in another world. He inclined his head slightly to the side. It was as though he was listening, waiting for something.

'Detective? Do you want me to make a statement? About my husband, or to report Tess missing?'

Stuart Adams leapt into action again, poising his pencil and firing another question her way. 'Did you see or hear anything last night, any noises perhaps, coming from Tess's flat?'

'I was in France,' said Sarah holding up the ticket. 'In fact no one yet knows I am back.'

'Really?' The man visibly relaxed.

'Tell me, Detective Adams, why did Mr Kruszynska have all of Tess's things piled up on the floor? What is going on? Do you know?'

'I am simply trying to get to the facts, madam. And I can only do so if you fully co-operate.'

Sarah had an eerie feeling that this man was talking from a script, as it felt like he was recalling lines from some TV show. Nothing rang true.

She said: 'Why are you holding Martin?'

'Who?' The detective looked up from his pad.

'My husband, Martin Beaumont. You're holding him for murder. I thought that was why you were here. '

'Are you expecting the police?'

'I thought you were the police.'

'Did you phone them? You were on the phone just now when I followed you inside.'

Now Sarah was certain something was very wrong.

She was also sure that his man was no detective.

He could be anyone.

Sarah slipped from her stool, ready to make a run for it.

As though correcting himself the man added: 'I am simply doing a house to house, you see. Making inquiries. It's very important to correlate evidence.'

'I was just about to phone the police. That's why I was so amazed that you'd read my mind and come here so quickly.'

'We don't chop and change cases, Mrs Beaumont.' The detective rolled his pencil between his fingers, then glanced at his watch. 'I am on a different case. Not your husband's. I'm working on the Tess Brandon file.'

Before she made a total fool of herself by running out of the house, Sarah decided to test him.

'Are you from the local CID?' she said, and then she told him a lie—that she I knew most of the local officers there.

The man fell right into the trap. Of course if he was a phoney now he would now have to say that he wasn't from the local nick.

He put on a very serious face and said: 'They wouldn't know me there. I am not based round here.' As though to gild the lily, he added: 'I am from Scotland Yard, you see. Special Branch.'

Sarah was now certain he was lying.

'Could I see your badge again, detective?'

'Sure.' As he reached into his jacket pocket the man stood up and took a step towards her.

Sarah only had enough time to see his fist before it hit her in the face, knocking her to the floor.

As she scrambled forward, her head throbbing, she didn't feel quite so smug about being right.

The "detective" ran past her into the hall. She could hear him calling back towards the front door. It sounded like he was crying out for 'Carol'.

Using the knobs on the kitchen cabinets, Sarah hauled herself to her feet.

It was only when she turned round that she saw, standing in the doorway, Kevin Kruszynska.

Sarah looked to the "detective", who was now cowering like a naughty child before the bank manager.

"The detective" raised his hands to Kevin Kruszynska in what looked like appeasement, opened his mouth and said something which sounded like a tape reeling backwards.

Shit.

They were talking Czech or Slovakian or Sudetan, or whatever the fuck they spoke over there. They stood there in her kitchen talking rapidly and incomprehensibly.

They really were accomplices.

From the split second glances they both made in her direction Sarah knew that they must be referring to her and what they were saying was not in her best interests. Her instinct was to run for the front door, but Kevin blocked the doorway and the "detective" stood between her and any hope of exit.

She glanced over her shoulder. Perhaps she should turn and run into the garden?

Sarah realised she could possibly make it out there and have enough time to yell. But, once outside, she would be utterly cornered and there really was no hope of escape. It was dark too. No one would even see her or what these other two were up to.

If she was to have any hope of surviving, the only thing to do was make a run past them into the hall and get out into the street.

Sarah made sure she was facing the men, as slowly she pulled open a drawer behind the small of her back.

Kevin was still shouting at the "detective" and he was shouting back, using urgent sounds and wild gestures. She felt sure she heard the phoney detective say her husband's name, and then Mr Kruszynska indicated a slit throat.

Oh god almighty.

They were going to kill her.

Jesus Christ.

Sarah slid her hand deep into the drawer and felt around till she found a knife. She knew exactly which one she wanted.

She wrapped her hand firmly round the handle and slid it out, holding it hidden behind her back.

Leaving her hands behind her, as though grasping the counter's edge, Sarah sidled along so that, instead of taking the run across the kitchen at a diagonal, she would be directly opposite the route out, with a protective wall on one side of her.

The two men were still furiously rattling away in their strangely strangulated language, gesticulating and flashing their eyes.

It was now or never. Sarah took a deep breath and darted forward.

As she ran, in the corner of her vision, she caught the jerky signals as the two men co-ordinated their attack.

Kevin Kruszynska held out his arms to block her exit.

Sarah pushed him aside.

He lunged at her, grabbing her by the hair.

Sarah managed to jerk herself free and made it into the hall.

A few feet from the front door she span round and faced him, thrusting forward, slashing the knife out in his direction, trying to drive him back.

Kevin Kruszynska put up his hands, mollifying, and danced away, as Sarah continued to edge herself backwards. When her back was against the front door, she turned briskly, fingers groping for the latch.

Damn.

The snib was on.

Her hand, sweating and slippery, fumbled.

Damn the lock.

At last she managed to release the catch, pull the handle down and tug the door open.

She heard Kevin yell: "Do something, Tony!"

Simultaneously she was thrown forwards and crushed flat against the door, which slammed shut under the impact of her own weight.

Tony pressed himself close, exhaling foetid smoky breath into Sarah's ear.

'Fuck you, bitch.' He reached out and snatched the knife from her hand. 'Turn round and do as I tell you.'

'No.' Sarah's voice was no more than a whisper. 'I will not.'

She turned her head to spit at him.

Tony swung the knife back.

She threw up her hands to hit it from his hand.

He stepped forward, swinging the knife towards her abdomen.

She twisted round, hoping to make a final attempt at escaping. But her sudden movement caused him to shunt into her, the knife walloping into her side.

Pain seared through her.

Gripping her flank, Sarah slumped down, landing on the wooden floor with a dull thump.

'Oh my god,' she cried, looking up into his eyes. 'What have you done?'

Sarah looked down at the red stain which spread across her white cotton blouse.

When she looked up again she saw, as though through a mist, the two men huddled together, staring down.

Tony gripped the knife, Kevin Kruszynska peered over his shoulder.

To Sarah they seemed fuzzy, their voices faint, bubbling, as though they were underwater.

Why were they talking gibberish?

Why were the lights suddenly so bright?

Kevin shouted at the other man, then stooped and grabbed hold of Sarah's ankles.

She could see the ceiling moving, sliding away from her, then Tony's startled face as he stepped back to let them pass.

Sarah was aware of shadows moving past her, of table legs and chairs, of the light becoming brighter and brighter, then slowly dimming.

She felt a dull thud beneath her head as she was dragged over the threshold of the back door then a cold rush of air and damp against her back as she was pulled across the lawn.

She could smell the fresh green smell of grass and the faintly mouldy aroma of soil, and somewhere heard the rhythmic sharp ring of a spade digging.

Then she seemed to be falling, tumbling round and down into vertiginous darkness, and finally she felt cold rough grit between her teeth as the first shovel full of dirt covered her face.

23

The Can-Can

Raucous French dance in which
women kick their legs in the air

'THEY'RE UNRAVELLING, THOSE two men. That's what's coming to pass.' Tess sat on the floor of the container, shaking her head, her forehead cupped in the palms of her hands. 'It eventually happens with all serial killers. When they don't act to plan it causes a domino effect. I'll tell you this, Lisa: They'll want to dispose of us pretty fucking fast. And I can't believe I just blew our greatest chance of escaping by not letting you holler.'

'We've to get someone's attention. Anybody's. We could take it in turns and simply yell till someone gets fed up with it and comes to investigate.'

Tess didn't say anything. Lisa knew she wasn't listening. She had noted at that awful dinner party that whenever anyone else was speaking Tess's feet were always tapping under the table and she seemed to be taking part in some kind of internal chase, fidgeting with nervous energy as though she couldn't wait for them to finish so that it would be her turn again. Lisa imagined Tess's brain was always racing, but imagined that she wasn't much of a team player.

'I know you love all this analysis stuff.' Lisa continued, running her fingers along the walls, desperately but methodically searching for weak points. 'But you do know that what we really need is action.'

Lisa's hair caught on a little hook which she hadn't seen before. She tugged to disentangle herself, and the diamante barrette she had been given at the hairdressers fell to the ground. 'I'd forgotten I was wearing that.' She stopped to pick up the sparkling gewgaw. 'That bloody psychopathic swine gave it me. Or rather shoved it on my head and put it on Max's bill.' She flicked open the strap, held it tight between her fingers and used the clip to start scratching away at the metal wall round the hook

'You'll never get through solid metal with a hair-grip.' Tess said wearily as she climbed to her feet and leaned against the door. 'God help us. How are we going to get out of this fucking thing.' She kicked her leg rhythmically backwards against the door, donkey style. 'Shit! Fuck! Bollocks!'

She twisted round and leaped into the air, slamming both feet at the door.

Lisa screamed. 'Tess? Look!' She lurched forward. 'Did you see that?'

She stooped and pointed her hand down towards the bottom of the door, beneath the spot where Tess had been kicking. 'Hit it again, only once you make contact, keep up the pressure.'

Tess slammed her shoe flat against the door.

'Of course you won't be able to see it from where you are.' Lisa scrambled onto her knees and crouched at Tess's feet. 'The thick end of that blanket is jammed into the bottom of the bolt hole. We need a knife, or a screwdriver or something to make sure it doesn't go back in.'

'Yeah,' drawled Tess. 'Or the key or a genie of the lamp or a fairy fucking godmother to come let us out.'

'Shut up, Tess.' Lisa tucked her head down, and pushed her shoulders flat against the door, all the while trying to work the ornamental barrette into position beneath the bolt. 'Just keep pressing. Now we need something to push the bloody bolt right out of the socket.' Lisa pulled off her belt and crammed the buckle into the sliver of dim light at the bottom of the container door. 'How about the heel of my shoe? Can you reach it, Tess? Without lessening any pressure against the door?'

Tess stretched out one leg, fishing for the shoes with her toes.

'Don't stop pushing,' shrieked Lisa, still shoving her shoulder against the metal.

Tess kicked, sending the shoe skittering along to Lisa's side.

Lisa grabbed it, hooked it under the door and pressed it further into position.

'Push hard, Tess, when I say three: one—two—three.'

As the gap widened Lisa gave an almighty shove, thrusting the shoe into the gap.

'Damn!'

The shoe snapped in two, but the heel remained wedged, holding the door firmly open by one inch.

'Considering how much they cost they're not very well made are they?' Lisa threw the body of the shoe over her shoulder.

'Hell, lady, you got your entire wardrobe under that door. It's a pity that pretty women like y'all don't wear corsets anymore.' Tess laid it on thick. 'All them fancy whalebones from your stays would have been just dandy to winkle under that bolt and set us free.'

'Don't mock me, Tess. I'm only trying to help.' Lisa stood and grasped one of the metal ribs of the door. 'Another shove. On a count of three, OK? Right.'

Both women put all their weight behind the door.

'One, two, three...LIFT!'

With a great clank the bolt fell into the space behind the socket, thus holding the door open at the bottom.

'Great,' said Tess. 'Now if one of us turned into a leprechaun we could nip through that three inch gap and inform the authorities.'

Lisa was about to hit Tess, when the gap was suddenly flooded with the flickering light of a fluorescent strip light firing up. The flashes penetrated deep into the box.

'Listen!' Lisa held her hand over Tess's mouth and whispered low: 'Someone's there.'

Tess shook her head free.

The light steadied.

They could see each other's eyes. They both glanced down. Through the tiny breach they watched the three inch strip of oil-stained garage floor.

The shadow of a leg crossed the space.

Lisa and Tess watched intently as the shadow moved away.

'Holy crap,' mouthed Tess. 'We're dead women.'

'No we're not.' Lisa mouthed back.

They heard stealthy footsteps, then someone on the other side of the door, breathing.

Their eyes locked in panic. Both women realised the one thing they had not decided on was the plan of action for the moment when the door opened.

Then the bolt creaked.

Someone was moving its handle slowly, stealthily.

From behind them came a booming sound.

They both knew it was the garage door swinging into operation.

Tess grabbed Lisa's hand. 'When it opens, push out and run for it. OK?'

Lisa nodded.

With a sudden metallic crank the bolt slid up, the container door burst open and bright light blinded them.

Tess hollered. Lisa tumbled out, tripping on the blanket. She landing on the garage floor at a woman's feet. The woman, small, dark and angry, held a large claw hammer which she swung dangerously.

Lisa, crawled along, flinging herself out of the way, and narrowly avoiding a crack across the skull.

The silver car pulled into the garage. Tony and Kevin were in the front seats.

The dark woman lifted her arm, ready to take another bash at Lisa, but Tess pushed her from behind, causing her to lose her balance and fall into the path of the vehicle.

They both heard Kevin curse as he swerved and slammed on the brakes.

Tess dragged Lisa to her feet. But by the time they spun round Tony, eyes blazing, stood between them and the street.

While the dark woman clambered out from the space under the front fender, Kevin concentrated on bringing the garage door down behind them, before they had a chance of getting out.

'This way,' screamed Tess. She turned and ran further into the garage.

'But...' Lisa panicked, but followed.

Tess ran on through an open door into ante-room, which was stacked with boxes.

'What the fuck?'

They both ran on through another open door into a sitting room, with a sofa and a TV which was turned on and showing an episode of some police series.

'The hall has to be this way.' Tess ran through the next door. 'Come on, Lisa. Let's get out of here.'

They darted along the hall, out of the front door and down the path into the dark street.

They could hear the garage door lurching up again and saw Tony duck beneath and run out after them.

Tess sprinted along the pavement, heading towards the bright lights of the main road with its small mall of run-down stores.

She heard Lisa yelp, and turned to see her stumble. She lay on the ground. She had no shoes.

'Come on, kid.' Tess darted back, put out her hand and hauled Lisa to her feet. 'I ain't going nowhere without you.'

Tess thrust her hand round Lisa's waist. 'Put your weight on me.'

Tony was closing on them.

Tess and Lisa stumbled towards the main road. As they rounded the bend at the top of the cul de sac, they could almost feel Tony's breath on their necks.

Lisa pointed towards a foreign-looking convenience store. 'Someone in there will help.'

As she hesitated, Tony grabbed out and caught hold of Lisa's blouse.

She screamed.

A woman coming out of the shop stared.

Tony fell back a step or two.

'Come on.' Tess tugged Lisa onwards. 'Look!'

A few doors along a yellow lamp flashed in the darkness. From her months in London, Tess knew that this signalled a minicab office.

'Only a few more yards.' Tess grabbed hold of Lisa and dragged her onward towards the car which waited at the kerb, its taxi lamp lit.

'There are two men chasing us.' Tess wheezed as she shunted Lisa into the back seat of the cab. 'You gotta help us get away.'

The driver turned. 'You want me to call the police?'

'Just drive,' shouted Lisa.

The driver didn't move.

Tony stood on the pavement, shouting.

Just as Tess slammed down the lock, he yanked at the passenger door handle.

'Shit, Mister, are you deaf or something?' yelled Tess. 'Drive!'

Lisa started to cry.

'Police!' Tony, slammed his phoney warrant card up against the driver's window. 'Don't go anywhere, mate. Not if you want to keep your license. These women have just burgled a house in The Close. Why else do you think they're running away from me?'

'Please, please, sir,' sobbed Lisa. 'Save us. He's a rapist and a killer.'

'He says he's police.' The driver shrugged. 'I don't want to lose my license.'

Nearby, a car's horn blared. Lisa turned to see Kevin at the wheel of the same silver car Tony had been driving earlier.

'Look, Mister,' Tess said quietly. 'Take us to the police station nearest to Clapham Common, then, either way, you're covered.'

The driver turned the ignition.

As the cab pulled out, Tony started banging against the windows, running after it, thumping the bodywork.

'Would a policeman act like that?' sobbed Lisa.

'In my experience,' said the driver, 'yes. However I am going to get the office to call the police station.'

As they pulled onto the dual carriageway the driver talked to his controller.

Lisa turned to look out of the back window. 'That horrible Czech's following us.'

'Let him.' Tess dug into her pocket, pulled out a business card and handed it over. 'Oh, driver, please tell the police it's me. I'm missing, you see.'

'Hey!' The cabby glanced down at the card. 'You're not Tess Brandon, the mystery writer?' he asked. 'Wow! I love your books!'

For the first time in her life Tess didn't care a jot whether he did or didn't.

'I suppose you couldn't give my phone a quick charge?' she said. 'I need to get my messages.'

The driver took the phone and plugged it in. Once it was attached to the charger, Tess dialled her mailbox and heard the message Sarah had left.

She gasped.

'If you're talking to the police tell them to go urgently to my address—well, anyhow, to the house next door.'

24

The Twist

*Rock'n'roll dance in which partners dance
separately, with much hip swivelling*

MARTIN GULPED AS the police detective led him, hand-
cuffed, through his own house and out into the
garden. Everything looked so cold, and strange, like
a film-set. The police were calling 'Sarah!' But Martin knew
they were wasting their time.

'As for burying your wife,' said DI Butler, 'you'd better show
us where you think you buried her.'

As Martin walked on towards the back door, he saw the
detective turn to his partner and wink. He also heard him
whisper: 'With any luck the sucker will take us to the place
he hid the librarian.'

A young officer came into the kitchen as the DI led Martin towards the garden and said: 'The SOCO team are all ready and waiting, guv.'

Martin stepped outside. The lawn was littered with trailing cables leading to lamps on tripods. Men were out there, wearing the white suits with hoods. They looked to Martin like spacemen. In the blanching white light, the garden seemed eerie too, like a moonscape.

It was all so unreal. Like being an actor on a film set.

In many ways, as he shuffled past the line of policemen, Martin felt relieved. The game was up.

He would be reunited with Sarah, albeit a dead woman, and finally take the rap for what he had done.

'There.' He took a step forward and pointed down towards the flowerbed. 'That's the spot. I buried her there.'

Martin noticed that the soil was all over place, and that the pansies and snapdragons he had planted on top of her body only a few days ago were nowhere to be seen.

He saw Detective Inspector Butler exchange another sly look with his colleague.

Martin knew no one believed him. But in a minute they would have to.

Unless...unless they had planted something on him. Maybe they had been here while he was being questioned and had buried the clothing of one of the woman in his back yard, just so they could put him down for it. He'd seen them do this all the time on TV cop shows.

'I didn't kill those women on the common, Inspector,' Martin turned and said very loudly to make sure that everyone there would hear him. 'Whatever you find here.'

As the men in white thrust their spades down into the loose soil, Martin started to cry.

'You see, I didn't have time to murder any strangers that night,' he sobbed. 'I was too busy killing my wife.'

'Stop!' One of the diggers raised his hand. 'We've got something.'

Two of the spacemen fell to their knees and started scraping away the soil with their bare hands.

'Why did I do it?' Martin turned away, retching. 'Why?' He didn't want to see Sarah all green and bloated, decomposing before his eyes.

'Camera!' The spaceman shouted the order and a flash exploded into the night. 'Here's a foot.'

Martin hung his head and wailed as he watched the men slowly expose Sarah's body.

'My god.' DI Butler stepped forward. 'We've got a bingo!'

Through his tears, Martin marvelled at how beautiful Sarah looked, lying there in her bed of loam. Not at all like those horrible pictures of dead bodies in the library book.

'When was the bloke supposed to have buried her?' whispered one of the SOCO officers, kneeling over the body, scooping the soil from her face. 'This woman's still warm.'

Martin wiped the tears from his cheeks with the back of his hand, flung himself to his knees, and, reaching down into the soil hole wailed: 'Sarah, darling, I am so, so sorry.'

The corpse opened its mouth and said: 'Martin?'

Martin screamed and leapt into the air, tumbling backwards through the spacemen onto the lawn.

Sarah's eyes opened and she blinked a few times. 'Martin!' She spat out a mouthful of grit. 'You bloody bastard.'

She raised a hand for assistance and started coughing.

'Well, I suppose at least this time you brought the police.'

The scene of crime officers helped Sarah to her feet. She leaned against the senior officer, who looked down at her bloody blouse and asked: 'Who stabbed you? Your husband?'

'Well, yes, actually,' said Sarah. 'But that was last week. This time it was a only a frosting knife. Blunt as fuck. As you see, it didn't even get through the dressing. Then I was buried alive by a Czech bank manager called Kevin and another Czech, a man masquerading as a Detective Inspector Stuart Adams.'

Sarah limped slowly through the parting crowd of astonished policemen.

'But the sod certainly burst my stitches. I think I'd better get to hospital and get my wound checked out.'

'Thank you everyone for getting here so quickly.' Sarah looked around, mildly surprised by the turn-out. 'I have to say, this time I really thought I was going to die.'

Aided by the SOCO man, Sarah hobbled into the kitchen just as the front door burst open and Tess and Lisa, with another batch of policemen, ran in through the hall from the street.

'Sarah?' cried Lisa. 'Are you safe?'

'We worked it out,' Tess panted: 'We came as quick as we could.'

'Look everyone!' Martin staggered into the kitchen. 'I didn't kill my wife!' he called weakly. 'Wait! I demand a solicitor. Call Max Latham.'

'Don't you dare,' snapped Lisa, looking around. 'If I never see that buffoon again it'll be a moment too soon.'

The two detectives sniggered.

'Oh, no, Sarah,' Lisa ran her hands back through her hair. 'What a mess they've all made of your lovely kitchen.'

'That's crime for you!' Nodding, Tess gave an insouciant shrug. 'Hey, Sarah, while we wait for the paramedics, is there anything I could get you?'

'Do you know,' Sarah wiped the mud from her lips with the back of her hand. 'I could murder a battered haddock.'

SOUTH LONDON
EVENING CHRONICLE

COMMON KILLERS CAUGHT

Monday 30ᵗʰ July 2011 Late Special

Yesterday a local bank manager and his brother were charged with the murders of librarian Jane Grimshaw (28) and Marina Sutton (29). Karel Kruszynska, (37) known to his co-workers at the bank as Kevin, and his brother, hairdresser, former actor and male model, Antonin, (32), who used the stage name Stuart Adams, and had appeared on *Casualty* and *The Bill*, were captured in the early hours of Saturday after two women, photographic model Lisa Pope (24) and American thriller writer Tess Brandon (30) managed to escape from an old shipping container in the garage of Kruszynska's Streatham home.

Police have consulted with forces in the Czech Republic and it appears that other similar cases may come to light. The brothers moved to the UK 15 years ago, shortly after

A shipping container, similar to the one above, was brought over from Czech Republic full of furniture by Karel Kruszynska's wife.

the fall of the Iron Curtain. They return home regularly, bringing with them charitable gifts for the people of their local village in the Silesian mountains. The items they donate are thought to have been stolen from the murdered women.

Jane Grimshaw was held inside the container for a week with little or no food before being sexually assaulted, killed and dumped on Clapham Common last Tuesday. Marina Sutton, herself a Czech, was briefly married to an Englishman. She is believed also to have been held inside the container last year before the Kruszynska brothers dumped her body in a ditch on Tooting Common, where it was found by an early morning dog-walker. Tony Kruszynska used his prop police badge from *The Bill* to gain women's trust. Karel Kruszynka had used documents from the bank, including an officially held copy of Martin Beaumont's signature to take out incriminating library books.

His wife, Marta (38), moved to England a year ago. She speaks little English and attends evening classes each night, followed by work as a night cleaner. She is being comforted by a neighbour who is also caring for the couple's 2 children.

The Kruszynska brothers are being held in remand at Brixton prison. They appeared in court today and their case was referred to trial in the Old Bailey in early September.

A spokesman for the bank had no comment.

LAWYER DISBARRED

Moves were put in place today to disbar senior partner Max Latham of Latham & Co for unprofessional conduct and bringing the bar into disrepute. Latham (59) said he was going strenuously to fight the decision and intended to win.

MURDER COUPLE FILE FOR DIVORCE

Martin Beaumont (35), who was wrongly held by police last week in the librarian murder case, is being petitioned for divorce by his wife Sarah (31) on grounds of his unreasonable behaviour. Mrs Beaumont's mother died earlier this week. The funeral will take place next Wednesday. No flowers; donations to The Fox Protection League.

MODEL JOB

Lisa Pope, recovered from her ordeal of being held in captivity by the Kruszynska brothers, today landed a two book contract plus a TV deal advertising hair clips. 'It's true what they said', bubbled Ms Pope (24) 'every clown has a silver lining.'

THRILLER WRITER HELD CAPTIVE BY KILLERS

Best-selling author Tess Brandon talked animatedly today about her time being locked in the container by two brutal killers. 'Hell, I thought I was going to die in there. I must thank Lisa Pope for her help. If it hadn't have been for her fancy barrette we'd still be in there—or dead.' When asked whether she would be going to use any of the experience in a novel, Tess was thoughtful. 'It's pretty painful stuff, but I suppose it is a writer's duty to share their experiences, be they good or bad. I've spoken with my agent back in the States and she is already talking with two major publishers, and I hear the TV rights to my story are being talked about too.' When asked about her role in pinpointing the killers, and advising police on the attempted murder of Sarah Beaumont, Ms Brandon said 'Hell—why don't they make those batteries on cell phones last longer? I knew his voice and heard him use the same name he used on me just as she hung up the call. So I got onto them. Then I called my agent,' she joked. Over the weekend sales of her books have surged.

Acknowledgements

Thank you to the staff at the Isle of Wight Coroner's Court, to Jackie Malton, ex-DCI in the Metropolitan Police, and to Celia Imrie and Lynda La Plante who read *The Murder Quadrille* at an early stage and persuaded me to finish it. And thanks also to Keith Snyder who wrestled with all the typographical problems thrown to him by the various layouts demanded by this book.

About the Author

FIDELIS MORGAN is an actress and writer

On TV she has appeared in *Jeeves and Wooster, Mr Majeika, As Time Goes By;* On stage she played leading roles in works by Schiller, Massinger, Fetcher, Webster, Brecht, Goldoni, Chekhov, Wilde, Coward, Shaw, Lorca, Genet, Orton.

Her plays *Pamela* and *Hangover Square* have won awards and nominations. Fidelis's 17 published books include the ground-breaking *The Female Wits*, the work which uncovered the Restoration women playwrights for the first time in 300 years. She also wrote historical biographies *The Well Known Troublemaker* and *A Woman of No Character* and edited various anthologies of plays and quotations for Virago, Faber and Jonathan Cape. Fidelis has contributed to many encyclopaedias and guidebooks, and has lectured across the world from the Stanford University to the University of Utrecht.

Fidelis's series of four historical crime novels featuring the Countess Ashby dela Zouche and her sidekick, Alpiew, sprang from her vast knowledge of the seventeenth century. The novels have been translated into seven languages. *The Murder Quadrille* is her first modern day mystery

Website: fidelismorgan.com
Twitter: twitter.com/@fidomorgan

Lightning Source UK Ltd.
Milton Keynes UK
UKOW042020200912

199346UK00001B/20/P